"...UNTIL YOU ARE SAFE"

"...UNTIL YOU ARE SAFE"

TONY SQUIRE

S.A.Squire & T.Squire

Contents

Dedication		vii
Cover Information		ix
Foreword		xi
1	One Man, One Gun	1
2	The Journey	32
3	Egypt	53
4	Lemnos	97
5	"Come on, Queenslanders"	123
6	A New Day Dawns	167
7	Patrols, Supplies and New Mates	194
8	Rough Winds do Shake the Darling Buds of May	216
9	The Long Dusks of Summer	260
10	The Break Out	291
11	August, The Summer's Last Messenger of Misery	307
12	Do Not Stir in Discontent	333

About The Author 364

I dedicate this book to all who have served in the armed forces, whether it be in a combat or support arm, each person is part of a well oiled machine, each dependent on one another. When you were needed you were ready. Let no man put asunder.

Copyright © 2023 by Tony Squire

All rights reserved.

Some of the characters and events portrayed in this book are based on real people and events from history, whilst others, including spoken word, are fictitious. Any similarity to real persons, living or dead, is coincidental and not intended by the author.

No part of this book may be reproduced, or stored in a retrieval system, or transmitted in any form or by any means, electronic, mechanical, photocopying, recording, or otherwise, without express written permission of the publisher.

No part of this book may be reproduced in any manner whatsoever without written permission except in the case of brief quotations embodied in critical articles and reviews.

First Printing, 2023

Cover Information

Cover design by Tony Squire.

Cover photographs are courtesy of the Australian War Memorial, Canberra.

Front Cover:
Accession Number - H10324
Maker - Ernest Brooks
Place Made - Gallipoli
Australian War Memorial Description - An Australian trench at the Dardanelles, showing a soldier using a periscope rifle, and another keeping watch by means of a periscope. Identified from original Australian War Memorial documents are, left to right: 274 Sergeant Ernest William Crain; unidentified; 313 Trooper Arthur Snowdon Demaine; Lieutenant Joseph Burge (killed in action 7 August 1915). These men belong to the 2nd Light Horse Regiment. These identifications are from a G series key sheet. Immediately after the First World War the Australian War Museum (now the Australian War Memorial) sought identifications from veterans to augment official captions. These identifications were recorded in the key sheets.
Copyright – Item copyright: Copyright expired: Public Domain.

Rear Cover:
Accession Number - J02601.
Maker - Unknown.
Place Made - Gallipoli.

Australian War Memorial Description - The Cemetery on Shell Green, Gallipoli in 1915 (Donated by Lieutenant Colonel A M Martyn).

Copyright – Item copyright: Copyright expired: Public Domain.

Foreword

In my early years of primary school, I couldn't comprehend why we were taught so little about the Great War and the ANZACs. It always puzzled me why our focus on ANZAC Day centred around the evacuation rather than delving into the valiant soldiers and monumental battles that took place at Gallipoli. It seemed as though Australia and New Zealand's contribution to the war abruptly ceased in December 1915, with the end of the Dardanelles campaign. However, history reveals a different narrative - a tale of how the ANZACs fought tenaciously until the war's end, making significant contributions on the Western Front and in the Middle East, often turning the tide of battle. This historical injustice has fuelled my desire to rectify the oversight by crafting a novel that interweaves fictional characters into true events.

In my novel, I set out to explore the experiences of regiments and battalions hailing from Queensland, particularly focusing on the 9th Battalion (Infantry) and the 2nd Light Horse Regiment. While numerous books have been written about Gallipoli, my intention is to take my characters on a journey that spans the entirety of the war. To aid in my research, I have turned to two remarkable books:

'History of the 2nd Light Horse Regiment A.I.F. – 1914-1919' by Lieutenant Colonel G.H. Bourne, DSO, and 'From ANZAC to the Hindenburg Line – The History of the 9th Battalion A.I.F.' by Norman K. Harvey, BA, AACI.

These invaluable accounts, chronicling the formation, trials, and eventual return of the units, have provided me with incredible insights.

By weaving together the threads of history and fiction, my aspiration is to shed light on the often-overlooked aspects of Australia and New Zealand's involvement in the Great War, honouring the sacrifices made by the ANZACs throughout the conflict.

In this novel, a significant portion of the characters are based on real individuals. The focal points revolve around my fictional characters Archie, Percy, and Rueben Taylor, alongside their comrades Freddy Ponsonby, Stowie, Clancy McBride, Taff Williams, Dave Li, Boggy Marsh, Jacko, Dave Devereux, Sergeant Mac, and several others. The names of most of these characters are inspired by personal friends I had the privilege to serve alongside during my time as a soldier. One exception is Greg Stowe, a childhood friend from my school days. Additionally, one of the characters, Samuel Ford, is based on a real soldier who valiantly served during the Gallipoli campaign - my wife Sheila's grandfather. He is pictured here. His poem too is real, written at Gallipoli in 1915, and this is the first time it has appeared in print.

The names of battles, dates, and locations depicted in the novel are authentic, as I sought to stay true to historical accuracy. However, there is one exception: the "smoke and mirrors incident," which is a fictional addition. Additionally, certain individuals, such as Albert Jacka and John Simpson Kirkpatrick, are integral to the story. Including my own characters within the context of their heroic deeds was the only means by which I could properly acknowledge these extraordinary figures.

By blending real historical events with fictional characters, my intention is to honour the bravery and sacrifice of those who fought and endured during the war, as well as to highlight the exceptional acts of valour displayed by renowned individuals throughout this tumultuous period.

I hope I have done them all the justice they deserve.

I

One Man, One Gun

It is truly astounding how the bullets fired from the gun of a single man in Sarajevo, on the 28th of June 1914, could wield such immense influence, not only over world history, but also on the lives of countless individuals; in an instant, extinguishing an entire generation yet to be conceived, while simultaneously giving birth to a legend that would endure as that of the ANZACs.

In 1914, Kilcoy, in rural south east Queensland, was a thriving outback town. The year had begun as normal with the summer rains falling fast and furious as they had always done. The countryside was green and lush, the creeks were flowing, and the dams were full to the brim. It looked to be the start of a prosperous year for all of the station owners of the area with food and water in abundance for their livestock. Everyone was content.

The third month of winter had just begun, and the temperature had dropped considerably. The horses and livestock, however, were set for the winter with plenty of hay to keep them fed, due to the bumper rains and wonderful green pastures that had grown up as a result.

Doriray Station was situated on a vast area of land around Sandy Creek, not far from Kilcoy. The owners, Doris and Raymond Taylor, had arrived in Australia from London, England, in 1885, hoping to make a better life for themselves. Raymond had worked in a foundry, but prior to that was a tenant farmer in the county of Essex, raising dairy cattle. Life was hard in the slums of London, and advertisements calling for able bodied farm workers to settle in the colonies were a great pull in such terrible times. With the money they had managed to save over the years, they purchased two hundred acres of land and set up their cattle station, clearing the land of trees in order to create pastures for grazing. In the years that followed they raised two sons, Archie and Percy, who were born in 1889 and 1890 respectively. They were happy young fellows who loved the countryside and, when not helping on the station, enjoyed climbing trees and swimming in the creek. In 1902 they had the addition to their family of their cousin Rueben, following the death of his parents Inala and Tom.

Rueben's mother Inala was an indigenous woman from the local Jinibara people. For Tom, Ray's brother, and Inala it was love at first sight, a love which resulted in the birth of their son in 1894. Rueben, or Roo for short, was truly a refreshing sign of racial harmony and the joining together of cultures for the good of all. He was a handsome fellow, his facial features being that of his Jinibara mother, whilst his skin colour was a mid dark brown. Roo's Jinibara family would often joke that he was not a black fella but a brown fella. In the end, like all people in the World, he was just that......a person, a member of the Taylor and Jinibara families, and that was that, and that is all that the families saw; and that is how it should be everywhere. Raymond and Doris loved Rueben and, although their nephew, they always thought of him as a third son, as he too thought of *them* as second parents.

Ray, and the three boys, now strapping young men, spent most of their days repairing fences, and ensuring that their vast herd of cattle were in good health. They were hoping for a pretty profit at the cattle markets in November. By now they were all expert stockmen and bushmen, thanks to the years of working their station, and to their Jinibara family who had imparted thousands of years of knowledge about how to treat and respect the land. Archie was twenty five, Percy twenty four and Roo was twenty. They were men. They had to be, in this unforgiving country. Percy had responsibilities too having married his childhood sweetheart Lil in December of 1910 and producing their son, Frank, who was just shy of his fourth birthday.

As they took a moment to survey the landscape to their front, they watched as a small willy willy, a mini tornado of dust, swept across the paddock lifting fallen leaves in to its cone shaped funnel, swirling them round like a mass of butterflies.

"I always used to love standing in the middle of those when I was younger," said Archie, "just to feel the breeze on my face and half hoping to be lifted off the ground".

"I still do it. I love it," announced Roo.

"Well, you've just missed your chance then fellas," said Ray.

"No you haven't...look!" said Percy as he pointed to a distant dust cloud.

As all four turned their gaze to the crest far out to their front, sure enough there *was* another willy willy, swirling around on the horizon.

"You're right Perce!" Archie exclaimed.

As Roo focussed his eyes on the swirling cloud *he* could see something quite different, and for some reason sensed that something wasn't right.

"Hold your horses everyone, that's not a willy willy, it's Lil, and she's galloping in pretty fast," said Roo.

"How can you tell?" asked Percy, "that dust cloud must be a couple of miles away".

"I eat a lot of carrots," replied a smiling Roo.

Ray tried his best to stop himself from laughing by changing the subject.

"Well, if it *is* Lil, then at least Percy here will be pleased," he said.

Percy could not help but notice how Archie and Roo were now giving him a bit of a funny look.

"What?" asked Percy.

"Nothing, just wondering....you know," replied Archie.

"No I don't!" Percy retorted.

"I think Arch is in awe of the giddy looks you still give Lil, even after all these years" said Roo as he patted Percy on the back, "Lil is a goodun. You hang on to her mate".

"I will..er...I do," replied Percy.

"I think it's more like Lil will hang on to him. She sure is smitten," laughed Archie.

"And there's nothing wrong with that *eh* Percy?" said Ray reassuringly, "that's what loving someone is all about, just look at your mother and me".

Percy smiled and nodded his head.

The foursome gazed out as the dot on the horizon that was Lil, drew nearer. As she finally arrived, she almost flew over the horse's head as her mount came to a sliding halt in the dusty ground.

"That was a close call," said Ray, with arms outstretched just in case he needed to catch a flying Lil.

"Thanks father, but I'm good," said Lil as she glanced around at her audience, touching the brim of her hat and nodding a greeting to each of them, "I've been looking for you fellas all day, but Ma wasn't really sure of exactly where you would be".

"Well you've found us lass, but what's the rush?" enquired Ray.

"Something terrible has happened, and I am scared," said Lil as she glanced towards Percy.

"Scared?" asked Archie, "scared of what?"

"Scared that the news I have will send you *all* away and put you in danger," replied Lil, trying to hold back the tears.

Lil climbed down from her horse and imparted her news that Australia was now at war with Germany.

"With *Germany*; how did *that* happen?" asked a shocked Ray, glancing across to his three sons, with a feeling of dread.

"I'm not sure. Something about the British having a treaty with Belgium and the German's attacking them to get to France," replied Lil.

Ray was disappointed and angry, throwing his hat down on to the ground. There had been rumours of upheaval in Europe for weeks now but, secretly, no one expected or wanted this news.

"So of course *our* government has said it would help! Well, *they* won't be helping *will* they? Just sending *others* to do their bidding. Bloody politicians, they're *all* the bloody same!" said Ray.

None of those present had ever heard Ray raise his voice, let alone curse; but he was right.

Centuries of conflict had plagued Europe, consistently instigated by those in power who possessed wealth and privilege, yet employed those they despised and looked down upon to fight their battles. Whether the disputes revolved around land, borders, culture, race, religion, or ethnicity, the pattern remained unchanged. As the new century dawned, regrettably, little had changed. Certain nations harboured expansionist ambitions, having honed their armies through smaller conflicts in the preceding decades.

The dominant forces in Europe during this period included Great Britain, France, Austro-Hungary, and Russia. The oncemighty Ottoman Empire, which had exerted its influence for four centuries and occupied numerous southern and Mediterranean countries, was beginning to decline. The Balkan Wars, which had taken place a year earlier, witnessed the defeat of the Ottoman Empire by the four Balkan states: Serbia, Montenegro, Greece, and Bulgaria. These events triggered substantial political upheaval across the European continent.

Empires like Austro-Hungary felt a loss of control over their southern neighbours and grew concerned about potential expansionism from that direction. Consequently, mutual defence treaties were established among various nations, some of which had existed for decades. The assassination of Archduke Franz Ferdinand, the heir to the Austro-Hungarian throne, during his visit to Serbia, acted as the catalyst for the ensuing conflict. In response, the Austro-Hungarian Empire accused the Serbian government of involvement in the assassination. These veiled accusations and demands served as a pretext for Austria to launch a brief war against Serbia. However, they had not anticipated Serbia's connections with Russia—a formidable force in its own right. As a precautionary measure, Austria sought assistance from its ally, Germany, which had eagerly sought a fight for many years.

The first spark was ignited when Russia mobilised in support of Serbia following Austria's declaration of war on the Serbs, resulting in Germany declaring war on Russia on the 1st of August. France, bound by a treaty with Russia, found itself at war with Germany and Austro-Hungary as well. The dominoes began to fall, and the final piece tumbled when Germany took a shortcut to Paris by invading neutral Belgium.

Though Great Britain had a precarious treaty alliance with France, it felt compelled to defend its French allies. However, the tipping point came with a seventy five year old defence treaty with Belgium. Following the Belgian King's desperate pleas for help, Great Britain entered the conflict on the 4th of August 1914, with its eager colonies also joining the fray. In fact, just weeks earlier, the future Prime Minister of Australia, Andrew Fisher, had famously declared, "Australians will stand beside the mother country to help and defend her to our last man and our last shilling."

It was late afternoon and, as the five members of the Taylor clan rode towards the homestead, the fading light cast long shadows which seemed to merge with each one's sense of foreboding. The world around them felt quiet and still, as if nature itself was holding its breath in anticipation of what lay ahead, the beauty of the rolling hills and plains, once a source of solace and tranquillity, now serving as a bittersweet reminder of what may be lost.

The conversation at dinner was quite muted, the family members exchanging concerned glances, their minds racing with the gravity of the situation. Archie, Percy, and Roo's inwardly felt excitement at the prospect of war weighed heavily on *their* minds, mingled with a sense of guilt about potentially leaving behind their responsibilities on the cattle station, for they understood the immense amount of work involved in its upkeep and organisation. Meanwhile, Ray, Doris, and Lil were hesitant to address the subject, unsure of how discussing it might steer the conversation.

It was Ray who finally broke the silence, "Well, it seems our worst fears have come true".

"You know, *I've* been thinking about enlisting. It's a chance to show how great this country is, and make a difference," announced Archie, trying to hide his excitement.

"I feel the same...and think of the adventure," added Roo.

Percy was always the practical one of the family.

"Adventure?! I'm worried about leaving Lil and young Frank," he said hesitantly, "and what about the station? We have so much work to do here. It feels like we're abandoning everyone and everything that is dear to us".

Lil gently grasped her husband's hand.

"Percy my lovely, I love you, and the thought of you going to war terrifies me, but you need to do what you think is right," she said, whilst looking towards Archie and Roo, "you *all* do; and, besides I'm sure mother and father can sort something out with the station".

"They reckon it'll all be over by Christmas anyway," added Roo.

"Look, the station will always be here, and I'm sure all of the other stations will band together somehow to help each other," said Ray.

"Don't forget there are plenty of swaggies who pass through and need the work," said Lil, "*and* the young fellas still at school".

Ray looked towards Lil and smiled.

"Lil's right. We'll sort something out, so you boys do what you need to do," he said.

"Where there's a will there's a way," added Doris, trying to fight back the tears.

Although the boys felt a mix of excitement and guilt, they also recognised the gravity of their decisions, whilst Ray, Doris, and Lil were a little more cautious about the whole matter, wanting to protect their loved ones from harm.

So, the decision had been made. The Taylor boys were going to war.

The news of the war quickly spread around the region with many of the local men and women wanting to do their bit for King and Country. The next train to Brisbane was not until Monday so the family enjoyed some precious time together, with a family picnic near the dam on the station. Archie, Percy and Roo were excited and proud to be going to war, but the mood was still a little sombre.

"All I ask is that you do yourselves proud and return home safe," said Ray to his sons.

"We'll be back Dad, don't you worry," said Archie, "you taught us many things Mum and Dad and we will always be grateful. It'll all be over in a few months anyway".

"Yeah, watch out Kaiser Bill because the boys from Kilcoy are coming," laughed Roo.

The next morning an impromptu parade was held. The Kilcoy volunteers formed up by the bridge then marched proudly up William Street, along Mary Street and Hope Street to the train station. They were led by the local brass band, resplendent in their uniforms. Local families lined the streets holding banners wishing them luck, and waving the relatively new Australian national flag. Lil, with Frank sat on her shoulders, waved vigorously at the marching men. Frank too had a flag which he waved proudly at his Dad and uncles as they marched past him.

At the station the Mayor gave a rousing speech about patriotism and honour, and the crowd applauded and cheered. Kilcoy was very proud of its menfolk. Speeches and cheers gave way to tears as the volunteers hugged their loved ones and bade them farewell.

"Don't worry we'll be home in a few months," said one young soldier to his family.

"Come back to me and Frank safe my darling Percy," said Lil, holding back the tears, "and don't forget to write".

"Don't worry about me and these two my lovely, we'll do our duty and keep our heads down," Percy replied.

The boys gave final hugs to their parents, who were putting on a brave face.

As the new recruits boarded the train, a quiet descended on the families as the huge steam locomotive chugged gradually out of sight. The people of Kilcoy slowly dispersed to their homes with heavy hearts wondering if they had said all they needed to, and fearful of their loved one never returning. Like all of the other passengers, the boys hung out of their windows for as long as they could, waving frantically and blowing kisses to their family, but as they sat down a sombre reality overtook them.

"Are we doing the right thing?" asked Percy.

"I hope...well...I think so," replied Roo.

Archie surveyed the carriage.

"Look around you. All of these blokes are going. How could we have *ever* looked them in the eye again if *we* hadn't gone too?" said Archie.

"You're right mate," said Roo, as he acknowledged friends and former schoolmates.

As the passengers sat in quiet contemplation, the door leading to the adjoining carriage was suddenly flung open and in stepped a burly and rough looking fellow, standing around 6 feet 2 inches tall. He seemed to be looking round the carriage, possibly for a seat. The man immediately caught Roo's eye.

"Oh bugger, look who's on the train," he said, sinking slowly down in his seat.

Archie and Percy turned their heads in the direction of the newcomer and eyed him up and down.

"No idea mate. Give us a clue," said Archie.

"Do you remember me telling you about a boy at school who used to pick on me?" asked Roo.

"Yeah...used to call you Tar Boy as I remember...is that *him*?" asked Percy.

Roo nodded. "Yep. Clancy McBride," said Roo, "I hope *he's* not enlisting too. Quick put your feet up on the seat, he's coming this way!"

Clancy had noticed Roo, and his cousins, and began striding confidently towards them.

"Well, if it isn't me old mate Rueben Taylor," announced Clancy, holding his hand out in greeting.

Percy immediately rose to his feet.

"We're *not* your mates!" he said.

"Oh come on fellas, don't be like that," Clancy pleaded.

Roo could see the concern and disappointment on Clancy's face.

"Hang on a sec Perce, let's see what he has to say," said Roo.

Clancy gestured to Percy to make some space on the seat, then sat down.

"Listen mate, I was a proper bastard to you when we were at school and it has always been on my mind. When I heard you were enlisting I just had to find you and say my peace," explained

Clancy, "both my Mum and Dad were a pair of drunks. They hated everyone, especially Abos, and it...well...it sort of rubbed off on me...not that it makes it right of course".

"Well for a start I'm not an Abo, that's a word that you white fellas brought with you. Before you arrived we were just people, and *I* am a man, just like you; simple as that," replied Roo.

"I know mate, I know, and that's just it, we *are* men now, I've worked all over Queensland and New South Wales, and met many people, many *different* people, and I have learned that really we are all the same deep down," said Clancy, "and all I wanted to do...er to say...oh bugger it...I am so sorry for making your life a hell........mates?"

Clancy held out his hand again in friendship to Roo. Roo smiled and rolled his eyes, accepting Clancy's hand.

"Thanks mate, that means a lot...mates it is," replied Roo.

As the tension subsided Clancy introduced himself to Archie and Percy.

"We were going to meet you years ago and give you a bashing for Roo, but he wouldn't have it. You were lucky," said Archie, "he said he could give you a good thump anytime if he wanted to, *and* he could".

"But I didn't want to," replied Roo.

"Well I wish you had. We'd have been mates then. Anyone who fights back is a good bloke in my books, and I reckon I needed some sense knocking in to me," said Clancy.

During the third week of August 1914 a small number of uniformed officers, and men in civilian clothes, were pitching tents in Bells Paddock, Enoggera, a pretty spot five miles north of Brisbane, ideal for the location of a military training camp.

There was a train station and good road links, making it easy for new recruits to find their way there.

When Britain declared war on Germany, the state of Queensland immediately resolved to play its part. Men from all walks of life at once offered themselves for active service and within a week over fourteen hundred had volunteered at the Brisbane Town Hall.

The first men, including the Taylors, arrived in camp on 17th and 18th of August, and three days later another three hundred recruits from the Tweed, Richmond and Clarence River districts joined them, followed on the 22nd by thirty volunteers from the Oxley Regiment.

The new Australian force, which was rapidly growing throughout the country, was first known as the European Expeditionary Force, but by the end of August it had become the Australian Imperial Force, or AIF for short.

Following the recommendations put forth by Field Marshall Kitchener, in 1911, a form of mandatory military training was implemented in Australia, targeting all males aged twelve to twenty six. However, this form of conscription was for home defence only, thus these troops were legally restricted from serving overseas. By the end of 1915, an impressive number of over one hundred and seventy five thousand young men had registered. So, in reality, by the outbreak of war Australia had a sizeable force of trained men who were ready to use their skills in the defence of Australia and the Mother Country. The Taylors were amongst these numbers and possessed prior military experience with the 9th Battalion, The Moreton Bay Regiment, a unit with a notable history dating back to 1867, whilst Clancy had served with the 1st Australian Infantry Regiment in Sydney.

On arrival at Enoggera, the train was bursting with men who had boarded at stations on the way, all hoping to enlist and join in the great adventure. As the men crowded on to the platform they were met by uniformed soldiers of the Infantry and Light Horse, who somehow managed to arrange the men in to three ranks and ushered them out to the barracks.

Bells Paddock was a hive of activity with large white bell tents scattered in neat rows, and many which still needed to be erected. The men were led to a holding area where they joined several queues which ended at wooden trestle tables manned by a Sergeant or junior officer.

As the group drew closer to the table Clancy appeared nervous. This didn't go unnoticed by Roo.

"Are you right mate?" he asked.

"Yeah, I just don't write too well and all that paperwork looks a bit frightening," replied Clancy.

"Don't worry, I've been watching, and it looks like you just have to sign your name," said Roo reassuringly.

"Oh, that's good then," replied Clancy, feeling somewhat relieved, "that I can do".

Pretty soon they were at the desk, with Roo at the head of the line.

"Next!" the sergeant shouted.

"Good morning sergeant, I've come to join the Infantry," Roo announced proudly.

"Name?" the sergeant asked, still looking down at the mass of paperwork in front of him.

"Rueben Taylor, sergeant," Roo replied.

"Age?" said the sergeant as he changed his gaze and looked up at the new recruit, "hold your horses, no black fellas allowed".

"What do you mean?" asked a surprised Roo.

"Just what I said. Now go home to your tribe, or whatever you call it lad, you're not wanted here," said the sergeant.

Roo was stunned. Did this great country truly not want his services just because of his colour?! As Roo turned to walk away the others stopped him in his tracks. Archie and Percy were furious.

"Why can't our cousin join the Army? What's the problem?" demanded Archie.

"Your cousin?! No Abos can join the Army. Them's the rules. I don't make 'em. Sorry," replied the sergeant.

"You'll be sorry in a minute mate if you don't let my mate join," said Clancy, waving an angry fist at the sergeant.

"Don't bloody mate me soldier or you'll be on a charge," replied the sergeant.

"A charge?" growled Clancy, "I'd like to see that one. I haven't even signed up yet!"

"And we *won't* be unless Roo here can come with us!" announced Archie.

"You men, what's going on here?" came a voice from behind the sergeant.

Roo's face lit up when he recognised the Captain as Doctor Butler from Kilcoy. The doctor had been a member of the Citizens Military Forces for two years and had joined the 9th Battalion, as a medical officer, when war was declared.

"Doc! I didn't recognise you there," said Roo with a big smile on his face.

"Rueben Taylor...Archie...Percy. Come to join up have you?" said the doc.

"Yes sir but this fella won't let me," replied Roo.

At this the doctor turned to the sergeant saying "why ever not?"

"Because he's a black fella sir and the rules say they can't join," replied the sergeant, "personally sir *anyone* with the guts to sign up is good enough for me, but like I said, I don't make the rules".

"Well I brought this young man in to the world and can vouch for his father being white and his mother being a native woman, so I think you'd better let him in don't you?" said the doctor.

"So he is a half caste? Whatever you say sir is fine by me," replied the sergeant as he offered his pen and the enlistment form to Roo, "just sign there at the bottom, son".

Happy to enlist but still disappointed at being labelled due to his colour, Roo stepped aside and waited for the others.

Clancy was next in the queue and after the usual barrage of questions, signed his papers and joined Roo in their newly formed platoon. Archie soon followed, but to the surprise of the others Percy joined a different group.

"What's happened Perce? Have they rejected you?" asked Archie.

Percy laughed. "Rejected? No. I've joined the Light Horse".

"What did you do that for?" asked a surprised Archie.

"Promised Mum," replied Percy.

"Mum? What do you mean?" said Archie.

"I told her we'd join different units, giving us a better chance of at least one of us getting back home," replied Percy.

"Good idea, but I intend for us *all* to come back mate," said Archie.

"Yeah, me too, but...you know," said Percy.

The next few days were spent getting familiar with military procedures and their new mates. Little military training was undertaken at this point, but those with military experience, along with the regular soldiers and non commissioned officers (NCOs), began instructing those new to the army in the basics of drill and military etiquette.

The remainder of August saw a vigorous enlistment both in country and city regions with another one hundred and thirty three men arriving from far north Queensland. Of that number seventy seven joined the 9th Battalion, whilst the remainder went to the 2nd Light Horse Regiment and other units.

The new enlistments brought with them new friends. There was Steve "Jacko" Jackson, Gregory Stowe and Rhys "Taff" Williams who joined the 9th Battalion, whilst Wilbert Awdry, or Chugger to his mates, and David Li, enlisted with the 2nd Light Horse Regiment. Whether in the infantry or the light horse they were all mates together, with the new additions becoming part of the Taylor family circle, meeting up in the camp canteen during down times.

"I'm Rhys Williams but you can call me Taff," said Rhys as he introduced himself to the group.

"Taff? What's a Taff?" asked Clancy.

"A Welshman," replied Rhys.

"Welshman? *That's* nothing special, New South Wales is only a few miles down the road," replied Clancy.

"No...*not* a New South Welshman. Can't you tell by my accent boyo? I'm from Anglesey in Wales. It's a country," said Taff.

"Oh right. What town?" asked Clancy.

"You didn't even know it was a country mate, so I don't think his home town will make you any wiser," laughed Roo.

"Llanfairpwllgwyngyllgogerychwyrndrobwllllantysiliogogogoch," announced Taff.

"Clan fair...what? Hey Roo this bloke speaks your lingo," Clancy remarked as he nudged Roo in the side.

"What, English?" asked Roo.

"No, the Abo language. Say it again slowly so I can have a go," said Clancy.

"Bloody hell man! I'll break it down easy like for you...Clan fair pull gwingeth clan drobel clanty sillyog go go go," replied Taff, shrugging his shoulders.

"Fair dinkum I'll never get my tongue around that mate," said Clancy, scratching his head.

The AIF was quite a cosmopolitan bunch with over thirty percent of its number being born overseas. Gregory Stowe was an American from Texas, whilst David Li was Australian born, of Anglo-Chinese descent. Roo was curious about David for although he had European features his skin was lightly tanned.

"So, what's your story Davo?" asked Roo.

"What do you mean?" asked Davo.

"Well, you look a bit brown like me," said Roo.

Davo explained that his mother was English and his father Chinese, having come to this country in search of Gold. He had heard that the Chinese weren't being allowed to serve so had banked on his European features to get him through, as well as changing the spelling of his last name from Li to Lee; and it worked.

"Bloody hell...that is a disgrace! Any bloke willing to fight for his country should be good enough!" shouted Clancy.

"Hey, calm down mate, I don't want my secret to be known," said Davo.

"Sorry mate but these bastards really get my goat," replied Clancy, "they even tried it on with my mate Roo here".

By now Clancy and Roo had become good friends, but Clancy *did* have a bit of a problem with his occasional bursts of bad language.

"Perhaps we should start calling you Blue, mate," joked Roo, "on account of the colour of your language".

"Yeah, mum would give you a clip round the ear if *she* heard it," laughed Archie.

Just then the huge figure of Sergeant MacDonald appeared in the canteen. A veteran of the British Army, the sergeant stood six feet seven inches in his bare feet and, although a gentle giant, he struck an imposing and fearsome looking figure.

"Lads, I've got a new pal for ye," he said in his broad Scottish accent, "this fella here is Frederick Ponsonby, I think you'll find him a wee bit of a novelty...be nice".

Ponsonby had quite an air about him, seeming confident before he had even spoken.

"Ponsonby? What sort of name is that?" asked Clancy, "I think I'm just gonna call you Freddy".

"Yeah, sounds good," said Archie.

"If you must old bean," replied Ponsonby in a very upper class English accent.

"Are *you* a Pom?" asked Chugger.

"No. I'm English," replied Ponsonby.

"Yeah....definitely a Pom," replied Chugger.

"I do believe that Pom stands for prisoner of mother England......so that would be you chaps," replied Ponsonby with a wry smile.

"Well, I beg to differ on that," said Chugger.

"Now, what are *your* names, seeing as you already know mine?" asked Ponsonby.

Archie held out his hand, "I'm Archie; this is Percy, Roo, Chugger, Taff, Davo, Jacko and Clancy....although we're thinking of calling *him* Blue".

"Oh I see, you all seem to use nom de plumes," said Ponsonby.

"Nom de what?" asked a confused Clancy.

"Nick names old boy. Now let me guess, Chugger. I take it you have some connection with locomotives?" said Ponsonby.

"Spot on mate," said Chugger, "I used to drive a sugar cane train, up Bundaberg way, that pulled the bins".

"Hmmm, let me see. Archie. That would be short for Archibald no doubt?" asked Ponsonby.

"No mate, just plain Archie, that's me," replied Archie.

"Now, Clancy, or is it Blue? I *am* a little perplexed. Don't you chaps refer to a fellow with red hair as Blue?" said Ponsonby, "well, you haven't got red hair, and *I* haven't a clue I'm afraid".

Clancy nudged Archie with his elbow.

"See, I knew he wouldn't get it. It's on account of my bad language," replied Clancy proudly.

"Oh, that's unfortunate. Do you utter many profanities?" asked Ponsonby.

Clancy felt a little confused. "P...P...P...what?"

"He means swear words mate" said Percy.

"Oh, right. Well, why didn't you just say? We don't put on the dog here ya know," replied Clancy, "and my favourite word is......"

"Bastard" said all present in unison.

Ponsonby then turned his attention to Roo, giving him a disdainful glance.

"And who is this fellow? Is he your *man*?" he asked.

The atmosphere dropped and the tension suddenly rose.

"*Man*?" asked Clancy.

"Your servant dear boy" said Ponsonby quite thoughtlessly.

Ponsonby didn't see Clancy's fist as it suddenly caught him square on the chin knocking him back a few paces.

"This bloke here *is* a man, simple as that, and not only that, he is *our* man. He is my best mate. No truer friend ever walked this earth than Roo, and don't you forget it," exclaimed an annoyed Clancy.

"I do apologise, that was very rude and presumptuous of me" said Ponsonby, reaching out to clasp Roo's hand.

"Oh by the way Clancy," said Ponsonby, "I will allow you that one, but I used to partake in pugilism at school you know, and was quite good at it. Queensbury rules and all that you know".

"I don't know what you are going on about but if you want to go again let's go for it," said Clancy clenching his fists.

Archie jumped between the two men. "Save it for the Germans fellas".

"So what do you do for a living mate?" asked Roo.

"I am an accountant.....a keeper of books," replied Freddy.

"What's a book keeper doing in the army?" asked Percy.

"Long family tradition of soldiers, just doing my bit for King and country and all that?" said Freddy.

Archie was a lover of history and had read many books about the British Army.

"Wasn't there a Ponsonby at Waterloo? Any relation?" he asked.

"Yes a distant relative. He was commander of the Scots Greys. Got himself impaled by a Lancer don't you know," replied Freddy, "my family has a bit of a history of being stabbed by sharp objects. My own dear father was also impaled by a Zulu at Isandlwhana when I was just a babe in arms; not very lucky in that respect".

"Isandla what?" asked Chugger.

"It's a place in Africa," said Archie as he placed his arm around Freddy's shoulder, "well mate, stick with us and we'll see you through it and break the moz eh?"

"Yes, that would be agreeable," said Freddy, nodding his appreciation.

"Shouldn't you be an officer with that accent?" asked Davo.

"Accent? You are the fellows with the accent, not I," Freddy replied, "an accent does not an officer make...no I joined to fight like a real orstralian".

"What the bloody hell is an orstralian? Its astrayan mate," announced Clancy.

"Australian," said Freddy, trying to imitate the accent.

"That's close enough. We'll make you in to a true blue dinkie dye Aussie by the time this is all over," joked Clancy.

"Wonderful," said Freddy, "another reason I am in Australia is that the English upper class are bullies. It's in their nature and they seem to find it funny. I went to school at Eaton and was bullied and beaten by other boys nearly every day. After that I vowed that I would just be an ordinary fellow like you men and never let those people hurt me again, hence I came to this fair land".

"Well good on yer," said Clancy.

The 2nd Light Horse Regiment came in to existence with the appointment of its Commanding Officer, or CO for short, Lieutenant Colonel Stodart, whilst the 9th Battalion was officially born with the arrival of its CO, Lieutenant Colonel Lee, and a handful of officers on the 21st of August. The 9th Battalion was destined to form part of an Infantry Brigade along with the 10th, 11th and 12th Battalions, whilst the 2nd Light Horse formed part of the 1st Light Horse Brigade.

Both Commanding Officers held formal muster parades to welcome the new troops. They were fully aware, and indeed fortunate, that most of their number, including the officers, had served in some way or other, whether in the cadets, militia, Citizens Military Force (CMF), or the British Army. There were also a large number of veterans of the South African War. One officer of the 9th Battalion, Lieutenant Boase, was a recent Duntroon graduate. All Senior Non Commissioned Officers (SNCOs) and Warrant Officers (WOs) were members of the CMF; the CO of the 2nd Light Horse Regiment was a regular soldier and veteran of the South African War, whereas the CO of the 9th Battalion, a

Maryborough school headmaster, had been posted from the 23rd Infantry (Port Curtis) Regiment.

From the outset both the 2nd and the 9th were confident that, with their wealth of experience, they were ready for the task ahead of them. As a result, little drill was undertaken in the first few weeks, with Lord Kitchener's words *"Never mind the drill; teach them to shoot and do it quickly"* echoing throughout the AIF. Construction of the camp was their priority, involving the pitching of tents, erection of cook houses, and the unloading of the influx of stores. There was, however, always a veteran on hand to prepare those with no experience for the training that was soon to come. As of yet no uniforms or equipment had been issued as the rapid enlistment of vast numbers had far outweighed the expectations of the government and the factories who produced them. Currently the troops were dressed in a variety of clothing ranging from variations of the Australian Army uniform to dungarees and civilian attire. On the very first muster parade the endless variety of hats, from bowlers, straw boaters, panamas, caps and felt hats, was particularly noted. They looked a rag tag mob but were fast becoming a cohesive unit, a unit of mates, who relied upon each other, from the humble soldier to the CO himself.

Once the camp became more organised, squad, platoon, company and battalion drill began. Rapid progress was made, for all were volunteers and were keen to learn, help their less able mates, and quickly deploy to France to show the Germans a thing or two.

Physical fitness was a key for all soldiers and involved a variety of exercises to improve strength, endurance, and overall fitness; distance marching with heavy packs being the major focus. Most of the men had been using weapons of various types for most of their lives but it was learning how to properly maintain, clean, and fire these weapons, which was the order of the day, combined with the knowledge of how to use them effectively in combat. The weapons too were different to what the men were used to, the modern battlefield being overtaken by the use of Lewis and Vickers machine guns, as well as trench mortars. The soldiers' old friend the bayonet certainly was not ignored, as the type of warfare the AIF would be involved in called for the skilful use of this deadly and terrifying weapon. Infantry and trench warfare tactics were something which would be taught on arrival in England, but right now the priority was the assembly and shipping out of an army.

Despite their unwavering dedication and professionalism towards their cause, the men of the Australian Imperial Force maintained an unmistakably civilian essence. Their intention was not to conform to the norms of regular soldiers, as they had responded to their country's plea as men called upon. While they were more than willing to engage in the fight, they failed to see the purpose behind the strict discipline and trivialities of the parade ground. This perspective would eventually transform as they experienced frontline action. Nevertheless, at this very moment, they perceived their involvement in the army as a mere occupation, with any time spent outside of it belonging to themselves.

Within a month each man was issued with the uniform and kit that they had been longing for. This kit consisted of tunic, trousers, singlet, shirt, underwear, socks, boots, laces, hat khaki fur felt, chin strap, puttees, braces, dungarees, white hat, balaclava cap, bronze badges and collar titles, sewing kit (or housewife), brush, comb, holdall, razor, shaving brush, knife, fork and spoon, mess tin, water bottle, kit bag, sea kit bag, rifle, bayonet, webbing and shovel...soldier for the use of!

Each man was also issued with the latest incarnation of the Rising Sun Cap badge.

"Hey, have you seen this? Our badge is from a flaming jam jar!" exclaimed Clancy.

"Yeah, Dad loves a bit of Rising Sun marmalade on his toast," said Archie.

"Oh well, at least it is something uniquely Aussie eh?" replied Roo.

"Too right mate," said Clancy, nodding proudly.

The 9th Battalion was now officially part of the 3rd Brigade, its commander being Colonel Sinclair-MacLagan, an officer of fine quality. The Colonel was a regular army officer in the British Army, having served since 1889. The men felt blessed to have him, because he was a *real* soldier, and veteran of many battles in India, and the South African War, where he had been mentioned in despatches and awarded the Distinguished Service Order. He was also no stranger to the Australian soldier either, having been seconded from 1901 to 1904 as Adjutant of the New South Wales Scottish Rifles. In 1910 he was invited by the then Brigadier William Bridges, who knew him from his time in Australia, to take up an instructional position at the newly established Royal Military College at Duntroon. When war broke out, the Defence Act of 1903, precluded the Australian military from serving outside of Australia. To counter this, a totally separate, all volunteer force, was raised....the Australian Imperial Force. Bridges had been selected to command and form this force specifically for overseas service, and had personally selected Sinclair-MacLagan to be the commander of the 3rd Brigade of the 1st Division. Sinclair-MacLagan was the only brigade commander of the division who was a professional soldier.

By the first week of September the 9th Battalion consisted of sixty five officers and one thousand seven hundred and eighty four other ranks. During the same period, the 2nd Light Horse Regiment received their first horses from the Remount Section.

Many men had brought their own horses with them, these being purchased by the army and issued to their previous owners. However a large proportion of the government issued horses were wild and unbroken, so the Regiment set to the task of breaking them. Once this task was complete, it was time for the obligatory riding test of sitting astride a bareback horse and taking it over a water jump and a log fence, which revealed a few non riders who had joined the light horse because it was too tiring to walk as an infantryman. These "tired" men were transferred to the 9th Battalion, who rapidly educated them in the ways of staying awake.

On the 19th of September the 3rd Brigade marched from Enoggera to Brisbane and back in full marching order, with fixed bayonets. Crowds greeted them with tremendous applause and cheering. They arrived back at camp with no complaints and as fresh as they were when they had departed; proving that these men, pioneers of a harsh country, were not only extremely fit, but were born soldiers.

The men of the light horse and infantry were also treated to inspections by the Governor General and State Governor.

"I reckon we'll be off to France soon boys, what with all these inspections," said Roo.

"I agree. I think we are being paraded as the final product of our training, before we go," said Archie.

"I'll drink to that," said Chugger, clanking his glass against Freddy's.

"I think you chaps are correct," added Freddy, with a solemn glance.

"Have you turned in to a horse mate?" asked Clancy.

"What do you mean?" said Freddy.

"Why the long face?" replied Clancy as he ducked to avoid the many swipes across his head for his bad joke.

"I have been found out my friends," said Freddy.

"Found out?" enquired a surprised Roo.

"Have you done something wrong?" asked Percy.

"I wasn't exactly honest," said Freddy.

"What are you...a bush ranger or something?!" exclaimed Clancy.

Reaching in to his pocket Freddy produced four pips and looked towards his 9th Battalion mates. "I'm your new Platoon Commander".

"Well bugger me, Lieutenant Freddy Ponsonby" said Clancy, shaking Freddy's hand vigorously, "good on yer mate".

"Really? I thought you'd hate the idea," said Freddy.

"Mate, we knew from the start you had it in yer," said Roo.

But there was more to it, as Freddy had been a regular officer in the British Army prior to coming to Australia, a graduate of the Royal Military Academy, Sandhurst no less, as well as a veteran of the South African War. Joining up for the war as a Private was through a sense of duty, *without* the responsibility, but his record had caught up with him and the CO had insisted that he accept a commission, which he did with the promise that he could command his current platoon.

"Well bloody double bugger me you bastard!" exclaimed Clancy, "at least we'll have an experienced officer leading us".

"It means I'll have to move to the officers' lines, but I will still come and visit," said Freddy.

"At least we'll get some sleep now," said Archie, "you snore like a pig with a blocked nose mate".

By the middle of September the second expeditionary force was already forming, with three hundred and ninety two men in camp, to commence their training. This could only mean one thing. The AIF was finally on the move.

2

The Journey

The 22nd of September was a busy day for all at the camp in Enoggera, with 'H' Company, of the 9th Battalion, along with the band and drummers, entraining at the local station for the trip to Pinkenba Wharf at the mouth of the Brisbane River. That afternoon too, saw 'C' Squadron of the 2nd Light Horse, riding out to Pinkenba. To the civilians who ventured out to cheer them it was just another daily exercise run for the horses, but nonetheless it was a welcome sight *and* distraction for the soldiers who privately hoped that their families would be present to say farewell and wave them off. The date of sailing had been kept secret from all, including the press, and at 0230 hours the following morning the remainder of the Light Horse departed for a night ride to Brisbane, arriving at the wharf at the crack of dawn.

The A14, or 'Star of England', was a cargo ship which usually carried frozen meat, but today it was a troop and horse carrier, having been fitted out with horse stalls on all of the decks which could be ventilated.

The advance party of the 9th Battalion had been tasked with preparing the Orient liner 'Omrah', known as transport A5, for the embarkation of the remainder of their Battalion. The 9th Battalion had struck it lucky with *their* ship, the 'Omrah' being a comfortable passenger liner which had operated between England and Australia for many years.

The Light Horsemen's first task was the loading of the regiment's horses. As luck had it, a number of the regiment had worked in the business of shipping horses to India prior to the war, so were well practised in the art of loading horses on to a ship. The rest of the men simply observed and copied their methods, resulting in the fast and efficient loading of their mounts, which were soon stalled and fed. The rest of the morning was spent loading saddles and all manner of Quartermaster stores.

Like the 2nd Light Horse, the 9th Battalion had departed camp during the night, at 0414 hours, on the 24th of September, arriving at Pinkenba as the sun was rising over Brisbane. Approaching the gang plank the soldiers were in awe of these great iron vessels which towered above the wharf, the sight of them evoking a sense of anticipation among the Australian troops. They knew that these ships would take them on a journey to a foreign land, where they would be engaged in a monumental conflict. The anticipation of what lay ahead, both in terms of the challenges and the unknown, filled their minds and hearts.

There was one, however, who was not so much full of anticipation or awe, just fear. Private Jackson, like most of the troops, had never been on a ship, let alone seen the ocean. Pausing at the gang plank he turned to his mates.

"I can't do it fellas".

"Do what?" asked Archie.

"I'm not getting on that bloody thing," he exclaimed, "what if it sinks?"

"Well, I think you'll have to mate," explained Archie.

"What *are* you on about yer banana bender?" asked Clancy.

"Nobody told me we had to go on a ship. No mate, I'm not getting on *that* bloody thing. Father read about that ship the Titanic a few years back and all those folks who were drowned. Nope, not for me mate," said Jacko nervously.

As his mates tried to usher him up the gang plank, the panic on Jacko began to set in, with him physically pushing and shoving in his attempts to avoid the inevitable.

"Well, I don't think you have a choice mate. England is a long way," explained Archie, indicating with a flick of his head that it was time to board, "besides, that ship was all alone in the middle of the ocean; we will have a Navy escort, so if anything did happen they'd be on hand to rescue us".

"All aboard!" the Company Sergeant Major shouted.

All of the excitement was causing a stir in the ranks as

impatient men formed up behind were desperate to board the ship and get their heads down.

"Come on you blokes" and "chuck him off the wharf", were some of the cries coming from the crowd.

Try as they may the boys could not convince Jacko to step any further.

"What the hell is going on here?" thundered the voice of big Sergeant MacDonald.

"Its Jacko sarge he is terrified....look," replied Roo

As the huge Scotsman stared at Jackson he could see the fear in his eyes.

"Look yer wee beastie are yer getting on the boat or what?" asked the sergeant.

"I...I...I can't," shrieked Jacko.

"How in God's name did yer think we were going to get to France? Walk?" growled Sergeant Mac, as his huge fist struck Jacko, knocking him to the ground; unconscious.

All present were shocked and impressed at the same time. One blow to knock a man out?

"Bloody hell sarge, remind me never to get on the wrong side of you," said Clancy.

"Well, it did the trick did it not? Now, you men carry him and his kit on to the ship then we can all have a snooze just like he is," said the sergeant.

The 9th Battalion were finally all on board by 0800 hours, along with detachments of the Australian Army Service Corps and Australian Army Medical Corps, plus four nurses from the Australian Army Nursing Service. The officers, nurses and a section of NCOs were accommodated in cabins whilst the remaining NCOs and troops were to be housed in the cargo holds which had been converted in to troop decks. Wooden staircases had been constructed between the decks, and electric lights installed in the otherwise pitch black living quarters. Wooden tables and benches had also been installed as a makeshift dining area. The troop decks held up to three hundred men. Hooks had been fitted to the ceiling and each man issued with a canvass hammock, which, during daylight hours would be stowed at the sides of the room, and fitted to the hooks at night when the individual chose to go to bed.

"Bloody hell I've seen better cattle sheds than this," said Stowie.

"Yeah it is a bit grim," said Roo, "but how are we going to get Jacko down these stairs? They're a bit steep".

"Pass him to me and I'll stick him over my shoulder," Clancy suggested.

After a bit of a heave ho Jacko was soon draped over Clancy's shoulder like a rag doll, his arms swinging freely with every step that Clancy took. Once on their allocated deck they laid Jacko gently on the floor and surveyed their surroundings.

"Hammocks?!" exclaimed Clancy, "that'll certainly rock me to sleep".

After some trial and error the men finally worked out how to hang their beds and clambered uneasily in to them for a short, but well earned, cat nap.

The departure of the ships had been kept a secret so, at first, there were no family, friends, or well wishers to wave them off, but word soon spread and by the time of departure at mid day there were over two hundred well wishers crowding the dock.

The morning sun cast a warm glow over Pinkenba Wharf, as the sound of bustling activity filled the air. The air was thick with a mix of anticipation, pride, and a tinge of sadness, as the momentous day had arrived. The ships that would carry the soldiers to war were standing tall and resolute, ready to embark on their solemn journey.

Both Percy and Archie stared down at the gathering throng on the wharf, not thinking for one minute that their families would have heard the news of their departure, let alone made it to the port on time. But the whispers of troop movements over the past few days, as well as the armada of ships which now filled the Brisbane River, had spread quickly to the country towns, with relatives and friends, feeling the pull to catch just a small glimpse of their loved one; quickly filling up the carriages of the trains heading in to the city.

Amidst the crowd gathered below, Ray and Doris stood with a mixture of hope and worry etched on their faces. Ray, a sturdy man with greying hair, wore a worn-out hat that hinted at his days of hard work on the station over the many years, whilst his wife Doris, a kind-hearted woman with gentle eyes, held a handkerchief tightly in her hands, prepared for both tears of joy and longing.

From the 'Omrah', both Archie and Roo stood tall and proud, in their uniforms, their eyes scanning the crowd, searching for the familiar faces of their loved ones, whom they did not even think would be there. Whilst Percy onboard the 'Star of England" did the same, his face etched with determination and a touch of nervousness.

Stowie, and Jacko, now recovered from his "sleep" and

resigned to his fate, felt a sense of calm, and strained their eyes, hoping to catch sight of family members in the crowd. Stowie's gaze finally locked onto his parents, who had come to bid him farewell, their eyes filled with a mix of pride and worry, whilst Jacko recognised a familiar figure, that of his younger sister, who had travelled a great distance to be there, her unwavering love shining through her teary-eyed smile.

As the time for departure drew near, the atmosphere crackled with anticipation. The 'Omrah' began to slowly pull away from the dock, her engines rumbling and fog horns bellowing a farewell salute. The sound resonated in the hearts of the departing soldiers, a mix of bittersweet pride and the weight of duty.

Amidst the cheers and waves of countless onlookers, Archie and Roo at last caught sight of their family. Ray's weathered face lit up with a proud smile as he waved his hat high in the air, whilst Doris, overcome with emotion, clutched the handkerchief to her chest, tears streaming down her cheeks. Lil stood beside Ray and Doris, her expression full of worry and pride, her hand resting on Frank's tiny shoulder, the young boy oblivious to the gravity and history of the moment. But she could not see Percy anywhere.

"Archie! Roo! Where's Percy?!" she called out.

As Archie and Roo exchanged a glance at Lil, who was waving frantically, they could not make out her calls.

"Do you think she's wondering where Percy is mate?" asked Roo.

"You know you could be right there," replied Archie as he leaned forward across the ship's railing, pointed down the wharf and began to shout, "PERCY'S DOWN THERE ON THE STAR OF ENGLAND LIL...DOWN THERE!"

Lil couldn't hear Archie above the noise of the crowd but from the way he was forcefully gesturing to her left she somehow understood that her husband was on another ship. At that moment only the 'Omrah' was moving, so Lil knew that she would have time to search for Percy, and blew a kiss in thanks to Archie and Roo. The two men raised their right hands in a unified salute, their hearts brimming with a mix of relief, determination, hope, and a touch of sorrow.

Meanwhile, Clancy, stood alone on the deck, having neither seen nor expected anyone to be there to wave *him* off, and as the ship began its departure, his gaze remained fixed on the receding dock, devoid of any familiar faces; yet, despite this, Clancy stood tall, resigned to the fact that his journey would be a solitary one.

As the 'Omrah' sailed slowly away from the dock, the sound of her horns merged with the deafening applause and cheers from the crowd. Ray, Doris, Lil, and Frank stood waving until the ship was a mere speck on the horizon, their presence a symbol of pride and love. The cheers from the crowd continued to echo, as another ship roared in to life, preparing to embark on its own journey. This ship carried Percy, Chugger and their mates from the Light Horse.

"Quick! I think that's Percy's ship," exclaimed Lil as she lifted the bottom of her dress above her feet and began to run towards the departing vessel, Frank in tow, and Ray and Doris running closely behind.

As the 'Star of England' cast off and began to pull away from the dock, Percy's heart sank a little deeper. He strained his eyes, desperately searching for a glimpse of Lil, Frank, or his parents in the crowd, but there was no sign of them. Doubt gnawed at his mind, wondering if they had missed the news of his departure, or worse, if they were unaware altogether.

Just as Percy was about to turn away, accepting the reality that they weren't there, he caught a movement in the corner of his eye. Turning his head, his eyes widened with astonishment and hope. There, running frantically along the dock, were Lil, Frank, and his parents. Lil, her face flushed with exertion and tears streaming down her cheeks, clasped Frank's tiny hand tightly, urging him to keep up, whilst Ray and Doris, followed in her wake.

Percy's heart swelled with a blend of emotions, for he could hardly believe his eyes as he watched his family racing against time to bid him farewell. As he raised his arms high into the air, waving vigorously to catch their attention, Lil's face lit up with relief and joy as her eyes met with Percy's. She waved back with all her might, her voice lost in the distance between them but her emotions clearly conveyed. Ray and Doris, breathless but filled with pride, waved their arms and shouted words of encouragement to their son, their voices barely reaching his ears; whilst onboard, Chugger couldn't help but share in Percy's happiness, vigorously slapping him on the back. It may not have been the farewell that they had imagined, but it was a moment that would forever be etched in their memories, carrying them through the hardships and uncertainties that lay ahead, until they could be reunited once again.

The 'Omrah' became the first troop ship to depart Queensland, for the war, with the 'Star of England' following ninety minutes later, and the 'Rangatira' the following day.

On the 28th of September the convoy anchored at Hobson's Bay, Port Phillip, then moved to Port Melbourne Pier on the 30th, where it remained in situ for three weeks whilst awaiting the arrival of the New Zealand contingent. Due to the threat from two German warships in the Pacific Ocean, the New Zealand government had delayed the departure of its troopships until a naval escort could be provided to Australia.

The 9th Battalion CO's vast military and training knowledge, combined with the ability and drive of Captain Ross, ensured that their valuable time in Melbourne did not go to waste. Dressed in their adopted training uniform, of dungaree trousers, jersey and white cloth hats, the battalion carried out long route marches around the areas of Albert Park, Fisherman's Bend and Heidelberg, as well as undertaking practice attack drills, and entraining and detraining drills. This on the move training was to stand them in good stead and prepare the men for future battles.

The 2nd Light Horse disembarked at Williamstown where they were billeted at the local showgrounds for the next few weeks and it was during this time, after petitions from the CO, that permission was finally granted for the Light Horse to wear the coveted Emu Plume in their slouch hats; a proud moment in the history of the Light Horse, the deal being finally sealed by a visit from the Prime Minister and other dignitaries.

Whilst in Melbourne the 9th Battalion was inspected again by the Brigade Commander who was impressed by what he saw, especially after barely a month of military service. Leave to visit the city was soon permitted during off duty hours, which were few and far between, and many made use of the sea pool at Stubb Baths. Major Harvey became the victim of officer high spirits after being ambushed by subalterns, emerging with one side of his bushy, waxed moustache clipped off.

"Hurry up and wait" was now a familiar saying, but waiting became very tedious to the men who had volunteered to fight the Hun. But, finally, at 1525 hours on the 19th of October, the A5 slipped out of Port Melbourne like the escaped convict, William Buckley, had over a hundred years earlier, when he had taken his famous chance. They were followed the next day by the 2nd Light Horse who had changed vessels to one, the 'Anglo Egyptian', which proved more fit for purpose for both the troops and their horses, being larger and less crowded.

Although conditions were cramped, everyone gradually settled down to what became normal life. The scramble for a shave and a wash was always a chore, but Archie and Roo soon discovered that getting up thirty minutes before reveille was the only way to beat the inevitable rush.

During the voyage each unit carried on training their soldiers in general battlefield tactics, rifle drill, weapon handling, physical training and, in the case of the Light Horse regiments, stable duties.

Five days later, on the 24th of October, the convoy dropped anchor in a bay surrounded by hills on all sides. This was King George's Sound, the harbour of a small town called Albany in Western Australia, a town soon to become synonymous with the ANZAC legend.

The respite for the infantry troops on the sea journey through the Great Australian Bight was soon broken after breakfast by a route march. The 9th Battalion was ferried to shore via the tender boats. All soldiers were dressed in full battle order and had been issued with rations. The days of wearing of dungarees for *real* soldiers work were long gone, for the battalion now needed to practise and prepare themselves properly for what was to come. Captain Butler, the Kilcoy doctor and Medical Officer for the 9th Battalion, had that day fallen foul of his own recommendations. Having determined that all soldiers should sterilize their water bottles with condy's crystals, otherwise known as potassium permanganate, and allow them to stand for twenty hours before thoroughly rinsing them out before use, he had neglected to carry out the latter part of his own instruction. During the march he took two generous gulps of his water only to realise that he was in fact drinking the condy's crystals. Needless to say the taste was foul, and observing his reaction and his spitting the crystals out was a source of entertainment for both officers and soldiers, sitting by the roadside, who cheered and applauded loudly. Doc Butler obliged with a bow of appreciation as soldiers came forward to share their water with the well respected MO.

"I think the water being pink was a clue doc," chuckled one soldier as he handed the doctor his water bottle.

"It's a good job you don't need a doctor or you'd be buggered eh doc?" added another.

"You could be right there son. You could indeed," replied the slightly embarrassed, but grateful, doctor.

During their time at Albany, most days were spent on board ship, apart from the 31st of October, when the various regiments and battalions were allowed to stretch their legs ashore. There *were* the occasional on board sports days which, combined with training, proved a good tonic for the camaraderie and team spirit of the men. The tug of war was particularly popular, with the occasional bet being put on the side.

Orders were also issued that all personal mail should now be unsealed, or were to be written on postcards. Censorship was now upon them, and for good reason, which *all* understood only too well. But to all on board it was the first acknowledgement that they would soon be sailing to who knows where. The arrival of the New Zealand contingent, on the cruisers 'Philomel' and 'Pyramus', escorted by the Japanese warship 'Ibuki', seemed to confirm this.

The harbour was now as busy as downtown Brisbane on market day, with four mighty warships and thirty six transports now docked in the Sound, waiting patiently for the "off" like the jockeys in the Kilcoy Cup.

Tensions were now running high, for it was indeed a serious time; this being demonstrated a day earlier when a steamer entered the harbour and failed to reply to a signal to "lay to". For its non-compliance it was greeted by the duty warship at the harbour entrance, with two loud and terrifying salvos across its bow.

On the same day Archie, Roo and Clancy were taking some air on deck, hoping for some more naval gun action, when they noticed about one hundred and fifty men coming up the gangplank.

"What's that about do you reckon?" asked Roo.

"Buggered if I know mate," replied a just as curious Clancy.

It transpired that, due to overcrowding on the 'Horatio', 'A' Company of the 6th Battalion was being transferred to the 'Omrah'. Apart from disrupting the members of 9th Battalion, who had been, until that moment, occupying the lower troop deck, and had to now be re-housed on the upper deck guard room, the 6th Battalion also brought an unwelcome bout of measles with them. This soon spread to a few members of the 9th Battalion, who were none too pleased.

"Thanks for sharing fellas!"

The day that all had been waiting for arrived on the 1st of November; departure day. As the 'Omrah' was to be the penultimate ship to leave, the men of the 9th Battalion watched from the upper deck as the great fleet steamed slowly, yet gracefully, out of the harbour. All in all it was a mighty feat, and at seven miles long, took over three hours to complete.

"If Mum and Dad could see what we are seeing now," Archie uttered.

All who stood in awe on deck gave a silent prayer of hope, wondering secretly if they would ever see these shores again.

Clancy could sense the feeling of gloom.

"Cheer up you bastards," he announced whilst holding up a bundle of bank notes, "two up anyone?"

"Clancy me old mate, got any grog to go with that?" asked Roo.

"Might have mate, might have," Clancy replied with a sly wink.

"Then let's get to it," said Archie.

Like the fading Australian coastline as it disappeared over the horizon, the feelings of gloom were soon just a distant glimmer. As some of the troops enjoyed their "sport", many others watched the Australian coast fading away, until the curtain of darkness finally shut it out. The next morning the ships were out of sight of land, with nothing but the calm blue sea all around them, like a sheet of shimmering glass. At last everyone felt that they were finally on their way to France, via England, but, unknown to them, on the very day of departure, Great Britain had declared war on the Ottoman Empire of Turkey. Their destiny was now set.

With its precious cargo of twenty one thousand five hundred Australian, and eight thousand five hundred New Zealander troops, twelve thousand horses from both countries, and a huge array of medical and military equipment and supplies, the vast flotilla steamed cautiously westwards. Once out in the Indian Ocean the convoy adopted its defensive formation, with the Australian troop ships forming three long lines, and the Kiwis stationed two lines behind them. The four escorting warships, the 'Melbourne', 'Pyramus', 'Minotaur' and 'Sydney' were stationed at posts to the front, rear, port and starboard sides. The convoy soon increased by two to thirty eight when the Western Australian contingent arrived from Fremantle, in two transports, very ably escorted by the 'Ibuki', which had slipped out of port, undetected, a few days earlier, for this specific task.

For the first few days the weather changed and the glass like sea soon became a rough, torrid soup. On deck, sports had to be postponed due to the rising and falling motion of the ship. A player could jump in to the air to retrieve an incoming rugby ball and have the deck meet his feet before he had a chance to fall back to the ground. Clancy and the boys, who were enjoying their temporary power of flight, were disappointed by the postponement, but soon found other ways of occupying themselves. Many, who had never left Australia before, let alone set foot on a ship, were feeling sick and at night took to sleeping on the mess tables, rather than swing back and forth in their hammocks. As it turned out, this was not the solution as many, including Roo, simply slid up and down the table top with the motion of the ship, or rolled off, plummeting on to the hard floor below. Either way, there was much swearing and cursing going on, much to the delight of Clancy who even learned a few new words; some of which even made him blush.

Although Jacko had now resigned himself to being a temporary "prisoner" aboard ship, it transpired that he was *not* a good sailor and certainly did not immediately acquire his sea legs as his mates had. Three days of sea sickness and the remainder of the mid tropical heat on the troop deck had left him feeling like a beetroot coloured skeleton, with but two cravings - iced water and shade. Sadly there was no iced water but his mates *did* manage to rig up some shade on deck with some canvass they had scrounged.

Jacko was grateful, "as long as I'm alive I can't complain, and it's a jolly sight better than being dead".

The nights were the redeeming feature of this voyage. After a day spent amid blazing canvass and sun baked decks, with the sea shimmering like a vast sheet of steel, it was doubly enjoyable for the men to lean over the rails at night, whilst the vessel slipped with a hiss through the almost motionless ocean, letting the cool breeze fan their faces.

"This is the life eh?" said Roo, as he gazed at the moon rising splendidly over the horizon.

The group of friends were all standing bare-headed, coatless and bootless, lining the rail, mesmerised at the tiny swell the ship sent racing out over the face of the sea.

"To think, rich people go on sea voyages for the fun of it, and we're doing it for free," remarked Clancy

"Them's the perks of the army," added Stowie.

The moon had now risen high in the night sky, its beams lighting up the countless miles of ocean creating a silver road ahead of them, in which the ripples crossed and glinted, and now and then a flying fish flew up the radiant track, its transparent wings scintillating in the soft light. As the men marvelled at the sight, their troubles departed. Even Jacko's thoughts of bringing up his dinner completely left his mind. Whilst on another ship, Percy cast out thoughts of his arms, tired with swinging his rifle about in the merciless sun, forgot his burning feet on the steel deck, and gazed silently, imagining being home with his wife and young son. Had he done the right thing? Should he have stayed at home with his family? Could he have lived with himself, and the guilt, if he hadn't volunteered? No doubt each man was harbouring similar thoughts, but there was nothing for it than to soldier on, get the job done, and go home.

The roaring seas were not the only peril to be had, for two enemy warships, the 'Emden' and 'Konigsburg', were believed to be lurking somewhere close.

Things were now becoming real for all on board the ships. Within days, as they entered warmer climes, the ships' companies and passengers were regularly paraded on deck at night, during which the ships' lights would be switched off for a time, in order to practise for night manoeuvres, to lessen the danger of being seen at night by enemy vessels.

On the 8th of November the 'Sydney' broke away from the convoy and headed off towards the Cocos Islands. The German warship 'Emden' had landed sailors on the islands with the intent of destroying the wireless station. Naturally the said station was manned, the operator managing to send off a brief distress signal on sighting the approaching enemy. As a result the 'Sydney' was dispatched and, during a brief one hour battle, the 'Emden' was destroyed and its crew captured.

All battles, it seemed, must have a positive, especially for the 9th Battalion, who were excused duty for the afternoon and given an extra beer ration.

"This is good eh boys?" said Stowie.

"Yeah, I wonder what we'll get when *we* win a battle?" laughed Clancy.

After the usual initiations by King Neptune, for all who were crossing the equator for the first time – which was just about the whole of the AIF, as few had left Australia before – the convoy called in for coal and water at Colombo, Ceylon, before continuing their journey towards the Suez Canal.

The temperatures were much the same as those in Australia, so did not bother the troops too much, however, many had taken to sleeping out on deck to avoid the sweltering heat and stench from the inside of the iron juggernaut. Archie and Roo, again, became very wise to the situation and ensured that they were amongst the first out in the open air to hitch up their hammocks, or even find a comfy spot on the wooden deck, before the hoards of sweating soldiers swarmed anxiously, and eagerly, in to the fresh air to find a suitable place to lay their clammy bodies. The breeze too, from the movement of the ship as it cut through the Indian Ocean, was a welcome addition to their attempt at a restful sleep. Percy and his mates did much the same each night, the stench from the horse droppings adding to the incentive to sleep outside.

After six weeks aboard ship the men were looking forward to completing their training on terra firma. Although, for the most part, the majority of the AIF had some form of military experience, all were impatient to revise their skills and get on with the job at hand. Life on board had comprised of physical training and the occasional classroom lecture, but more work was yet to be done.

An announcement came on the 28th of November.

"Righto men, some news......"

"The Kaiser has surrendered and we're sailing home tomorrow," shouted one hopeful soldier from the ranks of sweaty troops, as they paraded on deck.

"No such luck I'm afraid. We are not going to England. We are disembarking at Port Said," said the officer.

This excited Archie, who, along with his brother Percy, was a bit of a history buff.

"We're staying in Egypt? Bugger me! Think of the history to be seen there," he said.

The 1st Division had been redirected to Egypt as a result of overcrowding on Salisbury Plain. Colonel Harry Chauvel, a regular soldier and veteran of the South African War, had sailed for England with his wife and three children to assume his appointment as the Australian representative on the Imperial General Staff. Whilst on route, war broke out, and on reporting for duty he was directed to assume command of the 1st Light Horse Brigade of the Australian Imperial Force on its arrival in Britain. Becoming concerned with the slow progress of construction of the AIF's proposed quarters, he made frequent visits to Salisbury Plain, accompanied by Major Cecil Foott, of the Royal Australian Engineers. Having witnessed, personally, the general appalling weather conditions and hardships being suffered by British and Canadian troops, Chauvel was convinced that the huts would not be ready on time, and that Australian and New Zealand troops would therefore have to spend a winter under canvas. Having relayed his concerns to the High Commissioner for Australia in London, former Prime Minister Sir George Reid, Chauvel convinced him to approach Lord Kitchener with an alternate plan of diverting the AIF and NZEF to Egypt; which was done.

"So, we get the sun and they get the rain and mud? Fair swap I'd say," said Chugger.

"No doubt we'll experience similar conditions soon enough, so enjoy it while you can boys," added Percy.

3

Egypt

On arrival at the southern entrance to the Suez Canal, Division staff had learned that rebel Arabs had been firing upon ships transiting this great waterway. A decision was therefore made to traverse the canal during the hours of darkness. With the number of ships in the convoy this would be carried out over a few nights. At 2200 hours the 'Omrah' set off on its precarious journey, complete with a platoon of twenty armed soldiers on deck with orders to return fire on any shots from the canal bank. The night, however, was uneventful, but as they docked at Port Said to collect mail and provisions from Australia, a soon to be familiar enemy, in the guise of Arab hawkers, invaded the ships. "Hey, Australia! You buy this antik. Very, very old," was a common cry, or the sale of what Clancy called "smutty" post cards, of naked or semi-naked women. Not having seen a naked woman before, Archie and Roo were eager for a squizzy.

"You'll go blind if you look at those mate," said Clancy as Archie and Roo half heartedly waved away the eager, and disappointed vendor.

"What? You no buy? Very naughty ladies……..look".

"Bugger off with your filth Abdul, before I drop you mate," said Clancy, fists clenched.

The unsuspecting hawkers very quickly learned that the Australian soldiers were not to be messed with. They believed in free enterprise, but also in fair play and decency. Despite this, the hawkers remained a part of daily life for the AIF's stay in Egypt, even managing to profit from the sale of silk, fruit, antiquities, and not to mention their foul tasting cigarettes, which became affectionately known as camel dung.

On the 4th of December the 'Omrah' slipped out of Port Said and sailed on to Alexandria, named for the Macedonian King, Alexander the Great, who had conquered these lands more than two thousand years earlier. The area had been the scene of many a battle throughout the centuries, the prominent structure of Fort Marabout being one such player during the Napoleonic Wars, when, in August 1801, the British had encountered fierce opposition from the defenders, but eventually carried out a successful assault on the fort. The ship arrived at Alexandria just at the peep of day. The beautiful harbour was almost crammed with shipping of all descriptions, including twenty five large steamers, which had been captured from the Germans. As the 'Omrah' pulled alongside the wharf, the weary troops proceeded to disembark. Walking down the gang plank, the obvious history of the place, gave way to a dirty hay-strewn wharf, a high concrete wall which enclosed the harbour area, and the dowdy office buildings of the Egyptian State Railways. Everything was done safely and without a hitch, with all being pleased to be ashore again. There was excitement too as on arrival more letters from home awaited the troops. There was, sadly, no time to read them though as the Division was off to Mena Camp, near Cairo.

Upon disembarking, yet again the men were surrounded by hawkers calling out "Australia! Australia! Looky, looky".

Some were selling food items such as fruit and flat breads, which caught the eye of the CSM.

It's going be a long journey to camp boys, so grab some of these dago rations while you can".

The announcement was music to the mens' ears, and much to the delight of the many Abduls, Omars and Mohammeds, who were soon liberated of all of their wares. Their money belts were bursting; for them it had been a profitable day. But now it was time to restock and find out where the Aussies were going.

'B', 'C', 'D' and 'E' Companies arrived at Mena Camp just before midnight, with 'A' Company, who had been detailed for guards on the ship, reaching camp at around 0220 hours in the morning. Four days later the battalion was complete with the arrival of its Transport Section.

During the train journey the troops hung out of every

window and door admiring the greenness of the fertile lands of the Nile, as well as the villages with their white stone houses, with flat rooves. Egypt was a marvel, a wonder, to those who had never left Australia before. The journey was through a level strip of intensely cultivated land divided into small patches of clover, beans, barley, and occasionally artichokes and onions. The stock too was very numerous – sheep of some unknown breed, humped cattle, buffalo, donkeys, camels, mules and some domestic fowls, usually perched on the top of a mud hut. To the men, who expected a barren desert, Egypt seemed at first sight to be the most heavily stocked of all countries. As Archie leaned out of the train window his eyes were wide with wonder.

Roo stood beside him, taking in the sights with equal amazement. He nudged Clancy, "would you look at that, Clance! This place is like a bloomin' paradise! I never thought I'd see such greenery outside of our little town back home."

Clancy nodded his agreement, a wide grin stretching across his face.

"You're right mate. Egypt is nothing like what I imagined. It's like a whole different world out here, and just look at all those animals!" Clancy exclaimed, pointing excitedly at the array of creatures passing by, "I bet we could fill a whole zoo with the ones we've seen already."

Stowie, who had been leaning against the door, chimed in with a chuckle, "and don't forget those chooks perched on the huts, strutting about like they own the place".

Canals were everywhere, with many different beasts walking round in circles pumping water out of the canal for irrigation, like a never ending circus parade. The villages appeared very compact with the houses adjoined in terraced rows, which reminded Taff of the workers cottages back home on Anglesey. Sometimes there were chimneys and occasionally a glass window. But there were no fences to be seen anywhere and very few wheeled vehicles, all produce being carried on the backs of the animals. The roads too were very narrow with only enough space for one way traffic. The villages, themselves, were constructed on raised land added to by the refuse heaps of the ages. The banks of the Nile were raised to prevent serious flooding, and the masts of the boats could be seen over the tops of the banks, as if they were floating above the land on a magic carpet. Trees were few and far between, and those that the men *did* see were mostly ugly looking specimens; except the date palms, which were graceful enough.

As the train chugged along toward Cairo, the soldiers continued their light-hearted conversation, their spirits lifted by the unexpected sights of this new land.

At Cairo the men each received a meagre, yet welcome, meal which consisted of a pint of cocoa, a long bread roll and a generous piece of Dutch cheese.

"Hey fellas have a go at this bread," said Archie.

"Yeah, it would make a great cricket bat eh?" joked Clancy.

"Well, it's certainly hard enough," replied Archie.

It was a stroke of luck that most had brought along rations from the ship, or those that they had purchased from the eager street pedlars. Those who were unfortunate *not* to have any did not go hungry as there was always a benevolent mate at hand. The cooks did their best with……nothing……but did manage to get some welcome hot tea on the boil.

"Nothing like a hot cuppa to remind you of home, eh boys?" said Roo.

The final leg of the journey was completed in open topped electric tram cars.

Mena Camp, to some, would have been a disappointment, especially to some *other* armies, but not to the Australians or New Zealanders. On arrival the men were each issued with two blankets.

"Behold, Mena Camp," said the Q Sergeant, as the men gazed out in to the darkness.

Archie, Roo and Clancy strained their eyes trying to see the camp, but all they could make out was sand and gravel.

"Sand!" exclaimed Clancy, "it's just like the showgrounds at Nanango when the camp draft is on".

"Yeah, bloody hard to get a good spot!" a voice responded from the darkness.

"This'll do me, cobbers," announced Roo as he dropped his kit, shook out his blankets and laid them on the stony ground.

Not needing an invitation, others followed, and the battalion, apart from the sentries, was soon sound asleep under the night sky of Egypt, oblivious of the ancient wonders to be revealed in the morning.

Owing to the quick re-routing of the antipodean forces, there had been no time to construct a camp, or even to provide tents for shelter. It had been a cold and wet night sleeping under the stars of the Egyptian desert, but the troops were treated to a magnificent sight as the sun slowly crept over the horizon, for the camp was situated right at the foot of the Pyramids.

"We must be in the Valley of the Kings!" exclaimed Archie

as he gazed in awe at the massive stone structures looming above them.

"I'm gonna climb that," said Roo, as he pointed excitedly at the largest and tallest pyramid, "not today though eh?"

"Gosh, that is incredible!" exclaimed Archie as he cast his eyes on the great structure before them, "it must be over four hundred and fifty feet tall".

As each man rose to their feet and looked upon the huge pyramids, they marvelled at their construction, offering opinions and theories about how the many large stones with which they are built were lifted to such a height, as many of the stones must surely have weighed seven or eight tons. Mena Camp itself was on the western side of the Nile valley, with sand hills approximately one hundred feet high to the rear. The countryside was quite open and the troops could see the sandstone cliffs on the east side of the valley about eight miles away.

During the next night the heavens opened and it poured with rain. Ordinarily, on the stations back home the rain would be a welcome sight, but when you are sleeping under the night sky with only a woollen blanket to protect you, it certainly *was* not. Apart from a few moans and curses the men just got on with it. Archie, Roo and Clancy huddled together under four blankets whilst using the remainder to construct a makeshift shelter, using their packs and webbing to give the "tent" both some walls and height. It did the job well enough, but it soon became sodden, with rain water dripping on to the sleeping occupants below.

The 'Anglo Egyptian', complete with its cargo of two regiments of Light Horse and their mounts, docked in Alexandria on the 9th of December at 1400 hours; its passengers having been on board for seventy days. Not only the men, but the horses had done amazingly well, the horses having stood for the entire voyage; but they were in no state to be ridden, and wouldn't be for several weeks. As soon as the ship docked the mammoth task of unloading the horses began. The trucks were already lined up on the wharf next to the ship. For the most part the unloading was a fast and simple task, the horses probably feeling some relief at being on the move. But there *was* one horse which behaved somewhat rowdily, that horse being Bill the Bastard. Bill was a chestnut Waler who stood over fourteen hands. He was the most obnoxious horse in the AIF, refusing to let *any* man ride him, and a horse guaranteed to give you a well timed and accurate kick should you venture behind him. Percy, it seemed, had somehow been given the dubious honour of leading Bill from his stalls and out in to the fresh air of Egypt.

"Come on mate, it's all good," said Percy in a calm voice, "let's go; come on boy".

After a few snorts and stomps of his hooves Bill had proven his point and casually followed Percy down the gang plank and on to the waiting truck. Although still outwardly annoyed, Bill seemed to sense that life was about to improve.

"Good lad Bill. I bet you are all worked up after being couped up on that ship for all this time, eh mate?" said Percy, reaching in to his breast pocket for some licorice which he had bought from the ship's canteen.

Bill's ears pricked up as he smelt the odour of the licorice.

"Hey boy, do you like that?" said Percy as he offered Bill a morsel of the sweet.

Bill did indeed like licorice and eagerly took it from the palm of Percy's hand, then nuzzled his nose against Percy's tunic pocket as if asking for more.

"Sorry mate, that was my last bit," announced Percy whilst showing his empty hands.

Bill snorted his disappointment and shook his head. As Percy stroked Bill's face he promised him that they would meet again and that he would bring him more treats.

By 1600 hours the first train, loaded with two hundred and thirty horses, and half of the regiment, departed for Cairo; the remainder leaving just over an hour later. The journey took five hours and, on arrival, the troops were greeted with muddy streets, the latter having been caused by a combination of heavy rainfall and poor street drainage. Because the horses were too weak to be ridden, the troopers marched on foot to the camp at Ma'adi, with an Egyptian police constable as a guide. The journey of nine miles, but estimated by the soldiers at twenty, took all night, the men loaded with full equipment and each leading two horses.

As Percy plodded along the dark, unfamiliar terrain, his eyes strained to make out the surroundings in the dim moonlight. Turning to Chugger and Davo, who were marching beside him, their faces shadowed by exhaustion, he whispered "bloody hell fellas, this night march feels like it's been going on forever. Can't even see where we're heading half the time".

Chugger, his voice laced with fatigue, nodded in agreement.

"Yeah mate, it's a fair dinkum task, this march, and we can't even rely on our horses to carry us," he replied, "but mate, look on the bright side, we'll be fit as racehorses after dragging these beasts for miles".

Davo, struggling to keep his balance as he led his two horses, chuckled to himself. "Fit as racehorses, you say? Well, I reckon we'll be thoroughbreds by the time we reach that Ma'adi camp, then. But I'll be glad when we can finally see where we're going!"

As they trudged on, the conversation shifted to the unfamiliar surroundings and the difficulties they faced in the darkness. Percy, peering ahead, tried to make sense of the barely visible roads.

"Anyone else finding these roads a bit tricky to navigate? They're narrower than a bandolier strap, and no lights to guide us! Good thing we've got this Egyptian constable bloke to show us the way," he said.

Chugger, squinting through the darkness, replied with a hint of frustration. "Yeah, mate, I can barely see me own boots, let alone the road. But I reckon we've got it lucky compared to the rest of the regiment leading their horses through this night."

Davo nodded in agreement. "True that, Chugger me old mate; half a regiment of blokes pushing on through the dark? Let's hope this constable knows where he's taking us. I'd hate to end up in some Pharaoh's tomb by mistake!"

The trio shared a tired laugh, finding solace in the camaraderie that eased the weariness of the night march, striding on, each step bringing them closer to their destination.

The town of Ma'adi was barely eight years old and was under the jurisdiction of a major London based land and investment company. It appeared spick and span and well cared for. Many of the occupants were British, mostly glorified administrators in the employment of the Egyptian government, and were not expecting the sudden arrival of soldiers on their doorstep; let alone *colonial* soldiers.

As with the infantry, yet again there were not enough tents to house the men, but they made do, spending the next week erecting tents as they were delivered, creating a neatly laid out camp that any commander would be proud of.

The 9th Battalion too, received a welcome delivery on the 10th; four bell tents per company had arrived. Sadly each tent could only house twelve men so the troops drew lots or tossed coins to ascertain who the fortunate occupants would be.

"Roo you couldn't win a cold on a wintry day mate!" laughed Clancy.

Fortunately, the few rainy days on their arrival were the only days of wet weather that they would experience for the remainder of their time at Mena Camp.

Welcome news was soon received that a fifth of each company were to be granted five and a half hours leave to Cairo that evening. Things were looking up for the section as they were all on the list. Curfew was 2200 hours.

"Plenty of time for a bit of mischief," said Clancy.

Before arriving in Egypt the troops had been paraded in front of the Regimental Sergeant Major, another veteran of the British Army, and one whom had previously served in Egypt, and were given the sage advice *"nothing in Egypt is ever free, so beware and be on your guard at all times"*.

As they stepped off the electric tram, on arrival in the city, the boys encountered their first enterprising local. Cairo was a bustling metropolis, dating back four thousand years. To the country boys from Queensland it was hell on earth.

"I bloody hate cities," said Clancy.

"Me too," responded Archie.

"Yeah? How many cities have you been to then mate?" asked Stowie.

"Brisbane and this place," replied Archie, feeling quite satisfied with himself.

"That many eh?" said Stowie.

Clancy glanced around for a bit of assistance.

"Hey! Abdul!" he shouted at an unsuspecting passerby.

"Eshaq," replied the young Egyptian.

"What?" asked Clancy.

"Eshaq, that is my name, not Abdul," the young man replied.

"Oh right, sorry mate…er…Eshaq. Now, where can me and me mates go for a bit of grub and some fun?" asked Clancy.

"You must go to Khan El-Khalili sooq, just that way. Many shops and much food," replied Eshaq, his hand outstretched anticipating monetary compensation.

"Thanks mate," said Clancy, shaking the outstretched hand in gratitude.

"Wait! My tip. Two shillings," Eshaq called out.

"Two bob for giving us directions. You know where you can stick that mate. Cheeky bastard!" growled Clancy.

Archie felt a twang of guilt so reached in to his pocket and flicked a sixpence in the direction of Eshaq.

"You know, my mum always says that a little kindness goes a long way. Here you go mate," said Archie with a smile.

Eshaq scanned the coin with disdain.

"Sixpence? A very rare coin and not often seen in Cairo," he said sarcastically.

"Really?" replied Clancy as he snatched the coin from Eshaq's grasp.

"We'd better hang on to it then, it might be worth something. Here you go Arch," responded Clancy as he handed back the coin to his friend.

Cairo has for centuries been considered the centre of ancient civilization, and a destination which Archie had dreamed of visiting since reading about it in history books at school. But it was not the magical place that he had imagined. With a population four times the size of Australia, each struggling to earn a living, it was absolute mayhem. The city itself contained *some* very fine buildings, but as Clancy put it, "Cairo is a rotten place". There were few, of what the boys thought as, decent streets in the city, and certainly nothing to compare with the streets of the small towns which they had come from; although there was a very fair tramway system, which had apparently improved the city.

"I hate to judge boys, but this place reeks with filth," said Archie, feeling a little disappointed, "how can a country which was so advanced thousands of years ago be in such a state?"

As they walked around they noticed that the streets all over the city were mostly paved in tar, but in reasonable order, but the footpaths were only of the natural earth and piled high with refuse. The rules of the road were exactly the opposite of what they were in Australia, the roads being open to all alike; camels, horses, or donkeys. It was also a common thing, when traffic was heavy, to see camels and donkeys parading along the footpaths.

The many street hawkers too made a nuisance of themselves,

roaming the city in their thousands, from the small child of seven or eight years old, to old and infirm men and women, latching on to all foreigners, hawking everything imaginable. Clancy was becoming particularly frustrated with them and slapped several hands away which were touching his uniform, no doubt hoping to liberate him of his wallet.

"Bugger off yer thieving little bastards!" he shouted, waving his two clenched fists about for good measure.

This tactic worked at first but the boys discovered that unless you send them off they will follow you for hundreds of yards in the hope of making a sale; Clancy's remedy being to swipe each one on the head and plant his large boot up their backside.

Despite their disappointment, the group of friends walked, for what seemed like miles, through open air markets, admiring the hanging racks of beef suspended from the beds of rickety carts, the smells of fresh citrus and strawberry mixing with the pungent odours of what must have been years of accumulated animal and human excrement. Despite the stench, the boys enjoyed their night at the market, perusing old artefacts and admiring the colourful, yet crumbling shops, despite having to dodge the overzealous vendors who insisted on showing their goods to all and sundry. The boys, feeling hungry, paused at a streetside cafe, strewn with sawdust, to sample the local fare of fresh falafel made with fava beans, and grilled pigeon stuffed with aromatically spiced rice, whilst admiring the colourful carts serving dollops of flavourful beans, and hot tea served with mint and a fresh falafel wrap. All of this, whilst being treated to a show of battle-scarred cats, fighting over the best scraps, in a mountain of rubbish piled at the roadside.

"Just like the pub on Friday night eh?" joked Stowie.

For the 9th Battalion, pretty soon everything began to come together in camp. Meals were plentiful, and eaten in the open air, until the various messes and cookhouses were constructed. Morale was high and boosted by the daily afternoon parades at the fine swimming baths at the Mena House Hotel. The hotel itself, however, soon becoming a casualty of the war when it was commandeered and transformed in to both a hospital and Divisional Headquarters.

Although a new Army, the majority of its recruits had some sort of military background, some being compulsorily enrolled in to the cadets at the age of fifteen. Much training had taken place at Enoggera prior to setting sail, as well as on board ship and on dry land, wherever possible, during the journey. The AIF were volunteers to a man and were eager to take on as much knowledge as they could. They had heard whispers that the British officer class considered them second class soldiers only fit for garrison duty.

"How bloody dare they! We'll show them.......the bastards!" said Clancy.

The Australian and New Zealand troops had even gained a new title...ANZAC, which was short for the Australian and New Zealand Army Corps. No one knows who came up with the term, but it is likely that Sergeant Little, a clerk in General Birdwood's headquarters, thought of it for use on a rubber stamp; the abbreviation was convenient shorthand, and became the telegraph code word for the corps.

Training re-commenced in earnest on the 10th of December in order to make the 9th Battalion fit for active service. At first the battalion trained as individual companies, refreshing their field craft, attack formations, setting up defensive positions, and familiarisation with each weapon that the army would use on the battlefield; ensuring that a soldier could pick up *any* weapon and be able to use it proficiently when required. Once the companies were considered to be effective, the battalion began to train together as one unit. By the 14th of December the battalion was training for days at a time in the desert, entrenching in the sandy ground, practising attack and defence, with half of the battalion acting as the foe. They would often leave camp at 1700 hours, and march through the darkness, until about 2200 hours, across the sand until they came to a suitable area on which to set up a defensive position. Here they would dig themselves in, and with the platoon acting as reserves, managed to sleep until 0200 hours the next morning, their slumber being interrupted by a 'stand to arms' for an hour...just in case they were needed. Throughout the entire time mock attacks were taking place, with blank cartridges being used for a bit of added realism.

"Sand, and these bloody blanks!" Clancy would complain, "just another excuse to make a man clean his weapon!"

On completion of the first training exercise the men, on their return to camp, were pleased to find that not only had they been erected, but there were now sufficient bell tents to house each man. A home from home!

Each tent was occupied by a Section, who slept in a circle with their feet pointing towards the centre. The men now only had one blanket each, the second having been withdrawn, so on their visit to Cairo the boys had each purchased a sleeping bag at a cost of £3 and more; the price dependent on which stall you went to and how expert you were in the art of haggling. The price *was* quite hefty but the weeks aboard ship had allowed each man to accumulate some savings, which they put to good use. The boys were all impressed with the warmth that the bags provided, with Stowie commenting that "it is about the most useful article I have", all being certain that they would have no difficulty in taking them wherever they went. The tent, with ten great lumps in it, was a sight to see each morning before parade. Stowie had the place near the door, slinging himself and his belongings inside and out. Next was Taff, who was always rooting around in his sleeping bag for his belt and shirt, and, at the same time, stalking round the pole to find his tunic. Archie would be attempting to get a shave in, putting his equipment together whilst not even dressed. Meanwhile Clancy would still be in bed, cursing at everybody for disturbing him, but somehow just managing to slide on to parade as the boys moved off. Roo slept beside Clancy and got up about five minutes before him, usually spending his time chasing his hat. Whereas big Sergeant MacDonald would dress quietly, wondering how to encourage these boys to become a bit more organised, keeping his cool whilst doing all his shaving sitting on the sand outside; whilst he and Jacko carried on a sparkling conversation all the time. Jacko had been impressed with the huge sergeant since Enoggera, constantly referring to his height; having christened him 'Big Mac.' Kenneth Thornhill was a rather quiet chap, whilst Dave Devereux and Brian McGregor slept near the opening on the other side, with Dave keeping up a good witty speech about everything he knew, and didn't know. The whole show would finally end with Sergeant Mac jumping into his equipment calling out, "Fall in, Number 1". Needless to say, nobody heeded him, taking about four minutes to exit the tent.

"You wee men had better start livening up in the mornings or you'll have me to answer to. DO *YOU* UNDERSTAND?!!" shouted Big Mac.

Knowing that the sergeant was referring to one of his famous "chats", each man vowed to do better in future.

It was well known that the war in Europe was at a standstill with both sides living in a network of trenches which stretched from the English Channel to the border of Switzerland. It was, therefore, essential that the art of trench construction was learned by all. The man for this was a certain Major Clogstoun, a British officer, who commanded 3 Field Company. The Major was a down to earth fellow and became popular with the Aussies with his easy going nature and fun, hands on lectures. He introduced them to the latest tool for the war, an entrenching tool.

"Now, you chaps, some bright spark has made your lives a little easier," he announced as he held up the new tool, "as you can see it is robust and compact, making it easy to carry".

Indeed it was, for it was a collapsible tool with a round wooden handle and a folding cast iron head with pointed shovel at one end and pick at the other.

"Ripper! Will we *all* be issued one of those sir?" asked an excited young soldier.

"Ripper? I do love your turn of phrase," replied the Major, "and in reply to your question, yes you will, very soon".

Groans of appreciation from the audience of the battalion, who were seated on the sand, followed. The Major then gestured for all to stand and told all present to follow him. He led them to a spot approximately one hundred yards away. On arrival the men were impressed to find a pre dug small system of trenches.

"As you can see, as a good boy scout, I always like to be prepared," announced Major Clogstoun.

Over the next few days the troops were taught the workings of a good trench system and given ample opportunity to practice digging. It was hard work in the blazing heat, but all present knew well that it was an essential piece of learning.

"I never realised there were so many types of holes that you could dig," uttered Archie.

"Yeah mate, I think I'm turning in to a bloody great Wombat," Clancy chuckled.

"Bless your cotton socks," said Roo as he playfully pinched Clancy's cheeks.

Although he saw the joke, Clancy was not impressed and quickly brushed Roo's hands away.

All in all there were four types of trench, starting with the front line or firing and attack trench. This was where the main fighting occurred, with the trench being located anything from fifty yards to a mile from the enemy front line defences. The trench was not dug in a straight line, but in zig zags, in order to prevent attacking enemy firing straight down the line of the trench. This was known as enfilading fire. Being dug in these zig zag sections also meant that if a shell exploded in a section, or the enemy managed to occupy that section, only *that* area would be affected. Next was the support trench, which would be to the rear of the main trench and would house men and supplies which could be brought to the front at a moment's notice. Behind this trench was the reserve trench which held yet more men and supplies should the front trenches be overrun. All of the trenches were connected by communication trenches which provided a safe corridor for the movement of men, supplies and messages. There was also a trench known as a Sap. These saps were dug usually at night as, in effect, they were a corridor to push forward and develop a new front line, or to move artillery pieces in to better range of targets.

Major Clogstoun was a "pacer", in that whilst he instructed he would pace up and down the ranks of his students. He also wore a monocle. On one occasion a few of the Aussies had placed their Identity Discs in their eyes, playfully mocking the Major. Not to be outdone he remarked "Yes old man, but I bet you can't do this", whereupon he tossed his monocle skywards and caught it again with his eye. The Aussies were indeed impressed and whooped and cheered their admiration. "He's a good sport".

At Ma'adi the Light Horse soldiers spent the first ten days carrying out dismounted drills as well as exercising their horses daily over a period of a few hours across the sandy terrain. By the 18th of December the horses were finally rideable, having regained their land legs; the event being marked by a mounted parade when Colonel Chauvel arrived from England to take command of the Brigade.

Vigorous training for all continued throughout December, with the occasional break to travel the ten miles in to Cairo, via the local tram. The trams were quite comfortable but the motormen would constantly bang the gong from start to finish of the journey, which to some could be quite annoying.

"What else did you get for your birthday you noisy bastard?!"

Cairo may have been a cosmopolitan city dating back

centuries, with its spectacular and beautiful buildings, influenced by the architecture of ancient Rome and Greece, as well as Europe and Britain, but Archie and his mates had not been impressed by their first visit. Food, however, was their main enticement. The many and varied restaurants were a welcome change from the sometimes mundane food back at camp; although the battalion cooks did their best with the ingredients at hand. Cairo was also full of many bars which gained many new found, and reasonably wealthy, patrons in the ANZAC troops. Street pedlars were still an ever present annoyance to the men, who would wave them away with a shout of "imshee" or "imshee yalla", some following through with a fist to the more persistent salesmen.

Most, though, were happy with a quieter lot, and settled with their towering neighbours, the pyramids and the sphinx, marvelling at the mighty structures and offering theories on how they were constructed. A few were so taken by the pyramids they decided to climb them for a better look. At a height of around four hundred and thirty feet and an angle of fifty two degrees, this was no easy feat. Archie, Roo and Clancy even had a crack, in search of some graffiti by Napoleon himself, but, as the day was a scorcher, and each step was around four and a half feet in height, they were forced to pause for a brief rest. What appeared on the huge stones to be a plaster covering was gradually crumbling off the stone blocks, and there were large heaps of it lying on the desert sand below. The threesome felt quite awe struck at their first glimpse of the pyramids, but they were even more impressed to be sat half way up one of them admiring the panoramic landscape. However, after a hard, and sometimes dangerous climb, all were disappointed in not finding Napoleon's signature, but very satisfied with the magnificent view that the apex of the structure offered; but then came the descent, which was much worse than going up! Being from a nation of sportsmen, others even took part in races up the pyramids, the fastest time recorded as four minutes; only to be beaten by a group of Ghurkhas who were observed ascending the Great Pyramid of Giza in a time of only two minutes. All in all, Egypt was a place of discovery for many of the men who had never been to a town or city, until they enlisted, let alone another country.

Christmas was looming which, for the ANZACs, meant thoughts of home and their loved ones. Archie and Roo were also missing Percy, not having clapped eyes on him since prior to leaving Brisbane. With the Light Horse Brigade camped on the other side of the Nile it was a day out for Archie, Roo and Clancy who had been training hard since their arrival; however, they were not looking forward to the journey, which would take them to within a stone's throw of Cairo.

There was no rest, even on the tram. The boot blacks had become quite cheeky and regularly took advantage of the good nature and "fair go" attitude of the soldiers. Quite often on the tram they would locate an unsuspecting victim engaged in conversation, and quietly and gently polish one boot, meaning that the victim would end up paying to have the other boot shined. Except Clancy of course who would clip the offender round the ear, then polish his other boot himself......."cheeky little bastard!" On this particular journey he was at the end of his tether when, yet again, a young boot black began to polish his boot. Grabbing the boy by the scruff of the neck it was time to teach him some manners.

"Look you little bugger," he growled, "in *my* country we *ask* before doing this sort of stuff. It's called manners. Do you know what they are?"

The boy was indifferent to Clancy's explanation, instead holding his hand out for payment.

"Bugger this, and bugger you, you little bastard!" exclaimed Clancy as he threw the boy's polish and brushes from the train, closely followed by the boy himself, who bounced and rolled along the street as the tram continued its journey.

Archie and Roo were slightly shocked but not surprised, glancing at Clancy who was still fuming about the incident.

"What?" Clancy exclaimed on sight of his mates staring at him, "the bloody tram is only going about five miles an hour; he'll be right".

The Australian Light Horse Brigade was camped at the edge of the desert just south of Ma'adi, linked to Cairo by a railway line which passed through the sleepy Ma'adi train station. As the train pulled in, the three mates stepped on to the dusty platform, and were immediately set upon by hawkers. Clancy was livid and began throwing punches in all directions, the hawkers soon getting the message and backing off. In the rail yard to the side of the platform were mountains of fodder, rows of field equipment, and mounds of baggage and foodstuffs, all of which were guarded by Australian sentries who were posted on both sides of the railway lines, their eyes keen to discover any gyppo loiterer intent on stealing the military supplies before they could be transported to the nearby camp.

To capitalize on the beer drinking troops there was even a cafe and tavern purposefully situated next to the station.

"That's more like it. Fancy a beer?" asked Clancy.

"Maybe later mate. Let's get some directions from the blokes over there," suggested Archie, pointing to the Light Horse sentries.

As they approached the soldiers Archie's face lit up.

"Davo! Chugger! Good to see you both," he said, excitedly shaking their hands.

"Archie...boys," replied Davo, acknowledging them with a nod, "how have you been?"

"Pretty good. Getting sick of these flaming hawkers though," replied Archie, "Clancy here just chucked a young boot black from the tram".

"And walloped a few fellas over there at the station," Roo added.

"Good on yer Clance. The thought crossed *my* mind a couple of times too I can tell yer," replied Chugger.

Archie looked around at the other soldiers.

"Is Percy not here?" he asked.

"No mate, we drew the short straw," replied Davo, "he's back at camp having a day off".

"Oh right. Is the camp far from here?" asked Archie.

"It's a bit of a walk but you can hire a moke from that Gyppo over there," Davo replied.

"Bloody hell!" said Clancy as he shook his head, for across from the station was a seething mass of Arabs and soldiers, all haggling away about the prices of donkeys and guides.

"It's got to be done mate, c'mon," said Roo as he ushered the angry Clancy towards the mayhem.

"I'm staying in camp from now on boys!" he exclaimed.

In fact Clancy was so tired and annoyed with the hustle and bustle and rudeness, that when a fresh cavalcade of donkeys appeared from nowhere, he eagerly seized them without bothering to enquire about the fare.

Archie and Roo picked out the finer specimens, whilst Clancy's donkey was a moth-eaten looking customer, who badly needed clipping and brushing. She had a small saddle, with no bellyband, or other means of fastening, and rusty stirrups which were a tight squeeze for Clancy's big feet. The saddle continually slipped from side to side throughout the journey until he got used to it, having to indulge in violent gymnastics to retain his seat. He was just about to give himself up for lost, when a Lighthorsemen passing by on another nag advised him to "sit far back, lean back, grip with your knees, and keep your feet well in front of you". It worked and Clancy's final leg of the short journey was far more agreeable than the start.

"Thanks mate. You beauty," he said, in thanks to the soldier.

The Light Horse camp was a blanket of white bell tents neatly laid out in rows, regiment by regiment, and squadron by squadron, all conveniently sign posted.

"Here you go, 2nd Light Horse Regiment, 'C' Squadron along here," announced Roo.

Making their way along the rows of tents, waving off the hordes of flies as they went, they called out for Percy Taylor.

"Three tents down fellas," announced a helpful voice.

"Percy...Percy Taylor!" shouted Clancy.

As Percy stuck his head out from inside the tent he could not help but smile.

"Archie, Roo, Clancy! Good to see you," he said as he shook each man's hand and hugged them tightly.

"Mate...I like you, but not that much," laughed Clancy.

"Fair enough mate," replied Percy, "what brings you fellas here?"

"We came to see you of course," replied Roo, swiping at yet another fly.

"Yeah, sorry about that, thousands of horses means tons of horse manure, which means flies," said Percy.

"That must be a pain mate," said Clancy.

"It is," replied Percy, "unless you have a Goliath".

"A Goliath?" asked a confused Roo.

Percy beckoned the boys in to his tent, "come on in and I'll show you". Once inside Percy produced a lizard, which was around eighteen inches in length, "boys, meet Goliath, he's a Chameleon".

"Crikey!" exclaimed Roo, "he's a big ugly fella".

"He is but he's great for keeping the flies down," Percy explained, "look, Goliath's normal colour is a kind of sandy green but he doesn't stick to it and can change...you know a bit like Lil does her frock. Here, I'll show you. If you put him on this blanket, in about five or ten minutes he takes the same colour. See, he's changing already".

The boys were impressed with Percy's ingenuity as Goliath's chief virtue in the men's eyes was his diet, which consisted mainly of flies.

"He eats about twenty of the buggers in one go, but the best bit is watching him go at it," said Percy, "he'll just sit there, absolutely still until a fly comes anywhere within six or eight inches of him. Then his mouth slowly opens and a tongue, coiled like a watch spring, slowly comes out. Then, like a flash, it shoots out and back and the fly has gone to meet his maker".

"So what do you blokes do for fun here?" asked Archie.

"Training, mostly. We *did* have a look at Cairo but we won't be going back. Besides there's loads to do here," replied Percy, "it's a shame the local Poms aren't friendly".

The Anglo-Egyptians, as the British administrators were called, lived in the town of Ma'adi. They were not amused by the arrival of the Australians, whom they regarded as rowdy, undisciplined and unkempt men who couldn't even speak proper English, and as a result were constantly making complaints to the senior officers.

"Perhaps we should let the Turks take over the place, then see how the bastards feel," said Clancy.

Percy agreed, "too right mate, too right indeed".

The camp, itself, wasn't without its own amenities and there was plenty for the soldiers to do in their off duty time. There was a cinema tent, which also doubled as a church, a boxing ring, and a billiard saloon, plus the Ma'adi Soldier Club had been opened that month; all of which impressed the infantry men.

"Hey Clance, I see your favourite word hasn't changed," Percy remarked, a mischievous glint in his eye, "I've got someone I think you'd like to meet".

Clancy's curiosity piqued as Percy beckoned the boys towards the area where the horses were stabled, although calling it a stable *was* a bit of an exaggeration. The horses were known as "Walers," New South Wales stockhorses specially bred for the demanding task of mustering in the harsh highlands of the state. They embodied strength and courage, with a blend of thoroughbred and semi-draught bloodlines granting them remarkable endurance, power, and speed, and each horse bore the Government broad arrow branding and an army number on one hoof.

There *were* no stables for them in Egypt, for there weren't the materials or manpower to construct them, so in camp, the horses were tethered by head and heel ropes between long ropes called picket lines. As the boys approached, they were greeted by the breathtaking sight of hundreds of horses before them.

"I never thought I'd see such a sight," said Roo.

As the boys strolled along the line, they couldn't help but admire the magnificence of every horse they passed, pausing to pat a select few.

Clancy couldn't resist a light hearted remark, "these horses are bloody marvellous. Perhaps we should have joined the Light Horse *eh* boys?"

"No fear mate, I'm happy where we are," Roo promptly replied.

Towards the end of the picket line, their attention was drawn to a soldier grooming an exceptionally large horse.

"Brace up boys, its Major Paterson," announced Percy as he straightened his tunic and threw up a salute to the officer, "morning sir, how's Bill today?"

The Major greeted Percy, acknowledging his salute.

"G'day, young Taylor. Bill is still as grumpy as ever, but your idea with the licorice worked wonders. He loves them," replied the Major, "and he's found a new friend in Lieutenant Shanahan."

Percy's curiosity got the better of him.

"Do you reckon Mister Shanahan might try and ride him sir?" he inquired.

The officer chuckled in response, "well, he might give it a crack, but I don't think he has a chance in hell of staying on. I hear the only person who did was a young recruit by the name of Towers. Needless to say they signed him up on the spot".

Apologising for his oversight, Percy introduced his companions.

"Sorry Major I forgot my manners, this is my brother Archie, my cousin Roo and our mate Clancy; they've come to meet this big fella here...Bill the Bastard," said Percy.

The Major extended a welcoming greeting, "Good to meet you boys," he replied. His attention then turned to Clancy, remarking, "Clancy, that's a strong name, a bit like Clancy of the Overflow."

Clancy, puzzled, scratched his head and asked, "Clancy of the what?"

Roo jumped in, explaining, "It's a poem about a drover, by a bloke called Banjo...Paterson". The penny finally dropped. "Are *you* Banjo Paterson sir?" Roo asked; his surprise evident.

"That I am. Are you familiar with my work?" Banjo inquired.

"I am sir. Us Taylors love 'Waltzing Matilda' and sing it all the time when we're mustering," Roo replied.

Clancy couldn't contain his excitement, exclaiming, "*You* wrote 'Waltzing Matilda? Well bugger me! I've never met anyone famous before". He reached out to shake the Major's hand, saying "pleased to meet you, sir."

As a patriot and a fervent horse enthusiast, Banjo Paterson

had enlisted in to the Light Horse as an honorary veterinarian, and it was during the voyage from Australia that he had the opportunity to become acquainted with Bill. Aware of the horse's notorious reputation, Paterson approached him with caution, and it was through this careful approach that a mutual respect had blossomed.

"So, what brought you fellas to Bill then, might I ask?" said Banjo.

"Bill's last name happens to be Clancy's favourite word, so I thought I'd bring him along sir," replied Percy.

"Really? Perhaps you'd like to ride him?" inquired Banjo.

Clancy glanced round at his mates who had suddenly gone silent.

"Yeah, I'll give it go," he replied.

"Let's get him saddled up then shall we?" replied Banjo.

Bill was very calm as the boys tacked him up, almost lolling them in to a false sense of security and normality, as he allowed them to lead him in to the riding arena. As Clancy approached the formidable figure of the huge horse that was Bill the Bastard, a sense of anticipation mingled with the watchful gazes of Archie, Percy, Roo, and Major Paterson. They knew the legendary reputation of the horse, his wild spirit, and untamed power. Concern etched their faces; a shared worry for Clancy's safety as he prepared to mount the mighty beast.

Clancy, who was oblivious to the horse's reputation, took a deep breath, his hands trembling slightly as he grasped Bill's reins. Looking into the horse's eyes, he spoke softly, as if trying to forge a connection.

"Easy there, boy," he whispered, a mix of respect and determination in his voice.

Bill snorted; his breath hot against Clancy's face, a reminder of the raw power that lay within.

With a final glance and wink at his companions, Clancy placed his left foot into the stirrup, the metal cool against his boot, and hoisted himself up, his muscles straining, until he found himself perched on the saddle; his heart pounding in his chest. His three mates, and Major Paterson, watched with bated breath, their concern growing with each passing moment.

At first the huge horse stood like a statue, a pillar of defiance, but then suddenly Bill exploded into action, his powerful muscles launching Clancy into a whirlwind of motion. The onlookers held their breath, their eyes fixed on the daring rider atop the untamed steed, every buck, twist, and sudden movement of the horse sending a ripple of concern through their collective being, their hands involuntarily clenching and releasing.

Clancy's grip tightened on the reins, his body instinctively reacting to Bill's relentless defiance. Major Paterson's eyes narrowed; a mix of admiration and anxiety evident in his gaze. Archie's knuckles turned white as he silently urged his mate to hold on, whilst Percy's face contorted with a blend of worry and determination, and Roo's breath caught in his throat, his eyes wide with a mixture of awe and concern for his friend.

But then, in a heart wrenching moment, the inevitable happened. Bill's power proved dominant, and Clancy was forcefully thrown from his back. Gasps escaped the onlookers' lips as they witnessed Clancy's fall, their hearts sinking as one. Major

Paterson's hand instinctively moved to his chest, a gesture of concern for the young rider's well being.

As Clancy lay on the ground, pain etching lines across his face, his audience rushed to his side, their worry turning to relief that he was bruised rather than broken.

"That looked fun," joked Archie, his voice conveying a mixture of humour, relief and reassurance.

As Clancy clambered to his feet and brushed himself off he could not speak, as the heavy fall had knocked the wind out of him. Instead he waved a two fingered salute at Bill and his small band of supporters. Falling off Bill didn't mean he was defeated, but he would definitely think twice before riding him again. Finally regaining his voice Clancy managed a quick retort.

"Thanks Bill...Major...you sure know how to show a fella a good time".

"Any time Clancy," laughed Banjo, as Bill too could apparently see the funny side shaking his large head and snorting with apparent satisfaction of a lesson well taught.

Bidding Major Paterson and Bill farewell, the four mates strolled back to the tent lines.

"You did great there mate," said Percy as he patted Clancy on the shoulder.

"Yeah. I reckon after riding that bastard I've done *my* bit for King and country," replied Clancy.

"Perhaps we should sing the National Anthem to celebrate," announced Archie with a cheeky wink.

Clancy stopped suddenly in his tracks and looked confused.

"What's an anthem? Is it a dirty song?" he asked quite innocently.

Now even his mates were confused.

"It's a patriotic song about your country," replied Archie.

"Is it? I didn't even know there was such a thing. What's ours?" Clancy enquired.

"Why, God Save the King of course," replied Archie.

"God Save the King? What's it about?" asked Clancy.

"It's about the King and wishing him well and stuff," said Roo.

"You're joking mate. What's that got to do with us and Australia? He sounds like a bit of a vain bastard to me having a song about himself," Clancy announced, "we should be singing about our country and all that is good about it, not some bloody King on the other side of the world who only cares about himself, and doesn't give a stuff about us!"

"Clance, when we get home you should run for parliament," said Percy, rolling his eyes.

"No thanks mate, those blokes are a bunch of lying bastards too, just out for themselves. I'll stick with droving; it's honest work," replied Clancy.

On the 23rd of December there was movement and activity in all allied camps. Officers and non-commissioned officers were bustling around, rousing the troops and organising them into columns of route, shouldering their weapons in preparation for the march to Cairo. Archie, curious about the commotion, turned to Freddy for answers.

"What's going on mate?" he enquired.

"I'm not entirely sure, old chap," Lieutenant Ponsonby replied. "But it seems that both the infantry and the light horse are marching through the city".

Indeed, it was an impressive spectacle, a show of strength as every available soldier and horse paraded through the capital of Egypt. With each step, the soldiers wondered if war had finally reached their doorstep. Were they truly prepared? Would they prove themselves worthy? Yet, amidst their anxious thoughts, a wave of pride washed over them. Instead of a battle, cheering crowds lined the streets, greeting them with enthusiasm.

The reason for this grand display soon became clear. The British had quietly removed the pro-Turkish Sultan of Egypt, establishing a new Protectorate and installing a *new* Sultan. To ensure a smooth and uncontested transition of power, all available British and dominion troops were paraded, asserting their authority in a resounding manner. And the strategy worked flawlessly, capturing the attention and respect of the people.

Christmas came and went, with a fancy feed being put on by the regimental and battalion cooks, and served by the Officers, Warrant Officers and Senior Non Commissioned Officers. There was even a well received appearance by Sergeant Major Christmas who roamed around the tables of seated men distributing gifts of fruit, whilst playfully poking fun at individuals as he passed. A good time was had by all present and helped to break the monotony of continuous training and thoughts of the dangers which were soon to come.

"Almost as good as Mum's Christmas Chook, eh Roo?" said Archie.

At this time of merry making it was the officers and not the ordinary soldiers who got up to mischief, with the 9th and 10th Battalion Officers Mess combining forces to attack the Mess of the 11th, which then became a domino effect, resulting in the storming of the 12th Battalion Officers Mess. As is the norm, this behaviour was attributed to "high spirits", whereas lesser mortals would certainly have been placed on a charge.

Being under the auspices of the British Army, on the first of the New Year, each infantry battalion was re-organised, changing from eight Companies to just four, with each Company consisting of four Platoons. The 9th Battalion didn't escape this reshuffle. 'A' and 'C' Companies became 'A' Company, 'B' and 'D' became 'B', 'E' and 'G' became 'C', and 'F' and 'H' became 'D' Company. Clancy, although slightly annoyed, was happy that he had remained in his original Company with his mates.

Following their intensive training throughout December, the battalions were now at a point where they began to train as a Brigade; a brigade comprising of four infantry battalions plus supporting arms such as artillery, supplies, engineers, pioneers, transport, cooks and medical. Major General Bridges, who had raised the AIF, built his force based on a defence scheme that he had created in 1908. His main desire was for Australian troops to fight together, separate from British army units. Bridges and his Chief of Military Staff, Lieutenant Colonel White, had planned the order of battle for the AIF. Their initial idea was to recruit members of the citizen army and men with experience in militia units, cadets and rifle clubs, and to form military units with territorial connections, with men drawn from the same regions. This would aid with the cohesion of men drawn from similar places and backgrounds, with the infantry battalions and light horse regiments recruited from their own states throughout the war. However, specialty units, such as the artillery, medical and engineers, were drawn from men from all over Australia.

Training, for the lighthorsemen, now began in earnest with

the 2nd Light Horse engaging in patrols and conducting mock reconnaissance (recce) and attacks in the challenging terrain of the Mokattam Hills. These exercises were intense and brief, but packed with action. In the first attack, 'C' squadron launched an assault on a position held by 'A' squadron among the hilly landscape, whilst, in the second, 'A' squadron pursued 'C' squadron, who skilfully fought a rearguard action back towards the camp. The pace was swift, leaving most of the men and horses breathing heavily by the end.

The senior officers were impressed by the dedication and professionalism displayed by the men during training. They wholeheartedly embraced the challenges, approaching each engagement with a spirited and vigorous attitude. Notably, the lighthorsemen remained vigilant, keeping a watchful eye for potential threats from all directions. They were not content with merely scanning the expected areas where the enemy might appear; instead, they remained alert, ready to respond to trouble from any quarter.

Signallers and stretchers bearers too were receiving detailed training in their trades, whilst musketry practice, an essential skill for all, was also carried out.

Over an hour's march from Mena Camp was a jagged rock formation nicknamed the Tiger's Tooth. There was a rifle range nearby where weapons training would take place on a regular basis; not that any form of target practice was required as most of the ANZACs were crack shots, having been born with a rifle in their hands. The Tooth, however, with its steep, rocky slopes, and all round views, was used regularly in attack and defence scenarios, at the end of which the "Gyppo" pedlars would appear from nowhere to sell the troops oranges and cold hard boiled eggs, which they referred to as "eggs-a-cook".

Officers, unknown to themselves, were often the brunt of jokes from the men. The biggest object of the men's humour was the map reading and direction finding skills of officers, especially the inexperienced Platoon Commanders.

"Hey Arch! What's white and stuffs officers?" enquired Clancy, "a map!"

On one such day, 'A' Company were to head off to the Tooth for a range day. During the night a heavy fog had descended in the valley, completely shrouding the pyramids and the surrounding hills and mountains; including the Tigers Tooth. The OC, Major Salisbury, was very concerned and decided that it was too dangerous to try to find the track that led to the range.

"We'll have to march on a compass bearing," he was overheard saying to Lieutenant Chambers.

"Oh bugger, we're in for it now," uttered Clancy.

Prior to departure, a map was laid out on the sand and a grid and compass bearing were taken with a prismatic compass and a bit of mathematic know how. Unusually for the company their route, through the thick fog, was down rocky slopes and along uneven valley floors. Throughout the journey the officers would pause, re-check their bearing, then carry on their journey.

"He's bloody lost," announced Corporal Harrison.

"I don't think he is mate. You'll see," said Roo.

Ten minutes before their planned arrival the fog miraculously cleared and, to the amazement of the soldiers, just three hundred yards to their front, lay their destination. The men sporadically began cheering and whooping, some even patting Lieutenant Chambers on the back.

"He's a bloody marvel," said Stowie.

"Yep, our officers are good blokes. I'd follow them anywhere," said Archie as he looked over to Lieutenant Chambers, "you're not just a good looking rooster, eh sir?"

"That's the benefit of sailing at night on Moreton Bay young Taylor, you get to know how to find your way out of a sticky spot," said Major Salisbury.

"Well, I'm glad you're with us sir," replied Archie.

"Groveller!" exclaimed a smiling Roo.

It was indeed a strenuous time, with the battalion returning to camp caked in sand, which had stuck to their sweaty bodies.

On the 30th of January, a significant disruption unfolded for the men of the Light Horse. There was a reorganisation underway, accompanied by a change in location to Heliopolis. As they arrived at their new campsite, they found themselves surrounded by vast stretches of sandy desert. Everywhere they looked, it was sand, sand, and more sand. The barren landscape offered no signs of vegetation, as nothing could grow in this inhospitable environment.

However, it wasn't all desolation and despair. Their camp was situated about a mile away from the town of Heliopolis, which had earned the nickname "Garden City" for its remarkable beauty. The town boasted exquisite buildings, mainly constructed from sand brick, concrete, and cement. These structures appeared pristine and impressive, adding a touch of elegance to the surroundings.

Despite the challenging desert terrain that engulfed them,

the Lighthorsemen found solace in the proximity of Heliopolis, appreciating the allure of the town's picturesque charm and the sight of well-crafted buildings amidst the vast sandy backdrop.

The 1st Light Horse Brigade had now become part of the New Zealand and Australian Division, led by Major General Godley. With this new alignment, each unit within the division began a collaborative training programme.

The soldiers in the Light Horse were already skilled horsemen and marksmen. As a result, the focus of their training shifted towards drill exercises and honing their expertise in mounted infantry offensive and defensive techniques. The regiment adopted a tactical approach known as the "four man sections," where each unit functioned as a small, yet efficient, team. During engagements, three soldiers would dismount to fight as infantry, while the fourth soldier assumed responsibility for safeguarding the horses until they were required for further advances or withdrawals. This method of fighting had proven effective during the South African war.

By embracing this refined fighting style and training alongside their fellow divisional units, the men of the Light Horse prepared themselves for the challenges that lay ahead. They understood the importance of mutual support, coordination and adaptability on the battlefield, drawing upon the lessons learned from past conflicts to enhance their effectiveness in future engagements.

All allied camps were now rife with rumours and furphies circulating with regard to deploying to the Western Front, or even local areas.

On the 1st of February a Turkish Army Corps launched a

surprise attack on the Suez Canal. Under the cover of darkness and during a sandstorm, they made their advance, reaching the Canal between Ismailia and Suez. To aid their attack, they brought along boats and pontoons, which they deployed on the Canal.

Their attempt, however, did not go unnoticed by the vigilant allied troops and warships, one of the warships swiftly sinking all of the pontoons, causing the drowning of a number of enemy soldiers. The Turkish attack caught the allies off guard, as the Turks entrenched themselves for miles, right up against the allied defences. Yet, the Turks soon discovered that they had underestimated their opponents. The attack turned out to be a failure, and the allied forces successfully repulsed them. While the Lighthorsemen felt a sense of envy, knowing that their New Zealand comrades had participated in the battle and gained experience for the upcoming fights, they recognised the Turks' defeat. Approximately six hundred Turkish soldiers were taken prisoner, appearing as a motley group, poorly clothed and equipped. Surprisingly, they seemed content with their capture and the prospect of receiving proper food. The Turkish casualties too were significantly higher, with several hundred lying dead or wounded on the desert sands.

As the enemy quickly retreated, leaving only a few stragglers behind, the land became clear for a distance of twenty miles on both sides. The ANZACs understood that this would not be the last encounter with the Turks, as they had proven themselves to be formidable fighters. However, reports from the New Zealand units indicated that the Turkish soldiers seemed fearless under command but surrendered swiftly when on their own. It was evident that fear played a significant role in their actions, as many Turkish soldiers were found shot, with their hands tied behind their backs, suggesting they were being led through intimidation.

Mena Camp, over time, had metamorphosised into a large and recognisable army barracks, with the mile long infantry road, lined with its neatly whitewashed stones, running down its centre. The camp was home to the 1st, 2nd and 3rd Infantry Brigades, plus many other arms and specialties. Reinforcements were arriving regularly too, with Lieutenant Koch and a hundred men arriving from Australia on the 9th of February; each man being welcomed and quickly absorbed in to the battalion.

By mid February, 3rd Brigade training was complete, missing and old kit was being replaced, and rumours were rife.

"We're off to Southampton mate, and that's a fact".

On the 27th of February the Brigade was informed that it was deploying..........but to where? The destination, it appeared, did not matter to the thousands of ANZACs who had been waiting, training, for a chance to prove themselves to their British mates – the "Chums" - and the rest of the world. Whatever the destination, all were relieved to be finally going. That evening sporadic bouts of cheering and singing could be heard throughout Mena Camp.

As the boys prepared for their departure Archie felt an overwhelming desire to see his brother Percy one last time before they sailed, but to leave without permission would be desertion.

"Go and ask Freddy mate, he'll understand," said Clancy.

Determined, he approached his officer and friend with anticipation, knocking on the post of his tent to attract his attention.

"Archie. How are you dear boy?" asked his friend, a smile beaming across his face.

Archie was nervous for he knew that the question he was about to ask would put his friend in a difficult position.

"Freddy...er...sir. I've got a favour to ask," said Archie nervously, "I'd like to visit Percy in Heliopolis before we leave. It would mean the world to me, and I reckon Roo and Clancy would love to come along too".

Ponsonby, a thoughtful look crossing his face, understood the importance of family, but was also aware that all leave was now cancelled and no one was permitted, for security reasons, to leave camp. He pondered for a moment.

"There must be a way," he thought to himself, as he took out his writing pad and ink pen. "Archie, go and round up Roo and Clancy and bring them here. I have an idea," announced the officer as he waved his friend away.

The three mates were soon stood to attention outside Ponsonby's tent.

"Right; take this and follow me," he said as he thrust an envelope in to Archie's hand.

At great risk to himself the officer had written a note addressed "To whom it may concern" explaining that the three men had his permission to visit the camp at Heliopolis for the purpose of delivering an important message. At the camp gate he stated the same to the Military Policemen who accepted the explanation.

As they set off Freddy whispered to Archie, "ensure you return before dawn and bring this note back with you, or I am for it. Now off you go and give my regards to Percy".

Their visit with Percy was a brief one, and amidst the laughter and conversation, there was an unspoken acknowledgment of what was to come, their bonds growing stronger as they exchanged stories, cherished memories, and wished each other well.

Percy, raised his cup, offering a heartfelt toast which resonated with all present.

"To our family, and the best mates a bloke could ask for. May we find strength in each other, courage in the face of battle, and the good humour to lighten even the darkest moments. Look after yourselves boys, see you soon, and leave a few of the bastards for us. Cheers!"

"I'll drink to that," announced a proud Clancy.

The clinking of cups and resounding cheers filled the tent, a testament to the unwavering mateship and the unyielding spirit they carried within.

4

Lemnos

Since the rain on the first evening at camp, the weather had remained hot and dry, apart from the occasional sand storm, and plagues of locusts.

"Bloody hell boys will you look at that, and on our last day too," said Clancy as he stared indignantly at the dust storm which arrived just in time for their departure, "well goodbye Egypt you old bastard!"

At 1700 hours the 9th Battalion marched out through the

storm, to Cairo, to the cheers and friendly taunts of the 10th and 11th Battalions.

"Don't get lost 9th Battalion will yer?" shouted one soldier, whose reply from the 9th was a couple of friendly two finger gestures.

From Cairo the battalion boarded a train to the ancient city of Alexandria on the Mediterranean coast, where the troopship 'Ionian' was waiting for them. Jacko stepped on to the gang plank quite willingly today as the long voyage from Australia had cured him of his fears, plus he didn't think his jaw bone could stand another thump from Sergeant Mac. They were later joined by the 10th Battalion, which did not help the already cramped conditions.

"Bloody hell, this ship stinks to high heaven. A bit like rancid butter or onions," said Clancy.

"I know. I think we should call it the 'One Onion" replied Roo.

"Yeah, good one mate, I think that's all it deserves," said Clancy.

The terrible odour on the ship was apparently due to its not being cleaned properly after its previous voyage, when its cargo was horses. The smell was appalling and most men chose to sleep on the outer deck; if they could find a spot that is. The ship was not suited, or even adapted, to be a troop ship and, with its unsanitary conditions, soon became a hive of illness, with over a third of the men becoming sea sick. The lack of fresh air and instability of the vessel was also a main contributing factor in this.

The ultimate destination of the 'One Onion' was the island of Lemnos which lay approximately forty eight miles from the coast of Turkey, in the Aegean Sea. The Battalion arrived on the evening of the 4th of March, the journey having taken two days. Mudros was an ancient town standing on a natural deep water harbour, ideal for a large military fleet. The bay itself was a fine anchorage, around three miles wide, and, although basic, had everything required by a large armada, including fresh water. It was a chilly evening when the ship docked in the harbour, joining two other vessels which had already weighed anchor. The men out on deck stood in silence, marvelling at the island that lay before them, as had soldiers, centuries before, from the Greek, Roman and Ottoman empires. Lemnos, a rugged, fertile island of about twenty miles in diameter was a Turkish possession until the recent Greco-Turkish war. Its hills appeared to be very rocky, and the valleys and slopes well cultivated, the island dotted with tiny old world villages, built of stone, with narrow, rambling, cobbled streets. The harbour, almost circular and reached by a narrow passage, was a perfect natural haven, its surroundings resembling that of Albany.

"Why are we here Freddy?" asked Archie, of Lieutenant Ponsonby, who had arrived at the railing.

The officer explained that there was a stalemate on the Western Front and the Russian army had been unable to assist the allies due to it being involved in fighting with the Turks in the Caucuses, a region along the east coast of the Black Sea and Turkey's northern border. As a result the decision had been taken to knock Turkey out of the war.

"But how?" Archie enquired.

"That's quite simple," explained Freddy, "by invading Turkey and capturing its capital, Constantinople".

"Simple", however, was not the right choice of word as an attempt by the Royal Navy had already been made in late February, with some success, but a land assault was required to not only silence the forts which lay at the entrance to the Dardanelles, but also to take the country by storm with an overwhelming force.

By the morning of the 5th of March ten warships had arrived in the darkness, adding more fuel to the rumour mill.

"Hey! The CO is a lucky bugger!" said Clancy.

"Why's that?" asked Stowie.

"The battalion's going ashore because he won a coin toss. Grab your kit fellas," replied Clancy.

The CO, Lieutenant Colonel Lee, had indeed been lucky as it had been decided that, to alleviate the cramped conditions on board the 'Ionian', one battalion should bivouac ashore. The two battalion commanders had therefore tossed a coin, and ashore went the 9th.

An advance party landed on 6th of March with the remainder of the battalion disembarking the following day. Although the temperatures on the island were extremely cool in the spring, Lemnos was, in parts, an arid, dusty and rocky island, quite the opposite of Egypt, although the land was generally flat with the lowlands being quite fertile. The hillsides afforded good pasture for the many sheep and goats that grazed there, with their milk ensuring a rich and bountiful cheese and yoghurt industry for the local population. Fruit and vegetables such as almonds, figs, tomatoes, pumpkins and olives were also in plentiful supply as were wheat, barley and sesame. The troops would also be pleased to learn that the island had produced its own wine for centuries.

The 9th Battalion marched to a reasonably flat piece of ground not far from where the ship was docked.

"Righto lads, don't drop your kit just yet," announced Sergeant Mac.

"Where's the tents sarge?" enquired Roo.

"Still on the ship. So, while we are waiting, we'll go on a nature walk shall we?" replied the sergeant, a satisfied expression on his face.

"Nature walk?" exclaimed Roo.

"I think that's sarge language for route march mate," replied Clancy.

"Come on you men, look lively!" shouted Sergeant Mac.

Roo had a cursory glance inland and gave Archie a gentle nudge in the ribs.

"I'll bet you tuppence that we are headed that way," he said, pointing in a south easterly direction towards a distant mountain range.

Roo was right, for the battalion stepped off in the direction of the high ground. As they marched the men admired the surrounding countryside and savoured the sea breeze which was keeping them cool. As Archie surveyed his surroundings he noticed many ancient foundations of buildings which had once stood on the island and he thought of the civilisations that had lived here over the centuries.

"Hey Roo, did you know that as the first troops on Lemnos we are an occupying force?" said Archie.

"But this is a Greek island is it not?" replied Roo.

"Yeah, but the Turks have claimed it for their own for a while now. The Ottoman Empire has conquered and ruled this region for over four hundred years you know," said Archie.

"Well *we're* here now and if they want it back they'd better ask nicely," added Clancy.

After months in the dry desert of Egypt the troops took in the beauty of the island as they marched. Like most of the Mediterranean islands Lemnos had been formed through violent volcanic eruptions, the explosions and shock waves creating a mountainous landscape and leaving huge boulders everywhere. Passing through the occasional village conspicuous by their white houses with blue doors and window frames some of the men began to think that blue and white were the only colours of paint available on the island.

By nightfall, their "nature walk" complete, there was not a tent to be seen at the makeshift camp, but it did not matter to any of the men who were content with camping out under the stars, as many had done on the cattle drives at home, and whilst walking through the outback seeking out seasonal work as shearers, fruit pickers and the like.

"The stars are different here Arch," said Roo.

"Yes, no Southern Cross above us here," replied Archie, "but it's a good omen though. It means the Cross misses us and one day will welcome us home".

Like Egypt the weather could be a little unpredictable. On Sunday evening a storm blew in and soaked the soldiers of the 9th Battalion, who now lay in pools of water, grasping their sodden blankets tightly, whilst trying to make the best of it. When dawn broke, so did the storm and the diggers rose up from the wet ground, soaked but cheery. However, the wringing wet battalion was not impressed when it was greeted by the early morning arrival of their elusive tents.

"Wouldn't you bloody believe it?!" Clancy groaned.

A breakfast of sodden half loaves of bread was distributed amongst the men.

"I don't think I'll be eating in this establishment again fellas," said Clancy.

"Hey, what's going on over there?" said Roo, as he spied a group of locals who had arrived at the camp armed with cold boiled eggs.

"It's another gyppo shop; let's go and have a squiz," said Clancy, checking his pockets for loose change.

"You ripper!" exclaimed Archie.

The eggs were certainly a welcome accompaniment to the half soggy bread. Despite the fact that the village of Mudros, with its seventy or so houses, was not a particularly clean place, the villagers certainly were *not* gyppos, in the sense that they had grown to know the Egyptians. In fact, they were quite a wildly good looking folk and not at all pushy like the Arabs. But they were definitely enterprising, and the sight of locals peddling such food stuffs as apples, dates, figs, nuts, biscuits and other goods became a regular daily occurrence, and one which was welcomed by the Australian troops. The Aussies learned quickly too that the Greeks knew *how* to charge for things; the people being very different from the Egyptians. There was no haggling here. If you went to buy, and tried to battle them down, they simply put the article back and told you to go somewhere else for it.

The soldiers, too, quickly discovered that the local population was a world away from the Arabs of Egypt, both in dress and attitude. They were simple, and sometimes primitive folks, who took life very easily, dressing as their forebears must have done – the men in baggy pants, stockings, or bare legs, wearing greenhide sandals or slippers and sporting fur caps, the women in loose, baggy print or rough cloth dresses, a coloured handkerchief tied over the hair, and the children mostly barefooted, the boys with sheepskin jackets and half-mast pants with ornamental patches sewn on to the knees and seat, and the girls, with short frocks and long pants. The men were mostly of a rugged complexion, whilst the women were, for the most part, baggy dames, with plain tanned faces, looking very stolid. The majority of the women seemed to be middle aged, old, or very young; the soldiers noting that the blushing damsel of fifteen to twenty did not seem to exist, possibly being kept under lock and key while the troops were present. Their farming methods were also primitive, the earth being tilled by rough wooden ploughs pulled by a cow or bullock. Donkeys were the chief means of transport, the soldiers marvelling at the great loads which they carried. Washing days seemed a great feature of the villages, with every village having a common wash house, usually near a spring or creek, the tubs being huge troughs hewn from pieces of solid stone. To these places the women would take the family washing, where the process was carried out in the orthodox fashion, where they depended on elbow grease rather than boiled water. The surrounding hills were dotted with a series of round stone mills, with sails like those of a ship, and here the grain was turned into the rough dark flour, from which they made their heavy dark bread. Goat and sheep's milk was extensively used on the island, from which they made a peculiar soft white cheese which was not of unpleasant flavour, but rather salty.

The camp was situated near the natural harbour and just short of the village, by a ploughed field, between two rows of ancient looking windmills, which had turned for centuries.

Since the battalion's formation, the men had done nothing but train, from Enoggera, throughout their journey to, and during their stay in, Egypt, to this rough and dusty island in the Mediterranean.

"We must be the best trained army in the empire boys. I don't envy anyone we come up against. What do you reckon Roo?" Clancy asked.

"I reckon when they clap eyes on *you* mate they'll turn tail and run" replied Roo.

"I hope so mate. I hope so," said Clancy.

Training on Lemnos was the final touches to a well oiled machine. The 9th Battalion continued to train in tactics, weapon handling, signals and all manner of tasks, but on Lemnos things were a little different with the battalion, and all other units, concentrating on landing from boats, laying communications wire from the beach head to the hillside positions, and fetching and carrying stores and ammunition to the units in their forward positions.

"This is bloody impressive and well organised," Clancy noted.

"It is, but as the CSM says, the best laid plans go to hell in the first five minutes of any battle," replied Archie.

"Thanks mate. That's very reassuring," said Clancy.

As well as training for their inevitable entry in to the war, the army had quite a few feats of engineering to undertake, especially as Lemnos was to be the staging post for the invasion of Turkey.

When the ANZACs arrived on Lemnos the natural harbour of Mudros consisted of the beach and a few rocky outcrops, from where the locals had launched their tiny fishing boats for hundreds of years. Mudros needed a substantial harbour to accommodate the troop and cargo ships which would require somewhere to unload their valuable "freight". Being the first allied troops to land on Lemnos the task of constructing a huge jetty fell to the 9th Battalion, under the supervision of the Field Engineers. The jetty was to be constructed a short distance from the camp and Lemnos, being a rocky island, had the perfect natural resource from which to build it; rocks. The whole battalion was set to work, scavenging boulders of all shapes and sizes from the surrounding hillsides. As there were very few tools available, most of the work was done by hand, with some of the rocks being a two or three man lift. The villagers assisted where they could, very kindly lending the soldiers their wheelbarrows and carts; for a small fee!

When complete, the new structure was indeed a thing of beauty, the main body of the jetty being constructed from the scavenged rocks and stretching out two hundred feet in the harbour. Being around twelve feet in width and three feet above the high tide level it was an ideal and necessary thing. The Engineers had added the finishing touch of a wooden T head, constructed from island timber, at the end.

The jetty, completed in record time, didn't signal an end to the work, or training. The troops preferred to be kept busy, but did enjoy their half, and occasionally a full, day of rest each week, when they took part in swimming, and visiting the village and local countryside.

It was quite a relief to be able to venture out in to the streets and not be plagued by nuisance hawkers, and Clancy, for one, seemed much keener to visit the island than he did Egypt.

"You know I was never one for book learning but I do feel a bit disappointed that we never got to see much of Egypt, so what do you fellas reckon about a bit of a trip to the city?" he asked.

"That would be great mate," replied Archie, "I don't think we'll ever be here again once we've left, so why not?"

The next day was their day off so they ensured that they got a good night's sleep and were up bright and early.

The three mates departed camp just before 0900 hours, their destination being the capital of Lemnos, Myrina, which was approximately seventeen miles away as the crow flies. At a village near camp they secured three ponies, and commenced their journey, travelling on a well formed road for several miles. Leaving the road, they continued along a rough, stony bridle track, for over two hours, winding through valleys and along hillsides. It was a beautiful but barren landscape.

"Hey this countryside and the hills is a lot like Kilcoy, don't you reckon?" said Roo.

"A little, but there's not much bush is there?" replied Archie.

"Or cattle," added Roo.

Alternating between riding and walking, they eventually arrived in the city at 1230 hours. On their approach they saw that the settlement stretched around two beautiful bays with an imposing castle standing proudly between, and surrounded by massive formations of volcanic rock.

By now their stomachs were rumbling with hunger after their arduous journey, so they immediately sought out the best hotel and enjoyed a good meal, followed by a rest and Turkish coffee.

Clancy patted his belly, feeling quite satisfied.

"Well that filled a gap," he said.

"It did. I'm stuffed mate," replied Roo.

Archie, by now, was becoming impatient to partake in some sightseeing.

"Come on boys, forget about your fat guts, let's go and explore," he said excitedly.

Myrina, as with Egypt, was like no place they had seen before. The residences, which lay on the outside of the town, were surrounded by high stone walls. The streets were narrow and paved with stones, whilst the shops were small, and the prices high. The best buildings, the old neoclassical mansions and Ottoman buildings, were to be found on the sea front, being usually three storeys high, graced at the front by wonderful fountains. As they walked along the esplanade, they acknowledged the numerous Greek soldiers, dressed very smartly in their uniforms. The population of the city was around two thousand, consisting of Greeks for the most part, with a fair sprinkling of Turks, who appeared to be quite content to stay where they were instead of being press ganged in to what they deemed as a foreign army; for they were Lemnians, not Turks. As Clancy surveyed Myrina he felt a sense of calm.

"If this is a city, then I love it," he said, "it beats the crowds in Cairo, and Brisbane for that matter. I think I might come and live here after this is all over".

"Well, just in case that doesn't happen I think we should get some souvenirs to remember the place by," suggested Archie.

But this was 1915 and Lemnos was not a place for tourists, so naturally had no souvenir shops.

"They're not as enterprising as the Gyppos are they?" said Roo.

Looking over towards the castle a thought occurred to Archie.

"How about a small rock from the castle over yonder? We can carve all our names on them too," he suggested.

"If it doesn't cost anything then I'm up for it," agreed Clancy.

"I'm going to start calling you Scrooge," laughed Roo.

"Who?" asked Clancy.

"Bloody hell...never mind," replied Roo shrugging his shoulders in disbelief.

It was now 1700 hours and as the day gradually turned to evening, the trio set out on their return journey, the boys, each armed with a rock the size of their hand. At around 1900 hours they found themselves passing through a small village called Thermu. The villagers, recognising the travellers' tired and dusty appearance, warmly welcomed them, offering information about the village's renowned healing hot springs. Not having had a hot bath since Australia, the boys paid the small fee, shed their clothes and submerged themselves in the soothing, mineral-rich waters of the hot springs. As the warmth enveloped their bodies, tension melted away, and a sense of tranquility washed over them, the boys reclining in the comforting embrace of the waters, gazing upwards at the expansive, cloudless sky.

"This place gets better and better," said Clancy as he lay in soothing mineral waters, staring upwards.

Engrossed in their peaceful state, Roo broke the silence, his curiosity piqued.

"What shall we write on our rocks then?" he asked, his voice carrying a hint of excitement.

Archie, with his eyes closed, contemplated for a moment before responding, "I don't know... maybe something simple, like our names and "mates together, Lemnos, 1915"...what do you think?" he asked.

A smile graced Clancy's face as he nodded in agreement.

"That sounds just the ticket, mate," he replied.

As the boys revelled in the hot springs, their peaceful sanctuary was interrupted by the unexpected arrival of a group of local women who giggled like school girls as they approached.

"Bloody hell!" Roo called out as he instinctively sank lower in to the water.

Roo's sudden shout had awakened Archie and Clancy from their blissful daydreams.

"Oh my giddy aunt...women!" said Archie as he too ducked down in to the spring water, using his hands to conceal his modesty.

Clancy, however, wasn't so modest, for his eyes were apparently bigger than his belly, as he spied the platters of food that the women were carrying; mandarins, figs, nuts, local cheeses and freshly baked bread.

"You beauty!" said Clancy, "jut set it down over here please".

The women, seemingly unaware of the boys' discomfort, set the platter down nearby, inviting them to partake in the feast.

It soon became apparent that the supper was an unexpected inclusion with the bath, catching them off guard. Grateful yet slightly flustered, they expressed their thanks while trying to wave away the women, and their wandering eyes, with a little tact. Finally the women seemed to understand and, after a few sneaky downward glances, they departed, still laughing as they went.

"That was embarrassing," said Archie with a relieved sigh.

"Yeah mate...they were definitely laughing at you and your little John Thomas there," joked Clancy.

"Bugger off! They'd have needed a magnifying glass to see yours mate," replied Archie.

Feeling suitably cleansed and well fed it was time to get back to camp.

The rest of the return journey lay along a rough track, scarcely discernible in the dark, but their surefooted mounts, it seemed, were used to both the dark and the tracks, bringing the threesome safely back to camp just before 2100 hours.

"That was a good day boys, but I need my beauty sleep. Tomorrow is going to be a long one," said Clancy as he clambered in to his warm sleeping bag.

Lemnos was certainly cooler than the oppressive heat of northern Africa and the boys were soon sound asleep, no doubt dreaming about what had turned out to be an interesting day in one way or another.

Clancy was right as the next day certainly was going to be a busy one.

As it transpired, not all of the work was popular, especially when poorly timed.

"Psst! Hey, *you* blokes, wake up," came an unwelcome voice in the darkness.

"What is it sarge?" said Roo.

"Captain Fisher needs five blokes for a work party, and you're it. Come on, get a wriggle on," replied Sergeant Mac.

Arch took a glance at his watch, holding it up so that he could read it by the light of the night stars.

"Flaming heck sarge, its ten o'clock!" he exclaimed.

"Well the army doesn't stop, and besides, you men are paid twenty hours a day, seven days a week, all year, so come on," growled the sergeant.

"That sounds like a piss poor hourly rate to me. I'll have to have a word with the union rep," joked Clancy.

Unfortunately for the boys, a supply barge containing sacks of oats had docked at the jetty. It needed to be unloaded urgently so that it could slip back out to sea, as easily as it had arrived, thus avoiding prying eyes and enemy submarines.

The boys moaned and grumbled all the way to the jetty.

"I'll have a bloody question asked in parliament....the bastards," announced Clancy.

"Yeah, we build the new dock and now they expect us to be wharfies!" Roo replied in agreement.

Not feeling particularly confident that his small band of workers would indeed work, Captain Fisher turned to his two fellow officers.

"Somehow I think that these blokes are strong union men, but I have an idea; follow my lead," he whispered.

On arrival at the jetty Captain Fisher adopted a sudden jovial persona as he walked up the gangplank, followed by his two officer mates. The three men returned from the vessel, each with a huge sack slung over their shoulders.

"Come on you blokes, this cargo won't shift itself," the Captain joked.

Archie and his group could not believe what they were witnessing; officers doing manual labour!

"Come on boys, if they can do it so can we," he announced.

"That's the spirit. The sooner we get this done, the sooner we can get back to dreaming of home," said the Captain.

With the help of all, the unloading was soon complete, a grateful Captain bidding the men good night. Back in their warm beds, the men were soon sound asleep, enjoying the few hours that remained of the night.

Dawn seemed to arrive suddenly, with the bugle calling Reveille, and the Duty Sergeant roaming the lines shouting "wakey, wakey, rise and shine".

Rubbing his eyes as he peered out through the flaps of the tent, Clancy noticed that the barge that they unloaded had departed, but many other ships had arrived during the night.

"Hey fellas, take a look, the harbour seems to have got busier lately," he said.

Indeed it had, for, with the new jetty, came numerous ships; troop ships, cruisers, battle ships, some showing signs of war damage on their weary exterior. With the ships came more soldiers, Greeks, French, British and many other nationalities from both the Empire and allied countries. Lemnos was now quite the cosmopolitan island.

Since their arrival, one item, which had been scarce, was now in plentiful supply.....alcohol. By the end of March just about every shop in Mudros sold it, ranging from brandy, wine and beer; though the beer wasn't as good as that from home.

The villagers had been encouraged by the local Bishop, who had obviously seen a market, so took the chance. Temporary booths were popping up along the harbour selling items such as post cards and chocolate covered figs. The wine was sold for a penny a glass and, although some had described it as "fearful stuff", it soon became a big seller with the troops.

"I think the wine and beer is bloody marvellous," said Clancy, who fancied himself as a bit of a connoisseur.

"Oh mate, if I peed in your cup and told you it was beer you'd believe me," joked Roo.

Clancy suddenly wore a shocked and worried expression as he paused and spoke.

"You haven't though, have yer?"

The three slouch hat missiles which bounced off his head in unison gave him his answer.

Food was also becoming irregular in both amount and type. There was either bread or biscuits, but not both, on any given day, and fresh meat was becoming a luxury item, with serving sizes decreasing somewhat.

"Clancy mate, I think the army suspects you are getting a bit fat. They want to make sure you can climb those hills unaided and don't need a shove up," said Archie.

Towards the end of March the ANZACs soon became very popular with the High Command. On the 23rd the 9th Battalion put on a display of a bayonet attack for the Commander of the Mediterranean Expeditionary Force, General Sir Ian Hamilton. The troops were eager to impress this highly decorated British officer.

"Blimey, Birdie yesterday and now the Big Wig is here to see us," said Clancy.

"Well, then let's show him what we can do," replied Freddy.

In four waves of companies, the battalion charged across the open space, bayonets gleaming in the bright sunlight, screaming all manner of obscenities as they ran. Reaching the sacks stuffed with straw and sawdust, which were suspended from wooden frames, they were unable to parry against the inanimate "defenders" but instead eagerly thrust and lunged at the marked vulnerable points on their "enemies" bodies. By the time the last wave had arrived to wreak death on the defenders, the sacks lay in shreds on the dry ground, but none the less still bore the brunt of fearsome stabs from the last attackers.

Impressed by their blood curdling display the General addressed the Battalion, giving them a rousing speech about defeating the Hun and the Turk. The General then inspected the troops. During the speech Private Devereux, a veteran of the British Army, whispered something to the soldier next to him, convincing him to pass the message down the line. By the time the inspection party had reached the first rank the scene was set. Now, British Officers are quite out of touch with the lower class soldier and only have a small repertoire of questions and comments to the men who they are inspecting, such as "where are you from?", "what do you for a living?" or "how are you enjoying army life?" Hamilton's question appeared to be about what the individual soldier did for a "crust".

As he walked along the front rank he eyed the troops up individually, "A fine body of men you have here Colonel", pausing to speak to individual men.

Halting in front of Devereux he uttered the words "and what do you do for a crust soldier?" unknowingly setting in motion the wheels of a humorous conspiracy of replies.

"Book binder sir," came the immediate reply.

The General, nodding his approval at such a useful trade moved on.

"And you Corporal, what do you do for a living?"

"I'm a Book Binder sir".

"Really? You must know the other fellow I just asked".

As the General moved through the battalion lines, receiving the same response, it became apparent that something was afoot, but, being a good sport, he played along. The Colonel could see the funny side and found it difficult to keep a straight face whilst turning to the RSM with a raised eyebrow.

"There certainly are a lot of book binders in this battalion Colonel. Do they read a lot in Australia?" asked the General, with a wry smile.

Clearing his throat, and managing to sneak a quick wink and nod to his battalion, the Colonel replied, "Yes we *do* find time between cattle herding and sheep shearing sir".

Unknown to the rank and file D-Day on the prospective target had been set for the 19th of March, but a severe gale had resulted in its postponement. A number of ships had been washed ashore by the rough seas, not good for the Navy but a bonus for the Army who eagerly rescued the occasional barrel of rum, or crate of delicious chocolate, which had made its way ashore with the assistance of the roaring surf. Of course the enterprising platoon were there gathering up the spoils.

"We'd better get this barrel secured away out of sight. I heard that an officer the other day ordered that a barrel be poured away," said Taff.

"What?" said an appalled Clancy.

"Yeah, probably one of those holier than thou temperance types," added Roo.

"You can bet he filled his hip flask up first though eh?" said Archie.

"Too right he did; the bastard!" Clancy exclaimed.

On the 31st of March the first mail since the ANZACs landed on Lemnos arrived – one hundred and ten bags of it. The queue for the many letters and packages stretched from the tented camp to the makeshift postal and courier office. Archie and Roo both received letters and a parcel from Doriray Station. As Roo marvelled at the fine pair of knitted brown woollen socks, Archie held up a similar pair.

"You've gotta love Aunty Doris and Uncle Ray," said Roo.

"Yep, they always send useful stuff," replied Archie.

"Did they send any cake but?" enquired an eager Clancy, "I love your mum's cake Arch".

Delving deeper in to the brown paper package Archie produced a tin, and inside, a fine rich, fruit cake.

"Just the ticket. What did you get Roo?" asked a hungry Clancy.

"A bloody great tin of homemade biccies mate. Here you go, help yourself," said Roo, as he passed around the tin, "and don't forget to leave me some you buggers!"

"No mail for you Clance?" asked Archie.

"Naaa mate. I've got no family to speak of, or any that I speak to anyways," replied Clancy.

"That's a shame mate. Hey, why don't you write to my mum and dad, they would love to hear from you?" Archie suggested.

Clancy smiled. "That would be very kind mate. Very kind. I will do that".

Archie handed Clancy a post card and pencil. "Here you go mate. No time like the present. I'll let them know you are writing".

"Bugger!" exclaimed Clancy, looking embarrassed, "my secret is out".

"What secret?" asked Roo.

"I can't read or write. I never tried at school, work on the farm was always more important, so Dad said there was no need to learn," Clancy explained.

A moment of silence followed, only to be broken by Roo. "Don't worry mate I can teach you, but in the mean time you can tell me what you want to say. What do you reckon?"

Clancy felt emotional, his voice quivering, "after the way I treated you all those years ago, and you'd do that for me?"

"Water under the bridge...and besides you're my best mate now," said Roo, nodding.

"Then that would be much appreciated. Thanks Roo," said a grateful Clancy.

April Fools' Day was one of great strain and stamina as the battalion headed off on a picnic at the local beach, or so Sergeant Mac had told them. Ten hours of traversing up and down steep and rocky slopes it certainly was not a picnic, but it was preparing them and getting them fit for the task ahead.....and fit they were!

"These bloody hills seem to go on and on," moaned Clancy.

"Stop your whining Sassenach, it's all in your mind," said an unsympathetic Sergeant Mac, "just look down at the ground, lean in to the hill and your wee legs will do the rest".

"Wee legs?? Cheeky jock bastard!" whispered Clancy.

Sergeant Mac may have been a lot of things, but deaf he wasn't.

"You'll keep wee man, you'll keep," said the sergeant to a surprised Clancy.

The following day was a day of rest unless you count the Good Friday Church Parade, where all attended, the padre preaching about the crucifixion and resurrection; each man secretly praying for their own salvation from the storm which would soon be upon them. The Easter weekend was a time of relaxation too and marvelling at the Greek custom of the colourful dying of eggs, which the locals presented to the grateful soldiers on Easter Sunday.

This was also a time when advice from old soldiers became very useful. Sgt Mac, a veteran of the British Army, gathered together the men of the company.

"Listen you blokes; our entry into this war will be with us soon," he said, "food and water will be scarce on the first day so any non-perishable rations which you can scrounge, plus an extra water bottle, will be useful things to have......so get to it".

Within days, 3rd Brigade Headquarters received confirmation that the Dardanelles was the objective, and that they would be the covering force for the invasion.

On the 8th of April, following yet another gale, the battalion embarked on the 'Malda'. The British India Liner was crowded with the 9th Battalion as well as some members of the 11th.

Portholes and hatches had to be left open to allow in fresh air to the stifling vessel. The ship, still in the bay, ready to move at a moment's notice, was soon joined by numerous other vessels. The day that the troops had enlisted for would soon be upon them. The remainder of the 1st Division began to arrive, including Lieutenant Warren and the 2nd reinforcements; a welcome sight to all.

The ANZACs were soon joined by French troops, the Royal Navy Division and the 29th Division of the British Army.

If the 9th Battalion were wondering why they were still bobbing up and down in Mudros Harbour instead of on terra firma, their question was very quickly answered – disembarkation practice. Loaded up with their eighty pounds of equipment, the troops practised day and night time drills of scrambling quietly down a highly animated cargo net in to the small boats waiting at the side of the ship. Once aboard, the troops, and their small Navy crew, would row silently, but quickly to shore, re-organise and regroup on the beach, then scramble up the steep slopes which towered over the shoreline. It was exhausting, yet necessary, work, charging up one hill and then another, until every muscle in their legs ached and felt like they were going to explode. Despite the agony and the hardship, the men got on with it, with little complaint, for they knew they were being preparing for something big, and this training could save their lives.

Over the next few days there were numerous issues by the Quartermaster. Emergency rations of bully beef, biscuits, an Oxo cube, tea and sugar. Peak caps were given out with orders to remove the wire which gave them their shape, so they would be less conspicuous to the enemy. This brought a few laughs from the ANZACs.

"I think that shooting at the bastards would give them a bit of a clue!"

Something which would become dear to each man was their new regimental patches, which were to be sewn on the sleeve just below the shoulder seam. The 9th Battalion's patch was black over light blue, the black denoting the battalion, and the light blue the 3rd Brigade. To the Aussie diggers the battalion colour patch was treated with the same affection as the British metal cap badge.

From the 16th of April, for two to three nights, parties from the battalion left to practise landing from battleships. Three days later the troops began to live on bully beef and biscuits. No fresh meat was issued.

Divisional training for the Light Horse back in Egypt was also now *very* real, every day spent in the desert practising protection on the move, at rest, attack, defence and night operations. They were soon an efficient fighting force and, in addition, began to practise swimming their horses across the Nile as well as ferrying them across on native barges.

"They reckon we might be deployed to southern Europe...maybe Hungary," said Chugger.

For those on Lemnos the invasion became elusive. The 23rd had been set for the big day, but violent gales on the two days prior had put paid to that. Postponed again!

5

"Come on, Queenslanders"

The ANZAC's role in the landings had been meticulously planned by Major General Bridges and Lieutenant Colonel White, making effective use of intelligence gathered by the Royal Navy Air Service aircrews, who had conducted a total of one hundred and ninety six aerial missions over the Gallipoli peninsula during the first few months of 1915. These missions had included thirty eight aerial reconnaissance and eighteen photographic aerial reconnaissance missions.

This was followed up on the 14th of April 1915, when Major Charles Villiers-Stuart, an intelligence officer from ANZAC HQ, embarked on a significant mission over the peninsula. Despite having no prior experience in aeroplanes, he courageously took off, as a passenger, from the island of Tenedos with the objective of conducting aerial surveillance over the designated landing beaches. His primary goal was to identify any concealed Turkish defences and artillery batteries. Remarkably, his mission was a resounding success. The valuable information he obtained, combined with previously reported intelligence, ensured that when the attack eventually took place, the troops not only knew their destination but also had a solid understanding of what they were up against.

Lieutenant General Birdwood had also conducted a recce, by ship, of his own in February of 1915 noting the terrain and the logistical issues that his Corps may have.

The Gallipoli Peninsula itself is a hilly outcrop of land shaped much like a foot, with its toes pointing downwards and its front facing the Straits of the Dardanelles. Suvla Bay is the heel, Cape Helles is the toes and Gaba Tepe is a cape on the sole. The undulating landscape is characterised by valleys and numerous spurs that extend towards the coast. Almost the entire surface of the region consists of ridges and plateaus with irregular elevations. It is covered in places by scrub and sparse vegetation, but largely comprises bare and arid rock. The rock is fissured and marked by a complex network of deep ravines, whose sides are as craggy and precipitous as sea cliffs. A beach stretches northwards from Gaba Tepe to Ari Burnu and further on to Suvla Bay; Ari Burnu soon to become known as ANZAC Cove. The entire surrounding range is referred to as Sari Bair on military maps, but in reality this was the Turkish name for the high, steep, yellow cliff which was known from day one of the invasion, by the troops, as the Sphinx.

The plan to seize the peninsula, gain control of the straits, and ultimately capture the ancient city of Constantinople was an audacious and intricate endeavour that involved various strategic manoeuvres. One of these tactics involved the French landing at Kum Kale, located at the southern entrance of the Dardanelles, while the Navy staged a compelling display of firepower at Besika Bay to the south. Concurrently, a feigned landing was planned at Saros, situated to the north of Suvla Bay.

The French forces stationed at Kum Kale had a specific objective: to secure their positions for a few days before re-embarking and proceeding to Helles. Their purpose was to reinforce and provide assistance to the 29th Division in that area.

The 29th Division was to land at Cape Helles and progressively move along the peninsula, systematically clearing out Turkish artillery and infantry along their path. Meanwhile, the ANZACs were tasked with landing on the beach between Gaba Tepe and a location referred to as Fisherman's Hut, positioned three miles north along the coast.

Initially, a covering party would seize and occupy a line extending from Gaba Tepe to Koja Chemen Tepe, also known as Hill 971. Once this line was secured, the main ANZAC force would land and advance up the steep slopes towards their objective line, which traversed through Mal Tepe, situated three miles away. The aim was to pose a significant threat and potentially disrupt Turkish communications. The success of the attack heavily relied on the element of surprise and the use of stealth.

The Navy was strategically positioned to unleash a powerful bombardment on the peninsula, but this was to be initiated only after the defenders became aware of the attack. Ideally, an artillery barrage directed at their position would give the Turks pause and dissuade them from deploying reinforcements at the risk of heavy losses.

General Bridges had selected the 3rd Brigade, from the 1st Australian Division, to land soon after dawn, an hour before the assault on Cape Helles. Immediately on landing, near Little Ari Burnu, the northern parties of the brigade were tasked to advance up Sari Bair, seize the heights near Hill 700 and extend their line to Hill 971, thus forming an impenetrable barrier in order to prevent the Turkish Army from rushing down from the heights and defeating the ANZACs at the shoreline. Simultaneously the remainder of the brigade were to capture all of the high ground stretching along to Gaba Tepe.

The 9th Battalion, on the extreme right of the landing, were given two objectives. Two companies were to swing right on landing, approximately a thousand yards north of Gaba Tepe and destroy the battery believed to be overlooking the invasion beach. The other companies were to advance about a mile, straight up the heights, to a knoll; later known as Anderson's Knoll.

The covering force was to be transported from Lemnos, split in to company groups, on three battleships and various transports. The fleet's destination was the island of Imbros, which lay half way between the peninsular and Lemnos. Once there the troops in the transports were to be transferred to Destroyers, and the remainder to Tows at a rendezvous point five miles west of Gaba Tepe; a Tow being a string of three ship's cutters, or other small craft, towed by a steam launch, and carrying approximately one hundred and thirty men. The battleships would then closely escort the Tows as far as they could without being detected. Once they had reached their safe limit they would stop whilst the Tows made their silent dash to the beach. As for the Destroyers, each had a number of rowing boats alongside. Once near the shore, the troops would scramble down cargo nets in to the rowing boats, bobbing up and down with the waves, to begin *their* journey. Each ship would then tow its rowing boats as close to the shore as the sea depth would allow, the small craft then being cast off to row independently to the landing point.

Saturday the 24th of April 1915, the day of destiny for the ANZACs, and the rest of the allied forces, had finally arrived. Most of the company had slept out on deck in the cool air and, when they awoke, were met by an awe inspiring sight.

"Something's happening boys........look!" announced an excited Clancy.

Much had occurred during the night. The world's greatest armada of warships and transports was now assembled in Mudros Harbour.

"I bet you never thought you'd ever see such a sight, eh mate? I know *I* didn't," said Roo.

"I never thought I'd be this close to fighting in a war," replied Clancy.

There was now a sombre feeling in the air as the individual

soldiers contemplated their own mortality. The feeling was soon broken by the Company Commander, Major Salisbury.

"Come on you blokes cheer up and don't put the moz on the day. Let's shake hands as good mates and wish each other well eh?" he announced extending his hand to Clancy.

There were handshakes and pats on the back all round and the whispers of "good luck" and "see you in Constantinople". By mid day 'A' and 'B' Companies had been transferred by destroyer to the battleship 'Queen'. The rest of the Battalion remained on the 'Malda' which, along with the rest of the covering force slipped out of Mudros Harbour on route to Imbros Island.

During the afternoon Major Salisbury had re-iterated Sergeant Mac's earlier advice to scrounge as much extra ammunition and water as they could carry. Sergeant Mac, himself, did the rounds ensuring that each man had his "scoff bag" full of non-perishable food items such as broken biscuits, nuts and any dried fruit they could get their hands on.

"Keep the bag of treats in your tunic pocket so you can reach in whenever you feel a bit hungry," he told the men.

Pretty soon the ship's canteen was stripped of any foodstuffs the soldiers could use, and the cooks even tossed a few tins their way when they could.

The official mobilisation issue for each man was two hundred rounds of ammunition, full rations, a full water bottle, and two sand bags wrapped securely around their entrenching tools. The sandbags were to be used to throw across barbed wire in order to prevent the troops getting caught on the wire as they scrambled towards the enemy, and also to fill with soil when the time came to dig in.

During the short voyage few conversations were had. Each man sitting quiet with his own thoughts, wondering if he would acquit himself well and who in the group of brave fellows would find out the great secret.

Good officers and NCOs make it a point to inspire their men, and Major Salisbury certainly did that as he mingled with the troops.

"Bloody hell, what a maudlin lot you blokes are," he said as he glanced around his men, who had perked up a little, "is anyone scared?"

The men, surprised at this question, looked left and right.

"Come on, stick your hand up if you're scared" he asked.

Again no one moved, except for the OC and Sergeant Mac, who both raised their hands.

"Bugger me sir, if you two are scared then we've got no hope," said Roo.

"Well, not necessarily," replied the Major, "I've been in many battles, too many in fact, and, each time, I am scared shitless. Any of you who isn't scared is not only a liar, but a bloody idiot".

One by one each soldier raised their hand.

"Look fellas, war is a terrifying thing, that's for sure, but once it starts the fear disappears and all that you have learned begins to sink in and take over," said the Major in a calm voice, "just follow your leaders, keep moving forward, and don't stop for buggery. That's my advice. Stick with it and, God willing, we'll get through to the end. Together".

During the voyage the ship's officers and crew couldn't do enough for the Aussies. There was a service by the Royal Navy Chaplain on the Quarterdeck and later the men were showered with gifts of tobacco, cigarettes and pipes. There was even an all you can eat dinner and a concert later that evening.

"I feel like a condemned man with all of this grub," said Archie.

"Save any extras for your scoff bag mate," replied Roo.

"We've got a few hours yet, so grab some sleep boys," said Major Salisbury.

"Sleep? I don't need to be asked twice," said Clancy as he snuggled down on his folded tunic.

Not *all* could sleep, with many contemplating their future and whether or not they had one. But, despite this, the general consensus was that they wouldn't have missed it for quids.

As the armada sailed towards the Turkish coast light and noise discipline were now in force. No smoking or talking on deck, and certainly no white lights. All external doorways were fitted with canvass curtains so that when a door was opened no light escaped outside.

Minutes after midnight on Sunday the 25th of April 1915, Saint Mark's Day, two destroyers, 'Colne' and 'Beagle', drew up alongside the 'Malda' and the soldiers of 'C' and 'D' Companies dropped quietly over the side on to the deck. Accompanying them were two platoons of the 12th Battalion.

Lieutenant General Birdwood was very proud of how the ANZACs conducted themselves at this point, later writing:

"You will I know be glad to hear how extremely enthusiastic the Naval officers were at their behaviour on board. It took under ten minutes to transfer the whole of these men to their boats, and when this had been completed the Flag Captain said to me – "Your men are not quiet they are absolutely silent"."

At 0130 hours the men on the 'Queen' began descending down the cargo nets in to the cutters and lifeboats waiting below. 'A' Company alighted down the starboard side of the ship and 'B' Company the port side.

Before easing himself over the side Clancy offered his hand to Roo and Archie saying "It's not something I usually say to blokes, but good luck fellas, I love you both. See you in the boat".

The Taylor boys were lost for words acknowledging Clancy with a nod.

By 0235 hours the entire covering force was in their Tows, and not a sound had been made.

Sitting in their small craft the troops could now see the feint outline of the coast before them.....Gallipoli. All they had to do now was land, run across the open terrain ahead of them and on in to the hills. Constantinople would soon be theirs.

The sea was almost completely still, and the moon, which hung in the night sky to their front, was full. As soon as the men were safely aboard the Tows, the battleships began to move slowly towards the shore, the Tows and their picket boats advancing with them. By 0330 hours the moon had vanished and the battleships had moved forward as far as they could without being seen. From the bridge of the 'Queen' the order was given to land, and, as the Tows moved quickly away from their escorts, the crews waved their hats enthusiastically and gave the troops a whispered cheer.

The journey towards the enemy coastline was indeed a precarious one, and the atmosphere on the boats was tense. Not a word was spoken. Some clutched crucifixes, others rosary beads, muttering personal prayers to themselves. Others patted pockets and pouches trying to remember if they had everything with them for this day's work. Most stared at the approaching landscape to their front straining to detect any sudden movement or muzzle flashes in the darkness. For a moment everyone held their collective breath as two searchlights suddenly shone their beams ahead of the Tows, but, being located on the far side of the hills their lights fell short of the armada of small craft. Nonetheless, instinctively, the occupants of the boats ducked in unison, hoping to decrease the size of their silhouette.

"Phew Arch, that was a bit close eh?" whispered Roo.

A Royal Navy officer in charge of one of the 9th Battalion Tows had the task of guiding all craft to the designated landing area at Gaba Tepe. All Tows had been instructed to keep each other in sight and to follow at intervals of around one hundred and fifty yards. This was not an easy task as without the moon it was dark, and a thick early morning mist had descended on the surface of the sea. To compound the situation, at a point half way to Gaba Tepe the officer noticed that visual contact had been lost with the rest of the attacking force. It came about that the ocean current was too strong for most of the boats, which were comparatively light and small; resulting in the armada drifting north towards Ari Burnu, a mile away from the intended landing place. In desperation the officer quickly changed course and caught up with the missing force, managing to pass a message that they needed to turn southwards; but it was too late, for the battalions and companies had become mixed up and, with the waves pushing them ever closer, the shoreline was too close to avoid. To add to the issue the steam pickets had begun to cast off their Tows upon reaching shallow water and, as one of them did so, flames and sparks flew out of its funnel to a height of three feet, its light show lasting around thirty seconds.

As he stared at the flames Sergeant Mac was not impressed.

"Bugger! There goes the element of surprise".

At 0429 hours, on one of the hills, a bright yellow light appeared for a few seconds, and then, a single shot cracked overhead from out of the darkness; then a second.

"And so it begins," Archie whispered.

All at once the tension in the small boats disappeared and adrenalin kicked in. A shout from one of the Tows instructed the troops to make their way to shore and hold their ground.

The Queenslanders had been given the honour of being the first to land. As the first boat ran aground, Lieutenant Duncan Chapman, of Maryborough, an officer from the 9th Battalion, calmly drew his pistol, a Mark IV Webley Revolver, from its holster and turned to the soldiers in his boat.

"Righto boys, here we go. Remember, head across the beach and open ground and regroup at the base of the slope. Good luck, and give 'em what for!" he shouted.

As each boat ran aground, men began jumping into the shallow water. Sadly some jumped too early before their boat reached the shallows and were dragged below the surface by the weight of their equipment.

As Lieutenant Chapman stepped on to the beach, only yards away in the darkness, the feet of one Sergeant Joseph Stratford, also of the 9th Battalion, simultaneously touched the soft sandy shore.

Chapman knelt and took a quick glance to his front and knew at once that they had landed at the wrong beach, for there was no open ground, just a small beach enveloped by what, at first look, appeared to be mountains. He called back to one of the Coxswains of the Tows.

"We're on the wrong beach. Let them know, but tell them to send the next wave here. Got it?"

"Aye, aye sir," the sailor replied.

"Good on you," Chapman thought to himself, "this is as good a place as any".

As the shots became more numerous Lieutenant Chapman shouted for the men to form up at the base of the slope, fix bayonets and charge their magazines.

Archie, Roo and Clancy climbed over the side of their boat, along with the rest of its human cargo. In parts the water came up to the men's chests which, along with the weight of their weapon and equipment, and the slippery shingle under foot, made the going quite difficult. As they waded through the cool water the soldiers were almost convinced that the Turks were not there, until a single shot was fired. As if requiring an invitation, shots rang out from all directions. Roo must have had the luck of the ancestral spirits as one shot hit his cap and threw him back in the water. Archie and Clancy did not see it happen as they were just ahead of him, but a helping hand from Lieutenant Ponsonby pulled Roo back on to his feet, Roo nodding in appreciation. Once ashore the soldiers raced across the small beach to the base of the heights, as bullets cracked, thumped and whizzed around them. At the slope each man took off his pack and laid it neatly on the ground, remembering to remove anything which they might need during the next few hours. Archie had arrived at the wall of the slope in quick time. The CSM had been right about the battle plan going to hell in the first few minutes. The beach was a scene of chaos with no one taking charge. The men lay at the foot of the hill for about ten minutes, the bullets whizzing round like blow flies, men being hit as they stepped from incoming boats. As Archie fixed his bayonet on to his rifle he looked round in all directions and could see at once that the companies and battalions were intermingled.

"Are there any officers or NCOs here?" he called out in the chaos.

There was no response, for everyone else too was trying to get their bearings. There was a sudden thud behind Archie as Clancy flung himself on to the sand.

"Ah! G'day Arch me old cobber. How are yer?" he enquired.

"I've been better mate," replied Archie as he suddenly realised that his cousin wasn't with them, "hey Clance, have you seen Roo?"

"No mate, not since we jumped out of the boat," he replied.

Both men lay on their backs, straining their eyes in the darkness, searching the shoreline to their rear. It wasn't long before they located Roo, standing at the water's edge, puffs of sand exploding all around him. They watched as Roo calmly bent down and reached in to the shallow water at the edge of the beach, grasping hold of a smooth rock, which had been shaped by the movement of the water. He then stood on one leg with his other bent at the knee and the sole of his boot placed along the supporting leg. Next he placed the rock under his arm pit, and, after raising his eyes to the sky and uttering a few words in the Jinibara language, he cast the rock back in to the incoming surf, then, placed the foot of his bent leg back on to the sand; he seemed very content.

"Bloody hell...Roo! Come on Clance," exclaimed Archie as he grabbed Clancy's webbing strap and pulled him towards where Roo was standing.

"Roo! What the blazes?" shouted Archie, "we're not at home and the spirits of the ancestors aren't here".

"The spirits are everywhere Arch and, anyway, this is for the water spirits to let them know that we are around anyways," replied Roo.

Up at the rallying point an old goat track of sorts had been found, and the word was given to charge. As the troops began climbing towards the heights there was a great cry of "come on, Queenslanders, come on, the 9th!"

"Look boys our mates are moving forward without us. Let's go before we miss it," said Clancy.

"Hang on mate I haven't finished yet," announced Roo, "we are entering the lands of the great warrior Turk and must seek the protection of the ancestral spirits whilst we travel here".

"You get me killed and I'll never speak to you again Rueben Taylor!" said Clancy, rolling his eyes at his own nonsensical statement.

"Just let me finish and we will all be safe," said Roo.

Resigned to their fate both Archie and Clancy loaded and cocked their rifles as they knelt with their backs to Roo, scanning the hillsides for those in the darkness who intended them harm.

"Fire at the muzzle flashes and you're sure to get the bastards," said Clancy.

As the Turkish rounds peppered the beach around them, Clancy and Archie laid down a steady fire which was obviously working, as the shots in their direction became less and less. Scooping up some sand from the beach, Roo began to rub the sand under his arms so that the land would then take on his smell and that of all who came ashore that day. His little ceremony complete, Roo dusted himself off and sprinkled the sand back over the beach.

"There you go. Now we are all safe," announced Roo with a satisfied grin.

"Halle-bloody-lujah!" whispered Clancy, as he aimed another lethal shot in to the darkness, "can we go now?"

Suddenly an angry sounding voice came from their front. It was the doctor, Captain Butler, pistol in hand.

"G'day doc," said Archie.

"What the blazes are you three playing at?" demanded the doc.

"Oh, Roo's just making sure that the spirits are with us," replied Clancy.

"Really?" replied the doc as he gazed over at Roo, "that's good. Well, are the spirits happy Roo?"

"Yes sir," came the response.

"Right, stop firing up the hill for a start, our blokes might get in the way, and let's get on with this war," replied Captain Butler as he beckoned them to follow him.

"I wonder what's got him so arced up?" asked Roo.

In the first couple of minutes of the landing Doc Butler had watched as some of his stretcher bearers had been mown down by the deadly fire of a Turkish machine gun and, despite his Hippocratic Oath, he was out for retribution.

Many men had fallen before they left their boats, others on the sand as they ran towards the bank at the bottom of the hills. As the doc and his small party ran, they recognised faces of those who had been killed, men who they had known since Enoggera, and many whom they didn't know, for at that moment the 9th was mixed with the 10th Battalion. Yet, despite this, platoons and companies were forming from these rag tag mobs, led and inspired by officers and men who had simply put their hand up, moving forward and upwards towards their objectives. Prior to landing all had been told that they must advance quickly to the heights at whatever the cost, for they needed to clear the way for the main body which would soon follow.

"I think someone got our order wrong," joked Clancy as he began to climb.

"Order?" asked a confused Roo.

"Yeah mate, I ordered a starter of flat ground soup, followed by a medium hill slope," replied Clancy.

"Silly bugger," said Roo, "another rubbish joke like that and I'll shoot you myself!"

There was much swearing, cheering and joking as the troops pushed forward up the steep slopes, partly due to the rough terrain and the thorny vegetation which covered the ground. Their cries and shouts of "bum nuts", "imshee-yalla", and "eggs-a-cook" were thrown at any Turk they encountered and chased away.

Sighting the enemy machine gun post at the top of Ari Burnu, a hundred yards or so from the beach, the doc yelled "come on men let's take that gun!" Scrambling up the rocky slope, revolver in hand, he was soon overtaken by Clancy and the Taylors who silenced the gun by shooting the firer and bayoneting the remaining crew. A small victory for the battalion, a gun spiked and a trench seized.

The troops then carried on up to a triangular shaped plateau, flanked by two ridges, with a large gully and valley to its front, overshadowed by yet another steep hill. Later in the day it was to be christened Plugge's Plateau in honour of Colonel Plugge of the Auckland Battalion who set up his Battalion Headquarters on the plateau. But, for now, it was a rallying point and staging post for the 9th, 10th and 11th Battalions.

"This is as good a spot as any," said the doc, "now, my work is about to begin for these poor unfortunates, so you blokes look after yourselves".

Archie, Roo and Clancy thanked the doc and wished him well as he began assisting the wounded and ushering those who could walk, back down the slopes. He was impressed by the wounded who gently skidded and rolled themselves downwards, some even becoming entangled in the prickly vegetation, or hanging precariously on the edge of huge drops, until they could be rescued.

A zig zag shaped path lay on the slope of the inland side of the plateau, and the Turkish defenders were making a hasty withdrawal, slipping, skidding, and sliding down the rocky path.

"Hey, look at those cheeky buggers!" shouted Clancy, pointing at the retreating Turks, "let's give 'em what for eh?"

As Clancy fired at the enemy soldiers the rest of the men joined in, the Turks falling when hit, like targets at the local show; the rapid firing so intense that it sounded like the bursts of machine guns.

As all of this was going on, the second instalment of the

covering force, which consisted of 'C' and 'D' companies, had begun their landing from their Tows. The element of surprise had now gone and as they approached to within one hundred yards of the shore they were met with a perfect shower of lead; many being hit before they could land. Again the ocean currents were playing havoc with the landing vessels, with parties landing at different points on the coastline; 'D' company landing at Little Ari Burnu, parts of 'C' company approximately three hundred yards south of 'D', whilst other groups landed a hundred yards or so further south. Whilst some met with similar terrain as the first wave, for most the going wasn't too steep, although many had to climb up on all fours in places.

With true fighting spirit the second wave disembarked from their boats, throwing their heavy packs from their shoulders as they did so, and followed the muzzle flashes to the nearest enemy, quickly dispatching them with the bayonet. 'C' and 'D' companies were quickly reorganised by their officers and, through the dim early morning light, they managed to find their bearings, rapidly moving southwards to begin carrying out their objectives. Like the first wave the men cheered and cursed loudly as they saw off any Turk who came in to view. This noise combined with the flashes and cracks of rifle fire assisted greatly in guiding other water borne troops advancing in their small flotillas, to their landing positions.

In the mean time the majority of 'A' and 'B' companies were now on Plugge's Plateau, along with elements of the 10th and 11th battalions. For now, with the absence of senior officers, who were en route in the next wave, other officers and NCOs were rallying and taking charge of the three battalions. Major

Drake-Brockman of the 11th Battalion had organised the battalions into defensive positions, in readiness for them to go on the offensive, sending the 9th to the right, the 11th to the left, whilst keeping the 10th in the centre of the position. In order to conserve ammunition the men had been ordered to stop firing at the retreating Turks, as they would no doubt be dealt with by the ANZACs advancing from the south. Major Salisbury, being the most senior officer from the 9th Battalion present, assumed command of the battalion, taking charge of the right flank and appointing Captain Ryder to command the left.

Dawn was slowly breaking but vision was still limited to around fifty yards, making it difficult to accurately identify enemy targets to their front. As the sun finally breached the eastern horizon it became apparent to all who were formed up on Plugge's Plateau, based on pre-invasion briefings, that the ridge immediately to their right, known as 400 Plateau, should have been on the left centre of their landing place.

"Bugger!" exclaimed Lieutenant Ponsonby, pointing southwards, "right now we should have been down there, two miles distant at Gaba Tepe".

"We can't help the currents mate.....er.....sir," said Archie, "but now we know where we are, a quick trek south won't do us any harm".

"Well that's Major Salisbury's decision," replied the officer.

By now the Turkish defenders were beginning to feel a little outnumbered by the newly landed second instalment of Aussies and Kiwis, and began to flee down a valley to the rear and right of the 9th Battalion.

"Right, men of the 9th," shouted Major Salisbury, "there to

our right, the Turks have heard of us. Let's go and make their acquaintance."

"Good on yer," said Clancy, grinning.

'A' and 'B' companies advanced in extended line towards the 400 Plateau, whilst slightly to their south, elements of the 10th were moving forward in pursuit of the retreating Turks. 400 Plateau, named for its height above sea level, consisted of two spurs, one of which would become known as the Razor. Meeting light resistance and sporadic fire from the enemy, the 9th Battalion scrambled up the steep sides of the Razor, managing to reach the far side of the plateau. More dangerous than the Turks at this point were the loose rocks, which became dislodged under foot, sending miniature landslides hurtling towards their comrades behind. "Below!" would go the warning shout, to be met by "thanks you bastard", and other "grateful" obscenities.

For now Archie, Roo and Clancy had been enlisted by Corporal Harrison into his section, which formed part of a hodge podge platoon led by Lieutenants Ponsonby and Thomas. As the platoon reached the scrubby edge of 400 Plateau, it commenced re-organising and ammunition checks. The CSM and his party were then dispatched to the beach in order to gather up any battalion stragglers, and to bring back much needed ammunition.

Looking out over the platoon Lieutenant Ponsonby noticed that his three friends were missing, calling out, "has anyone seen Clancy McBride and the Taylor boys?"

"They were with Corporal Harrison's section sir, and *he* aint here," came a voice in reply.

"Thomo we've lost a section," said a concerned Lieutenant Ponsonby, "we need to find them".

"Mate, they'll turn up, but we need to keep moving," replied Lieutenant Thomas.

With many bands of soldiers cobbled together by officers and NCOs it was inevitable that some would be mixed in with other groups of men as they passed through; which is what happened to Harrison's section, being scooped up by Captain Milne.

The soon to be Victoria Gully was on the seaward side of the plateau and was separated *from* the plateau by a ridge. At the join there was an enemy trench. As soon as Captain Milne's men arrived at the top of the hill his party was fired upon *from* the trench. Captain Milne was wounded, but not seriously, and was able to carry on.

"Corporal Harrison! Deal with that will you?" he ordered, pointing at the trench.

Without hesitation Harrison signalled to his section to follow him, crawling on their bellies, working their way behind the enemy trench. Harrison gave a snap order to one of his fire teams, half of the section, to lay down suppressing fire on the trench, as he and the remainder of the section carried out a right flanking manoeuvre.

"BRAVO FIRE TEAM, TWENTY YARDS, ENEMY TRENCH AT ELEVEN O'CLOCK, AIMED SHOTS; ALPHA FIRE TEAM WITH ME, RIGHT FLANKING, MOVE!"

"Keep those Abduls heads down boys," Clancy shouted as he, Roo and Archie, followed Harrison on their deadly mission.

Once they were within a stone's throw of the trench the section second in command's team ceased firing, causing the Turks to raise their heads. Harrison and his group were straight on to them, firing and stabbing at the Turks as they leapt in to their trench. Apart from the machine gun squad earlier, this was the men's first real taste of the brutality of war; hand to hand fighting. Archie stumbled as he landed in the trench. One of the Turks was fumbling desperately to clear a stoppage in his weapon, then success, as he raised his rifle to take down Archie. Archie could not help himself as he froze in position awaiting the inevitable. But, in that split second, Clancy had landed in the trench and struck the Turk on the back of the head with the butt end of his rifle. As the stunned Turk hit the ground Roo finished the job with a swift and deep lunge of his bayonet.

"That was a six worthy of the Gabba, eh Arch?" shouted Clancy.

But their gruesome work wasn't over as they dealt with the remaining occupants, fighting like wild dogs over a scrap of meat. It seemed like a life time, everything moving in slow motion, but the fight was soon over, with all but one of the enemy lying dead.

"Hey Corp, look at this bloke," exclaimed Clancy, still pumped with adrenalin, "shall I send him to Allah?"

The young Turk was cowering in the corner of the trench. What little English he had spewed out in his pleas for clemency.

"No, no, no. Please. Prisoner. Please".

"Come on Clance, let's take him prisoner. He might have some good information," suggested a hopeful Archie.

Clancy gradually calmed down and relented.

"Fine mate. He put up a good fight eh?" he replied.

"Yeah mate, he's a bit of a goer," said a relieved Archie.

The remainder of the platoon advanced cautiously in an arrowhead formation which stretched almost two hundred yards from flank to flank. Moving in to a gully between the two spurs, Lieutenant Thomas suddenly halted the platoon, ordering them to go to ground. He signalled to Ponsonby, who crawled on his belly to Thomas.

"What do you see old chap?" enquired Freddy. Thomas passed Ponsonby his field glasses.

"It looks like someone's been digging. What do you think?" Freddy said.

"It's not so much the soil; look slightly right in the scrub," replied a concerned Thomas.

"Bloody hell, its Harrison's section!" exclaimed Freddy.

"Yes, and I think they are about to walk in to something. I'll get the signaller to warn them in semaphore," replied Lieutenant Thomas.

The signaller was a little aghast at the request, especially in such dangerous a position, but clambered to his feet nonetheless. But each time he stood up he was met with bursts of machine gun fire. Luckily he was out of range.

Having had his section "borrowed" by Captain Milne, Corporal Harrison was now leading his men back to the platoon whom, he had been informed, were somewhere in the gully.

"Keep looking boys, the boss is round here somewhere," he told the section.

As he spoke he saw a depression to his front, and signalled the section to lie prone. In that moment the section received three short bursts of machine gun fire from the scrub ahead.

"Did anyone see where that came from?" Harrison called out to the section.

"No mate, but there's some dead ground just ahead, maybe we can work our way towards the bugger," Clancy suggested.

Using a natural drainage ditch, which had been carved out by water runoff during the rains, the section crawled slowly along the ground making sure to keep their heads and bodies low, moving inch by inch, through the thorny scrub, to the edge of the depression. But there *was* no machine gun, just hundreds of spent cartridges lying on the dusty ground.

"The bastard's scarpered!" exclaimed a disappointed Clancy.

"He must have known *you* were coming mate, and was worried about your bad language," joked Archie.

"Yeah, they're a bit delicate these Turks," added Roo.

Whilst scanning the gully to their front, Roo saw a small group of tents, and then even further down the valley he could clearly make out yet more tents, and a smoky haze of a cooking fire drifting above the encampment.

"Hazza, look!" Roo called out as he excitedly pointed towards the tents.

"Yeah I can see them mate, but look left about two hundred yards, there's the platoon," the corporal replied.

"Mate, they're trying to signal something," said Archie, as he watched the signaller frantically waving his flags, in between throwing himself on the ground, trying to avoid being sniped or machine gunned.

"Did anyone get any of that?" asked Archie.

"I could make out "gun", but that's it," replied Roo.

"Gun?!" exclaimed Clancy.

Almost immediately there was a succession of loud booms directly above their heads, as the ground shook beneath them.

"Bloody hell, that was a bit close!" said Archie.

"Look, the cheeky bugger's just up there!" replied Clancy as he pointed in the direction of the battery of guns.

How they had gotten so close to the battery of field guns they will never know, but Corporal Harrison and the section were right on to it as they crawled gingerly up the embankment towards the gun emplacement. Once safely on the edge of the mound, and concealed by the thick scrub, the section could clearly see two artillery pieces, and their seven crew, along with parties of soldiers some fifty yards yonder, loading machine guns on to mules, and limbering up a third gun.

"That must have been their parting shot before withdrawing," said Roo.

"Well, let's give them a parting shot or two of our own," replied Harrison.

By some stroke of luck the Turks hadn't spotted Harrison's party, so he set to organising his small group. Very quickly he gave each of the seven Turks a number, then allocated each of the section *one* of those numbers.

"Right, get comfy and get your targets in your sights. When I shout fire, give it to them, then we'll rush the bastards,' Harrison told his men.

Each man tested and adjusted their firing positions, and carefully took aim on their selected victim.

"Ready?" whispered Corporal Harrison.

Each man nodded.

"FIRE!!"

Muzzles flashed and rifles cracked as the artillerymen fell to the ground. Each section member was struck by the knowledge that they had taken a life, face to face, just like in the trench earlier, for King and country. Quite a burden. But there was no time to ponder as the corporal shouted "up and at 'em boys!"

Without thought or hesitation the Aussies scrambled to their feet and, with bayonets glinting in the early morning light, sprinted like madmen towards the surprised Turks. A Turkish officer suddenly appeared from the command post and levelled his pistol at the charging men. Before he could get a round off he reeled backwards, dead before he hit the ground, as Corporal Harrison beat him in the race of death, firing his rifle from the hip. At the sight of the Turkish officer, the section lay prone and began to fire at the soldiers, who were loading the mules. All but one fell dead where they stood, whilst one terrified man ran, stumbled, crawled, and eventually managed to rise to his feet and flee to safety, screaming out a warning to those in the distance as he ran.

"All round defence, ammo check," shouted the Corporal, as each man interlocked their feet as they lay in a circle in readiness for a possible counter attack.

The attack didn't come, but the rest of the platoon did, much to the relief of the section.

"Well done corporal, and well done men," said Lieutenant Thomas, as he glanced around at Harrison's group, "how are the boys?"

"Very good sir. I'm proud of them all," replied the corporal.

Meanwhile Lieutenant Ponsonby felt a sense of relief as he shook hands with his three friends.

"You fellows had me worried, but I am glad you came

through," said Freddy, "a bit of a coup with the guns; no doubt the first captured today I'll wager".

A group of soldiers, in the mean time, were wheeling one of the guns round in order to launch a few rounds at the distant camp, but discovered to their chagrin that the Turks had begun to dismantle the firing mechanism, making the guns inoperable. There was, however, a reward of tobacco to be had in the small shelter, which appeared to be a cross between a Quartermasters Stores and a corner shop. Any paperwork or maps was quickly seized for onward transmission to the battalion headquarters. Anything else was either discarded or kept by the lucky finders.

The 10th Battalion was now on position and had eagerly begun finishing the task that the gun crew had started, by burring the screws inside the breaches of the guns.

The CSM and his ammo party, plus a few stragglers, arrived shortly after Lieutenants Thomas and Ponsonby had placed the platoon in a semi rest position fifty yards forward of the enemy guns. There was an abundance of natural cover to be had in the scrub, depressions and ditches, and the men had been carefully placed in a defensive line behind this. Unfortunately the CSM reported that up until now very little ammunition had been transported to the beach head, so he had scrounged as much as he and his party could carry. Apart from distant gun shots and explosions, the 9th, 10th and newly arrived 12th battalions were able to grab a ten minute respite; whilst staying fully alert. Most of the men were now low on ammunition, despite the CSM's resupply.

"I have an idea," said Ponsonby.

"I'm all ears," replied Lieutenant Thomas.

"The Turkish ammunition is a different calibre to ours so we need to glean what we can from *our* poor dead and wounded, but also make use of enemy weapons and the ammunition in their pouches," explained Ponsonby.

The CSM nodded his head in approval.

"Our blokes can sling their weapons over their shoulders and make use of the Turkish weapons until the bullets run out, or until we have a resupply. I'll pass the word," said the CSM.

The ridge very quickly became a hive of activity as the men collected enemy and friendly weapons, whilst delicately removing magazines from no longer needed pouches. Roo knelt down beside his enemy number from the gun crew, bowed his head and placed a hand on the dead foe as he removed the necessary spoils.

"Sorry mate. Please forgive me," he whispered, wiping away a tear.

Clancy noticed his mate's demeanour so, tossing some ammunition to Roo, tried to lighten the atmosphere.

"Hey Roo catch this and put it in your pouch will you mate?"

The rest of the brigade began to arrive, led by the Brigade Major, Major Brand, whose group came across Lieutenant Thomas's rag tag platoon by chance. The original battle plan was now changing and evolving and, with the arrival of the Brigade Commander and the main parties of the 9th and 10th battalions, new orders to dig in and reorganise on this, the second ridge, were issued.

Major Salisbury soon arrived, along with a collection of 9th Battalion men whom he had gathered up on route. He set upon carrying out the dig in order with a line facing south east, ensuring that the security of the position was tight, by placing a platoon under Lieutenant Fortescue as an outpost along the northern side of the gully.

The defensive line formed by the 9th and 10th battalions was long, with a few holes in it, but these were soon plugged by a company of the 12th Battalion.

As well as Fortescue's outpost there were a number of screening platoons placed a few hundred yards forward of the main body.

The dig in order had not reached all. Captain Ryder had passed through on his way from Plugge's Plateau prior to the arrival of the Brigade Commander. As he moved through he enlisted small groups of men, including Ponsonby and his three mates, and made his way to a point later to be known as Lone Pine.

"I don't think we're going to get a break today boys," said Harrison to his section.

A detachment of the 10th, plus some 9th Battalion men, under Lieutenant Loutit, had already made their way to the third ridge, coming upon a large enemy group, whom they promptly opened fire on. Noticing Captain Ryder's group down the slope he sent a runner to request their assistance.

"Once more into the breach dear friends," announced Ponsonby as they made their way towards Loutit.

Having joined forces with Loutit, Captain Ryder took charge, was briefed, and laid his men out in a defensive line to protect the southern flank. Glancing out over the landscape before them it became apparent to Ponsonby that of all the ANZACs, *they* had reached their final objective. They just needed to hold it. Shaking Archie's shoulder quite roughly, he could not contain himself at the sight of the waters of the Dardanelles on the far side of the peninsular.

"Look chaps, it's the Sea of Marmora. We've done it!" he exclaimed.

"Done what you maniac?" demanded Clancy.

"Carried out our objective," replied Ponsonby.

"Bonza, we can pack up and go home now then," said Clancy, rolling his eyes.

"Don't be silly, we need the rest of the allies to link up now, then it's on to Constantinople," replied an excited Ponsonby.

It was now around 0800 hours and the ANZACs had been fighting hard for three and a half hours. Captain Ryder's group was now in a very precarious position having reached the final objective. To hold or not to hold, that was indeed the question. The problem at this moment in time was that, being on the receiving end of an invasion of their homeland, Turkey was in a good position with regard to manpower, with almost endless streams of brigades and divisions being moved towards the peninsular. The ANZACs, and the whole attacking force for that matter, did *not* have that luxury. That, combined with the earlier confusion and, in cases like the unfortunate beaching of the 'SS River Clyde' at 'V' Beach, which was just downright murder, *and* the fact that the brigade was now digging in way to their rear, meant that they were on their own.

Messengers were sent to Brigade but most did not get there.

Like the rest of the peninsula the ridge was covered with dense low scrub, which in parts, came up to the men's chests. The Turks had very game snipers, who would stay behind in the scrub, sniping at the ANZACs until they came within ten yards of them, when they would try to make off, needless to say, not succeeding. Their artillery too was just as cleverly concealed, the heavy howitzers constantly firing shrapnel shells which flew over their heads by the hundred, making a peculiar noise like a rocket, each shell containing over three hundred bullets.

A heavy barrage of rifle and machine gun fire was being laid on Ryder's party by a far superior force. Time and again they were rushed by the Turks, who were repulsed by bullet and bayonet. In one particular charge Archie and some of the boys witnessed the huge Sergeant Mac bayonet a Turkish soldier, lifting him, screaming and kicking, high above his shoulders, as his body slid down his bayonet on to the stock of his rifle.

Sergeant Mac was heard to shout "get off my bloody rifle you wee Abdul bastard!" as he unceremoniously detached him from both blade and barrel with his size 12 boot.

Seeing *that*, was warning enough, as many of the enemy soldiers fled back to their lines.

No longer game to carry out frontal assaults, the Turks changed tactics and began working their way round the sides and rear of the ANZACs. After ninety minutes of constant fire fights they were now taking fire from the left and rear and were in danger of being cut off. Reluctantly, through a lack of reinforcements and dwindling ammunition, it was time to withdraw. As disappointed as the men were they could see the senselessness of remaining and, under the watchful eye of their officers and NCOs, made a steady withdrawal down the slippery slope, some men facing forwards, acting as guides and observers, and others walking uneasily backwards with their faces towards the foe, firing at any Turk who dared pursue them. But pursue they did.

Cover at the bottom of the slope appeared to be quite sparse. Not a good place for a withdrawing force. Captain Ryder immediately saw the increased danger ahead, as the marauding Turks clambered down the ridge towards them. Ponsonby, however, was ready for this very situation and imparted his plan to Captain Ryder.

"Really? Are you sure?" asked a surprised Ryder.

Ponsonby responded with a confident nod.

"Men!" shouted Ryder, "aimed shots only. When I tell you, cease firing and keep your heads down".

"Keep your heads down? He's off his rocker," whispered Clancy.

Prior to departing their Destroyer, Ponsonby had made a one-time arrangement with the gunnery officer of the 'HMS Queen'. Lieutenant Ponsonby scanned the sea below them, through his binoculars, until he found what he was looking for.

"What's going on Freddy?" asked Archie.

"Smoke and mirrors old boy, smoke and mirrors," replied Ponsonby.

"Eh? Well, whatever it is bloody hurry up, the Turks are nearly on us," added Clancy.

Reaching in to his map pouch, Ponsonby pulled out his shaving mirror.

On seeing this Clancy exclaimed "bit of a bad time to spruce yourself up wouldn't you say mate?"

"Not me who needs sprucing up dear chap," replied Ponsonby as he began flashing his mirror, sending signals to one of the ships below. Within seconds a signal reply of three flashes bounced back from one of the ships.

"That's it," he thought, then, turning to Ryder, shouted "THAT'S IT. THE SIGNAL!"

Ryder momentarily glanced up towards the advancing Turks, who were about two hundred yards away.

"CEASE FIRE! HEADS DOWN!" he called out.

Archie and Roo both looked towards the many vessels sitting just off the shoreline. From one of the ships came a sudden flash and plume of grey smoke, followed shortly by the loud thunder of its twelve inch guns. Next a whoosh and scream over head as the projectiles of death peppered the slopes above, sending huge clouds of dust and rocks skywards, and the enemy soldiers to Allah. Arms, legs and other body parts were flying in all directions, some even showering the Aussies below.

"Bloody hell, it's raining Abduls!" joked Clancy, which caused a chain reaction amongst the others who used humour and laughter to shield themselves from the reality of the savagery that was being unleashed above them.

"You've gotta laugh eh Arch?" said Clancy.

Archie nodded. "It's either that or cry I suppose".

What was left of the Turks, after the short barrage, halted in their tracks, stunned by the sudden ferocious and barbaric demonstration of naval firepower.

Captain Peck, the adjutant of the 11th Battalion, had been met by messengers, and wounded, from Loutit and Ryder's party and had gathered men together to go to their aid. But, as grateful as they were when he arrived, after the barrage, it was too late. It was 0930 hours and the battered band were withdrawing in the knowledge that, of all of the ANZACs, they had carried out the original plan of attack and had reached the nearest point to the Dardanelles; but simply could not hold due to superior enemy numbers. If only the brigade had not have dug in where they did. Oh what could have been.

Nonetheless the men were grateful to Peck and his group, joining forces and making their way back to 400 Plateau. Ryder was aware of the need to be out front and not giving back too much ground, so, on reaching the edge of the plateau, ordered his men to create a forward outpost fifty yards ahead of the main defensive line.

Much had been occurring along the ANZAC attack line in the hours since dawn. Captain Dougall had led a handful of men on a run towards Gaba Tepe. Near a place now known as Bolton's Ridge, close to the sea, they had seen a large enemy column moving along the third ridge. There was nothing else for Dougall and his men to do except withdraw in good order back to 400 Plateau, where the brigade was now digging in. It was mid morning and half of the 9th Battalion was now in situ on the plateau, observing the ant like figures of the Turks moving towards them. This was the same group that had caused Ryder and Loutit to withdraw, but had paid a heavy price with the barrage from the 'Queen'. Lieutenants Thomas and Boase remained with their platoons, still in advance of the brigade. They too observed and sniped at the advancing enemy. The Turks, who had been moving north along the ridge, changed tact and set their sights on those unleashing a heavy fire on them from the plateau. Advancing in extended line the Turks were dangerously close to the advance parties of Boase and Thomas, who then withdrew in stages of about fifty yards, each party halting to support the other's withdrawal.

Seeing that heavy fighting had again broken out on the left front, where the 2nd Brigade were moving up the slopes, McLagan ordered Salisbury to send men forward to meet the attacking force. The time was now around 1000 hours. The 9th Battalion quickly departed their unfinished trenches and moved off through the dense vegetation. Almost at once they were subjected to sustained and accurate small arms and machine gun fire and, as a result, became jumbled up within their own battalion. Losses were heavy, but the mixed up battalion battled through its own chaos and were soon advancing towards the guns, which had been captured earlier.

Corporal Harrison and his section were now back with Lieutenant Thomas; or thought they were. Being on the extreme right of Thomas and Ponsonby's platoon, Corporal Harrison's section were unaware of the platoon's withdrawal, or the Turkish advance. They were now isolated but were soon, again, blended with Milne's men learning of the withdrawal as Milne passed by them. Meantime, Thomas and Ponsonby had fallen back to a position about one hundred and fifty yards from the Turkish guns along with remnants of the 9th and 10th battalions who had re-enforced them earlier.

Somewhere between 1100 hours and noon an enemy mountain gun battery had come in to play, establishing a fire position on a knoll within striking distance of 400 Plateau. From this point they were soon in action, laying down a deadly barrage on the Australians to their front. The Turkish advance was now gaining momentum with some attempting to occupy their old trenches near a lone pine tree, only being stopped by unexpected fire from a party of the 12th Battalion.

Runners were sent out requesting re-enforcements, but none came, and the runners did not return, most likely becoming casualties themselves. Salisbury and Milne made the decision to retire three hundred yards to the rear, to the summit by the pine tree. Milne had already been wounded three times but had since received another two. But he remained at his post, having to crawl around to encourage his men. Major Salisbury too had received a wound to his hand but bound it with his field dressing and carried on.

During the chaos the 9th Battalion managed to advance forward, close to where Lieutenant Costin and his machine gunners were located.

"Look at the machine gunners go mate!" Roo shouted excitedly.

But his excitement was short lived; for the enemy fire was becoming murderous and he watched helplessly as one by one the machine gunners became casualties. Very soon there was only one gun in operation, manned by Sergeant Steele, who continued to work the gun, with Costin acting as his number two, untangling ammunition belts and reloading the weapon. As Roo and the rest looked on, an artillery shell landed close to Costin and Steele, killing Costin outright. Sergeant Steele was now in a precarious position and grabbed a few belts of ammunition and his gun, and sprinted to the captured enemy gun pit, joining Haynes's platoon.

The numbers of the 9th Battalion men were dwindling and,

where possible, the 2nd Brigade, who had been directed to re-enforce the front line, plugged the gaps.

At around 1155 hours the third ridge suddenly, and without warning, exploded in to clouds of dust and rubble, as the Indian Mountain Battery, which had landed and taken up position on the north side of the 400 Plateau, opened fire. Archie looked on in awe as he wondered how the gunners had managed to get their artillery pieces up the steep slopes.

"You bloody ripper!" shouted Clancy, echoing the feeling of fresh hope felt by many.

However, the endless tide of Turkish re-enforcements soon resulted in the ANZACs pulling back to the plateau, a line which they would occupy for the foreseeable future. To rub more salt in to their wounds, counter battery fire by the Turks forced the Indian Battery to retire to a sheltered position.

By early afternoon the two brigades were dug in on 400 Plateau. A formidable force, ammunition was now reaching them, and they were feeling both vengeful and vulnerable at the same time.

"The games up boys," someone shouted.

"Oh, get nicked!" replied a defiant Clancy.

As the Turks continued their advance towards the plateau many were bowled over by rifle and machine gun fire. Some managed to reach the top but were swept away by the hail of .303 rounds being spat from Aussie weapons. Many a good friend was lost that day.

Lieutenant Thomas eventually passed his command to Ponsonby, having suffered a severe shrapnel wound to the shoulder. Major Salisbury too had to retire to a dressing station. It had been a busy day too for the stretcher bearers who had been risking their lives to rescue and carry the wounded to safety; and it had been no picnic for the doctors and medical staff down at the cove either.

Apart from continual sniping and the occasional shot of artillery, the fighting on the plateau petered out; at least it appeared that way after more than fourteen hours on the continual offensive and defensive.

"Smoko time boys," said Clancy.

"I wouldn't mind some water mate," said Archie, draining the last drop from his canteen.

"Here you go Arch," said Roo as he tossed his canteen to his cousin.

"Freddy, what are we going to do for water, we're getting low?" asked Archie.

"For now you need to borrow from the dead," replied Ponsonby.

"The Turks too?" asked Roo.

"Water is water, and our need is sadly greater," replied Ponsonby, "I have an orders group soon so pass the word about the water, and make sure everyone keeps an eye out for a counter attack".

"I feel like I've been awake for a week, any chance of a sleep?" asked Clancy, yawning.

"Not just yet unfortunately," replied Ponsonby, as he headed off to the 'O' Group.

Enemy rounds were still whizzing overhead and thudding in to the earth around them, the troops being subjected to shrapnel from almost all sides, and machine gun and rifle fire from the front. The men just had to face it and dig in, which, given the circumstances, was done in record time.

"Time to dig a quick hole I think," said Clancy as he began cutting in to the hard earth with his entrenching tool.

In no time he had dug down about three feet, and was feeling pretty tired.

"Must be nap time. Wake me if anything happens," said Clancy.

As he curled up in his hole how ignorant he was of war, for, no sooner had he stretched himself out, there was a shout from their front and a call of "Stand to" along the line.

"Bloody hell, what is it now?" growled Clancy.

From out of the evening haze emerged two soldiers, carrying a wounded man on a stretcher. The men were dressed in the standard pattern British uniform but appeared to be of Middle Eastern appearance. The man on the stretcher, covered by a blanket, was groaning loudly.

"Stand where you are!" Clancy shouted to the men.

"I don't like the look of this," said Archie as he called out to the men, "are you Turkish?"

The men halted and looked at each other.

"Don't shoot, we are Indians," one of the men shouted, "hospital men".

"Hospital men? Who says that?" said a surprised Roo.

"I agree. The Indian medical blokes I have met say stretcher bearer just like us," Archie added.

All of the commotion perked up the interest of Private Devereux.

"Come on in mates," he shouted to the men, beckoning them forward.

"Hang on. Where are their Red Cross arm bands? STAND WHERE YOU BLOODY WELL ARE!" Clancy shouted at the men.

"Come on mate they've got a wounded bloke there let's get him in," Devereux insisted.

"Listen Dave, for once in your life shut your flamin' mouth and listen instead of talking bloody rubbish," growled Clancy.

Amidst the heated argument, the men had slowly continued moving toward the Australian soldiers, with one of them stumbling in apparent agony, causing the stretcher and the wounded soldier to fall to the ground.

"Stuff you McBride they need help. I'm bloody going," said Devereux defiantly as he walked toward the men.

Upon reaching the soldiers, he leaned down to lift the front of the stretcher. Without warning the wounded man cast off the blanket, revealing a rifle, bayonet fixed, immediately thrusting the bayonet through Devereux's throat, whilst simultaneously firing a round; the force of which catapulted the Australian soldier backwards with great force. Devereux was dead, killed by Turks disguised as Indian stretcher bearers.

"YOU MONGREL BASTARDS!" came a shout from the Aussie lines as they unleashed a barrage of bullets upon the Turks, obliterating each man with the mercilessness of their gunfire.

"You *bloody* idiot Dave!" Clancy thought to himself.

That night, similar acts of deception unfolded along the entire front line. The Turks had a substantial number of

German officers aiding them, and their tactics were far from gentlemanly. The Aussies, however, learned quickly, Turks and Germans alike feeling the cold steel of revenge.

As the excitement past, Roo noticed that another of their mates was missing.

"Hey," said Roo, "I haven't seen Taff Williams for a few hours; has anyone else seen him?"

"He could be anywhere, but I'm sure he'll turn up," said Archie reassuringly.

The tone of the conversation changed. Something had been playing on Roo's mind.

"Arch," said Roo in a whisper, "can I tell you something?"

"Of course you can," replied Archie.

"I was so scared when we first came under attack," Roo confided.

"Mate, like the Major said, anyone who says they weren't frightened is either a liar, or an idiot, or both," said Clancy, butting in to the conversation.

"You were scared *too*?" asked a surprised Roo.

"Bloody oath! I nearly shit myself!" replied Clancy.

"Oh Clance you sure know how to lower the tone of a conversation," said Archie.

"Well its true," replied Clancy.

"That's what I'm trying to say," Roo added, "when the bullets and shells began to fly, I, I........wet myself".

Clancy placed a comforting hand on his friend's shoulder. "Don't worry about it Roo, I pissed *myself* too," admitted Clancy, with a wry smile.

Roo turned to Clancy and smiled a relieved smile.

"Charming conversation boys. Thanks," said Archie, rolling his eyes and shaking his head.

As they lay, rifles at the ready, watching the ground to their front, they pondered the events of the day.

"A lot of good men died today, on both sides," said Archie.

"I feel guilty," said Roo.

"Guilty? About killing the Abduls?" asked Clancy.

"Yeah mate," replied Roo.

Clancy felt quite relieved at hearing this from Roo.

"Well, I don't feel good about it either, but the trouble is that you can sit here thinking I don't want to kill that bloke, and he could be thinking the same," announced Clancy, "but the truth is that neither of you know *what* you are thinking, so you have to believe that you *want* to kill each other. Nothing you can do really mate. You just have to live with it".

"*Those* are very wise words Clance," said Archie.

"Yeah, well, seven months of hanging round with you blokes I reckon. Rubs off eventually", responded Clancy.

Within the hour the officers returned from their orders group and imparted their information to the senior non commissioned officers and section commanders, who, in turn, briefed their men. Darkness was falling and although the battalion had been on the go for over twenty four hours, the orders were to make use of the cover of darkness and to dig a line of trenches, linking up with all positions on the peninsula. Quite a task.

"Right boys," Corporal Harrison told his section, "we'll join forces with the rest of the platoon and split in to groups of three. One can sleep, another can dig, whilst the third acts as a sentry. You'll rotate every hour. I'll sort out your arcs of fire in a sec. And boys; we need to dig down to a minimum of four feet before dawn. All spoil is to be piled at the front on the parapet to increase height and depth. Make use of sand bags if you still have them".

As dusk turned in to night the men set to linking up and digging in to the rocky soil. It was hard work but most of the Aussies had come from manual labour jobs, thus the trenches materialised very quickly. Archie took the first shift of digging, breaking the earth with his pick shaped entrenching tool then shovelling out the spoil on to the forward top edge of the trench. Roo slept, uneasily, as Clancy acted as sentry, crawling about six feet forward of the defensive line with a full sandbag to give a more secure rest for his elbow.

For now the Turks remained pretty quiet in this sector, but continued to snipe and lob shrapnel rounds from their mountain battery.

As the 9th Battalion, and the rest of the ANZACs, dug, slept and observed, their fate was being decided down at the beach.

Major Generals Bridges and Godley, the two division commanders, were concerned that over night the Turks would be able to bring up thousands of re-enforcements and sweep the ANZACS, who were hanging on to the steep inclines of the peninsula by a thread, back in to the sea. They relayed their thoughts to the ANZAC commander, Lieutenant General Birdwood, who decided that this was a decision for the overall commander General Sir Ian Hamilton. But, having discussed the possibility of evacuation with senior naval staff, General Hamilton decided that it was more prudent to carry on, as a withdrawal, under the eyes of the now superior Turkish numbers, would result in a catastrophe.

6

A New Day Dawns

It had been a cold night on the peninsula and, without their packs, trusty blankets and sleeping bags, the troops had had to curl up tight to keep warm. Although tiring work, it was almost a relief when the men's turn came to dig, as it was their only chance to keep warm.

Lieutenant Ponsonby seemed spritely at daybreak as he conducted his rounds, visiting his platoon.

"G'day sir," said Clancy, "so, what do you know?"

As he gazed down along the almost completed trench line he was impressed at what he saw.

"Well, I know you fellows have done a smashing job digging," he replied.

"So? What's happening? Some blokes heard a rumour that we are leaving," said Clancy.

"Well, old chap, don't believe everything you hear; but no, we are definitely staying. In fact General Hamilton sent *this* to HQ," replied Ponsonby as he flicked through the pages of his notebook.

"Here you go...'there is nothing else to do but dig. Dig, dig, dig until you are safe'....." said Ponsonby reading from his notes.

"Dig? Until you are safe?" exclaimed Clancy, "what a bloody drongo!"

"No mate, he's right. Digging trenches will keep us out of harm's way. And besides, I didn't come all this way to lose mates then bugger off after just a day," responded Archie.

Clancy pondered briefly, "I suppose you're right. With all those Abdul bastards out there, leaving will be harder than it was getting here".

Roo was sitting on the floor of the trench making billy tea. Pouring the hot black liquid in to his mates' mugs he looked towards Lieutenant Ponsonby with an outstretched hand.

"Want a brew sir?"

"That would be very kind Roo, thank you," replied the officer as he fumbled in his pouches to find his mug, "there you go".

Roo poured some tea in to his officer's mug and handed it to him. The officer sat on the trench floor with Roo and savoured his tea, then smiled and nudged his friend.

"Got any biccies?" he asked with a cheeky glint in his eye.

"Bloody hell mate, what did your *last* servant die of?" joked Clancy.

"Not having any biscuits as I recall, but, fear not, Freddy to the rescue," he replied as he pulled some slightly crumbling shortbread biscuits from his tunic pocket, and happily passed them around, "here you go boys".

"Ta, sir, you're not too bad for a toff," announced Clancy.

Ponsonby paused for a moment, replying "I think I'll take that as a compliment".

"So, what's happening today sir?" asked Roo.

"Today is a day of defensive rest I think," replied Freddy, "stagging on and sleeping is the plan".

"What about food and water?" asked Archie.

"And ammo?" added Clancy.

"The CSM is working on that. In the mean time ration what you have," replied Freddy.

"We could do with some blankets too mate," said Roo, "my sleeping bag is in my pack down at the beach somewhere".

"Yeah, mine too. Last night was colder than a mother in laws kiss," joked Clancy.

"How did you get to speak so proper sir?" asked Archie.

"Possibly the silver spoon or plumb that was in my mouth when I was born," quipped Freddy.

"By the end of this war you'll be speaking like us lot *I* reckon," added Clancy.

"Bonza!" replied Lieutenant Ponsonby with a wink, "perhaps I can refine you chaps a little too".

"Yeah?" replied Clancy scratching his head, "go on then".

The officer sat pondering for a short while. "Alright, repeat after me….air…" said Freddy, as the boys followed his instructions, "hair……..lair…"

"What's the point of that?" asked Clancy.

"Simple old chap, now say all three one after another," replied Freddy.

"Air hair lair," the boys repeated.

Clancy paused for a little then laughed, "I get it…….oh hello," he said giving Roo a nudge in the side with his elbow, "but it's not much to shite a bite is it?"

Everyone within earshot, laughed together, feeling a little positive and at ease with their situation; nothing like some friendly banter to cheer everyone up.

"That's it Clancy. Officer material I think," said Ponsonby.

"You'll have to take my brain out and replace it with my slouch hat first though but," replied Clancy.

Rifle shots and explosions reverberated all over the peninsula, with some Turks not game to move forward due to the heavy and accurate fire from the guns of the ships anchored off shore. This bode well for the allies as they were able to land personnel and stores on the beach heads.

At around 1600 hours on Monday the 26th of April the troops of the 9th and 10th Battalions, who were currently resting in reserve trenches, were ordered to move forward to the firing line which was near the pine tree, standing alone on the plateau. Half an hour later the line advanced a short distance. Ponsonby's platoon moved forward in extended line, keeping a watchful eye to their front and flanks. BRRRR! Rat a tat tat! came the hellish sound of a machine gun followed by shouts of "Allah! Allah!"

as a swarm of Turkish infantry rose up from nowhere and began running towards the advancing Aussies, pausing only to fire from kneeling or standing positions. Machine gun fire raked the plateau from left to right and ANZACs began to fall.

"Lie down men and give it to them!" shouted Ponsonby, immediately recognising the peril his platoon was in.

Although the advance was checked by the enemy, the accurate rifle fire and machine gun bursts from the ANZACs made the Turks think again, and soon the counter attack was over. The platoon withdrew to the fire trench, collecting wounded men as they went. Some Aussies, who were slightly forward of the main line of advance, now lay in the open. Some were dead, having been cut in two by the heavy machine gun fire. Others lay wounded, helpless and alone. Some said nothing, while others groaned and called for their mothers. Anyone who moved was hit from left and right by rifle fire; their cries and moans becoming silent.

One man began to crawl along the ground, back towards the battalion.

"Look," whispered Roo, pointing at the moving man, "its Stowie".

Archie and Clancy looked on helplessly, with Roo, as the fall of rounds on all sides of Stowie caused explosions of dust in the ground.

"Bugger this!" exclaimed Clancy as he slung his rifle over his back, "give me some cover boys".

Clancy winked at his mates then rose to his feet and, hunching over to make himself a smaller target, ran towards the wounded Stowie, zig zagging as he moved. Enemy bullets peppered the ground around him as he ran, but the platoon was now on to it, firing at those who would shoot at their mates. As Clancy reached Stowie he slid in towards him like he was scoring a try, ending up on his side next to him.

"Let's have a look at yer," said Clancy as he examined his wounded mate.

Stowie's trousers and lower legs were stained bright red.

"Have a guess where they got me?" whispered Stowie as he managed a smile at Clancy.

"It's not the time for I spy mate," snapped Clancy.

Stowie laughed and pointed to his backside, "in the arse mate….can you believe it?"

"Yeah, well, good job your mouth was shut then eh?" quipped Clancy.

"Cheeky sod!" laughed Stowie.

Clancy crouched as low as he could next to the wounded man and, as quick as he could, dragged him over his shoulder. Small arms fire was now coming from all sides but somehow wasn't finding its target. As he stood up Clancy felt the weight of Stowie and his webbing on his spine.

"You fat bastard Stowie, you need to ease up on the grub mate!" exclaimed Clancy.

As he began to run back towards the battalion lines Clancy's pace was helped along by the sudden burst from a machine gun which carved a jagged line in the ground to his left.

"Come on Clance!" was the cry from the Aussies as he ducked and dodged his way back to the lines, taking a diving lunge for the last ten feet, flying over the top of Roo, and landing abruptly on top of Stowie.

"Who's a fat bastard now?" groaned Stowie.

"Shut up you big galoot or I'll chuck you back over," laughed Clancy as he looked around the battalion men, then shouted "stretcher bearer!"

As he did so Stowie reached up with an open hand, "thanks mate. I owe you a beer".

"Make it ten and we'll call it quits," joked Clancy as he shook Stowie's hand.

"It's a good job the Turks can't shoot eh?" said Archie.

Clancy turned and looked out over the ground to their front where many a brave man lay.

"I don't think *that* lot will agree with you mate," said Clancy shaking his head.

As the medic gently lifted Stowie on to the stretcher and took him to safety, those who had witnessed Clancy's selfless act cheered, causing a usually boisterous Clancy to blush with embarrassment.

"I only did what anyone would do," said Clancy, "*you'd* do the same for *me*".

"Or maybe we wouldn't," came a comment from the battalion, which caused a great deal of laughter.

Once all of the excitement was over, another evening of defence followed. Still there were no blankets.

"It's cold again isn't it?" said Archie as he shivered, his teeth chattering uncontrollably.

"As long as we don't get any...........rain!" replied Roo in disbelief as there was a sudden downpour on the ridge, "bloody typical!"

"Bloody Egypt all over again!" exclaimed Clancy.

It was the early hours of the 27th when Archie felt someone shaking him. Fearing an attack, he awoke suddenly to see the shadowy figure of Freddy Ponsonby leaning over him in the darkness.

"Psst," whispered Ponsonby, as he attempted to attract the attention of the platoon.

"I haven't touched a drop," responded a still sleeping Clancy.

"Clance! Wake up!" growled Ponsonby as he stirred the troops, "come on, we're being relieved".

This news brought Clancy back to the land of the living.

"About bloody time!" he uttered, yawning and rubbing his eyes.

"We've been ordered in to reserve with the rest of 3rd Brigade," explained the officer.

"Reserve? Where we going?" asked Roo.

"Grab your kit boys we're off back down to the southern end of the beach," replied Ponsonby, pointing back down the slope, "I'm told it's a quiet spot".

"You ripper!" came a whispered shout of joy from the platoon.

"Yeah, we could do with some rest. We haven't stopped for three days," said Archie.

During those three days the battalions had fought many pitched battles on what was not ideal fighting terrain, but, each time, they had repulsed the enemy. During the hours of darkness they had taken their turn digging, guarding, sleeping, patrolling, and now there was an intricate system of ever evolving trenches, gradually linking to each other, making a good defensive line, and relatively safe corridor down to the Cove.

It soon became evident, however, that their new bivouac area was not that safe at all. In fact it was sited close to the entrance of what would become known as Shrapnel Gully, not far from a turning known as Hellfire Corner. The men were ordered to construct dugouts for themselves, in the sides of the embankment. Not surprisingly there were moans and groans, but the troops quickly got themselves organised and began digging like crazed wombats desperate for a sleep.

"This will be like a home from home when we've finished," said a cheerful Archie.

"Home? I haven't worked this bloody hard in my life. When do we get a rest?" moaned Clancy as he dug.

No sooner had Clancy spoken when the Turkish artillery opened up again with shrapnel fire, which exploded above the heads of the battalion, sending rounds in all directions.

As the men very quickly discovered, shrapnel was a horrible thing, exploding with a fearful noise, literally ploughing the ground, making strong men quail. Among its victims, there were often those who appeared unharmed at first glance, with only their demeanour revealing the profound toll exacted upon their minds. The relentless onslaught of shrapnel leaving them shattered, their nerves frayed and their sanity teetering on the edge. Then, the wounds it made were awful; men torn and mangled in the most cruel manner.

"Quick! Behind those sandbags!" shouted Archie, as he, Roo and Clancy sprang in to the cover, with everyone else following suit.

At this moment in time one of the staff sergeant majors, Sergeant Sinclair had been doing the rounds, encouraging the men, laughing and joking with them, and generally keeping them calm. Williams, one of the stretcher bearers was shovelling away at his dugout when the sergeant offered to give him a hand.

"That's very civil of you sir," uttered Williams, gratefully handing over his entrenching tool.

"More hands, less work mate, that's what my old mum used to say," said Sinclair.

Just as Sinclair took a step forward, preparing to commence digging, a series of explosions echoed through the air, erupting directly above them. In a harrowing instant, Sergeant Sinclair collapsed, landing face-down on the ground. His life had been abruptly extinguished before he even made contact with the earth, a shrapnel projectile piercing his forehead, obliterating the back of his skull as it traversed through his head.

As this latest bout of indirect fire subsided, some of the men gathered around their much loved sergeant.

"Poor bastard!"

"At least it was quick".

Williams sat in a daze.

"Here you go mate," said Roo, offering him a sip from his canteen.

A voice from behind opened up.

"Come on chaps I need some of you for a fatigue party," announced Ponsonby, feeling guilty when he came upon the gruesome scene.

"Oh God! I'm sorry boys. I wasn't aware," he responded.

"Don't worry Freddy, you weren't to know," said Archie, patting him on the back, "me, Clance and Roo will do your fatigues, but I think we need to get Williams here to the doc".

"You should probably take the poor sarge with you too," replied the lieutenant.

Luckily for the fatigue parties their task was an easy one, walking along the beach retrieving the battalion packs, which had been left there on the first morning. Sadly, very few packs were located, either washed away by the incoming tides or stolen by locals or unscrupulous soldiers. Either way the men were none too pleased.

"The damn scoundrels!" Ponsonby ranted, "I had a bottle of brandy in mine".

"If you were saving it to toast our victory then you were a bit early anyways mate," said Clancy, "and besides, we've *all* lost our flamin' sleeping bags, so we're going to bloody freeze our balls off again!"

Wednesday the 28th of April dawned with a fierce attack from the enemy, immediately followed by terrible artillery fire from both sides. Time after time the Turks were driven back with heavy losses. The warships were firing all day, and the soldiers marvelled at how the battleships could fire over hills miles away, and never see what they were hitting, yet landing shells with wonderful accuracy. They soon discovered that it was all done by communication and co-operation with aeroplanes, which droned high above the enemy positions. Since landing, the ANZACs had been under fire from six pieces of enemy field artillery which could not be silenced. At last the 'Queen Elizabeth' had got to work with her huge half ton shells, which contained thousands of bullets, her shrapnel exploding, raking the ground to the extent of two acres.

For the 3rd Brigade, still in reserve, there was a brigade

re-organisation and roll call on the beach. As the men paraded they were filthy, unshaven and stank to high heaven.

"We smell like a dunny in a heatwave," said Clancy in his usual refined manner.

Smelly, yes, but, above all, they were fit to drop, having been on the go for four days, snatching sleep whenever possible. Their uniforms too were ragged, torn and shredded by the thorny scrub which covered the peninsula.

Clancy nudged Roo as some of the officers arrived.

"Have you noticed anything mate?" he asked.

Being easily recognisable targets for enemy snipers, the officers had been ordered to remove all metal rank insignia, and to mark stars and crowns on their shoulder straps with indelible pencil. Archie nodded his approval, especially after roll call which revealed that the 9th Battalion could only muster four officers and two hundred and fifty one troops, out of a thousand strong battalion.

The temporary commanding officer was now Major Salisbury. Companies were reformed and a number of promotions made. Roo and Archie were both promoted to Corporal, whilst Clancy was raised to Sergeant for his cool, steady demeanour under fire, as well as his rescue of Stowie.

"Bloody hell I've won the chook raffle," joked Clancy.

"It's well deserved Clance. It really is," responded Roo.

"And it's more pay, so the drinks are on you," announced Archie.

Despite all of this the 9th Battalion were still in the line; until that afternoon.

Roo nudged Archie as he spied large groups of fresh looking, and very clean, troops heading their way from the Cove. As they drew closer the battle weary Aussies were thankful, but could not believe their eyes.

"Kids!" exclaimed Roo, who was only twenty years old himself.

"Kids?" asked Archie.

As Roo pointed at the two battalions of Royal Marine Light Infantry who had arrived to relieve them, all present were surprised.

"They're just boys! I bet they're only about sixteen. Look at 'em!" said Clancy.

He was right, as these were *indeed* boys, fresh from training.

"God help them," said Roo.

"And us mate, and us," Clancy added.

Once handover briefings on the position were complete, the men of the 9th Battalion struggled to their feet, some aided by mates, and began their trek down to the beach......again. Sergeant Mac collapsed on the ground. He and everyone else were hungry, thirsty and plain done in. As he began to crawl he felt embarrassed and exclaimed, "I've no got the energy to walk boys.......sorry to let you down".

Seeing his plight Roo and Archie linked hands and formed a seat, whilst Clancy gently lifted their sergeant *on to* the seat.

"There you go sarge.....and don't apologise. You've done your bit".

As the battalion reached the beach, most simply dropped, or crumpled, on the sand where they stood, and fell to sleep.

After five days of fighting, digging and setting up bivvies, it appeared that the brigade was actually able to get some proper rest. Unfortunately though, this was short lived as the 4th and 8th Battalions needed relieving at the southern end of the line, and in the early stages of the campaign, rest was a premium commodity. It was again time for the brigade to make the steep journey up the slopes.

As they walked, the men were impressed with the many corridors and mazes of trenches which had been dug in such a short space of time, set out in zig zags, with connecting saps, to prevent enfilading fire along the line, and to provide a pathway for re-enforcements.

"Looks good up here now eh?" said Roo.

As they relieved the weary battalions, men shook hands and exchanged pleasantries.

"Good luck boys".

"Keep your heads down".

As darkness fell, so did the commencement of night work, when the troops were less likely to be observed and fired upon by the Turks. Lieutenant Plant and fifty men, including the Taylors and Clancy, clambered quietly out of their trenches in to no man's land. Their mission was to retrieve what they could from their fallen comrades, food, ammunition, water and weapons.

"Bloody hell!" whispered Clancy as they commenced their grisly task.

Most of the bodies were by now unrecognisable as men for, after lying exposed for days in the hot sun, the bodies were swollen, bloated and had turned black.

"Some of these poor fellas look darker than me," announced Roo.

It was a terrible sight to behold, but certainly would not be the last.

Job done, the men stacked and sorted their haul, each in their own way haunted by what they had just done; a guilty feeling which would forever remain with them.

The sun shone bright the next day as the men manned the stepped parapets, ensuring that they kept their heads down and out of sight from the top of the trench, and the many loopholes, which had been constructed with sandbags as a safe observation and firing position. A few had fallen foul of Turkish snipers, but, lesson learned, the troops were now wise to these perils. Those who were tall in stature had to resort to walking slightly hunched forward, for risk of losing their head, Sergeant Mac being a prime example.

"I'll be hunched up like wee Quasimodo by the time we get out of here," he would often say.

"Quasi who?" asked Clancy, feeling a bit confused.

In between stags the boys sat on sandbags and, with wood scrounged from the dumps on the beach, built themselves a small campfire in order to boil up some billy tea.

"Ah, is that tea I detect there chaps?" asked Ponsonby as he appeared from around the zig zagged corner.

"Bloody hell mate," exclaimed Clancy, "you could sniff out a brew from twenty yards away!"

"Well I *am* English," he replied.

"Chuck us your mug then," said Roo.

"I don't mind if I do," replied the officer, producing his steel mug.

"I wish we had milk and sugar though," said Archie.

"I can't help you with the milk, but try some of this jam," said Ponsonby.

Archie scooped out some jam with his spoon and dropped it in to his hot brew, gave it a quick stir, and took a sip.

"Hey, that's not too bad," said Archie with a satisfied expression on his face, "bit of a strange tinge, but it will do".

"I'll have a go at that," said Clancy helping himself to the jam.

"Help yourself dear boy. Here you go Roo," said Ponsonby as he tossed him his tea ration, "I don't need it. There's plenty at the Command Post and everyone seems to offer me a drink when I visit, so there you go".

As the troops sat drinking their tea Roo asked of the officer, their mate, what the plan was now.

"Plan? No idea as yet," Freddy replied, "hold here for now whilst the big wigs devise some break out or other I imagine".

"Do you reckon we did good here?" enquired Archie.

"I do, and Birdie is *very* pleased," said Freddy.

"Yeah?" uttered a surprised Clancy.

"Chaps, we were doomed to failure from the start, but we have prevailed," explained the lieutenant.

"Pre-what?" asked Clancy.

"Done well," whispered Archie.

"How so?" asked Roo.

"Well the Royal Navy's attacks on the forts announced that we were coming. There are spies everywhere, from Lemnos to Alexandria; and to top it all the damn Egyptian newspapers were publishing troop movements and names of ships, for all to see," explained Freddy, "but look where we are now. We fought up this terrible terrain, repulsed everything the Turks threw at us, and now we have a strong foothold".

"Yep, we are just a hop, skip and a jump from Constantinople," added Roo.

"Yeah, and *we*," said Archie, pointing at all present, "even made it to the main objective".

"Don't remind me," said a disappointed Freddy, "if only more men were sent to consolidate the position and support us".

"I think the only thing that let us down was the sea currents sending us a bit further up the coast," said Archie.

"And that was no-one's fault," added Roo.

"Yes, all in all we still surprised the blighters. We *were* in fact lucky with the currents," said Freddy.

"Lucky? How?" asked Roo.

"Well, apparently Gaba Tepe, our intended landing point, was heavily guarded, and there is barbed wire all over the place, including in the shallows," explained Freddy.

"Bastards! So the boats wouldn't have got to shore, and we'd have been cut to pieces in the water by barbed wire and machine gun fire," said Clancy.

"Exactly," replied Freddy.

No-one was safe on Gallipoli. There was the constant hazard from marauding snipers in the day time. You were safe at night only because the Turks couldn't *see* you, but even then they had your exact location marked on their maps so were able to harass the ANZACs with shrapnel fire twenty four hours a day. Despite this the battalion settled in to life on Bolton's Ridge on the far side of the line. From here they had panoramic views of their intended landing site of Gaba Tepe, but were also in range of Beachy Bill, or Bills, which were concealed somewhere around Gaba Tepe, possibly in an olive grove.

On Saturday the 1st of May Sergeant Knightley, Lance Corporal Lynch and Taff strolled in to the battalion lines looking drained, dirty, hungry and exhausted. Roo ran up immediately to hug his mate Taff.

"Thank God you are alright," said Roo as he made towards Knightley and Lynch.

"Just a hand shake mate," Knightley advised, with a smile, "or I'll have to drop yer".

Knightley and his group had been fighting constantly since the landing, six days ago, his party being ordered to occupy a piece of high ground. The area was strewn with the dead of the 15th Battalion who lay where they fell. His group had been so weakened by hunger and constant fighting that in the end they only had the strength to advance in short bursts. During the hours of darkness Sergeant Knightley had moved around the area collecting ammunition, food and water, from the dead, a scene which was being repeated all over the peninsula. This is what had sustained them for the six days.

"You've been listed as missing sergeant, but it's good to have you back," said Lieutenant Ponsonby.

Due to the confusion of the first day, troops were scattered all over, forming hodge podge units, and fighting small engagements of their own. After six days, only Knightley, Lynch and Taff remained from their small group, their numbers having been depleted by the almost constant shrapnel which had been exploding above their heads.

The sound of a shrapnel explosion above a battlefield was

a terrifying and unforgettable experience to the soldiers, beginning with a sharp, piercing whistling noise as the shell hurtles through the air, the sound growing louder and more intense as it approaches, and, in a split second, detonating with a thunderous, deafening boom, drowning out all other battlefield noise. It is a cacophony of shattering metal, ear piercing blasts, and a deep, rumbling roar, as the air fills with flying shrapnel, debris, and dirt, the force of the explosion knocking soldiers off their feet, killing them outright, shredding their flesh and bones, or wounding and disorientating them, leaving them dazed and confused. The lucky ones manage to dive for cover or shield themselves with whatever they can find.

Needless to say, the three men were relieved to be back with the battalion.

"So what have you boys been up to?" enquired Taff.

"Not a lot. Although we *did* visit the Gallipoli constable to report you blokes missing," joked Clancy.

"Yeah, we were just about to come looking," added Archie.

The men set to work making the best of their lives in the trenches. For the foreseeable future the troops spent their time either manning the forward trenches, on the slope of Bolton's Ridge, or having a well deserved rest in the support trench just to the rear of the crest. Most, being country boys who liked their home comforts, even when droving cattle along the stock routes, cut bivvies in to hillsides, the rear wall being the actual hill and the side walls the slope of the hillside. The roof consisted of waterproof groundsheets or corrugated tin, if they could manage to scrounge it, and the height of all sides was levelled off nicely by the addition of sandbags. The men even tried to make the forward defensive trench comfortable but this was soon halted by order of the Brigade Commander as it was resulting in the occasional collapse of the trench walls. The one excavated luxury they *were* permitted was a single latrine dug in to the trench wall, walled in with sandbags and a roof of tin for good measure, with a hessian curtain for a bit of privacy. The toilet itself was a bucket, a wooden plank with a hole for a seat, much more comfortable than the communal latrines down at the cove where long planks over a pit were the order of the day. The buckets were emptied daily by the trench cleaning parties, who also swept out the trenches and removed all refuse, which included empty cartridge cases, which were sent back to munitions factories for recycling.

"Keeping a clean trench is like cleaning your house; it keeps your family healthy……..and, dare I say, happy?" said Ponsonby.

"I can't wait to the see the face of any Abdul who jumps in to our dunny!" laughed Roo.

"Hopefully it won't come to that mate as we'll *all* be in the brown stuff then, won't we?" added Clancy.

Water on the peninsula was always an issue, but the 9th Battalion were in the enviable position of having a small well to the rear of their lines, but, if required, the daily work parties would make their way through the maze of trenches to Shrapnel Gully to collect additional water, in four gallon petrol tins, from the tanks which had been constructed nearby. However, due to being in plain view of the enemy guns at Gaba Tepe, these work parties would attract the invariable six or seven shells, some of which inflicted a heavy toll. Pretty soon the water collection was carried out at night, with the Turks still sending over a few pot shots, hoping to score a few ANZACs.

"These cans are drewllyd they are boyo," announced Taff, giving the petrol tins a cursory sniff.

"Drew what?" asked Archie, scratching his head.

"Rank man. They stink of petrol they do," replied Taff.

"The water doesn't taste too good neither," added McGregor.

The men were right, but the tins were all they had for now, and the water *was* tainted.

"Let's get filling boys so we can get back to Bolton's and some sleep," said Archie to his section.

For the men, carrying an empty four gallon tin down from the lines was a simple task, but, once full, the cans were a different story.

"Crikey these things must weigh over two stone! I'll have arms like an octopus by the time we get back," joked Jacko.

"We could do with a pack horse or something or we'll be walking all night," said Archie.

"Did some fella say packhorse?" replied a Geordie voice from the darkness.

As the owner of the voice came in to view the boys saw a stretcher bearer leading a donkey, wounded soldier sat on the beast's back, supported by the medic; "I'll just drop this canny lad off at the dressing station, then me and Duffy here will give yers a hand".

True to his word the stretcher bearer and Duffy soon returned, and as he and his donkey halted he offered a hand of friendship to Archie and his mates.

"It's dinner time, I'm clamming for some scran," said the

medic as he sat down on a pile of earth, "have any of you lads got a snout?"

"Snout? You mean like a pig?" asked Archie, scratching his head.

The man laughed, 'yer silly begger, a tab……..a cigarette…."

"Ah, no sorry, I don't smoke," replied Archie.

"I do,' said Jacko, offering him a cigarette, "have one of mine".

"I'm John Simpson Kirkpatrick by the way, but me marras call me Simpson," said the soldier.

"Is that your nick name then?" asked Jacko.

"Na," he replied, explaining that he was a former merchant seaman who had jumped ship in Australia. He had worked for a few years as a cane cutter, miner and all manner of jobs, but now it was time to go home. He had altered his name on enlistment just in case he was in trouble with the Merchant Navy.

"I'm gannin yem to me mam in South Shields, but thought I'd do me bit on the way," John explained.

"So what unit are you with?" enquired Archie.

"The 3rd Field Ambulance but they just leave me to me self. I found it simpler to fetch these lads on a donkey, so they just let me get on with it. I camp out with the Indian transport fellas, they are good men and have plenty of fodder for me friend Duffy here," replied Simpson, "wanna come and say hello to them?"

"That would be good mate. We have much to thank them for," replied Archie.

"Crouch behind me donkey and walk with me, you'll be bonny. I'm bullet proof," said Simpson.

On the 1st of May the Indian Transport Corps had landed on the beach, between Brighton Beach and Hell Spit, bringing with them two wheeled mule carts which were employed to transport the huge array of engineering stores, barbed wire, timber and other equipment. It was here also that the Indian mule drivers camped, in relative safety from snipers and artillery, making it a little home from home. As they approached, the boys saw many Sikh soldiers, each bearded and wearing large turbans on their heads, all appearing quite exotic to the young Australians, much like the inhabitants of Cairo. They also eagerly inhaled the wonderful cooking odours which were coming from the pots on their camp fire. On seeing Simpson, the soldiers immediately stood and smiled, obviously glad to see him. One man shook Simpson's hand and patted Duffy, then gently taking his reigns from his owner, led him away to be fed and watered. They were introduced to some of the Sikh soldiers who had become his friends. The conversations that took place were a mix of awe and admiration for Simpson's courage and gratitude for his help in tending to their wounded.

"I have never seen such bravery in a man," said one of the Sikh soldiers, his eyes shining with respect, "he does not fear death, but he respects life. He is a true hero."

Simpson himself was humble about his role in the war, but he was happy to share his food and supplies with the Indian soldiers and their animals, and to partake of their delicious offerings.

"We're all in this together," he said with a smile, "and it's the least I can do to help me fellow man."

The three Australians were struck by the camaraderie and mutual respect that existed between the soldiers from different backgrounds and cultures. In the midst of the horrors of war, they had found a sense of community and shared purpose that transcended language and nationality.

"Would you like some dhal and a chapatti?" asked one of the corporals.

"My mum always said to ask a person's name before you take food off them, its good manners," said Archie, "no offence".

"None taken. I am Tarsam Singh Grewel. I am very pleased to meet you sir," replied the corporal as he shook Archie's hand, "your mother is indeed a wise woman".

The feeling of apprehension on the Aussies subsided and each man greeted one another and exchanged names.

"You have some wonderful sounding names, I hope I can say them right," said Taff.

"Yes, we have the same problem with English names," joked Tarsam.

"I am Welsh man, not English," said Taff, feeling a little insulted.

"Now, now Taff. You're an Aussie now and don't forget it," said Archie, reassuringly.

"I am sorry to offend," said a worried Tarsam.

"No worries mate. So what's in the pot?" asked an eager Archie.

"Oh. An aloo, saag and lentil dhal," said Tarsam, looking round at the blank expressions on his visitors' faces, "a curry, made from potato, spinach and lentils".

"Ohhh, right," replied Archie.

"I've never had a curry before," said Jacko.

"It's smashin' man, wait til you try it," said John.

All offered their mess tins, which were liberally filled, each was then given a fresh chapatti. As Archie fished his spoon from his pouch Tarsam explained that he must eat it with his fingers and the chapatti.

"I show you," said Tarsam as he broke a piece off his bread and used it with his fingers to scoop up some of his curry.

"That's easy enough," said Jacko using his chapatti like a shovel.

"Hey mate, what's the rush?" exclaimed Archie.

"I'm just starving mate, and sick of bully beef. This is bloody marvellous Tarsam. Cheers mate," said Jacko.

Tarsam and his comrades nodded their heads in approval.

"You blokes will have to come up to Boltons and have tea with us; we haven't got any fancy spices though," said Archie.

Tarsam reached in to a small sack next to the cooking fire and produced a small jar full of a reddish brown powder, and offered it to Archie.

"Here, take some curry powder, it is my honour," said Tarsam, half bowing his head.

"Oh mate, you don't know how pleased the fellas will be up there. Thank you so much. You come up to Bolton's any time and we'll do the same," said Archie.

"We'd better make tracks and get this water up top eh?" said Jacko.

"Why aye man, sorry, I forgot all about that," said John.

"No, no. We will take your water on our cart. We are friends now," said Tarsam ushering his men to help load the water cans on to a sturdy looking wooden cart.

"You mind out for Sniper Alley as you go boys, and I'll see yers again soon," said Simpson, shaking hands with his new mates.

The journey back through the gullies, sunken roads and labyrinth of trenches was uneventful, which was a good thing at ANZAC. The battalion men were grateful to see the arrival of the water but more interested in the Indian soldiers and their cart.

"G'day Johnny," came a few shouts from the parapets, but the Indian soldiers were not offended for they were used to the nick name that the ANZACs had given them, and knew that these big men respected them like brothers.

The Aussies in turn had the highest regard for the courage and professionalism shown to them by their Indian allies.

"This is Harpreet and Amrit, they're our mates from the Indian Army," said Archie, as he introduced the Sikh soldiers to all in earshot.

Clancy was quickly up on his feet and nearly shook the arms off both men with his enthusiastic greeting.

"G'day boys, fancy some billy tea?" asked Clancy.

The men accepted the kind offer and the men sat for a while exchanging stories about home and their present situation.

"You must come visit....eat food together," said Amrit, "but we must go. Much work to do".

"You're a bloody marvel mate. Look forward to it," said Clancy as he bid the men farewell.

"What a lovely people they are," said Archie, "you know I just can never understand why men can be equals in war but not at home".

"Well maybe this war will be the straw that breaks the camel's back on that front eh," added Roo.

Although the water was tainted with fuel it was all they

had. Because of this it was not to be used for any other purpose than drinking and cooking, so naturally the odour of the men, combined with that of the rotting corpses strewn to their front would make a muck spreader blush.

Sitting in the support trench the next morning, Clancy was prying open a tin of bully beef with his bayonet.

"I like a bit of bully but it gets a bit boring," he remarked.

"And these biccies are a bit dry and tough," replied Archie.

"Cheer up lads," came a hearty voice from the rear, "sustenance has arrived".

"Yeah, well I hope he's a good shot," said Clancy.

It was Lieutenant Ponsonby, he was singing the praises of the Quartermaster, and was followed closely by a fatigue party who became suddenly popular with the men resting in the rear.

"Look at that Arch!" exclaimed an excited Roo, "Jam, cheese, bacon, taters and onions".

"Once they dish it out we can make an all in stew with that lot and drop a little of Tarsam's curry powder in it for good measure," added Taff.

"Make sure you get it in to you boys, and don't forget we're on patrol tonight," said Clancy.

"You really know how to dampen a party mate," said Roo.

7

Patrols, Supplies and New Mates

"Right boys, empty your pouches and pockets of anything you don't need, or that rattles. Ammo is your friend tonight so grab some out of this box," whispered Clancy.

"What's the password tonight mate?" asked Roo.

"A good one. The challenge is dunny and the reply is ...."

"Can!" Interrupted Taff, "yeah I think we got that one boyo".

"Good on yer," said Clancy with a grin on his face, as he patted Taff on the back.

"Don't forget your water and your scoff bags too," Roo reminded his section.

As their mates in the front line trench held the ladders, Lieutenant Ponsonby did a quick scan of the ground to his front and flanks, then, stealthily, climbed out of the trench, pistol in hand, constantly straining to see in to the darkness. As he paused and squatted on the parapet, he signalled the platoon to climb the ladder. Roo was first with his section followed by Corporal Harrison and Archie's sections, with Sgt McBride taking up the rear.

"Keep an eye out for us when we get back," he whispered to the defenders in the trench, "and don't shoot me in the bum!"

The three sections were lying flat on the ground in a defensive line. The days had been warming up, but the evenings had a definite chill. Roo was shivering but managed to control it as Clancy gave the signal to move out. The sections rose quietly to their feet, as one, and set off along the seaward spur of Bolton's Ridge.

The section commanders had no official maps as they were few and far between; quite an item to be short of! But, through quick daytime observations between the NCOs and the Platoon Commander, they had managed to cobble together some very clever map drawings, which each officer and NCO carried. They weren't Ordnance Survey, but did the job, and their job now was to reconnoitre, or recce for short, the area to their front and flanks to ascertain the enemy's strength and positions. Seeing the odd wild goat here and there on the peninsula, Roo had devised a workable formation for sections to move as one during darkness. He called it the blob because the section moved together in a close diamond shape, which Roo thought resembled a blob of spilled jam. It was an ingenious formation because the Section Commander, and Second in Command (2IC), were placed in the centre for command and control, along with the Lewis Gunner who was able to step left or right to give a burst of fire if required. Clancy reckoned that in the dark the blob resembled a flock of goats, which was the intention.

Always full of praise, and humour, for his best mate, Clancy had remarked, "I bet you are looking forward to tomorrow Roo, because you get smarter every day".

This night the platoon was conducting a recce in the valleys to their west, just down from an area now known as Lone Pine. The group moved carefully and quietly along the rocky slopes, trying not to accidentally dislodge any stones or boulders and sending them crashing down the hillsides as they went. But this wasn't the only possible trigger to alert the enemy to their presence. Friendly Destroyers had been detailed to venture close to the shoreline at Gaba Tepe and to shine their huge search lights along the valleys in order to keep the Turks on their toes, whilst simultaneously alerting the allies to any possible incursions or attacks. The troops were all for the lights, except when patrolling, as they not only had the potential to expose them to the Turks, but also to ruin their night vision. The patrols had to constantly freeze in position and close one eye, their aiming eye, so their vision in the darkness wasn't compromised.

"Bastards!"

As the men moved carefully east of Pine Ridge, Roo signalled a pause and a squat down. About twenty yards above them, on the ridge, was a sizeable enemy formation; possibly a company. Ponsonby moved quietly towards Roo.

"What is it corporal?" he whispered.

Roo pointed west up the slope.

"At least a hundred and fifty men up there sir," he whispered in response.

As they conversed, a small number of the enemy paused and appeared to be scanning the area now occupied by the platoon. The platoon commander signalled to all to keep perfectly still. Each man could feel their hearts pounding in their throats as they froze in position. The small group of breakaway Turks now began talking quite loudly and pointing in an untactical manner in their direction. Surely they hadn't been seen or all hell would have broken loose by now. The platoon was ready for the worst. Suddenly, and without warning, one of the ship's search lights illuminated the enemy who were either too late, or too poorly trained, to protect their night vision. Roo and Ponsonby saw the opportunity.

"Right chaps, let's pretend we are a shepherd and get the flock out of here," Ponsonby whispered.

Roo gave the signal to slowly rise up and, as the Turks were staring and pointing at the ships below, the platoon steadily eased their way rearwards, disappearing in to the shadows.

The next morning the Turkish company paid dearly from their "almost" encounter with the platoon, as shell after shell from the Royal Navy slammed in to their last reported position. Roo and Clancy watched from afar as the Turks ran for their very existence, both uttering the words "poor bastards".

Although the nights were still chilly, the day time temperatures were definitely improving, so much so that the Aussies began wearing variations of their uniforms, tearing the tattered legs of their trousers off below the knee, forming shorts. Tunics were put aside in favour of their long underwear tops, and forage caps were adapted with material down the back to shield their necks from the raging sun; but most began to sport their slouch hats. They *were* Aussies after all, not poms!

The newspaper reporters had christened them the naked army as a result.

The ANZAC reputation as stubborn and determined fighters was not going unnoticed, resulting in two brigades being lent to the British during the second battle of Krithia, for two weeks in May. They were replaced on the line by two brigades from the Royal Navy Division. Many questions were asked by Aussie soldiers.

"What's the bloody point?" asked Clancy.

"The point of what?" replied Ponsonby.

"The pommy jokers. They send our blokes to fight *their* battle and replace them with these…..these bloody kids!" Clancy growled, quite angrily.

"Ours is not to reason why sergeant," replied the officer.

"Well it aint 'to do or die' mate either," added Roo.

"There's nothing we can do about it," replied their officer, "anyway……."

"Anyway?" asked Archie, sensing some bad news.

"Who wants a trip to ANZAC to fetch the mail?" replied Ponsonby.

"Well *I* don't need to be asked twice. You coming Roo?" asked Clancy.

"Bloody oath!" replied Roo.

"You'll have to go the long way, past Courtney's Post, as the quick way is in full view of Beachy Bill," said the lieutenant.

"Hey Roo," said Archie, "while you're at the cove see if you can scrounge some writing paper and pencils".

Practically the entire surface of Gallipoli is made up of a series of ridges and plateau of irregular elevations, overspread with scrub and scanty vegetation in places, but mostly bare and arid rock, fissured and cleft in all directions by a maze of deep ravines, the sides of which are as craggy and precipitous as sea cliffs. The previous day and night a failed, but brave, attempt by the 4th Brigade and New Zealand Brigade to take the hill known as Baby 700 had been made. This was one of the original objectives on the day of the landing and most likely could have been secured had the 3rd Brigade not been instructed to dig in at the 400 Plateau. The attack on Baby 700 should have been carried out by a Corps, the equivalent of nine brigades, forty thousand men, but now almost six hundred ANZACs lay dead on the hillsides, and a similar number were out of action due to wounds.

Making their way along the winding trench system to ANZAC, Clancy and Roo noticed many dugouts, wire entanglements to the front, as well as saps which had been dug out in to no man's land as listening posts, or start points of new trenches. The men were indeed industrious, digging deeper and tossing the spoil over the top of the trench, thus improving the height around the rim, to further protect the occupants.

As they approached the junction which veered off towards the beach, the thoroughfares were a hive of activity as a result of the aforementioned attack. Men were bringing up stores while stretcher bearers were ferrying the dead and wounded down the slopes. It was a terrible sight. Limbless and mangled bodies lay lifeless on the stretchers, whilst the wounded either lay silent or screamed for a loved one; the lads from the Field Ambulance consoling them as best as they could. As a soldier and his donkey, its saddle spattered in blood, approached them from the direction of the dressing station in Clarke Valley, Clancy could not help himself and grabbed the man's hand in thanks.

"You field ambulance blokes are a bloody marvel mate," he blurted out.

John Simpson halted, turned to Archie and Roo and said, "Nah man, away with yer. It's *you* canny lads who are the marvel, running into harm's way every day. Me and me marras just pick up the pieces and try to put them back together again. God bless yer lads"; and, like an angel, he was gone, continuing up the slopes to where shattered men needed him.

Nearing the dressing station the boys paused.

"Do you think Stowie will still be there?" asked Clancy.

"Don't know mate. Shall we go visit? They can only tell us to bugger off," replied Roo.

Upon nearing the entrance an enemy shell flew over their heads, and exploded directly in the doorway of the dressing station, knocking Roo and Clancy flat on their backs. Both struggled to their feet, ears ringing from the blast, but managed to stumble their way to the collapsed structure, fearing that Doc Butler would be dead. They were met with absolute carnage, but the doc was fine and was tending to Private Tyrell, one of his stretcher bearers. Seven had been wounded; three of whom would later die from their injuries.

"Doc, what can we do?" asked Roo.

The doc gazed at poor Tyrell.

"I don't know what I can do for this poor fellow, but see if you can check the bleeding of the others," replied Captain Butler.

Tyrell beckoned the doc to listen. Captain Butler leaned in placing an ear close to the man's mouth. As blood bubbled and gurgled in his throat, Tyrell knew he was mortally wounded and asked the doctor to tend to the others, as he was a lost cause. Smiling a proud smile at the soldier, the doctor made Tyrell as comfortable as he could; but in a few minutes Tyrell was gone. Three good men were dead and four others severely wounded, men who had risked all to save others.

"Crikey doc I didn't realise it was so bad here," said Clancy.

"Sadly it is, but it's no picnic for you men either, but for us, watching the suffering, is a long drawn out torture," replied the doc.

Covered in the blood of others, Roo, Clancy and Doc Butler carried the dead and wounded to the beach, where they laid them on the sand, with the many other broken men, waiting for the boat to take them to the hospital ships.

"The Turks don't usually shell us you know. Must have been a drop short," explained the doc.

The boys remained with Captain Butler for about fifteen minutes but, although still stunned by what they had just witnessed, it was on to collect the mail.

Up on the front line the men had heard stories of the beach at ANZAC being a place of tea parties and picnics. Those who had been there before knew this was not true, but this was Roo and Clancy's third visit, and this time they were arriving from a different direction than their first. They hadn't seen the cove in the daylight and were surprised at how small an area it was, only made smaller by the crates of ammunition and stores which were neatly piled on the sand.

"Crikey the beach at Kilcoy Creek is bigger than this," said Roo.

"Yeah, remember our swimming lessons with Miss O'Reilly?" replied Clancy, "those were the days eh?"

"Hey, fancy a dip now?" asked Roo.

The two friends quickly shed their blood stained clothes and dived in to the calm sea, splashing round like children. Other soldiers were also enjoying the cool waters, a break from the murderous life that awaited them in the hills above. A sudden explosion about fifty yards from the shore halted all of the frolicking, all bathers ducking down in the nonexistent cover of the sea. The worry of the moment, however, soon changing to laughter as the men spied an officer in a rowing boat scooping fish from the surface, which had been killed after he had thrown explosives in to the sea.

"He's bloody fishing!" exclaimed Clancy, "hey sir, chuck us a few of those later will yer?"

The officer replied with a thumbs up sign.

But even here they were always in peril, as the snipers took shots at the bathers.

"It's not safe here mate," said Roo.

"Oh bugger them, I'm gonna do my washing, besides Archie won't be pleased if you bring him back a stinky uniform will he?" replied an indignant Clancy as he dragged his uniform in to the salty water and began to scrub it as best he could.

As the blood seeped from his clothing the water turned red.

"Bloody hell," exclaimed Clancy as he watched the water change colour, "I bet it was like that when we first landed, you know, from all those poor blokes".

Job done the two mates lay in the sun behind some crates, out of the view of snipers, whilst their clothes dried in the sunshine.

"It's beautiful here," said Clancy as he gazed out to the horizon, "you know, until all of this I'd never seen the sea, let alone sailed on it".

"When *I* was a little fella my mum and dad moved to Bundaberg, that's where the work was you know....they had a dream of owning their own property, but they got sick and died. Anyway, I first saw the ocean when the Buthulla people took me in," said Roo.

He explained how, being half aboriginal, he was adopted and taken to K'gari, the original name for Fraser Island.

"All was well until a pack of white blokes and women turned up on a boat and stole away all of the children, including me. I remember the men and women from the village crying and wailing as we sailed away," explained Roo.

"They *stole* you?" exclaimed Clancy.

"Yes," Roo replied, feeling quite emotional.

"But how? Why? I don't see any sense in that?" asked Clancy.

"I think because they could," Roo replied, with a tear in his eye.

Roo went on with his explanation. Many years ago, laws were established in the Australian colonies that designated a Director of Native Welfare. This Director was given the legal responsibility for all indigenous children, regardless of whether their parents were alive. They were given the authority to separate Aboriginal children from their families and place them in dormitories. Essentially, certain segments of the white society considered the First Australians to be uncivilised savages, even though they had managed very well for themselves for thousands of years. Their objective was to eliminate Aboriginal customs, beliefs, and language, and instead educate and condition indigenous children to adopt the ways of the white people. Indigenous children of mixed parentage were specifically singled out in order to remove their non-European identity, often through physical means. They would be taken from their parents and transported to government institutions where they would receive training aimed at preparing them for employment in occupations that were considered civilised, such as domestic servants and labourers.

"That is a bloody disgrace, and un-Australian in my books!" responded an angry Clancy, "why is it I've never heard of it before?"

"I don't know mate, but these church and government people don't care about you or me mate," Roo explained.

"That is a terrible story mate, but how did you end up in Kilcoy and with the Taylors?" asked Clancy.

"My mum and dad used to tell me about their home in a town called Kilcoy and how, one day, we would return," Roo replied, "I knew I had family there at a place called Doriray, so I ran away from the home. It took me a few weeks to get there, but it was worth it. It turned out that my Uncle Ray was my father's brother and Archie and Percy my cousins. Aunty Doris and

Uncle Ray took me in and brought me up not only as a nephew, but as a son. I can *never* repay them for that," said Roo.

"And then *I* bloody picked on you at school," said Clancy, shaking his head.

"That's done mate. We were just kids, and now we are mates for life," replied Roo, reassuring his friend.

"I was a proper bastard, but I know better now. I just hope one day we can all just be good to each other, I mean look at where we are now. What's *this* all about? Idiots who can't live together. Makes my blood boil," exclaimed Clancy.

"Anyway, Freddy's blood will be boiling if we forget the mail," said Roo.

Three large sacks of letters were waiting for them in the postal tent.

"Do you have any writing paper and pencils at all please mate?" enquired Roo.

The postal orderly was quite taken aback, asking "what do you think this is mate? The corner shop or something?"

"That's a no then is it?" replied Roo as he and Clancy dragged the sacks out of the tent.

Noticing some crates full of cardboard and old orders notices, Roo and Clancy stuffed as much as they could in to the sacks.

While making their way towards the entrance of the sunken road, they caught sight of several small boats coming ashore in the Cove.

"There must be over a hundred blokes there mate," said Clancy.

There were one hundred and twenty to be exact, all wearing the battalion patch of the 9th Battalion. The re-enforcements were met by the beach master who was about to direct them up the hill when the boys arrived.

"We'll take them up sir," said Clancy.

"Thank you sergeant...corporal," as he nodded to both men in acknowledgement.

"Right men, how much ammo and water have you got?" asked the burly sergeant.

"Sergeant, I am Lieutenant Fowler, they have a hundred rounds each and a canteen of water...don't you salute officers?" said the young officer.

"Only if you want a bullet in the head from one of those snipers up yonder sir," Roo replied.

The officer, putting a hand to his head, accepted the reason and was thankful.

"Where are we going?" the officer asked, surveying the mountainous terrain to his front.

"Way up there to the right," replied Clancy, pointing in the direction of Boltons Ridge.

"It looks steep," said Lieutenant Fowler.

"It sure is sir. We landed right here and fought our way up there," added Roo, "saved you fellas a job eh?"

The rest of the men nodded in awe of the two veterans.

"Righto sir, boys, follow us," said Clancy.

Just then a shout rang out from another boat which had just beached.

"Hey Clancy, Roo! Wait for me!"

"I recognise that bloody Yank voice," said Clancy as he turned to see their mate Stowie limping along the beach.

"Got room for a little one?" said Stowie, as the friends hugged and shook hands.

"Tell me where this little one is and I'll think about," retorted Clancy with a broad smile, "all *I* can see is a fat bastard. How are yer mate?"

"I'm good," replied Stowie in his Texan accent, "my ass is a bit sore, hence my limp, but they said I was fine to come back to the battalion".

"That's bloody marvellous," replied Clancy, "glad to have you back".

Stowie, noticing Roo and Clancy's stripes, was impressed.

"Hey, love the new additions to your uniforms. Sergeant and Corporal eh?" he said.

"Yeah, they had a bit of a chook raffle while you were gone," laughed Clancy.

The young lieutenant was becoming a little impatient.

"Are we going or not?" he said gruffly.

"Keep your hair on mate," snapped Clancy.

"How dare you sergeant. I'll have you on a charge!" exclaimed the young lieutenant.

"Really?....good on yer mate," replied Clancy, "come on fellas let's be gone".

As they led the men and their indignant officer up the slope there were many sights to be seen as the company made their way through the sunken roads and trenches to Bolton's Ridge, passing men, stretcher bearers and their donkeys going the other way, pausing only at notorious sniper and machine gun corners, where Clancy had then men move past them in quick leaps and bounds. A few shots were taken by Johnny Turk but luckily the men reached Boltons unscathed.

The rest of the battalion was pleased to see the new arrivals. As the men halted Clancy went in search of an officer in order to find out where the men were being distributed.

Finding Lieutenant Ponsonby and Captain Ryder he announced, "morning sirs, got some new mates for you…just down here".

The two officers greeted the new arrivals.

"Welcome gents. Good to have you. The CSM will get you sorted then we can get down to some training," said Captain Ryder.

"Training? We *are* trained," exclaimed the Lieutenant.

"Really? Been in any battles lately? Know all about Abdul and the way he fights?" snapped Ponsonby.

"Well….no," replied the lieutenant, hesitating.

"I thought not. So *you*, second lieutenant, and these fine fellows will be receiving some training at Shrapnel Gully," said an annoyed Ponsonby.

"This sergeant here. I want him charged," Fowler blurted out.

"Charged? What for?" asked Captain Ryder.

"Insolence!" responded Fowler.

Both officers fought to suppress their smiles.

"Really?" said Ponsonby turning to Clancy, "Sergeant McBride have you been insolent to this officer?"

Clancy quickly turned to Roo and whispered through the corner of his mouth, "what's insolence?"

"Being rude I think," Roo whispered back.

"No sir, I'm *never* insolent," replied Clancy.

"Good sergeant. Thank you. There you have it lieutenant," said Ponsonby to the young officer.

"But?" the young officer protested.

Leaning in close to the inexperienced second lieutenant Ponsonby whispered in his ear, "grow up man. Look around and learn from these men. They have much to teach you and one day *may* save your life. Ah, Private Stowe, back from the hospital. Good to see you".

"Yes sir. Good to be home," Stowie replied.

Bringing re-enforcements *and* the mail made Roo and Clancy twice as popular. The troops hadn't had much news from home for a few weeks now and were eager to read the many letters, which had all come at once.

"Look at this! Ten letters and they are months old," came one of the many voices from the ranks.

But mail was mail, so the men got to it, finding a quiet spot to read news from home, and just daydream a little.

"Did you get any writing paper Roo?" asked Archie.

As he emptied the sack Roo handed around the scraps of cardboard and used paper that they had managed to salvage.

"Only this lot, but it's something," Roo replied, "no pencils though mate".

Archie and the others were grateful for anything they could use.

"We'll save on the dunny paper now eh?" came another voice.

"Looks like I'll have to write in blood if there aren't any pencils then," joked Archie.

"Well there's plenty of that to be had mate. Here, I've got a few spares," replied Clancy as he reached in to his pocket and pulled out a handful of pencils, tossing one to Archie.

"Cheers cobber," replied a grateful Archie as he caught the pencil with his free hand.

While they were on the mail run Archie had started an all in stew made up of anything they had, mainly bully beef and hard biscuits with a little bit of curry powder thrown in for flavour. A good old billy full of tea was also ready to be shared out amongst the boys. Roo tossed Archie his sea laundered uniform, which was still a little damp.

"Thanks boys, I'll hang that up to dry," said Archie, "did you drown the little buggers?"

"Eh? Oh, the lice? Yeah, but they'll be back soon enough," replied Roo.

After dusk the men were able to move around more easily and safely and would often congregate in small groups for a yarn.

Archie had received a small package from his parents which contained a letter and a pocket sized book.

"You beauty Mum," said Archie, as he excitedly showed the book to Roo, "just what I asked for, a diary to record all that happens to us".

"Hey, that's great mate. Will I be in it?" asked Roo.

"Of course you silly bugger. You, Clancy, Taff...all of you," replied Archie, "but you have to promise me something though".

"Promise?" said a surprised Roo.

"If I should fall, you have to ensure that this diary gets home. I want everyone to know the truth of what we did here, and may do in the future. Promise me?" insisted Archie.

"Of course I will...but nothing is going to happen to us, so you can take it home yourself," replied Roo, secretly hoping and praying to himself.

The conversation certainly had lowered the mood in their trench.

"What did Aunty Doris say in her letter Arch?" asked Roo, trying to brighten the atmosphere.

"Oh, the usual stuff, you know, the hay is in the paddocks for the winter, weather is pretty warm, oh, and Uncle Samuel is in Egypt at the moment," replied Archie.

"Yeah, she says that in my letter too, 'my brother Samuel Ford is with the South Staffordshire Regiment in Egypt at the moment, having a good time seeing the sights'. I wonder where *they* are headed?" said Roo.

"Hopefully here, God knows we need some help," replied Archie.

"Shift up," said Clancy as he plonked himself down next to the Taylors, "letters from home?"

"Yeah, from Mum and Dad. Nothing for you again?" asked Roo.

"Nah, they never were ones for letter writing," replied Clancy.

"What about Aunty Doris and Uncle Ray, have they written again?" enquired Roo.

"Not today, but they know by the writing it is Archie doing the talking, so they are probably getting bored now," replied Clancy, feeling down and left out.

"Cheer up Clance. You know what the mail is like here. They've probably lost it; plus Mum and Dad aren't like that, they love hearing from you," said Archie, reassuringly, "and anyway, don't you think it's about time you showed off your new writing skills? What do you reckon?"

"That would be ripper Arch, but do you think I'm good enough yet mate?" asked Clancy feeling a little emotional, but trying not to show it.

"Don't be silly, of course you're good enough; now get your pencil and paper out and start writing," replied Archie.

"Righto. I bloody well will then," said Clancy with a new sense of confidence in his writing skills.

The truth was that Clancy had been kicked out of home as soon as he reached the age of fourteen, which suited him as both of his parents were lovers of the bottle and used to beat him whenever they were drunk; which was every day. There would be no letters from family for him, and certainly no one waiting at home when this was all over.

Just then Taff appeared from the darkness.

"G'day mate, take a pew and warm yourself by the fire," said a jovial Clancy.

As Taff sat down there was a muffled shout from about twenty feet down the trench, it was Corporal Jones.

"Hey boys got any spare tobacco?" came the call.

The Taylor boys didn't smoke but always hung on to their tobacco ration should a friend need it.

"Yeah, hang on a jiffy," replied Archie as he fumbled through his pockets, "I'll bring it over".

The corporal waved his hand in grateful recognition as Archie began walking towards him. Suddenly there was a blinding flash and an almighty explosion. The ground shook violently as the force of the blast threw Archie back towards his seated mates.

Roo, Clancy and Taff were showered in debris, as they watched the corporal and his friends vanish in the cloud of dust, flames and flying earth. Even the Turks, who were within a hop, skip and a jump, were surprised, and peered over the top of their trenches to see what had occurred. As the smoke and dust cleared Corporal Jones's left boot was all that remained of him, standing straight and tall as if he had been lifted right out of it. His mates had gone too, replaced by a blackened crater. There had been no sound of artillery fire. The shell had been fired from a long range and had fallen perpendicularly like a mortar round, directly in to the trench. A lucky, or unlucky, shot. All around were in total shock at what they had witnessed. As Archie pulled himself to his feet, his ears were still ringing, but he managed to dust himself off.

"I suppose he won't be wanting the tobacco anymore then....." Archie blurted out, half laughing and half crying; still in shock and disbelief.

"Here have a sip of this," said Roo as he offered his cousin his canteen, "they didn't feel it mate; honest."

"Poor sods," added Clancy.

Indeed, no one even saw or heard it coming. As he surveyed the scene Lieutenant Ponsonby *had* to stay calm and collected. It was his job.

"Quick boys," he said, "I know this is a hell of a thing, but let's plug the gap eh? Sergeant McBride, let's get to it".

The 9th of May turned out to be a good day, for many reasons. The 7th Battery, Australian Field Artillery, now had a gun in the 9th Battalion's sector and, even though a little late in the day, the Company Quartermaster Sergeant (CQMS) and his storemen were doing the rounds and issuing each man with a blanket. All were grateful, as many had been keeping warm by wrapping themselves in their great coats; those lucky enough to have them that is.

Many new inventions and home made weapons were being manufactured in the factory down at ANZAC and disseminated around the battalions. The favourite was the trench periscope, which was constructed from pieces of wooden crates, and shaving mirrors. The periscopes had arrived a week earlier, only four per brigade, but it was a start. The men were now able to observe the enemy without having to expose themselves to hostile fire.

"We could do with something like this for our rifles so we can fire at Abdul without being shot in the head," said Archie as he admired one of the periscopes.

Mindful of the necessity for rest *and* organisation, the brigade adopted a system of dividing each company in to four reliefs, that is one platoon in the fire trench, one in the support, and one in the reserve trench (hopefully sleeping), and one on fatigues. These formations were rotated regularly, thus giving the battalion ample rest.

Patrols remained an integral part of daily existence on the peninsula.

But the 12th of May would become especially significant to the Taylor boys.

8

Rough Winds do Shake the Darling Buds of May

It wasn't until the 2nd of May that the first batch of casualties from Gallipoli arrived at the No1 Australian General Hospital at Heliopolis. Men from the ANZAC forces eagerly sought out information about friends and relatives on the peninsula, including Percy, who was relieved to find no trace of his brother or cousin on the casualty lists or in any of the hospital wards. Many also interrogated the wounded veterans about the terrain, and Johnny Turk, at Gallipoli.

The troops still in Egypt, including the 2nd Light Horse Regiment, were soon to become Gallipoli re-enforcements. On the 7th of May the light horse regiments were issued with improvised infantry equipment and, two days later, along with the 1st Light Horse Regiment, set sail aboard the 'SS Devanna' to the Dardanelles.

On the morning of 12th of May, as dawn broke over the rugged coastline, a flotilla of small boats silently cut through the calm waters, their destination, ANZAC Cove. Clancy was looking out at the blue sea to their rear, through his binoculars, when he saw the armada of small boats, Tows and steam pinnaces approaching the shore.

"Hey fellas look," said Clancy as he pointed, "some bloody new chums are approaching".

"That's a bit of a stupid thing to do in daylight, give us a squiz," said a surprised Archie, hand held out for the binoculars.

Tension filled the air as the men in the boats, clad in khaki uniforms and slouch hats with an Emu feathered plume, clutched their rifles tightly, their hearts pounding with a mix of anticipation and fear.

As the boats drew nearer to the beach, the soldiers could see the silhouette of the hills looming above them, shrouded in the misty morning haze. The sound of the oars slicing through the water was the only noise, but the eerie calm was soon shattered. As Archie watched on, shots rang out from the surrounding heights, obviously aimed at the approaching new comers, bullets whistling through the air, the senders praying to their God that they would find their targets. Chaos ensued as Percy and his mates ducked down in their transports scrambling for cover as the bullets began to fly, instinctively seeking refuge behind the sides of the boats or hunching down low to minimize their exposure. Some soldiers returned fire, their shots merging with the relentless rain of bullets, and amidst the terrifying cacophony, a strange mixture of emotions permeated the soldiers. Fear and determination intermingled as they pressed on, inching closer to the shore under the relentless hail of gunfire, drawing strength from one another, their unyielding spirit driving them forward even in the face of mortal danger. It must have been pure luck that only four men were wounded.

In the midst of the chaos, Percy and the others couldn't help but admire the young midshipmen who commanded the boats, and their steadfastness as the bullets flew; boys, but now veterans of war, it was just another day to them.

As Archie observed he couldn't make out the units but *could* see that there were at least two battalion sized battle groups in the boats.

"Perhaps they are coming to relieve us," said a hopeful Taff.

"Yeah mate, and if me mum had had a pair of balls she'd have been me dad," replied Clancy.

On hearing this latest from Clancy, Archie just rolled his eyes and shook his head in disbelief.

The newly landed light horse regiments were met on the beach by the Beach Master, who directed them to their bivouac area in Monash Gully. Having all become tired of Egypt, the troopers had been anxious to get to the front, but setting foot near the place where the Australians and New Zealanders had first landed, and to see the steep slopes and ravines which they had scaled, made the men wonder how *any* troops could possibly have taken this position, let alone hold on to it.

Although Percy knew it, Roo and Archie were unaware that there were now three Taylor boys on the peninsula. But, right now, this fact was far from Archie and Roo's thoughts for it was their platoon's turn on the rota to go out on a recce patrol.

On this night their mission was to scout the area around Weir and Pine Ridges, as sounds of digging had been heard the previous night. The ridges were spurs running south from Lone Pine, a bit too close for comfort; a spur being a narrow or elongated projection of land extending from the main body of a ridge, typically characterised by steep slopes on either side. In other words, mountain goat country. The suspicions were proven correct as the platoon came dangerously close to being seen by the enemy, who were indeed entrenching. Clancy quickly raised his left hand and halted the platoon, then giving them the signal to lie prone.

He then whispered "I need six of you to crawl up and see how many are up there, and what they are doing; any takers?"

All hands immediately went up. Clancy selected his six volunteers, which included Roo.

"I want you back here in ten minutes.....and no shooting, just looking; do you understand?" asked the burly sergeant.

All thumbs went up and then the six split up and moved towards the sound of digging. The recce, thankfully, was uneventful for the six, who diligently observed their foe, noting their gun pits and the fact that they were re-enforcing their overhead cover with pine branches which they had been transporting in by mule during the darkness.

"They're obviously here for the duration," whispered Roo as he reported his intelligence on his return.

All six men were soon back with the platoon, each reporting similar goings on. Mission complete, as one, the platoon disappeared slowly in to the night, unseen by the Turks.

Something big was coming, and soon.

Quinn's Post, located on the northern edge of the main ANZAC line, was the most dangerous and active position on the peninsula, forming the apex to the triangle of the front line. It was accessible by a long, straight staircase like path which was too steep for mules, let alone men, but they managed it, as soldiers do. The post itself was a line of single trenches on the crest of a crescent shaped ridge, and was divided in to six sub sections. The Turks were dug in less than thirty feet away, on ground which overlooked the ANZAC trenches, each belligerent clinging precariously to the edge of their own slope, a slight crest between them.

Because the post lay lower that the surrounding ridges, to raise one's head above the parapet to observe or fire, was to invite certain death at the hands of a sniper. The Turks, however, did not suffer this impediment and were able to hold their heads up to their heart's content and establish fire superiority, not to mention the regular throwing of bombs at the post.

In early May the defenders, the 15th Battalion, had for a short time captured and occupied the main enemy trenches, some twenty yards away. They had then dug communication trenches which were linked to what were, again, enemy positions. Two had been partly filled in, but one was still open, except for a three foot high sandbag obstacle, leaving a literal door between the two opponents.

At around mid day on the 13th of May, following a long and steep climb up the slopes, the 2nd Light Horse Regiment relieved the defenders of Quinn's Post. 'A' Squadron was in support whilst 'C' manned the right and 'B' the left. The regiment was ably supported by the 1st Light Horse who were the new occupants of Pope's Hill to the left of Quinn's.

"This is a bit of a scary place eh?" said Percy as he took a quick look at the enemy positions which commanded the area.

Within seconds of him raising his head above the parapet, the ground to his front suddenly spat dust clouds as the Turkish machine guns sent a few bursts his way. Percy didn't need an invitation as the adrenalin pumping through his body caused him to duck back out of sight.

"You bloody idiot!" shouted a sergeant of the 15th, "you gee gees are gonna get your heads shot off quick smart if you do that sort of trick again".

Feeling lucky to be alive, and foolish at the same time, Percy apologised to the sergeant.

"No need to be sorry son, you just need to box clever here," replied the sergeant, "come on boys and listen to what I have to say".

The sergeant beckoned the new arrivals to him then began to explain the position, its landmarks and, above all, its dangers. The nature of the ground meant that the Turks were in the best positions and were able to look down in to the Aussie trenches. What were known as The Chessboard and Dead Man's Ridge dominated the position to the left, whilst the German Officer's

Trench towered over the right. Because of this the enemy could enfilade, or fire straight along, the ANZAC trenches, from a distance of anything from one hundred to three hundred yards. The whole area, some of which had been in Turkish hands, was a maze of interconnecting communication and fire trenches, with all incoming and outgoing traffic having to pass through a corridor known as the water course. With the German Officer's Trench commanding the corridor which led in to number 5 sub section, it was an area with a high casualty rate.

"As you can see boys, this is a bloody dangerous place," said the sergeant as he held up a wooden periscope, "and this, this is your best mate when observing".

All nodded in agreement.

"Here endeth the lesson. Good luck gee gees; oh, and by the way, be alert to bombs, the Turks have an endless supply," said the sergeant as he made his way out of Quinn's.

"Why is this place called Quinn's Post anyway?" asked a curious Percy.

"Probably named after some silver spooned type. It wouldn't sound as good if they called it after one of us would it? Chugger's Post...mmmmm...I dunno, sounds good to me," joked Chugger.

The post was in fact named after Major High Quinn of the 15th Battalion. Sadly he was killed there later that month.

As the 2nd Light Horse began stowing their kit and making themselves comfortable there was a sudden thud, followed by a hissing sound. "Bomb!" someone shouted as the black ball of death came flying over from the enemy lines, hit the back wall of the trench and bounced unceremoniously on to the ground, rolling within a few feet of Percy's section. Instinctively Percy picked up the hissing cricket ball sized bomb and expertly bowled it back to the Turks. A dull explosion and cry of pain indicated that Percy had hit the enemy 'stumps'.

"Stick that up your bum Jacko!" shouted Davo as he reached out to shake Percy's hand.

A cry of "stand to" reverberated around Quinn's as the Turkish "welcome" began. These types of bombs were thought to be obsolete, not having been seen for sixty years, since the Crimean War. The Turks, however, were not of the same opinion, as bombs kept flying all that afternoon. The bombs themselves were filled with one hundred grams of TNT and were lit by pulling off a brass cap, with a flint and steel ignition for the fuse. The distance from the enemy and the large width of the trenches at Quinn's added to the danger, making the accuracy and surety of the Turks hitting their target a definite. Throughout the afternoon thirty four members of the regiment were wounded, including two officers. The men soon became experts in fielding the bouncing bombs from the dirt with their bare hands and lobbing them back to the enemy trench, whereas others would smother the bombs with sandbags. Percy was even able to catch the cricket ball grenades in mid air and chuck them back to their unsuspecting senders. The fuses of the bombs were abnormally long lasting giving the soldiers ample time to throw them in to strategic areas whilst limiting the chance of the bomb being returned by the Turks. The enemy soon learned a lesson, but, despite this, the bombing continued.

Silence was essential in the trenches and the numbers of men in the fire trench was reduced to prevent unnecessary casualties; not that any casualty was either necessary or welcome.

Re-enforcements were at hand in the reserve trenches, and the firing line was routinely strengthened at night as this was the most likely time of choice for an enemy assault. Each section on stag was allocated a position and their arcs of fire.

"Just fire at anything that isn't Aussie or Kiwi" was the order of the day.

Percy and his mates were on guard at a communication trench which led to sub section number 6. The men had scanned the area to their front, at dusk, via their best mate the periscope, but nothing seemed afoot. Perhaps the Turks had run out of bombs?

An uneventful night passed.

As dawn broke Percy observed no man's land, through the periscope, whilst his mates Troopers Butler, Rogan and Stark took a few minutes to rest following stand to.

"Hey Perce, wanna brew? Chuck us your cup," whispered Stark

Suddenly Percy's ears pricked up.

"What is it?" asked Butler.

"Sssh! Listen," said Percy pointing towards number 6, "someone's calling out; sounds like a Turk".

Only yards to their front, a hand, holding a white cloth, appeared from around one of the corners.

"Australia. Australia! Surrender...." came the voice, in broken English.

Percy looked back at his three mates.

"Roges, over here and keep watch to our front while I take a squiz," said Percy, handing over the periscope.

"It could be a trick mate," said Stark.

Percy shrugged his shoulders, then gently fixed his bayonet to his rifle and began walking in a ghost like fashion towards the voice. At the same time his mates pointed their weapons down the trench to give him some cover. Percy paused and knelt behind some sandbags, brought his rifle up to his shoulder, and called out in a low voice, "show yourself Abdul". Very slowly the Turkish soldier eased himself in to plain view of the Aussies. He had no weapon and held his open hands out to his sides. "Friend," he called, turning his head to the rear, ensuring he hadn't been followed; for surrendering was certain death should his own side be alerted. Percy beckoned the man to come closer, then held up his hand indicating for the Turk to halt.

"Hey Starkey, give this bloke a quick pat down will yer?" said Percy.

Stark obliged, gently passing his hands down the Turks back, then each arm and leg, grasping at pockets as he went.

"He's good mate," said Stark.

"Righto Abdul in here. Sit. Imshee!" said Percy, indicating for the Turk to sit, "go fetch the sarge, Starkey".

It wasn't the sergeant, but Major Bourne, who arrived on the scene. On seeing the Turkish prisoner he was impressed and excited.

"Good work boys. Hopefully this fellow will have some good intelligence for us," said Bourne enthusiastically, "see if you can entice a few more over eh?"

As the Major ushered the prisoner away all present shook their heads in disbelief.

"Entice? He's off his head!" said Chugger, as he called out

to the enemy who were only yards away, "hey Abdul! Wanna surrender?"

From the Turkish trench immediately opposite there was suddenly a bit of a verbal commotion, followed by much laughter.

"Obviously someone over there speaks our lingo," said Stark.

"We'll take that as a no then shall we?" yelled Chugger.

The Turks, in no mood for surrender, exercised their displeasure at such an insulting suggestion by bombing Quinn's for the remainder of the morning. No Aussie was wounded but the constant fielding of bombs kept them on their toes.

"Well one good thing that will come of all of this is a bloody good cricket team," said Percy.

By mid day the bombing had ceased.

"Must be smoko!" joked Chugger.

"Yeah, good union men the Turks," said Stark.

"More likely ran out of bombs mate," said Percy, "brew anyone?"

Chugger spied a familiar figure moving along the trench, followed by a small group of officers, including the Colonel.

"Just what we need!" said Chugger, nudging the others.

"Eh?" replied Percy, "oh bugger, it's Birdie!"

The boys quickly rose to their feet as the General approached.

"No, no, don't get up gentlemen, just an informal visit," said Birdie, in a friendly and calming voice, "I hear you've been playing catch with the Turks since you arrived. Well done".

"Yes sir," replied Percy, "we could do with something of our own to throw back, but".

"Indeed," the General responded, "that problem is being resolved as we speak".

Birdie was a soldier's General, and the men loved him for it; even though he was a pom! As he and his entourage carried on their tour Trooper Stark asked the sergeant what the General meant when he said they were resolving the problem.

"A bomb factory Starky me old mate," replied the sergeant, "down at the beach there are loads of blokes making bombs out of jam tins filled with all manner of shrapnel".

The men were impressed. A bomb factory had indeed been established just above the beach earlier that month and was producing almost two hundred bombs per day. Old tins were being filled with explosives and pieces of shrapnel such as nails, scraps of barbed wire, and live and used rounds. The final touch was a stick of gelignite jammed in the centre of the can. Just light the fuse and toss it, much like the cricket ball bombs which flew over from the enemy side regularly throughout each day. The only issue with these grenade-like weapons of Gallipoli was that they were improvised and at times as dangerous to the thrower as to the enemy, having only a three second fuse.

"Fellas, start collecting anything you can, scraps of metal, empty cartridge cases, even stones, and we can send them down to the factory.....and don't forget to save your empty tins," the sergeant suggested as he walked off to catch up with the General and his party.

As Birdie's tour of Quinn's Post ended he was very concerned that the Light Horse regiments, numerically fewer in numbers than the infantry, could properly defend this vital part of the front line. To their surprise, the Light Horse, later that day, were ordered to hand over to the 15th Battalion, whom they had only relieved twenty four hours prior. The 15th were exhausted, and the Light Horsemen felt ashamed. 'C' Squadron, however, remained in post, for they had been selected to carry out a night time raid.

The problem at Quinn's Post was that there were too many interlinked trenches which allowed the enemy to simply walk in to the ANZAC lines. 'C' Squadron's task that night was to mount a surprise attack, with no artillery support, on the enemy, damage their trenches, *and* fill in the communication trenches; all under the eyes and guns of the Turks.

"Bloody hell, what are we, soldiers or miners?" exclaimed Percy.

The raid was scheduled for 0145 hours the next morning. Between weapon cleaning and scrounging ammunition, somewhere during the evening the squadron managed to fit in some sleep. For the attack the squadron was divided in to four groups consisting of two assault parties and two digging parties.

As Starky disdainfully admired his shovel he whispered, "trust me to get the manual labour job eh?"

"If you want to swap with me on the assault team just say the word," replied Percy.

The raid which was about to be put in to action was nothing new at Quinn's, for the 15th had carried out several similar sorties over the last few days. As a result the Turks had skilfully placed machine guns in key positions to the north and south to sweep the area of no man's land between the opposing armies. As darkness fell the two assault parties were to clear the way for the diggers, so would be first out of the trench. Captain Burbeck and Sergeant Ogilvy were the assault commanders, whilst Major Graham and Lieutenant Potts led the diggers.

"Ready men?" Burbeck whispered.

The attackers signalled their readiness.

"Quietly now...let's go," whispered the Captain.

As the two assault parties clambered over the parapet they immediately re-organised and set off to their intended objectives. Almost immediately a shower of bombs rained down from the enemy trenches, quickly followed by hails of rifle fire. Not to be outdone, the Turkish machine guns joined in the chorus and raked the area to the front of Quinn's. Men began to fall, whilst others ran forward, zig zagging as they went. Four men, Lieutenant Ogilvy, Percy, Chugger and Davo launched themselves in to the enemy trench, stabbing and clubbing at the occupants with rifle and bayonet. It was a bloody scene. The surviving enemy fled along the communication trench, leaving the four attackers in control, awaiting their comrades. But none came, for they had been downed by the enemy volleys, lying wounded or dead in no man's land. Lieutenant Ogilvy, in the absence of the other assault troops, realised straight away that their position was hopeless.

"Right men, back down the communication trench to Quinn's!" he shouted, pointing towards their escape route.

As the small group moved they collected any wounded that they could. Major Graham could see that the attack had failed so ordered the digging parties to stand down. Stretcher bearers, without thought to their own safety, made their way in to no man's land under repeated enemy fire, and began collecting the wounded. Those wounded who were able, dragged themselves back to Quinn's and rolled themselves over the parapet in to the waiting arms of their mates. Major Graham felt helpless as he watched the stretcher bearers risking their all to bring in his men. He could bear it no longer. He had to do something, that something being to climb out in to no man's land to help. Bullets do not discriminate and, within minutes, Major Graham was dead; mown down by machine gun fire.

The raid was a good idea in theory but a costly waste in practice. Of the sixty men who leapt in to no man's land, twenty five were killed and twenty one wounded. Of the four officers Lieutenant Potts, who did not leave the trenches, was unscathed, whilst one was dead and the other two wounded. Later that morning 'C' Squadron, or what remained of them, was relieved by elements of 3rd Light Horse Regiment, and rejoined the 2nd Light Horse.

The next few days were spent digging trenches and creating a second line of defence. But it did not stop the snipers who accounted for three dead and nineteen wounded.

At the other end of the line on the 14th of May, one hundred NCOs and men from the 3rd Brigade were taken out of the line to act as beach fatigue party. Twenty five men from each battalion were seconded to the group.

"Who wants some time at the beach?" asked a cheery Ponsonby.

The platoon was at rest in the reserve trench, each man occupied by their own thoughts.

"I'll have some of that," said Clancy, as he deciphered the question.

"That's good sergeant, as the battalion is sending twenty five men, along with seventy five from the other battalions in the brigade to do some important work," replied Ponsonby, "and it looks like you've just volunteered the platoon".

"Thanks Clance. I was just enjoying a rest," uttered an indignant Archie.

"Cheer up chaps. I hear it is safe down there and there's lots of swimming to be enjoyed," said the lieutenant.

"I take it *you* haven't *been* to the cove sir?" asked Roo.

"Er....not since we landed , no," replied Ponsonby.

Roo rolled his eyes at the officer. "Enough said I think".

"Come on fellas, hands off cocks, on socks, gather up your gear. Let's go," announced Sergeant McBride.

"I'm with you sarge. Time at the beach," said Stowie.

"With *that* limp? You're no good to man nor beast at the moment. You can stay here and rest. It's probably safer here anyway," said Clancy.

"See you later mate," said Archie as he waved to the disappointed Stowie.

As Clancy and Roo had done a few days earlier, the rest of the men marvelled at the size of ANZAC Cove. It may be small but it was certainly making a good reputation for itself as a wharf, a hospital, General Headquarters, and a swimming pool, come laundry. The place was a hive of activity with soldiers carrying out their work whilst simultaneously dodging the constant artillery bombardments and sniper fire.

Lieutenant Ponsonby, as platoon commander, had joined his men at the beach.

"Come to give us a hand eh sir?" asked Clancy.

"You never know your luck sergeant," replied Ponsonby, "right men we are to be billeted just on the hillside over there, near to where the stores are to be landed, so go and make yourselves comfortable".

The men set to digging their dug out shelters in the bank, utilising whatever materials they could find - crates, sandbags, and canvas. That first night the men were even allowed an evening dip and a chance to wash their uniforms in the sea, taking advantage of the lack of visibility for artillery spotters and snipers.

"I wonder why they call it a fatigue party, because it's nothing like any party I've ever been to," asked Clancy.

"It must be army humour," replied Archie.

"Ha, bloody ha.....hold yer sides," joked Clancy.

"Er...it means tired mate," added Roo.

"Well I never; a let's get tired party," groaned Clancy, "it worked then...I'm bloody buggered".

The work may not have been enjoyable, but it *was* essential, unloading stores from small boats, carrying equipment, supplies and ammunition to anywhere in the ANZAC lines that it was needed. The men also worked on digging a sunken road from the beach to Shrapnel Gully; a concealed highway for men and stores to travel along in relative safety.

"This is thirsty work boys," said Clancy as he placed his entrenching tool on the ground and leant against the slope, "I wouldn't say no to a beer".

"You'll be lucky Clance," replied Archie, as he noticed a group of officers and stretcher bearers running towards them, complete with some unfortunate lying on the stretcher.

"Make way! Make way!" they shouted, waving all onlookers aside.

As the group past the fatigue party the men could see that the wounded man was an officer aged around fifty. He was bleeding profusely from his thigh, the medics trying to stem the blood flow as best as they could.

Lieutenant Ponsonby at first hesitated, but recognising the wounded man he quickly threw up a salute, momentarily forgetting that this action was the one thing that drew the attention of snipers. Quickly becoming aware of his error he snatched his arm away.

"Goodness. That was General Bridges," he announced.

"Bloody hell!" exclaimed Archie as he strained his neck to see.

"Even Generals are at risk here then eh?" said Clancy, "but he looked alright so should pull through".

Even though it was dangerous, Bridges had visited the front lines every day, but on the 15th of May he was shot in the right leg by a Turkish sniper, the round severing his femoral artery. He was pulled to safety and taken to the hospital ship 'Gascon' where he died three days later from an infection and severe blood loss.

His death was a great loss to the men.

Birdwood, while still commanding Allied troops on the ground at Gallipoli, took effective command of the AIF.

On the evening of the 18th of May there had been whispers of an enemy force being landed at the far side of the peninsula, and marching towards the ANZAC positions. The entire Corps was stood to, ready for the Turks.

All on the beach, who may have been asleep, were woken.

"What's happening skipper?" enquired Sergeant McBride.

"Something is stirring. The whole Corps has been stood to," replied Ponsonby.

"Great. We must be needed back on the ridge," said Roo.

"No Roo, we have an important role to play here. The Corps depends on us for ammunition, so we must keep it moving to them," the lieutenant explained.

Each battalion party was allocated a section of ANZAC to resupply, and were soon loading up pack mules in readiness for their silent journey to the troops above them. Number 1 Platoon was assigned the re-supply of the area of Pope's Hill, Quinn's Post and Courtney's Post; three vital areas of the front line.

"Hey fellas, want to load some kit on my donkey," came a familiar voice.

"Simmo! How are you mate?" asked Roo.

"I'm grand man. Looks like something big is happening canny lads," said Simpson.

"It is. We're re-supplying the area around Quinn's," replied Archie.

"Well, you're in luck lads, that's where I'm going, and I've got a new marra," said Simpson, pointing at a large horse, "this is Bill".

The boys recognised the large horse immediately as Bill the Bastard, whom they had met in Egypt. As Roo stepped forward to pat Bill's head, the horse began snorting loudly, his ears flattened backward and his huge hooves pawing and stomping menacingly on the ground, but as Roo spoke, in a calming voice, Bill began to relent a little and allowed Roo to stroke his neck.

"We know Bill from Egypt, don't we boy? He's part of the 2nd Light Horse.......hey, are they here?" asked Roo excitedly.

"I think they are man. Up at Quinn's. Why do yer ask?" enquired Simpson.

"Their brother, and cousin, is with the 2nd," interrupted Clancy.

"Oh aye? So I guess you might be renewing your acquaintance soon then?" said Simpson, "anyways, Bill here is a good pack horse and can carry four times what Duffy here can, just don't try and ride him. You can borrow him for tonight".

It was a long and steep trek, but once at the front the mules, and Bill, were relieved of their loads, and the fatigue parties journeyed back to ANZAC Cove for yet more supplies.

"This is where we part ways, for now, as I am needed here lads," said Simpson.

"Thanks for your help," said a grateful Clancy, offering his hand.

"Good luck Simmo. See you later mate," said Roo.

"You too lads, you too," said Simpson as he waved them off.

As the platoon journeyed up and down the sunken highway throughout the night, their mates back at Bolton's Ridge were on the far right of the line watching over the end of the ridge, whilst keeping an eye down the slopes at Gaba Tepe.

The 9th Battalion's strength was now down to just six hundred men, and the loss of a platoon for use as fatigues was harshly felt. The only reserve available to them was a section from the Engineers, who were placed with 'D' Company, defending the weakest point on the front line. Due to the shortage of men a new method of defence was enacted. The sector end of the ridge to the beach was held by a number of posts, which were manned by six to twelve men, led by a SNCO. The trench system was well sandbagged and loop holed but, due to a shortage of barbed wire, there were few entanglements to their front, giving the enemy a free run at them should they choose to charge.

Just after midnight on the 19th of May Stowie was surveying the ground to his front, through a loop hole, when the whole area erupted and the sky was illuminated with muzzle flashes from the intense Turkish small arms and machine gun fire. This was a prequel of what was to come.

"Shit!" shouted Stowie as he emptied his magazine in to the darkness.

An endless column of Turks, with bayonets fixed, appeared from the darkness, advancing down the gullies and up the slopes. The whole of the 9th Battalion line joined the fray and raked the ground to their front with rifle and machine gun fire. But the Turks came on undaunted, and other long lines of infantry began to swarm, line after line of the enemy coming steadily forward, while the Australians, standing or sitting on their parapets to get a better view, mowed them down with their murderous fire. The fire fight seemed endless, weapons were heating up and bolts were starting to jam.

"Bloody hell, my gun oil is getting low," said Stowie as he smeared the oil over the working parts of his weapon.

"Mine to," announced Private Thornhill.

But Stowie had an idea.

"Hey Brian have we got any bacon left?" he asked.

"Yeah, but this aint the time for a fry up is it?" exclaimed Private McGregor.

"You bloody dill. We can use the bacon fat to oil our weapons.

Mind you a bacon sandwich wouldn't go amiss either....if we had any bread of course," replied Stowie, winking.

Word quickly spread, and in no time the Aussie front line soon smelt of bacon.

"If anything the bacon should put Abdul off attacking for a bit," said a hopeful soldier.

Until the bacon fat was ready the troops had resorted to firing in pairs, one firing until his weapon overheated or jammed, then passing *that* rifle to his mate for it to cool down, whilst his mate then passed him a fresh rifle. Some of the "passers" complained that they should be shooting rather than gun bearing, but they soon sorted it out.

The Turkish attack eventually petered out. Stowie recalled Clancy's words just before he had departed for the Cove.

"Stay here and rest he says, you'll be safer here he says...not bloody likely!"

As the fatigue parties made their way from post to post the call went out for gun oil. Most parties had *some*, but ensured they stocked up for the next trip.

At 0300 hours, the 77th (Arab) Regiment began advancing across no man's land in two lines. Similar attacks were happening all over the entire front line, with a violent attack, being launched against Quinn's Post, while other assaults were made on the trenches opposite the Nek, on Pope's Hill and on Courtney's Post. This was the enemy's big attempt to drive the ANZACs back to the beach with the hope of surrender or total annihilation. The men could not believe their eyes as they observed the advancing Turks.

"What the hell?" exclaimed Stowie.

"They must think they are at Waterloo with tactics like that," said one of the officers.

The Napoleonic charge, much like the earlier attack, was met by a devastating fire from the ANZACS, who simply demolished the entire regiment. 7th Battery, Australian Field Artillery, who were positioned on the front line, added what can only be described as a huge shotgun, as they fired zero shrapnel, timed to explode on leaving the gun, in to the enemy line; in days gone by this was known as canister shot.

At one point in the battle near Bolton's Ridge a company of Turks were seen massing behind a stone hut in Poppy Valley. The Adjutant, Lieutenant Plant, had requested some co-operative fire from the Battery Commander, or BC, of 7 Battery, whilst also arranging for two platoons from 'C' Company to watch the sides of the building. As the shrapnel burst overhead, those sheltering behind the building ran in all directions, and were picked off by 'C' Company.

After hours of constant defensive fire, calls were going out all over the line for more ammunition. The fatigue parties were doing their best.

The area around Courtney's and Quinn's was the main objective of the enemy attack for, if they could drive a wedge of men between the two posts, it would open a direct path down to the beach and split the ANZACs in two.

As Clancy and his party reached Courtney's Post a huge battle was occurring.

"Right Arch, you blokes get these rounds to the units at Pope's and Quinn's and me and Roo will sort out this place," said Clancy.

The men parted ways and set off along the line with donkeys, and Bill, in tow.

As Roo looked around Courtney's, something wasn't right.

"Where *is* everyone?" he whispered.

There was much gun fire, explosions, and shouts of "Allah", but not an Aussie to be seen.

"They must be moving through the trenches," suggested Clancy as he listened intently to where the loudest battle sounds were coming from, "I think we need to go that way".

Moving left through the elaborate trench system they came across four 14 Battalion men in a reserve trench; solid looking Victorians to a man.

"9th Battalion? What are you blokes doing here? Have they broken through on the right?" asked Private Frank Poliness.

"Fatigues. Delivering ammo. Want some?" answered Clancy.

"Is the Pope a Catholic?" exclaimed Private Bill Howard," thanks sarge; it all helps".

"What's going on?" asked Roo.

"Our officer's just nipped up there to see what Jacka needs?" replied Howard.

"Jacka?" asked Roo.

"Bert Jacka. He's keeping the Abduls in check up there," said Howard.

"By himself? Bloody hell!" replied an astonished Roo.

"Coming over!" came a shout as Lieutenant Crabbe dropped in to the trench.

"Right, Jacka is down there in the communication trench keeping the Turks busy. He says he is willing to charge them if he has the men to back him up. Any volunteers?" said Crabbe, glancing round at the men before him.

The four Victorians volunteered to a man.

"Need any help from two banana benders?" asked Clancy.

"All assistance is appreciated sergeant. You stick with me for now. I'm sure there'll be a job for you soon enough," replied a grateful Crabbe.

"You beauties," said Poliness as he patted the sergeant on the back.

Jacka was close. Crabbe, satisfied with his volunteers, peered round the corner and gave the thumbs up signal to Jacka, who immediately leapt across the communication trench, in full view of the enemy, in to the reserve trench; narrowly avoiding a shot from a vigilant Turk. Jacka took a quick look at the six men, and one officer.

"Not quite the ten I'd hoped for, but beggars can't be choosers eh?" said Jacka as he offered a quick hand shake to the two 9th Battalion men.

Albert Jacka was a Lance Corporal, and a born leader. Because of this, and not out of disrespect to Lieutenant Crabbe, he ordered the men to fix bayonets and follow him. Crabbe didn't mind at all. He admired Jacka's initiative and, besides, he alone knew what awaited them.

Up ahead the Turks had managed to occupy a section of Aussie trench. Jacka intended to expel the interlopers by hook or by crook.

"Come on!" he shouted, racing along the communication trench and leaping over the forward trench on to the fire step.

A single shot rang out and missed. Privates Howard and

Bickley were close behind, but as they leapt in to the forward trench, Howard was killed by three shots to his torso, whilst Bickley was hit in the arm. The other two 14 battalion men saw what had befallen their mates and decided to stay clear of the forward trench...for now. Jacka quickly peered around the corner of the trench and could clearly see Turkish rifles and bayonets waiting for the next leaper.

"This is no bloody good," Jacka thought to himself, then called out to the others to stay where they were.

As suddenly as he had arrived, Jacka sprang from the fire step to safety, he and Private De Araugo dragging the lifeless body of Howard, by the legs, along with them.

Now back with Crabbe and the others, Jacka had a plan. If the others could keep the Turks busy with rifle fire, he would work his way along the reserve trench to the enemy's flank. If the boys could then toss a few grenades over, he would do the rest.

Crabbe looked over to the two Queenslanders.

"Can you blokes throw?" he asked.

"Sir, you're looking at two champion cricketers here," replied Clancy.

"Here you go. When I give you the signal pull the pin and lob these grenades over at the Turks," said Crabbe.

"Mills bombs! You ripper!" said an excited Roo, "I wish we had these up on the ridge".

Sadly, the Dardanelles to those in charge, was just a side show, and a badly armed and supplied one at that. Mills bombs were a rare commodity at Gallipoli, but gratefully received.

Jacka was off like a lizard up a drain pipe. Mindful of being seen he moved fast but stealthily along the main trench, then hoisted himself up on to the parapet, now lying prone in no man's land. As he crawled along the line of sandbags he could see at least half a dozen Turks in the twenty foot section of trench. Private McNally and Roo were detailed as "bowlers" for this over, whilst Clancy joined Poliness and De Araugo as they unleashed round after round up the communication trench in to the wall of the forward trench. It was working, for the Turks remained in the safety of their trench. Meanwhile Roo and McNally were now at the point where Jacka had made his initial lone defence. Jacka was becoming impatient for the diversion, but it was about to arrive. McNally clasped a grenade in his right hand and gripped the pin with the thumb and forefinger of his left. In seconds the pin was out and the grenade was hurtling towards the enemy, the handle flying left as it separated from the bomb, whilst simultaneously arming it. The grenade landed unseen in the enemy trench, but nothing; silence. It was a dud! As McNally cursed with disappointment, Roo lobbed his bomb, which overshot the trench and landed to the rear of the occupants. As it exploded it did not wreak the death which was intended, but caused much confusion and panic as a cloud of dirt and dust rained down on the Turks.

"Bugger!" thought Jacka, but that was it, he had to enact his plan.

Without a thought for his own safety he leapt in to the foggy trench, unseen by the defenders, who were pre-occupied by the hail of bullets coming from the other direction. Within seconds he had bayoneted two Turks, "stick it in, twist it, pull it out", and now commenced firing at the remainder who were packed tightly in the trench. With a 14 Battalion machine gun giving supporting fire above the trench, the Turks were oblivious to Jacka as he expertly fired his Lee Enfield .303 sending five of them to paradise. Five now remained alive, two of whom, in terror, clambered out of the trench, only to be shot by Clancy and Poliness. The remaining three, apparently thinking Jacka part of a larger force, threw down their weapons and raised their hands.

The sun was now rising and the mass attack by the Turks frittered away. Jacka remained on alert for fifteen minutes, whilst guarding his captives. When he was finally relieved by his fellow defenders, they were confronted by a scene of blood and guts, and an exhausted Jacka, who was grateful to his mates and pleased that his plan had worked.

"You are a bloody wonder Bert!" exclaimed Clancy as he reached out and shook his hand.

"I agree, and I'm recommending you for an award," added Crabbe.

"Cheers boss, but we were all just doing our jobs," replied Jacka.

"Hey," interrupted Poliness, "I thought you fellas were champion cricketers?"

"I think in Roo's case it's in his own head," quipped Clancy.

"You want to take some lessons from the 2nd Light Horse at Quinn's," said Jacka, "they've been fielding bombs now for a week".

"Percy's at Quinn's Post?" said Roo, beaming a smile and sense of worry at the same time.

"Percy?" asked Jacka.

"My cousin," replied Roo.

"It sounds like they've been busy up there like us," said Lieutenant Crabbe.

The 2nd Light Horse had indeed been very busy having been detailed to support the 1st Light Horse at Pope's Hill, with 'B' Squadron attached to the 15th Battalion who were holding Quinn's Post. Both were attacked before dawn but, as the whole Corps was on stand to, they were ready. The machine guns at Pope's and Courtney's had been angled to provide covering fire for Quinn's.

The battle along the front line began to peter out at dawn, lasting for about another hour. Of the forty two thousand Turks who dared to venture in to ANZAC territory, more than ten thousand were strewn in no man's land; over three thousand were dead and seven thousand were wounded. The repeated backwards and forwards motion of ANZAC rifle bolts had seen off the attackers, who now withdrew back to their own trenches, pursued hotly by .303 rounds which cracked and thumped in the hazy dawn light.

Simpson and his fellow stretcher bearers had been the unsung heroes, along with the ammunition bearers, journeying up and down the gullies throughout the night, the fatigue parties taking the occasional pot shot here and there at the enemy.

At Quinn's Post, Percy, along with the other defenders, was sending death to the attackers, using bullets faster than they could be delivered. In the half light he spied a party of Aussies, donkey in tow.

"Come on fellas we need ammo here before Johnny Turk gets us!" Percy called out.

"Keep your hair on mate," came a familiar voice from the darkness.

"Arch? Is that you?" said Percy, in disbelief, as he clambered down from the firing step to greet his brother.

As the two brothers laughed and embraced there was no time for pleasantries, for there was work to be done. Archie and his mates got on with the task of passing round the ammo, which was gratefully received.

"Mind if us blokes join in for a bit?" asked Archie.

"Fill your boots boys!" shouted one of the light horsemen.

Peering over the parapet Archie could make out the shadowy figures of hundreds of Turks running across no man's land. BANG! Up, back, forward, down went Archie's bolt as he ejected an empty casing and chambered a live round. BANG! Pretty soon he and his party got their rhythm as they began to drop Turks like rabbits back home on the station. He felt no remorse, for killing was a normal daily occurrence now, and not to be dwelt upon. Turning his head left and right Archie could see that all around him were now members of that fraternity, including his brother, and would deal with the consequences of their actions another day.

As Percy re-charged his magazine he managed a quick question to his brother.

"Where's Roo Arch?"

"Don't worry about him, he and Clance are on fatigues over at Courtney's Post," replied Archie.

Giving a relieved and approving nod, Percy continued his task to his front, unaware of Roo and Clancy's deeds that day.

Once the fighting had ceased along the front line the

ANZACs rested, uneasily, still keeping watch to their front, but glad to be alive. The Turks had managed to reach their objectives in some places, but not quite in others. In all though, they had been driven back by the defenders. Along Quinn's Post enemy bodies were piled high within three feet of the parapets, a sign of how determined an enemy the Turks were. Meanwhile, their faces blackened by the cordite from their weapons, the ANZACs resembled coal miners after a long day down the pit. At Courtney's Roo could see the funny side as he glanced around at the black faces.

"You fellas all look handsome like me now," he joked.

At Quinn's, Percy recognised the unseen danger of the enemy corpses.

"When it's safe we need to drag these poor beggars over and get them buried," he said.

"No point in encouraging the flies eh?" added Archie.

Just then Percy heard a whimpering, groaning sound coming from just over the parapet.

"Sssh! Did you hear that?" said Percy suddenly.

"Hear what?" asked Archie.

"Chuck me that periscope Arch," replied Percy.

As he searched the ground to their immediate front he could see a wounded Turk wriggling amongst the corpses of his comrades.

"Bloody hell. Here take this," said Percy as he offered his rifle to his brother, "everyone cover me but hold your fire, there's a wounded bloke just out here".

Archie grabbed for his brother's legs as he climbed out of the trench, but was too late. Up on the parapet Percy waved his arms high in the air and called out to the Turks who were only ten yards away; "hey Abdul....friend...er....sadiq...sadiq".

His words caught the attention of the Turks, who calmly watched as Percy knelt next to the wounded man, speaking gently to him.

"I'm not going to hurt you mate, I'm going to take you back to your friends," he said, first pointing at the wounded man then drawing his attention by pointing to the Turkish soldiers who watched on; "sadiq.....friend".

The young soldier seemed to understand as Percy gently forced his two arms under the Turk's body then stood up, lifting the man as he went. Walking towards the enemy trenches he continually called out that he was a friend, and as he reached the enemy parapet two soldiers climbed out, unhindered by the light horsemen who looked on.

"Thank you Australia," said one of the soldiers as they took charge of their wounded friend.

"No worries mate," replied Percy as he and the two men carefully lowered the wounded soldier down to the waiting arms of Turkish stretcher bearers.

Good deed done it was time to go. One of the Turks held out a hand of friendship and thanks to Percy, which he happily grasped and shook.

"Why you come fight in my country?" asked the Turk in good, but broken English.

"Buggered if I know mate," replied Percy, "I enlisted to fight the bloody Germans".

"Ah, the Germans, yes. You go fight them. Leave my country," said the Turk.

"I'd love to," said Percy as he waved, turned and strolled back to his own lines.

As Percy calmly dropped back in to the trench he was met with a cheer from some of the occupants, but not all.

"Bloody hell Percy you had us all worried there for a minute," said Trooper Marsh.

"Thanks Boggy but I knew it would be alright," replied Percy.

"How? They didn't know you were rescuing their mate. They could have shot you, then I'd have been another mate down, and I can't have that," said a worried Boggy.

"Don't worry mate I'm not going anywhere," replied Percy, 'oh, by the way, this is my brother Archie and some of his mates from 9 Battalion".

"Pleased to know you all. I'm Boggy," said Trooper Marsh, nodding and shaking hands with Archie and his party.

"I don't remember you from Egypt," said Archie.

"No, I arrived with the new draft just before we came here," replied Boggy.

"So...why the name Boggy?" enquired Archie.

"That's an easy one. My last name is Marsh, so Boggy Marsh.......do you get it?" replied Boggy with a grin.

"Ohhhhh yeah, I do. But that's not very nice is it?" said Archie, looking firmly at Percy who shrugged his shoulders.

"It wasn't me mate," replied Percy.

"Well, what's your first name? Surely we can find a better nick name than that," asked Archie.

"My name is Pete," replied Boggy.

The penny finally dropped.

"Pete Marsh? As in *Peat* Marsh?" asked Archie.

"Yep. So there was no escaping the name at all eh? Anyway, I like it," said the stocky Englishman, "and to make it worse guess where I was born?"

Archie scratched his head.

"England?" he replied.

"Of course I was born in England, but where?" asked Boggy.

"Buggered if I know mate," replied Archie.

"Norfolk," said Boggy.

"Is that significant then?" asked Archie, still none the wiser.

"Norfolk is famous for its waterways and marshlands, so as you can see, with a name like Pete Marsh my fate was sealed from the start," replied Boggy.

The time eventually came for the fatigue parties to regroup and return for more supplies. Each bade farewell to their new mates and, in Archie's case, to his brother.

"Say g'day to Roo and Clance for me," called Percy as his brother made his way along the trench.

"Great to meet you Bert.......fellas," said Clancy with an acknowledging nod.

"See you again boys," replied Jacka, with a cheeky wink.

The trench system from Quinn's to Pope's met at a junction to a sunken road, which led down to the Cove. Sergeant McBride had pre-arranged a rendezvous at the junction and, sure enough, the three groups met up and became one again, comparing the battles in which they had all taken part.

"Glad to know that Percy is alright Arch," said Clancy.

The small arms and artillery fire continued to echo along the peninsula, and the ever present danger from enemy snipers remained. As they approached Shrapnel Gully they were greeted by an unusual sight.

"Look," said Roo, pointing, "isn't that Duffy...Simmo's donkey?"

As they neared the animal he did not seem himself, a bit like a dog who had misplaced his owner. Clancy took hold of Duffy's reins and led him down the track, and there they found their friend, John Simpson, lying face down, with blood pouring from an exit wound on his back.

"Bloody hell mate!" yelled Archie as he and Roo ran over to their mate and gently rolled him over.

The hero of Gallipoli, a man who, in just a few weeks had become a legend to all, was dead, shot through the chest.

"Do you think he felt it?" asked Roo.

"I hope not," replied Archie, "looks like a single round through the heart".

"Poor bastard," said Clancy as he searched the heights around them, "it was probably a sniper, so let's grab poor Simmo there, and get out of here".

Loading Simpson gently over the back of his donkey, the boys walked solemnly back to the beach. All whom they encountered recognised John Simpson and removed their head dress in respect; some bowed their heads while others made the sign of the cross on their chest.

As they laid him down on the sand at ANZAC Cove, the platoon stood in silent thought as they honoured John Simpson with their own silent prayers.

"There'll never be another like him. I hope they remember

him. I hope Australia remembers him," said Archie, "his poor mother; what will she do now I wonder?"

"No mate. They reckon he personally saved three hundred of our blokes.......the man with the donkey eh?" said Clancy.

Turkish artillery had been dominant throughout the offensive, coming from all directions and landing in both the forward and reserve trenches. Thankfully for the 3rd Brigade, *and* the 9th Battalion, the Indian Mountain Battery had kept the guns at Gaba Tepe silent. The enemy barrage finally relented around noon, although they kept up their usual harassing fire. The Brigade had accounted for over six hundred enemy dead, with a third of that number lying to the front of the 9th Battalion lines. Although *never* good news, it was a miracle that the battalion had only suffered sixteen dead and twenty five wounded; the majority of those being attributed to the enemy artillery. Indeed, from the whole Corps, one hundred and sixty ANZACs were dead and four hundred and sixty eight wounded; a far cry from the Turkish losses.

At Quinn's Post it was time for a 'vigilant' rest, as things had quietened down; for Quinn's Post standards that is. All enemy attempts to break through had been repulsed. Even the ever present snipers seemed to have taken the rest of the day off. That said, the defenders rested whilst keeping a constant watch.

"I'm flamin' buggered," exclaimed Chugger as he slobbed down on to a pile of sandbags next to their mate Boggy Marsh.

"You're not the only one mate," replied Percy, handing Chugger and Boggy some billy tea.

"Cheers," said a grateful Chugger as he took a sip of the piping hot brew.

"They had Mills Bombs at Courtney's you know," said Percy.

"Lucky bastards. We could do with some of those; or just something," replied Boggy.

"Well, at least the cricket ball bombs haven't come over for a while eh?" said a relieved Percy.

"Bloody hell Perce, you've done it now….." said Chugger.

"Done what?" asked a confused Percy.

"Broken the moz…..tempted fate, as me old mum used to say," replied Chugger.

"You're not *superstitious* are you mate?" asked Percy, "just drink your brew. There's nothing like a good cuppa to make you feel good in yourself; and that's one from *my* mum".

"You're mum was right there mate," said Chugger.

"How so?" asked Percy.

"Well, this is definitely *nothing* like a good cuppa," joked Chugger.

"Cheeky sod," laughed Percy.

As the three men sipped their tea, something solid hit the back wall of the trench and bounced on to the floor. Percy was immediately up on his feet shouting "BOMB!" and pulling the sandbag from under his mates and tossing it on to the object, whilst instinctively throwing himself to the ground, dragging Chugger and Boggy down with him.

"Told yer…" whispered Chugger.

The three men, and those in close proximity, waited in anticipation for the explosion, but it did not come.

"Go take a look Perce," said Chugger.

"Oh, cheers mate," uttered Percy as he stood up and slowly edged his way towards the sandbag.

"Go on then...." Boggy called out.

Percy glanced back at Chugger and Boggy, made an obscene gesture with his fingers, then quickly picked up the sandbag and threw himself to the ground.

"It's not a bomb, it's a tin....look," said Chugger, pointing.

Climbing to his feet and dusting himself off, Percy bent down and picked up the tin. As he opened it he couldn't help but smile. The tin contained a pack of Turkish cigarettes, some herbs and spices, and a note.

"Listen to this," said Percy, "Australia are good soldiers. A gift from a Turkish friend".

"Would you believe it? Still what's a few bullets and bombs between friends eh?" said Boggy.

Thinking Boggy to be a bit ungrateful, Chugger promptly elbowed him in the sides, then called out "good on yer Jacko!"

"Hey, chuck us one of those fags mate. Anything's gotta be better than this camel dung that we've got," said Boggy.

"Here you go Boggy. I don't smoke anyway," said Percy, tossing the pack to his friend, "what shall we give *them*?"

"How about a tin of bully?" suggested Chugger.

"Really? Do you *want* them to attack again?" joked Boggy.

"You're welcome Jacko!" shouted Percy as he lobbed a tin of Fray Bentos in to the enemy trench.

"That's it mate. You've probably smashed some bloke's *head* in with that!" laughed Boggy.

Much discussion was heard coming from the Turks, then thud, the unopened bully beef tin was returned.

"There's no pleasing some people", came an Aussie voice.

"Yeah. We've got feelings you know," shouted another.

"You're lucky it wasn't a bomb," said Boggy.

"There's still time mate," came another voice from the Aussie trench; this was met with general laughter all around, even in the enemy trench.

"It doesn't seem right taking their stuff," said Percy.

"How about some of those biccies your mum sent?" suggested Boggy.

"Well, I was keeping them for us, but, bugger it," replied Percy.

Making use of the Turkish tin, Percy loaded it with as many biscuits as he could. Adding a note which said simply, "You're welcome Jacko," he tossed the tin over to the Turks. After a few minutes it was apparent that their enemy was pleased with *this* delivery.

"Thank you Australia.....very nice," came a shout from the opposing trench.

On the 20th of May the ANZACs were working hard, rebuilding their damaged trenches and dugouts, whilst the fatigue parties, along with the Indian Mule Drivers, were up and down the slopes re-supplying the battalions. Turkish medical staff, under the flag of the Red Crescent, were clambering out in to no man's land all over the front line, unhindered by Aussie gunfire, as were ANZAC stretcher parties, searching for those who were still alive and in need of medical aid. For the most part the ANZACs were rescuing fallen Turks, for their own side had remained on the defensive in the trenches. In the end, the uniform wasn't important, just a friend or foe in need of help.

Being at the far right of the line the 9th Battalion had heard nothing of the unofficial cease fires. During the mid afternoon

Turkish burial parties were seen to the front of Bolton's Ridge. They were allowed to carry on whilst the 9th Battalion tended to their own who had fallen to the front of the line.

At around 1830 hours Stowie spotted a worrying sight through his binoculars; large numbers of shining bayonets moving through the enemy trenches just to the rear of their stretcher parties.

"You cheeky buggers," said Stowie, to himself.

He reported the incident to Lieutenant Young. Apparently similar movements were occurring all along the Brigade front line, resulting in stand to being ordered. Within thirty minutes the Turks showed their hand, a company sized force rushing, bayonets fixed, towards 'C' Company. Firing immediately broke out, causing a knee jerk ripple effect along the Brigade front, the Turks replying with an artillery bombardment along the Brigade trenches. The Aussies were livid that their hard work rebuilding their trenches was being undone and let rip with volley upon volley of sustained and accurate rifle fire at the advancing Turks.

"Bastards!" was the general cry.

The attack lasted for an hour, the Turks gaining nothing, except more grieving families.

After this devious action by the Turks all temporary cease fires were halted by General Birdwood, who then sent a written communicate to the Turkish hierarchy telling them in no uncertain terms that if they wanted an armistice in order to bury their dead, it had to go via official channels.

As a result, on the 24th of May, all across the front line the guns fell silent and would remain so from 0730 hours to 1630 hours. At Bolton's, fifty 9th Battalion men were dispatched in to no man's land to keep the Turks away from the Brigade parapets, whilst two hundred Brigade men were sent out to bury the dead. Similar actions were repeated all over ANZAC.

At Quinn's Post it was more of a challenge to keep prying eyes away due to the short distance between the trenches. On all fronts the majority of the dead were Turks, with most of the remainder being ANZACs who had fallen on the first day. The bodies lay thick over the ground, causing the burial parties to step around or over their dead mates and comrades. The majority were buried just where they were lying, for when they started to remove the bodies the already terrible stench became worse. That said, the armistice was welcomed by all, for the smell of the rotting corpses wafting over the trenches, and the swarms of flies, was becoming unbearable.

The temporary peace that had broken out was also a great opportunity for the fatigue parties to continue their re-supply. The lack of sniper and artillery fire made movement along the gullies and tracks a much faster affair, so they struck while the iron was hot. The twenty five men from the battalion had now been detailed to re-supply their own brigade, something which didn't escape the attention of the men.

"I think we might be back with the battalion soon boys," said Roo.

"About bloody time too," added Clancy, in his usual colourful manner.

Pausing in the trenches to observe the events in no man's land they watched as foes exchanged pleasantries and souvenirs. But, all ears pricked up as a shot suddenly rang out. Two Turkish soldiers were making a dash for the 9th Battalion trenches; the enemy side was appalled, hence the attempt at shooting their own men. The soldiers were unarmed, so were allowed through. As they ran they called out in broken English, "surrender...not Turks...Armenian". As they dropped in to the trench they were confronted by Clancy and the boys, and began enthusiastically shaking hands with everyone, kissing the Aussies on the cheeks, much to their disgust and embarrassment. Instinctively Clancy held out a hand as a barrier.

"Kiss *me* and I'll drop yer, yer bastards!" he announced.

The two men seemed to understand and backed off. The Armenians may have begun to outstay *their* welcome, being escorted to the Battalion Command Post for interrogation, but the fatigue men were suddenly popular.

"What goodies have you got for us today boys?" asked one hopeful soldier.

"We've got some fresh meat and uniform bits and pieces," replied Roo.

"You beauty!" came a shout.

The next day the platoon was back in their own lines again.

"Must be time for a brew. Hey Stowie, you've been doing nothing while we've been gone. Make yourself useful and get the billy on," Clancy said to his mate.

"Would you like me to cook your dinner too yer lazy bugger?" joked Stowie.

"Yeah, why not? What are we having?" replied Clancy.

Sitting in the reserve trench eating lunch felt quite relaxing that day, especially considering the busy month they had all had. The views across the Aegean Sea were beautiful.

"The view up here is even better than from the beach eh Roo?" said Clancy.

Roo was in a world of his own gazing at the many navy ships off shore. A particular favourite for all was 'HMS Triumph', having done such splendid work at Gallipoli, especially for the infantry on the hills, with the most effective, and abundance of, fire support than any other ship. Roo suddenly rose to his feet, grasping Clancy's shoulder. Both watched in disbelief as a torpedo struck 'HMS Triumph' right mid ship on the starboard side.

"Bloody hell..." exclaimed Clancy as he and Roo watched the disaster unfurl.

Within eleven minutes the Triumph turned turtle and sank. Many sailors were swimming about, Torpedo boats and pinnaces trying to get as close as they could to rescue them. Artillery support from the Royal Navy was indeed a necessary thing to the allied infantry, but the Germans were putting paid to that, or at least attempting to. All who witnessed the attack fell silent, even Percy at Quinn's Post had been shocked and surprised at what he saw. But, sadly, the 'Triumph' would not be the last victim of marauding submarines with 'HMS Majestic' being sunk two days later off Helles.

By the end of May, the 2nd Light Horse Regiment had moved on to Pope's Hill. It was a much quieter spot than Quinn's, but no less dangerous, with snipers accounting for three dead and fifteen wounded. As Percy looked over the enemy trenches through his loop hole he was frustrated that the Turks rarely presented themselves as targets, so decided to take it out on a periscope which had suddenly appeared above the enemy parapet. Taking quick and careful aim Percy fired his weapon, shattering the offending instrument, resulting in much shouting from the Turks.

"Stick that up your Turkish arse!" Percy shouted, causing a ripple of laughter along the Light Horse lines.

Percy's actions did not bode well for *anything* which dared to rear itself above the sandbags, as both sides now entered in to a phase of tit for tat periscope killings.

9

The Long Dusks of Summer

On the 1st of June the brigade fatigue parties were returned to their respective units, having ably carried out their various manual labour, engineering and delivery tasks. Fetch and carry was now down to the individual battalions to organise. As the platoon, led by Lieutenant Ponsonby, arrived back in their lines they were greeted with applause and humorous shouts of "back from the dunny are you?" In reality the rest of the battalion knew what they had been about for the past month, and had heard of their deeds at Quinn's and Courtney's Posts. They were impressed and also grateful for keeping them re-supplied with all that they needed to survive and fight the Turks.

Life all over the lines became one of improving the trenches, mostly during the night, and digging saps, or corridors, forward of the firing line in order to create a new row of front line trenches. Men were also detailed to erect barbed wire entanglements in no man's land, a dangerous yet essential task.

Because of the low level vegetation, which was abundant on the slopes, observation and listening were the order of the day, as the vegetation could easily camouflage any enemy who may try to crawl towards their lines. From day one the men slept in their clothes, a normal practice for deployed troops, for fear of literally being caught with their pants down should they be attacked. Pretty soon the men became experts in recognising anything out of the ordinary in no man's land.

At 0500 hours the following day the boys were back to the reality of life on the front line. It was a beautiful morning, the sea like a mill-pond, but anyone lucky enough to be asleep was very soon awakened by a merry old artillery duel. The allied Destroyers were pumping them in, whilst enemy's replies were landing pretty close to where Clancy and his section were at rest, bits of lead and shell falling all around. Coupled with that was a perfect tornado of machine gun and rifle fire. The men had never heard such a furious storm before, and could scarcely hear the screech of the shells amidst the clatter and spit of the bullets.

"Welcome back boys," said Stowie.

"Do you think the Turks are getting a bit nervous," said Archie, "or is this a warm up before a big attack?"

All in all the counter battery fire was really making things somewhat uncomfortable for all in the trenches at that moment in time, with shells falling to the right, to the left, in front of, and behind the battalion positions; all falling within a hundred yards.

"Look, even the hospital ship is lying much closer in today, almost as if they know something we don't," said Roo as he pointed towards the ships anchored off the coast.

"I have my suspicions that there is a bit of subterfuge going on here chaps," said Lieutenant Ponsonby, "possibly getting the Turks used to fierce artillery barrages".

"So, you think something big is coming mate?" asked Clancy.

The officer nodded.

"Yes. Not just yet, but soon".

The cry of "STAND TO!" rang out along the front line...but luckily there *was* no attack.

Up at Quinn's Post a former miner, in the 15th Battalion, had reported hearing the sound of digging below the surface. He was correct as the Turks had begun to burrow under the allied trenches in order to plant and explode mines. The threat was taken seriously and soon volunteers were called for from anyone who had been a miner before the war. The 2nd Light Horse Regiment furnished twelve ex miners who, under the leadership and guidance of Sergeant Crain, worked exceedingly hard, succeeding to annoy the enemy by managing to detonate explosives and blowing in a few of the their tunnels which had come worryingly close to the trenches at Quinn's. Cheers and laughter regularly erupted around the post increasing the annoyance of the Turks.

As he sipped from his canteen, Boggy raised a cheeky toast to the Turks, crying out "up your bum Jacko," resulting in more cheers from all in ear shot.

As the laughter subsided one of the regiment's newly arrived officers, Lieutenant Cuthbert Jones, entered their trench from one of the saps. This young officer was of the old school and had not yet grasped the idea of the mateship which was developing amongst *all* ANZACs. He still believed in the *us* and them, and to know one's place.

"You men!" he growled, "keep the noise down! Do you want the Turks to hear you?"

"You've got to be joking mate!" replied Chugger, "take a look around you. The bloody Turks are ten yards that way, so I think by now they know where we are don't you?!"

Lieutenant Jones was taken aback by Chugger's anger, but could see from the expression on the soldier's face that he was not happy, and was not going to give any ground. Coupled with cries from all around of "does your mother know you're out?" he decided to carry on his tour.

"*Really?*" he replied, "I shall have to see for myself!"

"Don't go sticking your head up or Jacko will have it for brekkie mate," said Percy.

The young officer, having recently joined the regiment at Gallipoli was still inexperienced in the ways of the Australian soldiers, and those of the enemy. Like many of his, so called class, no one should tell their "betters" what to do, and he was certainly not going to take the advice of a mere soldier. As the officer neared one of the loop holes, Boggy prodded Percy to get his attention.

"He's going to get his head shot off if he isn't careful," he said, pointing at Lieutenant Jones.

"Bloody hell! Sir, get back!" Percy shouted to the officer.

But his cries were muffled by a sudden crack and thump from the Turkish side.

Lieutenant Jones died an easy, but unnecessary and stupid, death. He had his hands in his pockets, as he leaned in to the loop hole, when an explosive high velocity bullet struck him in the head. All around watched in horror as the bullet literally lifted the top of his head and laid it in his slouch hat. He still had his hands in his pockets as he crumpled dead on the ground. His death was instantaneous. Yet another senseless casualty.

Percy shook his head as the men gathered round the slain officer.

"When will they *ever* learn?" he thought to himself.

The officer's lifeless body was carried down to Shrapnel Green where, along with others who that day had learned the great secret, he was given a military funeral.

Midnight on the 29th was payback time by Jacko, as a large mine blew in part of Quinn's Post, sending rubble, sandbags, and an unfortunate Sergeant Crain flying; although he was not seriously injured. He did, however, earn the nick name 'Cyclone Crain' due to his fast and sudden arrival on the wind of the blast, which he accepted like the good sport that he was, wearing it like a badge of honour.

The shockwave of the blast reverberated all around the immediate front line and didn't go unnoticed at Pope's Hill. Shouts of "Stand to!" went up everywhere, as Jacko took full advantage of the dust and confusion, launching an assault, managing to occupy part of Quinn's Post. The 13th and 15th Battalions counter attacked with rifle and bayonet, firing, stabbing, clubbing, slashing. It was a bloody affair. At Pope's they were close enough to see what was developing at Quinn's. Percy, Chugger and Boggy were on duty in the fire trench and began to lay down rapid rifle fire at the attacking Turks. Pretty soon they were joined by the post's machine guns with their rat tat tat tat, spitting death at Jacko. Their fire, combined with the counter attacks by the infantry at Quinn's, succeeded in driving Jacko back to his own trenches.

The following day Pope's Hill and the gully between *it*, and Russel's Top, became the 'property' of the 1st Light Horse Brigade, which consisted of the 1st, 2nd and 3rd Light Horse Regiments, the three regiments rotating between support and rest; not that there was much rest to be had, unfortunately. On this day the 1st Light Horse relieved the 2nd from the firing line, much to the delight and relief of the men.

"Don't get too comfy boys, there's work to be done," announced a young Lieutenant.

"Will you be helping sir?" came a sarcastic voice.

There certainly was no rest for the wicked as the men dug new trenches and improved the old ones, as well as fetching essential food, water, ammunition and other items from the beach.

It was early morning, and Percy's section was lugging their precious cargoes up the steep slopes from the Cove, having set off in the darkness. In the first flush of the dawn the prospect on land and sea was beautiful, and everything seemed calm and peaceful. Looking south along the peninsula, it was difficult for the men to comprehend that the land before them was in the grip of war, and that hostile forces were facing one another. There was nothing that would indicate to the uninitiated that a great Turkish army barred the way of the ANZACs and their allies; no soldiers were visible, no camps to be seen. But it was all there, dug in and invisible.

"If I didn't know better I'd say I was back home in Kilcoy," said Percy as he gazed in to the distance, "a bit drier here though".

In the distance, out of shot from the soldiers and artillery, he could see tiny figures working, as they had always done, in the fields at the top of the slopes. War or no war, the work had to be done. Further round to the right he could just make out a handful of camels grazing peacefully, and the up-curling smoke wreaths revealed three small stone dwellings which had most likely existed in that spot for generations. His day dream was soon shattered by the vicious and deafening crash of an 18-pounder shell as it pitched into one of the enemy trenches at the top of the ridge. The war was definitely here, the reminder being the sight of a fleet of warships, pinnaces, hospital ships, transports, and smaller craft lying close in the waters around the various bays and coves. As the men continued their hard climb back to their post Percy couldn't help but wonder how the men on the first day had managed to scale these hills whilst under fire, all the time moving forward and up. But they did, and here they were scattered around this once peaceful land.

Percy and his party were greeted warmly by their mates for they had not only brought with them essential stores, but the mail, which was quickly distributed amongst the men.

Percy's face beamed as he read his letter from Lil and produced a small photograph.

"Hey look boys, this is Lil, and our son Frank," said Percy proudly, "isn't she beautiful? And look at Frank, he's learning how to ride".

"A chip off the old block eh? Can I see?" said Davo holding out his hand.

Percy passed him the picture.

"Wonderful mate," said Davo, "you must be proud".

Percy smiled and nodded.

"Jacko has been up to his tricks again while you were gone," said Boggy.

"The Turks? What have they done now?" asked Percy.

"Well boys, just after you left last night the Turks were holding up a shovel for us to shoot at; they like playing jokes, but they went too far," Boggy explained, "just when one of our blokes got a shot off a sniper got him clean through the head".

"So they were waiting for one of us to stick our heads up...the bastards!" exclaimed Percy.

"That's not the end of though mate," added Boggy, "this morning at stand to, we could see one of them walking along the top of their trench; we thought it was a daring thing to do. We shot at him and down he would go, and after a while up he would come again. Of course Jacko would return the fire. Well, it had us puzzled, and pretty soon we found out it was a dummy man; it looked like a genuine one in the dark. The sarge told us to stop firing at it because he reckons the reason they did it was so they could tell by the flash of our rifles the exact spot where we were".

"They must be getting desperate to kill us I reckon," said Chugger.

On the 3rd of June at Bolton's Ridge there was a sudden scream of "Allah!" as a company of Turks began racing towards the 3rd Brigade's lines. A cry of "Stand to!" went out to all. 'B' Company were resting in the reserve trench at the time, Roo making some tea, Clancy was sleeping, whilst Archie was writing a letter home.

"Bloody hell, can't a bloke get any sleep round here? Flamin' Abduls!" exclaimed Clancy as he picked up his rifle and, with the rest of the platoon, made his way along the communication trench to the fire trench.

As he rested his rifle on the sandbagged parapet Archie turned to Roo and said, "some people will do anything to make me clean my rifle!"

"Didn't Clancy say the same thing not so long ago?" asked Roo.

"Yeah mate he did," replied Archie, as he chambered a round and opened fire on the advancing enemy, "anyhow, let's get them dirty and see these buggers off".

"Come on, we'll give you Allah!" shouted Clancy, still reeling at having his sleep disturbed.

No matter how eager you may be to taste the experience of war, it is no sweet experience to be awakened from your short snatches of slumber by a shake and an order to "Stand to!" or "Every man to his post!" But here they were again, officers hurrying up and down the trenches and men springing to their posts, blazing away at the enemy, magazine after magazine emptied and recharged, each muzzle flash representing a swift messenger of death that perhaps will strike agony to some unlucky Turk who just happens to be in line with it. But strike they did, their rapid and accurate rifle fire downing most of the enemy in their tracks and sending the remainder scurrying back to whence they came. As fast as it began, the battle was over. Then came the order, "Cease fire!" Rifles hot to the touch, the boys collectively heaved a sigh of relief and felt safer, because looking left and right they knew that they were *all* still alive and uninjured. The floor of the trench gave a hint as to the enormous amount of small arms ammunition alone used in even so short a fray, as it was littered with heaps of empty chargers and cartridge cases.

"Well that broke the monotony didn't it?" said Stowie.

"Not for me mate, I was sleeping. Bastards!" replied Clancy.

"They certainly are goers the Turks," said Roo, "charging forward like that. They didn't have a hope in hell".

"Perhaps they'll learn a lesson and bugger off then," replied Clancy.

During the hours of darkness the artillery batteries to the rear of the 9th Battalion carried out fire missions on pre-arranged targets. The racket that they made was not welcomed by those, like Sergeant McBride, who were trying to sleep...again. On this evening a loud explosion was met by screams and shouts of "stretcher bearer!" as a friendly shell had exploded prematurely over Battalion Headquarters. Fifteen men, including Major Salisbury, had been wounded, as had several members of 7 Battery, whose positions were to the rear of the 9th Battalion.

The rest of the night was spent evacuating the wounded and shoring up the damaged trenches and dugouts; so not much sleep again.

Now that summer had arrived, the weather at Gallipoli had

suddenly become very hot, and was compounded more by the heat of the sun bouncing off the rocky and dry landscape, making life difficult for all. Another drawback was the scarcity of water and fuel, the lack of the latter meaning that the troops had resorted to burning the green scrub which grew in abundance everywhere, in order to cook. What wells they had were now drying up, so units had to rely entirely on water being transported to them from the beach. The majority of the drinking water came by ship from Alexandria, and each man was allowed a quart per day. Well water was used for the making of tea rather than waste the imported water. As a standalone liquid this well water was foul, but the men agreed that it was alright when boiled. No doubt if there had been some sort of Board of Health on the peninsula the water would have been condemned.

The supply chain for the MEF was also slowing down. The meat ration was reduced, whilst the sickly and watery jam ration was increased. The men were getting weary, and thinner.

Roo held out the waistline of his trousers to show how much weight he had lost since the landing.

"I don't mind hard work, but give me some grub," he said.

As Clancy entered from the communication trench he looked Roo up and down.

"Bloody hell mate if you turned to the side you'd look like a crack in the wall," he joked as he held up a huge sack, "but all might be saved. Look what I've got".

Archie's eyes lit up.

"The mail!" he said, "I hope there are a couple of parcels from mum in there".

"A couple?!" exclaimed Clancy, "mate, there are two for you, two for Roo, and, you'll never believe it, two for me as well".

The post was distributed quickly to the men, then, the three friends sat down and opened their various letters and packages. Clancy was particularly grateful to his mates who had introduced him to their family and had helped him with his new found writing skills.

"I wish I had known your mum and dad when I was a boy, they are wonderful people," said Clancy, "and they write very nicely in their letter".

"Thanks mate. Yes they are, but you *will* see them soon enough," replied Archie, "and besides they want me to pass on the offer of a job on the station. So how do you fancy being a stockman at Doriray when we get home?"

Clancy paused and a tear welled in his eye.

"That would be bonza mate. I can never thank them enough," Clancy said as he nudged Roo, "see mate, you've got me for life now".

"Well, you'd better write back and accept then mate," said Roo offering a brotherly hand shake.

"I'll do it now...er...if you blokes don't mind giving me a hand with spelling that is," replied Clancy.

"No worries mate," said Archie.

"Hey Arch, Aunty Doris says little Frank is doing well. He's learning to ride," said Roo.

"That's great news. I wish we were there to see it. Lil must be proud," replied Archie.

"Who's Frank?" asked Stowie.

"Oh, he's my brother Percy's young lad, and Lil is his wife," said Archie.

"I bet he's missing them like blazes," replied Stowie.

"We all are mate," said Archie.

Stowie was getting a little curious and impatient for the boys to unwrap their parcels.

"So? What's in the parcels boys?" he asked.

Archie rolled his eyes as the three ripped open the packages, "patience is a virtue mate".

"Oh beauty!" cried Clancy as he held up a huge fruit cake, "and look, some raw oats too".

"Oats?" asked Stowie.

All three had received the same.

"Hang on there's a note. Nope, it's a recipe," said Archie, "Mum says if we mix jam and butter with the oats we can make some tasty biccies; a bit like hers".

"We just need some butter," said Roo.

"I've got some," announced Stowie, "scrounged it from the cooks the other day".

"Ripper!" shouted Clancy, "let's get the pan on then".

Unbeknown to the troops at ANZAC there was some positive news which would soon be coming their way. Bread! The ANZAC cooks had set up a bakery on Imbros and had begun to ship bread every second day to the Australian and New Zealand soldiers at Gallipoli. The British, a little late in the day, soon followed suit. To all, the bread was very welcome.

One of the biggest problems that the troops had battled with since their arrival at Gallipoli was the flies. Now, because of the thousands of dead who still lay where they fell, the flies were swarming in their millions, moving from rotting corpses to the living...and their food.

As Archie prized open a tin of jam, the flies were already queuing up on his bayonet waiting to claim their prize. Once the lid was open, the top of the jam became a moving black mass of buzzing insects, each fighting for the delights that were before them. There was nothing to be done. The men were hungry and malnourished, so if a fly did not move quickly enough it was devoured by a hungry ANZAC.

Despite their malnutrition the fatigue parties had performed a marvellous task of constructing a sunken artillery road. This meant that the guns and ammunition could now be transported directly to the front line. Allied artillery at Gallipoli was not the big guns being used on the Western Front, for the terrain would not allow it. The Turks, however, did not suffer that handicap, having both large calibre guns and excellent positions, which commanded the peninsula. Luckily for the allies the Turks were not that flush with artillery ammunition, otherwise they could have blown the invaders off their shores with ease.

Periscopes had been in use on the peninsula for some time now, but Trooper Eubank from the 2nd Light Horse Regiment, had made them even better by creating a periscope rifle. It was such a simple, yet brilliant, device and allowed soldiers in the trenches to take accurate aim and fire without exposing themselves to the enemy. Eubank had adapted the periscope attaching the upper mirror in such a manner that it looked along the sights of the rifle. The view to the front was then reflected in the lower mirror, into which the firer would observe, then use an attached length of wire to pull the trigger...ingenious! The idea was quickly taken up by the "factory" down at the cove and was soon on general issue in many front line trenches; in particular places such as Quinn's Post, where the close proximity of the enemy trenches had made it virtually impossible to fire a shot during the daylight hours. Various other weapons were also reaching the defenders, such as the Trench Mortar, consisting of two feet of piping on a stand, and fired by a small charge. Tassie Smith and Trooper Birch became experts at Quinn's, regularly lobbing bombs in to the enemy trenches. They even had a go with the Japanese bomb thrower, another form of mortar, but much more powerful and effective, which Abdul came to fear, watching as its deadly projectile was launched high in to the air, falling straight down in to their trenches, smashing everything in its path. But, like the enemy artillery, bombs for it were few and far between.

For the rest of June the Australians and New Zealanders helped the Turks to remember that they were still there, by conducting night raids all over the front line.

Lieutenant Ponsonby and his platoon were out in no man's land again, but this time they were equipped with the newly issued Jam Tin Bombs. Crouching low as they left the trench they were all mindful that there was a bright half moon that evening, great for lighting their way, but just as good for any Turks who may be observing. It was an eerie night as the men looked out over the ground before them. They could see everything almost as plain as day, but nothing seemed out of place. As they crept slowly along in extended line, the moon began to wane and darkness began to set in. There was still no sound or sign from the enemy. What were they doing? Why were they so silent? Had they left their trenches? Were they silently creeping up to take ours? As each section moved in to their individual blob formation they drew closer to the enemy trenches, but still no sound, not a shout, nor a whisper. Lieutenant Ponsonby raised his hand and halted the platoon, then gave the signal. Every third man struck a match and lit the fuse on their bombs, then after a quick count to three, just to be sure, ten hissing jam tins were tossed all along the front line of the Turkish trench. There was no time for stealth now as the platoon ran like hell back to their own lines, giggling like naughty schoolboys, to the sounds of explosions and cries of pain to their rear. The enemy were sleeping. There would be hell to pay for someone!

As the last man dropped back in to the trench the Turks unleashed a volley of machine gun and rifle fire. But they were too late. The ANZACs were safely home, their *reminder* mission complete.

Home today for the platoon was the fire trench, but even here there was *some* respite.

"Hey Arch. What you got for brekkie?" asked Clancy.

"I've got the latest delicacy...blow flies and bully beef," Archie replied.

"Yeah? What's it like?" chuckled Clancy.

"The flies are fine, but the bully leaves a bit to be desired," replied Archie dryly.

"Yeah, same here," said Clancy, "perhaps we should say a few prayers for something a bit tastier".

"Just something *different* would do me boys," added Roo.

"Speaking of praying, the Turks must be really religious, calling out Allah when they attack," said Stowie.

"It's just another name for God, same as ours. We *all* think God is on *our* side," said Archie.

"Honest Arch? It's the same God?" replied Clancy.

Archie nodded.

"Well, I'll be buggered," said an astonished Clancy.

"Do *your* people have a God Roo?" Stowie asked.

"*My* people?" laughed Roo, "I was brought up a Christian, went to Sunday school and all that, you know. The Taylor family are *my* people".

"No, sorry, I meant your Mum's people," replied Stowie.

"The Jinibara?" said Roo, "they are more spiritual and about the land, but I *personally* believe that there is something or someone, a Devine being, but not what we are taught in church".

"What do you mean mate?" asked Clancy.

"Do you really think that the Bible is the word of God? It was written a thousand years ago by those who think they are better than us in order to keep us in line. They teach religion and God as something to be feared. But God, or the belief in God is about love, not hate or fear. Did you ever read or hear about Jesus preaching hate?"

"No mate. That's true, I never have," replied Clancy.

"Priests and the upper class call my people heathens, and punish them for their beliefs. *We* don't tell you how to live your lives and who to worship, yet you fellas are told that black fellas are bad people because we are not Christians. Hell, look at your history. None of you blokes from the northern lands can live together. You have different religions and types of Christianity and hate each other for it. You persecute other people for *their* religion and force *your* ways onto them. That's not love as I see it," said Roo.

"So, what do you think of our ancestors turning up in Australia?" asked Jacko, joining in the conversation.

"Look mate, I have no problem with it. All I ask is that you respect our ways and customs and work *with* us, not against us. Look at Archie here, and Percy. They are my brothers. They see me for *who* I am not what I am. Simple as that," explained Roo.

"Well, you'll always be *our* brother too mate," said Clancy.

From around the trench came shouts of "here, here," as all present shook Roo's hand and patted his shoulder.

"Let's hope that this war here changes things for the better and when we all get back home we can all live as one nation...Aussies together," said Stowie.

"It's a shame the curry powder ran out boys," said Archie, changing the subject.

"Yeah we sure need some herbs or something to liven up this tinned stuff," added Roo, "I sure miss Aunty Doris's Sunday dinners".

"Where ya gonna find herbs here you dill, I can't see any local stores about can you?" said Stowie.

"Dill? See you've found one already," laughed Roo.

"Well actually there *is* a local store about forty yards over yonder," said Archie as he began to slowly climb on to the parapet, "cover my backside will yer boys?"

"What the blazes are you doing Arch?" said Roo, but it was too late, Archie had crawled over the sand bags and out of the trench and was heading towards some plants he could see in the distance.

"Bloody hell….stand to," Clancy whispered.

"What's he doing?" exclaimed McGregor.

"Stuffed if I know mate," said Stowie.

"Heading for an early grave that's what!" said Corporal Harrison.

"Well I think we're all in *that* race don't you think mate?" growled Clancy.

As Archie dashed across no man's land, voices were heard coming from the Turkish trenches; but, strangely, no gunfire.

"Look at those cheeky buggers," Clancy exclaimed, "they must think its Grand Final day or something".

Carefully, the platoon, one by one, peered over their defences only to see several Turkish soldiers sitting on the parapet of their trench, in full view, cheering Archie on.

"Right I'm going to take advantage of this," said Private Thornhill as he aimed his rifle in the direction of the cheering Turks.

"What do you think you're bloody doing?" yelled Clancy as he knocked Thornhill's rifle out of the aim.

"My job," the soldier retorted.

"Your job?" replied Clancy, "and what exactly is that?"

"Killing bastard Turks," replied the soldier defiantly.

"Well right now the only person you'll be killing is Archie over there. You open fire on the Turks and I think they may take offence, don't you?" said Clancy, "now let's just enjoy this bit of sport shall we?"

Archie was oblivious as to what was going on to his rear and front as he dashed, crawled and dodged his way to his prize. Diving to the ground, within inches of the plant, he was relieved to find that it *was* what he had suspected...Rosemary. He had noticed it from afar growing wild on the whole of the peninsula. As he rubbed his fingers along the stem and leaves of one of the plants, and breathed in the wonderful scent, he was reminded of home.

"Mmmmm," he thought to himself, "smells just like one of Mum's roasts on a Sunday".

He quickly gathered up as much of the herb as he could stuff in to his webbing satchel and, as he turned to make his way back to his lines, he suddenly became aware of the commotion that he had caused, seeing men from both sides sitting on the top of their trenches cheering him on. For that short moment in time Turks and Australians were one.

"Well, I'll be buggered if I crawl back now," Archie said out load as he rose calmly to his feet and , with a brazen smile on his face, took several bows to his attentive audience.

In appreciation of this short truce he walked calmly towards the Turkish trench.

"*Now* what's he doing?" asked Clancy.

"A bit of diplomacy I think mate," replied Roo.

"What's that when it's at home?" Clancy asked.

"You'll see," said Roo, a big grin across his face.

Archie approached the Turks uneasily, but slightly confident, coming to a halt right in front of his audience.

"G'day fellas. Here," he said as he reached into his satchel and brought out a few sprigs of Rosemary, "share these out amongst yourselves. Makes your food taste better".

"Thank you, Australia," said a large Turkish soldier as he gratefully accepted Archie's gift.

Archie pointed to himself.

"Archie. Archie is my name," he said.

The Turk tapped his own chest. "Mohammed".

Archie reached out a hand of friendship and Mohammed happily grasped it and shook it firmly.

"Enjoy your dinner mate," said Archie.

"You go back now. It is not safe," replied Mohammed.

"Thanks mate. I will".

As Archie calmly dropped back into his trench Clancy slapped him firmly across the head.

"You bloody fool Taylor. I thought I'd lost yer," he shouted.

The cheering had alerted their officer who soon appeared in the fire trench.

"What's all the commotion about?" he asked.

"Archie was just doing some shopping," said Roo pointing at the bouquet of Rosemary that Archie was holding.

"Bloody hell corporal what were you thinking?" asked Ponsonby as he inhaled the aroma of the herb, "mmmmm, I look forward to tasting some of your fare...er, but no more private raids though boys".

"Righto skipper. Sorry mate," replied Archie.

"Archie...Australia!" came a shout from the Turkish lines.

"Bloody hell, what now?" growled Clancy.

"Hang on, gis a look," said Archie as he peered over the top of the trench, "it's Mohammed. He's got something in his hand".

Mohammed, hands in the air, climbed in to no man's land and began walking towards the 9th Battalion lines, constantly calling Archie's name as he walked.

"HOLD YOUR FIRE!" Archie shouted down the Aussie trench.

Arriving at the sand bagged parapet Mohammed crouched down and held out his hand, offering Archie a small cardboard box.

"For you my friend. Is good," said the Turk.

Inside the box were three crumpled brown paper bags each containing an aromatic powder of some sort.

"Smells wonderful Mohammed; what is it?" Archie enquired.

"Turmeric, Cumin and Garam Marsala; make food taste better," said Mohammed.

"Thanks mate. That's good of yer," replied Archie as he reached in to his pocket and produced a spare rising sun badge, which he gave to the Turk, "for you mate, it's our badge and represents the sun of Australia".

Mohammed smiled gratefully as he admired the badge.

"Beautiful! Thank you my friend," he said, "now we are friend we don't shoot if you don't...yes?"

"Look mate we can't speak for the artillery, but we'll do our best," replied Archie, "right fellas?"

"Anything for a bit of peace and quiet will do me," said Clancy.

"Good. I go back now; and thank you," replied Mohammed as he set off towards his lines.

It seemed that they could not *indeed* speak for the artillery, on *either* side, for that same afternoon at about 1700 hours, the cook had just brought round an urn of tea, when all of a sudden the Turks began to shell and fire at the Brigade trenches. It was so sudden that it gave the men a bit of a fright, as they instinctively tossed away their tea and grabbed their rifles; and there they stood with fixed bayonets, waiting for the enemy to charge. The barrage lasted about an hour, the waiting and uncertainty being the worst part of it. It was certainly a time to test a man when a charge was potentially going to take place, with the entire Brigade just waiting for the word to spring over the top to run at them. But the enemy fire gradually slowed down and it was then that the ANZACs knew that it was only to let them see that *they* were not asleep. Despite this, all night long the Brigade kept a very careful watch, the least little sound they heard causing each man to strain their eyes; but they did not come, and at daylight only a few Aussies had managed any sleep.

"Mohammed obviously has no say over there then eh?" said Clancy sarcastically.

On the 19th of June the 9th Battalion moved to new bivvies constructed along the ledges adjoining Shell Green, enjoying what was officially called a 'rest in reserve'. This "rest" consisted of going up to the line by night, as before, to dig in four hour shifts, or by day to the beach to carry back the tins of bully beef and biscuits, the '3-by-2' or '4-by-2' wooden beams, the bags of rice, or the sheets of corrugated iron, all past the many dangerous corners where a sniper's bullet could be waiting. The men learned over the months what it was to see rice leaking from a bullet hole in the bag of the man in front, or to lower a heavy beam of wood, wait for the crucial moment, and double across the thirty yards of exposed valley.

"I feel like a mountain goat!" said Clancy.

"Yeah, but at least we are safe," said Roo.

"Safe? You're having a laugh mate!" replied an indignant

Clancy, "*and* we are bloody knackered. This is *not* a rest in my books!"

The bivvie area resembled a terraced paddy field, but without the water, and being in reserve was definitely no picnic as, in addition to their fetch and carrying activities, the 9th Battalion were tasked with digging a sunken road from Shell Green to Shrapnel Gully. This was linked to the sunken road to the beach which had been dug the month before by the brigade fatigue parties, thus making the movement from the beach to the brigade sector less risky. But there was always a lot of noise from rifles, guns, and shrapnel going on all the time.

"Cheer up men at least the road leads to the "new canteen at the Cove," announced Lieutenant Ponsonby.

"Yeah, I've seen it mate, *and* the prices," groaned Clancy, "nothing like making life easier for your soldiers eh?

"I suppose not, but I do have *some* good news," said Ponsonby.

There was a pause as all present awaited the usual response, from Clancy, that the Turks had surrendered and the war was over. But nothing.

"Blimey! Fetch the doc I don't think he is well," laughed Roo.

"Yes, the thought *had* crossed my mind," added the lieutenant.

"All right, all right," said Clancy, "what's the good news then?"

"Company Sergeant Major Perrier is now the Regimental Sergeant Major," replied Ponsonby.

"That *is* good news," said Archie.

"Yeah, he's a good bloke...so?" replied Clancy.

Lieutenant Ponsonby looked around his small group of friends who were looking at him with anticipation, almost reading his thoughts.

"So...or sew, is actually the right word Sergeant McBride," said the officer as he reached in to his tunic pocket and tossed a crown shaped cloth towards Clancy, "you'd better get this sewn on because you are the new Company Sergeant Major; congratulations dear boy".

Clancy suddenly felt quite choked up, the feelings only added to by his mates' congratulatory smiles, hugs and handshakes.

"I've never felt so honoured in my life. Thank you for putting your trust in me sir; in fact thank you all of you," said Clancy, his chin quivering, along with his voice.

"In fact the colonel was feeling generous today," said Ponsonby as he handed out a few more material chevrons, "congratulations Sergeants Taylor...and Taylor, and Corporals Stowe and Williams".

"Stone the crows! Thanks sir," said Taff.

"It's time for a celebration I think," said Ponsonby, pausing for a second, "yes, what the hell, let's have a brandy shall we?"

As the friends savoured a small sip of brandy, a peculiar tranquility enveloped the world around them, the constant danger of shrapnel and snipers a seemingly insignificant part of daily life on the peninsula.

Any feeling of peace, however, was soon to be shattered.

At approximately 0830 hours on the 28th of June, Lieutenant General Birdwood received a message. The British were attacking Helles in just three hours, and high command wanted the ANZACs to make a minor attack on the Turks in order to prevent them from sending re-enforcements. This was extremely short notice and very unprofessional of the British commanders who *surely* must have known about their planned attack well in advance.

"Use the bloody ANZACs again!" exclaimed Clancy, his words and thoughts no doubt shared by others.

Brigade Commanders received their orders at 1030 hours so subsequently had to make a snap battle plan. Lieutenant Ponsonby informed his platoon that they were moving out now but that *he* knew very little of what, or where?

"Well, that's no bloody good is it?" said the new CSM.

The men hastily grabbed as much ammunition as they could carry, as well as their trusty scoff bags. 'B' and 'C' Companies, along with two companies of the 11th Battalion, plus elements of the Light Horse, had been selected for this dubious task. The 9th Battalion were to move towards the Knife Edge, travelling along Silt Spur. The two companies of the 11th Battalion would lie out on the spur, and Turkey Knoll, as a covering force, whilst simultaneously the Light Horse would advance to the right.

'C' Company had no chance from the outset. The British attack was well under way when, at 1315 hours, the two 9th Battalion companies climbed out from their trenches, at an interval of about a quarter of a mile, so as not to draw too much attention. 'C' Company, who had to pass via the shoulder of a hill, in full view of the enemy positions at Gaba Tepe, were soon subjected to a barrage of machine gun and shrapnel fire. Despite this they continued their advance up the hill through the thick undergrowth. Seeing the ridiculousness of the task, no doubt, a loud voice shouted "RETIRE!" Who called out? No one knew, but it was probably a disgruntled soldier sick of being used in diversionary attacks by the British high command. Nonetheless, the "order" was acted upon with the whole company withdrawing back to the start point. The terrain and the way that the companies were scattered during the advance, made command and control nigh on impossible, so the officers gave up trying. There was already alarm amongst the troops; causing a panic would not improve the situation.

The 'B' Company attack was more successful. Newly piled earth sheltered the troops as they left the safety of the trench and, although they came under immediate enemy fire, they sprinted across the dead ground of Cooee Gully and headed up Sniper Ridge. Protected by the cover of the ridge, they easily reached the enemy trenches. Because this was a diversionary action the troops, unusually, had been ordered not to enter the enemy trenches and, upon reaching them, they found them to be covered in pine branches.

"Bugger this! What's the point if we can't give them a nose bleed?" exclaimed Clancy, "get at them boys!"

The men shoved rifle muzzles and bayonets through the overhead cover, stabbing, bashing and shooting any Turk who came in to sight. They even chucked a few jam tin bombs in for good measure, some having difficulty lighting the fuse as their matches had become damp due to their sweat soaking their matches. A few choice words were uttered about that!

The light resistance from the trench that they had encountered soon petered out as the Turks retreated; running for their lives from these crazed antipodeans.

"They've buggered off!" exclaimed an annoyed Clancy.

With no opposition in the area the Aussies decided that it

was smoko time and lay along the parapet whilst having lunch and a brew of tea.

"Very civilised" said Lieutenant Ponsonby.

"Yeah, not a bad way to fight a war eh boss?" replied Archie.

The quiet, however, was soon shattered when the Turks began to shell the area. A Turkish battery somewhere beyond Lone Pine Ridge had decided it was *their* turn to give the Aussies a hard time. Shrapnel shells came over from the battery in abundance, and were well aimed, but exploded too high above the ground. Some men took shelter in the enemy trench, well aware that no trench was shell-proof, whilst others stood to along the parapet willing to suffer the shrapnel which, although uncomfortable when it struck, was falling like a gentle hail of pebbles from high up in the air. Although the company was suffering some casualties they held on to their ground. Private Latimer of the 2nd Field Ambulance calmly walked the line, tending the wounded and carrying them to safety. He was an inspiration to all, but like John Simpson, he met his death, killed by the blast of an artillery shell.

On seeing Private Latimer fall Clancy and Archie crawled over to the brave stretcher bearer, but were too late.

"Bloody hell!" exclaimed Clancy, "you bastards! A bloody diversion! Bastards all of you!"

As Archie tried to calm his mate down he noticed something unusual about Latimer.

"Hey Clance, look," he said, "not a mark on him. How can that be?"

As Clancy glanced over the stretcher bearer's lifeless body

he replied "buggered if I know mate. Maybe we should ask the doc?"

Archie nodded in agreement.

High Explosive ordnance and shrapnel was now falling heavily on both the attack and covering force, the barrage working its deadly path to all front line trenches in the area. Three shells tore into the trench to the company's rear, scattering a leaden hail in every direction. Cries of pain filled the air, as stretcher bearers leapt in to the trench, only to be seen again carrying away the remains of a member of 'B' Company. Roo glanced over his shoulder wondering who the poor unfortunate was, but he couldn't tell as the man's brains had been blown out.

"Poor bastard," whispered Roo.

The Turks kept on whanging the shrapnel at the attackers for some time. Most of the company men had by now taken refuge in the empty enemy trench and, as they sheltered, each man speculated, as they heard each boom of the enemy's guns, whether *that* particular shrapnel shell, with its deafening explosion, cloud of acrid, stinking smoke, and deadly balls of lead, was meant for them. To the men the explosions felt a bit ticklish; but as shell after shell missed them they laughed, and cheered, calling out insulting remarks and opinions concerning the gunnery skills of the Turkish gunners.

"My granny can shoot better than you lot, and she's been dead ten years!" shouted Clancy.

Naturally, the men had to do *something* under such conditions; stay sane by acting insane. After over two hours on the objective, the commanders in over all charge agreed that the men had met their mission of holding back any possible reserve forces, so ordered a withdrawal.

"About bloody time!" said Clancy, "come on boys, let's get the hell out of here".

'B' Company was shelled all the way back to Bolton's, by the guns in the olive grove, as well as receiving small arms fire from Lone Pine. Despite this they remained steady, carrying out a text book withdrawal, retrieving .303 rifles and ammunition from the dead as they went. By 1630 hours they were safe, back in their own trenches. The men were aware of the reasons for the action but could not condone the cost of thirty seven dead and sixty two wounded.

As the fighting at Gallipoli progressed it became more important to conserve equipment. That evening parties were dispatched to recover the dead and wounded, plus weapons, ammunition and webbing. On the evenings of the 29th and 30th further attempts were made to recover bodies, but were halted by intense enemy rifle fire.

Padres Dexter and Fahy conducted the funerals of those who *were* recovered, in a small cemetery near Shell Green.

The attack had resulted in the postponement of a large Turkish offensive on the ANZAC line for twenty four hours. Birdie was pleased with what the men had accomplished and visited the 9th Battalion to tell them. This personal connection between the men and their General was the glue which kept the ANZACs going.

But the attack *did* come.

10

The Break Out

"Hey Clance, do you know what day it is?" asked Archie.

"The first of July, why?" asked Clancy.

At that Archie began his minor assault on his mate.

"A pinch and punch for the first day of the month......." said Archie, laughing.

"What the?!" exclaimed a surprised Clancy, "are we still back at school or what Arch?"

Archie and Roo stopped laughing and were somewhat surprised.

"Have you not heard of that before?" asked Roo.

"Yeah, mum and dad always used to get us on the first of the month," said Archie.

The cogs were now turning in Clancy's head as he plotted his revenge.

"Nah, but I've got one for you," said Clancy, smiling as he slapped the cousins round the head and kicked them up the back side, "a hit and a kick for being so quick".

The Tom foolery by the friends was soon interrupted by distant explosions, rifle fire and shouts of "Allah! Allah!" A large attack by the Turks was taking place somewhere on the far left of the ANZAC line. Everyone stood to. Clancy, Roo and Archie, along with the rest of the 9th Battalion took up their posts behind the earth wall, with its parapet of sandbags, and, in turn, observed the Turkish lines and the ground to their front and flanks through their periscopes. Occasionally a head would bob up, and disappear in a second, from within the Turkish trenches, a few hundred yards away. The enemy made no signs of leaving their lines to attack Bolton's, whilst the 9th Battalion took care not to show themselves.

The battalion fired perhaps not a dozen rounds between them all day, whereas the Turks kept their rifles working continually, now and then ripping open the sandbags half a foot, or a foot, above the men's heads. Meanwhile the sounds of a great battle were echoing across the peninsula.

"Someone is getting their arse kicked," said Clancy, looking towards the area of Quinn's Post.

The 3rd Light Horse Brigade valiantly held their positions at Walkers Ridge, Russel's Top, and the Nek, while the Auckland

Battalion ensured the security of Quinn's Post. It was in this vital sector of the ANZAC line that the enemy launched a ferocious assault. The 2nd Light Horse Regiment occupied the valley between Pope's Hill and Russel's Top, with 'B' Squadron positioned there and 'A' and 'C' squadrons providing support. The 3rd Light Horse Regiment stood ready in reserve, while the 1st Light Horse Regiment guarded Pope's Hill, reinforced by a squadron from the 3rd Light Horse.

The Turks initiated their attack by shelling the Nek, followed by a massive infantry onslaught. Despite their initial success in occupying some of the trenches, the determined 8th Light Horse launched a swift counterattack, driving the Turks out of the ANZAC lines and reclaiming what the enemy had seized. Simultaneously, a sizable enemy force descended upon the valley, aiming to seize Russel's Top. However, 'B' Squadron of the 2nd Light Horse Regiment, supported by machine guns stationed at Pope's Hill, forcefully repelled the attackers. 'C' and 'D' Troops then swiftly launched a counterattack, wielding bayonets, pushing the enemy forces back up the valley from whence they came.

In the midst of the chaotic battle, the toll on both sides was heavy. The Turks suffered devastating losses, their positions on the imposing hill that the ANZACs fought to secure bearing witness to the awful toll of the conflict. The ferocity with which the Australians and New Zealanders fought surpassed that of their adversaries. On the right flank, a band of Maoris, their spirits ignited, surged forward with an almost supernatural fervour. Relentless in their pursuit, they seemed unstoppable, their unwavering goal to press onward, even to the gates of Constantinople.

In the gripping clash of bayonets, the 2nd Light Horse charged, pushing back the disoriented Turks, fear gripping their souls as they dropped their rifles and fled, desperate to escape the promise of cold steel that loomed over them. The lucky ones who managed to evade the ANZAC bayonets disappeared into the distance, their terrified cries reverberating through the air. As Percy and his mates pursued the fleeing enemy, he was sent spiralling through the chaos by a sudden blow to his shoulder, the fallout from an exploding cricket ball bomb. Momentarily dazed he awoke to find himself atop a mound of fallen Turkish soldiers. As he surveyed the scene his immediate thought was to scream out in terror like a small child in need of its mother, but he somehow managed to push aside the overwhelming sights and smells, and focus on the task at hand. For in that blood-stained moment, surrounded by the hideous sights of battle, he understood the unforgiving reality of war; the relentless pursuit, the precarious dance between life and death, and the unyielding spirit that propelled him and his mates forward, even in the face of unspeakable horrors.

The haunting scenes were everywhere, the lifeless bodies of countless Turks and ANZACs littering the ground, a macabre testament to the intensity of the fighting.

During the clash, the ANZAC forces suffered significant casualties, including the loss of Major Nash, the Officer Commanding (OC) of 'C' Squadron. Tragically, Major Nash was struck down by a chance stray bullet, his untimely death serving as a solemn reminder of the dangers faced by the brave soldiers on the battlefield.

For the next few days the 2nd Light Horse were rotated and became the Brigade reserve. *Their* "rest" time was taken up by heavy manual labour. The temperatures were very hot and sickness was rife – passed on by flies which had been feeding on the unburied dead.

Returning from the mail run, Percy came not only bearing gifts of letters from home, but also re-enforcements...two to be exact.

"That many? The war is won then," said Boggy sarcastically.

"Fellas this is Tubby Turner and Dave Evans," Percy announced as he introduced the two men to the section.

"Er-hum.....Id.......my name is Dave-id, not Dave," said an indignant Trooper Evans.

"Is it now? And what do *you* usually do for a crust mate?" enquired Chugger.

"I'm a Solicitor," replied the soldier.

"A Solicitor eh?" said Chugger.

"Hey Dave, I'd like you to represent me please," said Davo, joining in the fun.

"Look! It's Id, my name is Dave-id!" Evans growled.

"Ah right," said Chugger with a sly wink to his mates, "Id it is then".

"What? Oh I give up! Anyway, what would you need my services out here for?" asked Evans.

"I'd like to have General Hamilton and his cronies tried for murder," replied Davo.

"Here, here," came several growls of agreement.

"You can't do that," replied Evans.

"Why not?" asked Chugger.

"The King and our Prime Minister have given him legal permission to kill us," replied Evans.

"Is that right? Well bugger me. I'd better go and get killed then!" laughed Chugger.

"Don't say that you fool," said Percy.

Looking at the lean looking youth who had been introduced as Tubby, Boggy was a little perplexed.

"Mate! Why are you called Tubby? You're like a bean pole," he asked.

Tubby chuckled to himself.

"Well, when I first enlisted I was a bit stocky, you know on account of my Mum's great cooking, but with all of the army training and the fact that I shit my body weight out in Egypt, after getting Cairo belly, I am now a shadow of my former self, and I'd like to stay that way," Tubby replied.

"Well there's no fear of *not* accomplishing that. Have you met my mates Fray and Bentos?" Boggy replied, holding up two tins of bully beef, "and of course Bill the fly........and his *very* large family".

Rations were poor in quality and becoming monotonous; cheap bully beef, hard biscuits, and cheese that melted in the heat, fatty bacon and inferior jam, which was more of a liquid. Fruit and vegetables on Gallipoli were nonexistent and the men's health was suffering as a result.

Some, including Percy, however, were relishing the rather runny jam.

"Are you enjoying that?" asked Boggy.

"Yeah, it's not too bad," replied Percy, "it tastes a bit like fruit juice".

Whilst the folks back in Australia were fed news stories about great feats of heroism, the ordinary people in the street were unaware of what life was really like for their loved ones.

In the harrowing trenches of Gallipoli, soldiers endured the relentless torment of rats, lice and the persistent annoyance of flies. The battlefield, plagued by the unsanitary aftermath of conflict and overcrowded living conditions, became a breeding ground for these scavengers, drawn by the scent of death that permeated the air.

Lice, thrived amidst the cramped quarters, spreading through close contact and shared belongings among the soldiers, their bites causing incessant itching and skin irritation, adding to the soldiers' discomfort. The lack of proper sanitation and the inability to regularly change clothes or bathe intensified the prevalence of the infestations, as their eggs multiplied in the soldiers' uniforms and blankets.

The lifeless bodies of fallen soldiers lay scattered across the battlefield, a grim testament to the toll of battle. The decaying corpses, left unburied amidst the chaos, became a macabre feast for the flies, with swarms of these relentless insects descending upon the fallen, their buzzing wings and unforgiving pursuit adding to the anguish of the soldiers who fought on.

The flies were also drawn to the stagnant water and decomposing food, in the waste dumps, posing a health hazard, contaminating the soldiers' provisions and increasing the risk of illnesses such as dysentery, whose symptoms included bloody diarrhoea, abdominal pain, fever, and nausea, which further weakened the already exhausted soldiers.

On the 6th of July, following a similar "rest" to the 2nd Light Horse, the 9th Battalion were back in the firing line, whilst the 10th Battalion was moved to Imbros for a *real* rest, which cheered the men of the 9th Battalion as surely *their* time would soon come.

But sickness and the general hazards of battle was having a toll on the infantry too, with twenty three officers and three hundred and sixty eight men from the 9th Battalion on Imbros or in Egypt, sick or wounded, with no word of their condition or the date of their likely return.

In addition to the millions of flies buzzing around, the doctors *recognised* that the primary cause of the sickness was the inadequate and nutritionally deficient rations.

The men could not live by bully beef alone.

"I bet the generals aren't eating this rubbish!" was the consensus from the men.

Diarrhoea was prevalent everywhere, and Enteric Fever was also rife. Skin sores were developing on many, and healed slowly due to the breakdown of the individual's natural healing powers and immune system. But the men, despite their weakness from disease, soldiered on, sticking to their posts without complaint, not giving up; unless ordered to do so of course.

Whilst a weakened 2nd Light Horse began a quiet stint at Pope's Hill, on the 12th of July, yet another British and French attack at Helles called for more feints and night attacks by the ANZACs.

The Islamic period of Ramadan was also in full swing and an attack by one hundred thousand Turks was expected.

12th Battalion along with the 6th and 7th Light Horse carried out the feint. Whereas the 9th Battalion performed its *own* feint, forming up in their trenches with fixed bayonets raised high for the Turks to see, then marching through their trenches towards the 12th Battalion, hoping to fool the Turks in to believing that they were being re-enforced by a large force. As a bonus to their feint, the rear-side of the trench, known as the parados, had collapsed following the spate of artillery fire over the past week, the parados being constructed higher than the parapet so that the defenders were not outlined against the sky and therefore easy targets for snipers or anyone firing from the rear. Luck had it that the collapse had left a mound of earth as high as the natural terrain. The men used this to their advantage and, despite the obvious risk, ran over the ground in full view of the enemy, then disappeared down a communication sap, doubling back to the start to begin the process all over again. It was certainly a morale booster for the troops, along with the thrill of their actions, making it difficult for the troops to hold in their laughter and obvious enjoyment. This small body of men repeated this ruse over and over in order to trick the Turks, and it worked. Throughout the day the Turks aimed their rifles at the "re-enforcements" and dropped over 60 shells on and around the area; with no losses to the 9th Battalion. The enemy apparently reported it as a serious attack and genuinely believed that they had repelled it.

On the 16th of July the 9th Battalion were back in support,

but there was no rest to be had. They had even been issued an acetylene motor headlight for use as a search light.

Clancy was *not* impressed.

"What's the bloody point? As soon as you switch it on the Turks will shoot the bloody thing out and kill the bloke holding it!"

Throughout the rest of the month, their time was occupied with excavating and enhancing defensive positions in the front. However, it was inevitable and unavoidable that whenever the front line advanced, it would occasionally come across graves from two months prior. The overwhelming stench of death in the area between the trenches was already difficult to endure. Additionally, the soldiers would witness daily the sight of bodies reduced to mere skeletons, barely held together by tattered, rat eaten clothing that was once proud uniforms. As they dug into the ground, they would often uncover human bones, some of which jutted out from the earth like tree roots. To ordinary people, this sight would be horrifying, but for the soldiers who faced death on a daily basis, it was just another part of their routine. They relied on humour to cope, finding amusement in shaking hands with protruding limbs, or even using them as coat hooks.

Despite now being the Company Sergeant Major, Clancy was a hands on individual rather than a supervisor, willingly assisting his comrades in the digging process. While chipping away at the soil with his entrenching tool, he stumbled upon a skull, which promptly fell at his feet. Most people would have reacted with shock, but not Clancy. He had always felt responsible for maintaining high morale through any means necessary, so immediately picked up the skull, removing some dirt from it, and suddenly displayed it to his mates.

"Hey boys," he said, "I bet you didn't know that the Turks had Sheilas in their army?"

"What do you mean?" Stowie asked.

"Take a gander at this. It *must* be a woman... the mouth's open!" Clancy laughed, pointing at the loosely hanging jawbone of the skull.

This remark from Clancy elicited laughter from everyone present, which cheered him up greatly because, to him, he was doing his job.

"If Mum was here right now she'd clip you round the ear for that," said Archie.

"Na," Roo confidently replied, "I reckon she'd most likely chuckle and join in with the joke".

There was *some* good news towards the end of July, the first Victoria Cross to be awarded to an Australian in what had become known as the Great War. As their officer imparted the news to the platoon, Roo and Clancy, who had taken part in the action at Courtney's Post, were over the moon.

"I bloody knew it! Good on yer Jacka!" exclaimed Clancy, "if you blokes could have seen it. The bloke is just a bloody marvel".

"Well I am glad that you are excited sergeant major because you have been awarded the Military Medal for your bravery in rescuing our good friend Stowie here," announced Lieutenant Ponsonby.

As the lieutenant shook the hand of his friend there was applause and cheering from the battalion.

"Congratulations old chap".

But Clancy felt unworthy of such an honour.

"I was just doing my job, just like all of you blokes," Clancy replied as he looked around at all present, "I don't deserve a medal mate".

"Well, the generals, and the King, beg to differ dear boy," replied the officer.

Stowie clasped Clancy's hand. "You saved my life Clance. I can never repay you for that. Accept that you are a good leader and a brave and good man".

On the 29th of July the 2nd Light Horse Regiment was back on Pope's Hill. The enemy was causing casualties no matter what or where your situation on the line and, despite two drafts of re-enforcements since landing, the regiment was reduced to just one hundred bayonets. All were weak due to the lack of food and water, coupled with long night watches and heavy fatigue work.

Their one chance to improve their own hygiene and keep clean was a visit to the beach for a swim and a bath, and a chance to drown the lice which infested their clothing and bodies. But the journey to the beach was almost impossible now, the return journey for the weakened soldiers being the worst part of it.

With the Turks celebrating Ramadan the stand to was extended, for, although for Muslims it is a time of prayer and acts of charity, it also meant for the Turks that the gates of Paradise were now open, the gates of hell locked up, and the devils put in chains. So now, the already tenacious enemy was even braver knowing that paradise was a guarantee should he die on the battlefield.

"I wish I had *their* faith," said Percy.

The higher echelon had even ordered the Medical Officers (MOs) to leave all on the line who could hold a rifle, but this was a wasted order, as every soldier remained at their post until it was no longer humanly possible to do so *anyway*.

But, in reality the manpower and health situation was desperate.

Weak or not, improvement of existing trenches, the digging of new ones, as well as tunnelling and digging sunken roads, still carried on. The Turks were doing the same, with earth often seen flying out of their trenches, and the dawn of a new day revealing, through a periscope, an improved landscape on the enemy side of no man's land.

ANZAC snipers had been organised at the beginning of June and were taking their toll.

Most ANZACs were crack shots anyway and enjoyed tormenting the Turks. Their latest sport was the regular peppering of the loopholes in their parapets, destroying all attempts at improving them.

But it wasn't just the snipers who were taking some enjoyment out of their marksmanship skills.

"Hey Perce come and look at this," said Chugger, "what do yer reckon?"

Looking through the periscope, Percy surveyed the dark grey frame of the Turkish loophole to his front.

"Dunno mate. Looks a bit like concrete" Percy replied, "let's take a quick shot shall we?"

Using his Lee Enfield .303 rifle, fitted to a periscope frame, Percy took careful aim, timing his breathing, then...BANG!...he fired a single round in to the loophole frame, chipping some of the concrete from the side.

"Yep, definitely concrete," said Percy, marvelling at his work.

Word was passed around and soon the Aussies were intentionally firing at the concrete loopholes, hoping to get Jacko with a ricochet. From the agonising cries that they heard, they were obviously finding their mark. Pretty soon the concrete was removed and wicker frames installed. These now became a new toy for the machine gunners who cut through them like butter.

Destroying the loopholes was not only a morale booster but also an excellent way to deny the Turks the opportunity to take daily pot shots at them. The Forward Observation Officers from the Artillery had some good success too, via their field telephones, being able to direct a shell straight *through* the loophole.

By the end of July rumours were being tossed around about a possible push against the Turks. New Zealand scouts had been secretly penetrating the enemy terrain, exploring the ravines, gullies and heights to their front.

Despite their depleted numbers and sickness the men were heartened by the thought, and the numbers reporting sick dropped to nothing.

"You've gotta be in it," were the thoughts and conversations around ANZAC.

The already meagre water ration had been reduced severely due to destruction of tanks by enemy artillery, and partly because it was being stored for the new troops being brought in for the push.

Percy and his mates on a work party in the rear echelon area were employed in the construction of numerous bivvies. But, for who? The unanswered question only adding fuel to the rumour mill about something big.

"There's definitely something in the wind," said Clancy.

"Nothing that a good soak wouldn't cure...you smelly bugger," joked Roo.

"No...I'm serious mate," replied Clancy.

"What do you mean sir?" enquired Archie.

"Haven't you noticed?" asked Clancy, "and enough of the sir".

"Noticed? Just tell me mate, will yer?" exclaimed Archie.

"Have you seen anybody above the rank of Captain lately?" said Clancy.

"Come to think of it...no," replied Archie, scratching his head.

"*And* they disappeared for a few days a couple of weeks ago. I heard they were on a ship and went further up the coast to that bay...what's it called?" added Roo.

"Suvla I think," said Taff.

"Yeah, that's it, Suvla Bay," said Roo.

"See...told yer," said a triumphant Clancy.

Archie stretched his neck as he peered north along the coast.

Looks like a good spot for a landing," he said.

As they pondered, their platoon commander, mug in hand, came in to view.

"Is there any tea on chaps?" he called ahead of him.

As he halted and passed his cup to Roo he was bombarded with questions about the disappearance of senior officers, and Suvla Bay.

"Boys, you know I can't tell you anything...just yet...but I *do* know that there is a stunt on tonight," replied Lieutenant Ponsonby, "CSM..."

"Sir?" replied Clancy.

"Orders group at 1500 hours. Section Commanders too," replied the officer as he looked around at his friends.

As the Platoon Commander carried on along the trench, passing the word, Roo shook his head.

"Spoke to soon again eh?" he uttered.

The orders group revealed that an attack on the enemy to the front of a new post, called Tasmania Post, had been ordered. Two hundred men from the 11th Battalion were to carry out the assault as soon as the moon had risen, with the 9th Battalion tasked with repelling any counter attacks by manning the trenches to the left of the post. As soon as darkness fell the parties from the 9th Battalion, a platoon from each company, made their way through the labyrinth of trenches and on, just past Tasmania Post, leaving a significant sized defence force at Bolton's. By 1015 hours the next morning the Turks had been driven from the trenches, and the ANZAC front line had moved forward slightly. The Turks were good and brave soldiers but they despised mêlée attacks with the bayonet and, nine times out of ten, they would flee. As the elements of the 9th Battalion rested in the Tassie trench system a maelstrom of rifle and automatic fire erupted at Bolton's Ridge, driving off a large force of Turks who had been massing to the front of the 9th Battalion's positions.

"Bugger! Missed all the fun," said Taff.

Whilst this had been occurring fresh and untried troops had been landing in the darkness at ANZAC Cove, and all over the allied beach heads, occupying the newly constructed bivvie areas.

Finally, on the 4th of August the plan was revealed.

11

August, The Summer's Last Messenger of Misery

It would all begin on the 6th of August. The British forces would initiate an assault on Helles at 1550 hours. At 1730 hours, the Australian Division would launch an attack on Lone Pine. Later, at 2200 hours, the Australian and New Zealand Division, along with attached troops, were assigned to capture Chunuk Bair and Battleship Hill. Simultaneously, a new force would pose a threat to the enemy rear by landing at Suvla Bay during the night. In essence, the primary objectives were to secure the two peaks on the Sari Bair Range. Accomplishing this would safeguard the troops at ANZAC from enemy observation and attacks, while also providing the allies with a clear vantage point over the eastern approaches to the peninsula. It was an audacious plan indeed.

The 3rd Light Horse Brigade had the task of attacking the Nek and Baby 700. The 1st Light Horse Brigade was to launch an assault on the Chessboard area from Pope's Hill, while the trenches opposite Quinn's were to be targeted by the 2nd Light Horse Regiment. These attacks were intended to coordinate with the right flank of the Australian and New Zealand Division.

As Lieutenant Ponsonby briefed his platoon he intimated that this offensive had been planned for two months now, and that all of the attacks by the ANZACs on the southern peninsula had been a lead up to this day, by drawing the enemy away from the north.

"So, what will *we* be doing boss?" asked Roo.

"The 1st Brigade will attack Lone Pine as a diversion," replied Ponsonby.

"A *diversion*? They'll be bloody angry about that," noted Clancy.

"Indeed sergeant major, but between you and me, and all present of course, diversion or not, they intend to kick the Turks out of their positions," said Ponsonby.

"Good on 'em!" exclaimed Clancy with an approving nod to all.

"But what's our role mate?" enquired Archie.

"To cause *another* diversion by pouring heavy fire on the

enemy trenches opposite, thus preventing them from, in turn, firing on the 1st Infantry Brigade," replied the officer.

"So, *we're* not involved in any attacks?" asked a surprised Roo.

Ponsonby shook his head in response.

"Well that's no bloody good is it?" added Clancy.

"Boys. We haven't had a let up since we landed. We've been in many fights. None of us is in tip top shape, so let's just use our shooting skills to the best of our ability," said Lieutenant Ponsonby, "we'll still be in it, just not in the actual fray".

Clancy could not conceal his anger and disappointment, but resigned himself to the battalion's perceived minor role.

"We'd better stock up on ammo then boys, eh?" said the CSM.

"Well said dear boy," Ponsonby replied as he patted Clancy's shoulder, "all for one and one for all...as the musketeers would say".

The 9th Battalion may have been disappointed with the part that they would play, but for the 2nd Light Horse, at the other end of the line, it was a different story.

As the men of the 2nd Light Horse marched back in to Quinn's Post on the 5th of August, they were impressed, and grateful, to the Auckland Battalion, whom they were relieving.

"Hey Kiwis!" said Chugger to the departing New Zealanders, "I've never seen Quinn's look so good".

"You're welcome," said a passing Kiwi voice.

There was now a new fire trench and covered support trenches. To catch the bombs which regularly landed in the trenches, the Kiwis had installed wire nets. Apart from making it difficult to retrieve the bombs and throw them back, the drawback was that they prevented attack parties from exiting the trench, and if removed they would warn the Turks of a forthcoming stunt.

'B' Squadron was designated the left flank from which to attack, and was ordered to break in a tunnel in order to form a trench, to be used as their jumping off point. 'A' Squadron, the right attack party, prepared the netting in the trench for removal just prior to attack commencement. Communication trenches were also being dug in to no man's land for use following the success of the assault.

Lone Pine was a very strongly fortified Turkish position directly in front of the ANZAC lines. The distance between both sets of trenches was but one hundred yards, and in some places as close as thirty. Conversation could even be easily carried on by the two conflicting parties, and often was. The Turks had made elaborate preparations for this inevitable assault, and had three tiers of fire directed on the ANZAC trenches, so as to make it practically an impossibility for its capture. Machine guns were in great evidence, likewise bombs of every description, which the Turks knew the full value of, and could handle well, too. The advance on this position was the opening up of the general offensive all along the entire front.

Like clockwork, at 1730 hours, supported by a murderous naval bombardment, the 1st Infantry Brigade launched their attack at Lone Pine. The 9th Battalion unleashed volley after volley on the opposing trenches, thus keeping the enemies' heads down. Firing ceased when the 1st Brigade reached Lone Pine and began breaking through the overhead cover on the enemy trenches. Rifles cracked, jam tin bombs exploded, and men on both sides fell wounded or dead. Neither the 9th Battalion nor the opposing Turks could do anything now for fear of hitting their own men and, as firing at Bolton's Ridge subsided, an amazing sight unfolded.

"Look at those cheeky buggers!" said Clancy as he observed the Turks opposite climb out of their trenches, sitting on the sand bagged parapet, and watching the unfolding events at Lone Pine.

"Well, that's one for your diary eh Arch?!" exclaimed Roo.

As Clancy too scrambled out on to the parapet above, he called over to the Turks, "hey Abdul...don't shoot...me looky".

The Turks glanced across and nodded their approval and ambivalence to the situation.

"Hey Clance, gis a lift," said Roo, holding out his outstretched arm.

Very soon soldiers on both sides were seated on their respective parapets cheering their side on. The fighting at Lone Pine became a prolonged affair and would last for two days. But, as darkness fell on that evening, the audience of Aussies and Turks jumped back in to the safety of their trenches, keeping a watchful eye on their opponents to their fronts.

"Good night Abdul!" came a shout in the night.

The plan for the 2nd Light Horse was straight forward. In four waves of fifty men they would launch an assault on the enemy, who were only yards to their front. Similar attacks were being enacted all over the ANZAC front line. The attack was only to commence if the German Officers Trench had been taken, Chunuk Bair had been captured by the New Zealanders, and a thorough bombardment to the regiment's front had been undertaken.

The attack signal for the 2nd Light Horse was to be an explosion of a huge mine beneath Turkish Quinn's at 0430 hours.

Percy and Chugger were inserted in to the first attack wave, along with Id and young Tubby Turner. Bombardments to their front had taken place throughout the night. No information had been received about Chunuk Bair or the German Officers Trench. The assumption was that the attack was on. The men lined up in their four waves. The whispered order came to fix bayonets. Two hundred clicks sounded in almost unison as the steel blades of death were attached to their housings.

"I hope Jacko heard that," whispered Percy.

"Me too," said Chugger, "he might think twice and bugger off".

But Jacko wasn't going anywhere today.

As they waited with baited breath for the bodies to fly as the mine detonated under the Turks, they were disappointed that the explosion and impact was less devastating than a jam tin bomb. But nonetheless it *was* the signal.

Kissing the now tattered photos of Lil, young Frank, and his mum and dad, and placing them in his tunic pocket, Percy, in those few moments contemplated his past, his present, and his future.

"Is this it?" he thought as he awaited the attack signal.

"Cheer up Taylor," said Lieutenant Norris, "we'll be in Jacko's trenches in a moment and chasing the buggers off".

Looking left to right, Percy could see that everyone else was in their own world, locked in personal thoughts. Even Chugger was quiet; quite a first for him. But, it was different this time; their first *real* time out of the trenches and advancing to the attack.

"It'll be fine," he thought to himself.

"Good luck boys, we'll be with you shortly," said a friendly voice from the second wave, who were lined up ready for the off.

The dust cloud from the small explosion was still hovering over the Turkish front line like a sand storm when suddenly Major Bourne waved frantically to the officers of the first wave. The signal.

Let's go boys!" Major Logan called out, as he, Lieutenants Norris and Burge, scurried up the makeshift ladders in to the abyss that was no man's land.

Like obedient cattle dogs, the first wave followed in a split second, and were soon standing on the parapet, bayonets charged. As Percy stepped off the sand bagged rim of the trench and began to run forwards, he lost his footing, tripping over the body of a brave Turk who had been slain over a month ago. It was Percy's lucky day. Was he blessed by the Angels or a higher authority? As he rolled on to his front to stand up, a murderous hail of Jacko lead slammed in to the men of the 2nd Light Horse. Rifle fire. Machine gun fire. The air erupted with a hailstorm of bullets, each one carrying the intent to maim or kill, with Jacko's weapons spitting out a storm of deadly projectiles, turning no man's land in to a symphony of destruction. The piercing cracks and thunderous booms and rat tat tats echoed through the air, accompanied by the haunting screams of pain and anguish. It was a merciless barrage of gun fire, a malevolent symphony of death that sought to extinguish lives with every shot. Every man standing was hit, some multiple times as the rat tat tat and brrrrrr of the machine guns sent a wall of death towards them. Percy watched helplessly as men, his mates, were cut in half, others their entrails hanging out, or their limbs completely severed. This was war at its worst. *Everyone* went down. Nobody got further than ten yards. The Turks had been ready; waiting patiently to pay back the debt of thousands killed since April. To Percy it was all happening in slow motion. Blood, bones, limbs, guts, exploding in all directions. Chugger fell wounded, next to Percy, and as Percy reached out to his mate, Chugger snapped, "KEEP STILL MATE!" The Turkish guns soon fell silent, the only sound, apart from the groans of the wounded ANZACs, being that of magazines being recharged and rifle bolts being pulled back and pushed forward, ready for the next gallant charge. Sixteen men lay dead, including Major Logan, Lieutenant Burge *and* Troopers Evans and Turner; thirty six others were wounded. Those who were able rolled themselves the short distance back to the trench, dropping with a thud to the ground. Some Turks took aim and fired at them as they crawled or rolled. So, as it turned out, not all Turks were honourable; but *most* of the enemy watched in admiration as their foe scrambled to safety. What was the point of shooting them? Surely they could see that it was madness to charge again?

The men of the second wave were stood on the fire step covering the withdrawal, some of them becoming casualties as they attempted to protect their friends; one of them, Lieutenant Hinton being killed as he was firing over the parapet. Percy had only advanced a few yards before his life saving mishap. He grasped hold of Chugger's straps and dragged him along the ground until he reached the sand bagged parapet, many hands reaching up to pull him and Chugger to safety.

Attacking Turkish Quinn's was no longer viable. Major Bourne could see that.

"I'm not sending any more men to their deaths," he was heard to say.

The whole point of the attack had been to keep Jacko busy so that he wouldn't send men to the left where the main attack was happening. The men of the 2nd Light Horse were fully aware that it was hopeless, but were 'happy' to go.

"The next wave is ready sir, just tell us when," came a voice from the trench.

For the sake of his men and the fact that if he sent another hundred and fifty men to their deaths, Quinn's would be too weakened to fend off an enemy attack, he sent word to Colonel Stodart who, in turn, received authority from Regimental Headquarters to halt the attack.

The same luxury and commonsense sadly did not occur at the Nek for the men of the 8th and 10th Light Horse Regiments. Yet another diversionary action, the first wave of light horsemen was immediately mown down by a devastating hail of small arms and machine gun fire, the second wave suffering the same fate. Despite the obvious circumstances awaiting the next wave, the officer in charge refused to abandon the attack, resulting in the third wave also meeting the same tragic fate. The attack was eventually cancelled, but not before a few of the fourth wave went over the top. One hundred and thirty eight were wounded and two hundred and thirty four killed; two thirds of the attackers. Senseless!

For the rest of the day the 2nd Light Horse fended off attacks by the Turks on the 1st Light Horse Regiment. From the top outpost, Percy counted forty seven Australian dead. Percy and his mates concluded that this day, when the Turks charged all along their defensive line, was the "best ever," because they had left hundreds of dead in front of the Aussie trenches.

Although not a callous person Percy felt delighted with the slaughter; as did his mates.

"I hardly ever missed that running man target at Enoggera," said Percy, "but these buggers are just easy targets".

The Turkish soldiers all seemed big men, but the boys certainly wasted no time mowing them down.

"The bigger they are the harder they fall".

Boggy, it seemed, didn't know what it was to be frightened and took a delight in bomb throwing. When he threw one he would get halfway over the top of the trench to see what damage it had done, and when it exploded and the Turks screamed and yelled, he would laugh as if he was thoroughly enjoying himself.

As dusk fell, no man's land was no place for *any* man now, let alone stretcher bearers. The dead were never recovered and were destined to lie where they fell for another four years, along with thousands of others scattered around the peninsula.

The next day the Turks had erected a notice outside their trench, which read, 'Come again, Light Horse, and wear your white badges.'

"Ha! Look at this boys," shouted Boggy on seeing the sign.

Davo had a quick look through a periscope.

"They sure are a cheeky crowd," he said.

"Yeah but I admire the Turk on account of his being a fair

fighter. We've all seen our wounded bandaged by the Turks, and they have allowed bad cases to return to our trenches unmolested," Boggy added.

"I reckon they are fighting against their grain. The number of times I've seen German officers chucking rocks at them, forcing them to make attacks, then threatening them if they retreat," said Percy.

"I look forward to meeting *those* blokes one day mate," said Boggy.

Overnight another member of the Taylor clan, Archie and Percy's mother Doris's younger brother, Samuel Ford, had landed at Suvla Bay. This was not his first time at Gallipoli as only weeks earlier his battalion, the 7th Battalion South Staffordshire Regiment, part of the 11th Division, had taken part in its first significant action of the war. This was an attack on the Turkish positions at Achi Baba, a prominent hill which towered over the beach head at Cape Helles. The first casualties sustained by the 7th were in the Horseshoe, facing Achi Baba. This was the fourth attempt by the Allies to seize Achi Baba and the village of Krithia, but the heights remained in the hands of the Turks for the duration of the campaign. Following this action the battalion was withdrawn to Imbros in order to regroup for the Suvla assault.

The battalion arrived in pitch darkness on a hostile shoreline and, as the men waded ashore, through water five feet deep, they had to contend with sniper fire, along with land mines on the beach. Quite a welcome. Running out of the surf, Samuel and his muckas, or mates, could hardly see one another in the darkness. The Turkish snipers took full advantage of the situation, managing to mingle with the Staffords, shooting them from within.

The men of the South Staffordshire Regiment were recruited from the Midlands, an industrial area of England where one of the last examples of early English is still spoken today, that of the Black Country. Some of the men seemed shocked, and almost froze in position searching for the elusive enemy. Men kept falling and Samuel, not one to hold his tongue, began calling out in the darkness.

"The Turks am every which where, so stop yer ivverin' an' ovverin an' get on wi' it. Give 'em a right lampin' wi' yer bondook and bayonet!"

Samuel's calls in the darkness were all that the men required and, very soon, all of the snipers had been clubbed with rifles then dispatched with the bayonet.

Once the Turks had been dealt with, the companies regrouped and went straight on to the offensive, storming the Turkish outpost at Lala Baba. Whilst the outpost was being cleared other units moved north to destroy any other enemy nests.

Like the rest of Gallipoli, the ground was very difficult under foot, being sandy and covered with gorse bushes and other scrub. The Turks were dug in on Hill 10, a small promontory, only thirty feet high and three hundred yards long; situated half a mile from the landing area. There were an estimated two thousand defenders and two field guns in the general area when the British landed, compared to twenty two infantry battalions in the invading force. But, apart from the initial assaulting battalions moving inland, there was silence at Suvla with the exception of the occasional rifle shot from the surrounding heights. The landing at Suvla Bay was a surprise to the Turks, and there was ample time for the newly landed Corps to take the advantage before the Turkish reinforcements arrived. But, due to poor leadership, and communication, the landing was going astray, troops were milling around on the beach with no direction or orders. Crucial time was being wasted.

As dawn broke, the part battery of Turkish guns began shelling the beach and the gullies, the explosive blasts setting fire to the gorse through which the infantry were advancing. Some soldiers suffocated in the thick acrid smoke, whilst others were burnt to death, their cries piercing the battle field. During the smoky confusion the Turks attempted to take advantage of the situation, running hell for leather at the British, bayonets fixed, only to fall foul of the smoke and flames themselves, then being routed by the attackers.

The 10th Division was now landing. The tenacity and fighting spirit of the 11th Division had secured a landing place at Suvla Bay and had resulted in the path being cleared for the next north bound phase of the attack. But time had been lost between the original landing on the 6th and 7th and the occupation of the hills on the 8th and 9th. The troops had landed with no maps, no guides and no clear orders. As already mentioned, the terrain was difficult and slowed progress. Thirty thousand men had landed on the first day. The beach was a scene of chaos. Battalions were intermingled; the beach was crowded with stores, pack animals and even casualties from the hills, adding to their woes. By now the Turkish shells were falling on the occupied positions and all across the beach head.

Having not had time to acclimatise, the summer heat was

stifling, and the men from cold northern Europe were suffering; their water almost gone, and resupply a shambles. Chocolate Hill was taken by nightfall but the victors were now waterless, low on food and ammunition, unable to move against Ismail Oglu Tepe, and still two miles short from their link up with the Aussies.

The South Staffords were now making their way towards Scimitar Hill, the next valuable position to capture, as it would have made a perfect observation and artillery position for the enemy. Without maps or guides the battalion was having a hard time of it. Most of that night was spent slowly working their way back to the rendezvous with the 33rd Brigade. Although not a particularly long distance, the dense scrub dictated a single lined formation, increasing the delay even more. The battalion paused often to conduct a head count, and it was during these checks that exhausted men dropped down asleep, having to be picked up by their NCOs and officers. Despite their tiredness, having been in action for over twenty four hours, they were punctual for their rendezvous, linking up with the 6th Battalion the Lincolnshire Regiment and the 6th Battalion the Borderers Regiment.

The task for the right of the battalion was to direct the brigade on the line of the summit of Scimitar Hill, otherwise known as 'W' Hill. The leading companies were placed in to artillery formation, each company forming a diamond shape with its four platoons, covering a hundred yard frontage and thirty to fifty yard depth, with the rifle section up front and the rifle bombers and bombing section arranged behind, the Platoon Headquarters then followed by the Lewis Gun section.

It was hard going and Samuel was feeling it now, as was everyone else, but they were all focussed on their mission. Sadly, in the officer class there was too much bravado and thoughtlessness. So far the brigade had not been seen by the enemy. As Samuel looked to his left at a young Second Lieutenant who had been walking alongside of him, the officer placed a cigarette between his lips and began fumbling in his pocket for his matches.

"Yow doe wanna be doing that ar kid...sir," whispered Private Ford.

The indignant officer simply rolled his eyes at the soldier, tutted, struck his match and held it to his cigarette, and promptly dropped, with a bullet in his forehead. As the platoon carried on, stepping over the dead officer, Samuel shook his head, simply saying "yamp!"

At 0600 hours the brigade reached Hill 70 and almost immediately came under murderous shrapnel and small arms fire. In the first ten minutes every officer in 'A', 'B' and 'D' Companies was either killed or wounded. It was time for the NCOs to take charge and take the attack in. As the battalion advanced Samuel could see via his peripheral vision that comrades were falling all around him. Private Cooper from Tipton was marching opposite Samuel when he was grazed by a round on the left temple. At first he dropped to his knees, grasping the side of his head, but with a helping hand from Samuel he was up again and marching towards the fray. Shrapnel and bullets were flying everywhere, knocking dirt in to the men's faces. The air was hot with lead; then the bombs started. Such a row, just like a living Hell.

Samuel and his battalion marched on, not really thinking,

almost in a daydream. Then came the shout to charge bayonets. This was followed by a huge volley from the Turks causing the men, who survived, to throw themselves to the ground. Samuel being one of the lucky few kept his head down as he lay in the scrub. Looking around he saw that his platoon was quite a distance to the front of the battalion and he could see very few of his mates.

"Here's a 'ow do. We'em gooin to get ommered 'ere. If ar stay I will either get jed or bosted, and if ar get bosted I will lie here all day," he thought, "and ar aye got no waerter in me bottle, so I had better make a dash for our lines, and if I ketch merry hell, well, it cor be 'elped".

While debating this over in his mind Samuel was lying quite close to a chum called Michael Babb. He was badly wounded. Asking Private Babb where he was hit, Samuel almost revisited what little he had eaten that day, as he showed him his left hand, which was just a pulp. Then to worsen the situation, as Samuel was reassuring him, Babb was hit three times in the body; his groans were heartrending. Most were of the same opinion as young Private Ford, choosing to make a dash back to the main body of the battalion. Samuel rose cautiously to his feet and grasped hold of the yoke of Babb's webbing, but he was too heavy to shift. Samuel finally fixed a shovel to the equipment of his wounded comrade and, using this as a sledge, dragged the man back over one hundred yards to safety, being under fire all the way. As he moved rearwards he watched as another young soldier, by the name of Minshall, was shot in front of him when running past, the force of the bullet causing the soldier to jump about three feet as he was hit. Samuel was already busy with Babb, but was relieved when Private Minshall attempted to crawl back to the Stafford's lines. Sadly, Minshall was hit again and died within seconds.

At about 0800 hours support from the 10th Division arrived, but it was too late. The British line had begun to give way, mainly because the scrub had caught fire and the Turks were attempting a flanking manoeuvre from the left. Despite its magnificent behaviour on the battlefield, the battalion, and the rest of the attackers were overwhelmed at mid day by a far superior sized force, and forced to withdraw, with a loss of over four hundred men killed and wounded. They spent the next three days holding an old enemy communication trench running on to Chocolate Hill. Only then were they finally relieved.

The attack on the heights on the far left of the ANZAC line, the main objective of the operation, had been a disaster. The steep hills and valleys were unexplored and nigh on impossible to traverse at night. The New Zealand, Indian and Australian troops, like everyone else, were too weak and sick, but nonetheless advanced at a good pace, their movement being hampered continuously by the mobile Turkish forces who sporadically attacked them throughout the night, inflicting serious casualties. In the end they had to dig in short of their objectives.

Had precious time not been lost, the British and the Australians would have been on top of Chunuk Bair on the 8th. But Chunuk Bair *had* been taken, by the Wellington Battalion, and was held for a day, the Kiwis fighting a desperate hand to hand struggle with the Turks, losing only because of the failed link up, which meant that all other objectives which would benefit from the British divisions at Suvla, also failed.

The dry, scrubby, hills were in flames due to the constant artillery fire, naval gunfire, and bombing at close quarters, and, as those on the heights looked down at Suvla, they could see no movement of men coming their way. However, following the personal intervention of General Hamilton, they tried their best, struggling up steep and crowded narrow ravines in the dark, getting constantly lost, and, when in sight of the objective, being mistakenly shelled by their own side.

Those on Chunuk Bair were eventually driven off by overwhelming numbers, and friendly artillery fire, putting an end to any further attempts to secure the heights around Hill 971. A handful of Turks had been stationed at Suvla on the day of the landing, but instead of destroying them the commanders on the ground dilly dallied, choosing, in most cases, to dig in rather than advance.

Lieutenant General Stoptford, a professional soldier of forty five years, remained at his headquarters near the beach, largely ignorant of the state of the fighting, refusing to follow Hamilton's battle plan because there was not enough artillery support. Over twenty thousand men became casualties in the Suvla Bay action. Stoptford was relieved of his command on the 15th of August 1915.

Despite the failures at Suvla Bay, the reason for the feints by the ANZACs, the attack on Lone Pine, which lasted for two days, was a success. The hold on Gallipoli, however, was now a stalemate. The soldiers had done their best, and more. They had made their positions impregnable, but had been let down by the very politicians who had sent them there in the first place. Not enough men, and certainly very little artillery ammunition, which, had both been available from the outset, would have removed Turkey from the war. Unless Gallipoli could be garrisoned by another hundred thousand men, who were fresh and strong, the fate of the campaign was sealed. But, to the politicians in London, Gallipoli was a side show, and the Turk was an inferior fighter. Tell that to the men fighting in the Middle East, who respected Johnny Turk, and tell that to the nations who had been conquered and occupied by the Ottoman Empire for over four hundred years!

From the 9th of August the situation became calmer. The 2nd Light Horse Regiment transferred its responsibilities to the 3rd Light Horse and relocated to Pope's Hill. Over the next three weeks, a period of relative tranquility ensued. There were no further options for advancement, and the Turkish forces were aware of this. They continued to annoy with their artillery and snipers, but that was the extent of their actions, at least for the time being.

On the 12th of August twelve Aussie snipers were sent to Suvla to help clear out their Turkish counterparts. An important despatch was also required at Suvla and Percy and Davo were asked to volunteer to take it.

As the two mates made their way down the sunken roads and pathways they could see Suvla Bay in the distance. The beach appeared to be littered with cargo and there were many soldiers moving around, the occasional explosion of a shell flinging clouds of sand in to the air.

"Poor old Id and Tubby eh?" said Percy.

"Yeah, Id was a bit of a strange bloke, but he didn't deserve to die. Well, none of them did," added Davo.

"I'm glad Chugger is out of it for a while," said Percy.

"I wonder where they sent him?" asked Davo.

"Wherever it is it will be a darn sight safer than here," said Percy.

"Boggy is missing him. Pining like a lost dog he is," said Davo.

The trek to Suvla Bay from Pope's Hill was approximately ten miles, only made harder by the steep terrain down to the beach, but once there it was relatively easy walking along the flat coastline to Suvla Bay. The closer Davo and Percy got to Suvla the more annoyed they both became.

"Why the hell didn't *we* land here?" exclaimed Percy, "look at it! It's almost flat, and look how far you can see".

Percy was correct, in a manner, for *their* landing places were disadvantaged by the steep terrain and narrow beaches, not to mention the inadequate water supplies.

"Don't forget mate, we should have been at Gaba Tepe, which I've heard is similar to this place," said Davo.

"I suppose so. They were waiting for our boys there too I hear," agreed Percy.

Message delivered to General Headquarters (GHQ), Percy and Davo began their journey back to the ANZAC lines. As they navigated their way through the chaotic encampment at Suvla, Percy noticed a British soldier staring intently at him. The man's gaze lingered for a moment, and Percy sensed familiarity in his eyes. Davo had noticed too.

"That bloke over there is having a good look at us," said Davo.

Curiosity getting the better of him, Percy approached the soldier cautiously.

"Excuse me, mate," he said tentatively, "have we met before?"

The soldier, who was a member of the South Staffordshire Regiment, looked Percy up and down with a mix of surprise and recognition.

"Ar've got this photo 'ere ar kid and the more ar look," the soldier replied, his voice filling with astonishment as he showed Percy the picture, "is this yower faerce? Am yow Percy Taylor?"

As Percy was deciphering what the soldier had said in his mind, his eyes widened in wonder.

"You know my name?" he responded, his voice filled with disbelief.

The soldier nodded and smiled.

"Well blow me darn with a rag mon's trumpet," he replied, offering his hand, "Ar ay met yow in person, but yower faerce is familiar. Aerdew aer kid, aer bin ya? Ar'm yower uncle Sam".

Percy's confusion slowly turned into a mix of surprise and delight.

"Uncle Samuel! Blimey. Mum wrote and said you were in Egypt but I didn't know you were here at Gallipoli," said Percy, "oh, sorry this is my mate Davo".

Samuel nodded his acknowledgement to Davo.

"Yow am the spittin' image of yower muther," he said.

Samuel gestured towards a small pile of wooden crates.

"Shall we sit and cant awhile?" asked Samuel.

"Cant?" said Percy, looking towards Davo, "sorry Uncle Sam but I'm having trouble understanding you".

Sam laughed.

"I mean a chat ar kid," he replied, "to tell yer the truth I cor understand some of what yow blokes am on about either".

Eventually the three men worked it out, agreeing to talk

slowly and clearly in order to be understood. As Percy took out his diary to record the date of the meeting, Sam revealed that he too had a diary and had been recording his war in poetry.

"I'd like our Doris ter see this wun day," said Sam.

"She'd love that. Maybe I can copy it in to my diary?" asked Percy.

"Goo on then," replied Sam, handing the book to his nephew.

As he read the poem Percy was impressed and surprised, for despite his uncle's black country dialect, his written English was clear and concise.

"This is wonderful," said Percy, "can I read it out loud?"

Sam nodded.

The Landing of Gallipoli

Leaving their homes, forsaking all,
These were the lads, who answered the call,
The first of July they left England's shores,
For over the foam to some foreign floor.

Late in July we spotted the land,
Some looked happy and some dismayed,
I wonder who owns that beautiful land,
This question was asked by some at hand.

Hark at the guns cried one gallant lad,
Soon we'll be there all fighting like mad,
For this is Gallipoli where danger lurks,
For this is the land, the home of the Turks.

You talk of Balaclava,
And of Trafalgar Bay
But what of the 11th Division,
Who landed at Suvla Bay.

It was on the 6th of August,
And the night was dusk you know,
When the lads made that landing,
Prepared to meet the foe.

Through thick and thin, through shot and shell,
These gallant lads they stuck it well.
Brave officers fell as well as men,
But they still fought plucky after then.

The Stafford's were the first to land,
And this is what they met,
Turkish Sentry's on the beach,
Shouting "Halt! Hands up," you bet.

Then the order came along the line,
All bayonet work no shot,
And many a lad from Staffordshire,
Was killed upon the spot.

The Lincolns and the Borders,
Went mad and how they raved,
When the plucky Notts and Derbyshires

Came dashing to their aid.

Then a little higher along the beach,
There came a shout like thunder,
But it was the cry of our 34th Brigade,
Charging them asunder.

The Lancashire Fusiliers fought well,
And East and West Yorks too.
And the brave young lads from Dorset
Stuck to their tasks like glue.

The Yorks and Lancs were in it too,
Also the Fighting Fifth,
These men fought well on Chocolate Hill,
And many lie there still.

The Coat of Arms now had their turn,
As Chocolate Hill was rushed,
And the Turks who could not get away,
Were prisoners or else crushed.

Then on the Ninth of August,
I'll never forget the day,
We got the order to form up,
And get ready for the fray.

The hill called 971 by name,
Which had to fall at any cost,

Our General cried "Go steady lads
All bayonet work no shots".

The Lincolns were a sight to see,
All in a line they dashed.
Honour they won as well as fame,
For the Turkish line was smashed.

Well those are the lads, who left their home,
Their wives and sweethearts too
And many a lad was left there
But they died nobly for you.

So honour the 11th Division,
As well as the Light Brigade.
They joined and did their bit,
So never let them fade.

Private S Ford
South Staffordshire Regiment

Percy's voice quivered as he reached the last verse.

"Beautiful Uncle Sam" said Percy, wiping away a tear, "when all this is over I will type this out and frame it for mum".

Samuel shook his nephew's hand in appreciation.

"Mate, its getting dark so we'd better get going," said Davo, feeling a little concerned.

As the three men shook hands and bid each other good luck they vowed to meet again.

12

Do Not Stir in Discontent

Despite being weakened from sickness the ANZACs battled on, continuing their strenuous work of improving trenches, digging saps and tunnels, transporting food, water, ammunition and mail up the steep pathways which led to places like Quinn's Post and Bolton's Ridge, from the small beach at ANZAC Cove.

Dysentery, diarrhoea and general malnutrition were still rife in the ANZAC lines by the end of August. The lack of fruit and vegetables in the men's diet was a big factor, not to mention the lice, the flies that moved from the rotting corpses to the food of the living, plus the general stress of being constantly at peril for five months. Some men were just skin and bone, their limbs covered in open sores, prone to going septic. But the troops carried on, working in fatigue parties, existing on bully beef, bacon, hard biscuits and watery jam. By the end of August thirty per cent of the 3rd Brigade had been evacuated as sick from the peninsula. Those who were left struggled to stand up, let alone defend the line.

Roo was looking pale, and blue round his lips, nose and eyes.

"Mate, you look really crook," said a concerned Clancy, "you're so pale that if I didn't know you I'd say you were a white fella".

Joking aside, Clancy and Archie, weren't exactly feeling great either, the only *real* sustenance that any of them were receiving being Doris's fruit cake.

"You chaps look like death warmed up," said Ponsonby, "you need to report sick".

"Sir, you don't look too flush yourself," replied Clancy, "and we can't afford to report sick. The front line is weak as it is".

"We'll be right sir," added Archie.

Ponsonby was warmed with pride, a tear welling in his eye. Quickly wiping it away he reached for the old billy can.

"Tea anyone?" he asked.

"Bloody hell, that'll be a first!" exclaimed Clancy.

"Yes, well, don't get too used to it, I have standards to keep up don't you know," joked the officer.

At Pope's Hill Percy was suffering too.

Unlike the British officer class who considered sickness a weakness, labelling it malingering, the ANZAC officers were the direct opposite. In fact they were not immune to it themselves, with Brigade and Battalion officers being evacuated throughout the period.

Many men refused to be evacuated so were sent to rest areas on the peninsula. The line was now so thin that newly arrived units were split up temporarily to fill the gaps. 'A' Squadron and the machine gun section of the 11th Light Horse Regiment were attached to the 2nd Light Horse straight from the beach. They were very welcome indeed.

Prior to the sickness, the front line regiments and battalions were rotated, so that every unit got a regular rest; the "rest" being fatigue parties. But, with the heavily reduced manpower *every* regiment and battalion was manning the front line. The brigade sectors were re-evaluated. The 9th Battalion's line was increased by two hundred yards to its right, meaning that the already weakened men had to construct two hundred yards of new trench. Once complete they added wire entanglements and dug tunnels to within throwing distance of the Turks. Basically, the bombers would travel, concealed, along the tunnel to a hidden opening above them and toss their bombs at the enemy.

The 5th of September brought a visit from General Birdwood, who had come to see the newly constructed trenches. Although concerned for the wellbeing of the men he was both impressed with them *and* their excellent trenches.

Birdie must indeed have been impressed as nineteen days later, on the 24th of September, it was decided that a demonstration to draw Turkish fire, and their attention, was needed.

"What bloody for?!" exclaimed Clancy in his usual manner.

"Not another attack!" said a worried Archie, "we can't *walk* five yards, let alone advance at speed. Drongos!"

"Look chaps," said Ponsonby, "I believe something is in the wind again, and I think these demonstrations are to keep the Turks distracted *and* alert at the same time".

The good news was that it was not an attack, but a ruse. Bayonets and cut out figures were shown above the parapet, and dummy bombs in the form of burnt tins were lobbed as far as possible in to no man's land to add to the noise. Then the men, along with artillery and machine guns, opened up on Abdul, who replied with volley after volley from Hell itself.

The roar of the big guns, the whistling of the shells, and the bursting of shrapnel certainly kept everyone on the alert, including the Turks.

The 3rd of October brought some respite and entertainment for *all* on the peninsula. Each day a dispatch rider would make the hazardous five mile journey along the beach from Suvla Bay to ANZAC Cove. The task would need to be carried out at the gallop for the Turkish snipers, in the surrounding hills and ridges, would routinely take pot shots at the horse and rider throughout the entire journey. The event, to those not otherwise engaged, had become quite a sport, with bets being placed on whether the rider and horse would get through; the Turks also having a daily wager of their own. This day, however, was special, as was the horse that had been chosen to carry the mail…Bill the Bastard. The rider, one Captain Anthony Bickworth, an English cavalryman, had been selected for today's ride from the many allied troops who volunteered on a daily basis. The usual bet revolved around whether the mail would make it through or not, but once it became known that Bill was involved, the bet quickly changed to whether the mail would arrive *with* or without the rider. The odds from the various bookies around the peninsula were soon at twenty to one, the general consensus being that the mail would not get through at all.

"I'll have some of that," said Clancy, feeling confident that, with or without Captain Bickworth, Bill would do his duty and deliver the mail.

"How much are you putting on Clance?" asked Roo.

"A tenner," replied Clancy,

"Ten quid?" bloody hell you must be confident," exclaimed Roo.

"Look boys, we've met Bill, and seen him as a pack horse. He may be stubborn, but he gets the job done," Clancy explained, "and I reckon he'll throw the rider but deliver the mail".

"Yer know, there's nothing to spend our earnings on here so why not?" said Archie, "bookie, I'll have a tenner for the mail to arrive mate".

The soldier bookmaker smiled to himself as he accepted the same bet from Clancy, Roo and Stowie, remarking. "it's your funeral fellas".

The "race" was scheduled to begin at 1100 hours. The entire peninsula was silent. The only shots fired were from the Turkish snipers. Those who had them, watched through binoculars. From the off Bill ignored the directions of his rider, starting off at a casual trot, working his way up to a gallop. Faster and faster he went, seeming to sense the snipers bullets as he dodged left and right. The cavalry officer hung on for dear life and could not control Bill, for Bill was in charge. As the bullets whizzed and whined past, Bill was charging like a wild bull, head down and eyes fixated on ANZAC Cove. But, at about a quarter of the distance, Bill suddenly came to a halt. He'd had enough of the annoyance that was sitting on his back and bucked his rider high up in to the air, the Captain hitting the ground like a ton of bricks, unconscious. There was a muffled cheer from the hills as thousands of men, confident that they had won the bet, began to calculate in their heads just how much they had won. No thought was given to the poor lifeless rider now lying in the sand. But Bill was about to have his revenge, as he trotted a short distance then halted about then yards from the fallen captain, for he travelled this route on most days and knew exactly where he was going. Giving a snort and a few stomps with his front hooves for good measure, Bill casually turned south and began to trot, head held high in a sort of defiance, towards the Cove, where he was met and relieved of his saddle bags by the postal orderly. He had successfully completed the gallop and delivered the mail unaccompanied, albeit with a bullet lodged in his flank.

"Good on yer Bill," Clancy thought to himself.

Clancy's reading may not have been up to scratch but his arithmetic definitely was.

"Two hundred smackers! I'm rich!" he shouted, "now, where's that bloody bookie?"

The three mates couldn't believe their luck as they each collected their winnings.

"£200...that's two years earnings back home!" exclaimed Archie.

"If you're lucky," replied Roo.

"Well mine is my ticket to owning my own house and a plot of land," said Clancy, "there's plenty available in Kilcoy".

"I'm sending mine home for mum and dad to look after. Something to dip in to if they need it," said Archie.

"Me too. Good idea mate," replied Roo, "I wonder if Percy had a bet too?"

In early October the Turks were still busy all over Gallipoli. On the 5th of October an enemy fatigue party was seen working to the front of the 9th Battalion's lines.

"Hey Clance! Look at these silly buggers," said Archie, as he passed the CSM the periscope.

The Turks were working in plain view of the Aussies and were just asking for trouble.

"What the....?" uttered a surprised Clancy, who then whispered to the troops within earshot, "Stowie and Arch you cover left and right of them, Roo and Jacko get ready with the bombs".

On the signal Roo and Jacko struck their respective matches and lit the fuses on their bombs. "One, two, three!" The bombs were airborne, hurtling towards the unsuspecting Turks. BOOM!...BOOM! The bombs exploded, wreaking death and havoc amongst the men, flesh being torn and shredded by the shrapnel contained in the improvised devices. Six of the ten men were dead; the remaining four, at first stunned and shaken, now making a frantic run back towards their trenches. BANG! Up, back, forward, down, BANG! Stowie and Archie were doing their deadly work like well oiled machines, firing quickly and accurately at the enemy, the four men falling on their faces in to the dry soil of Gallipoli.

There was now silence on the ridge. Not a shot was received

from the Turks. Perhaps they were tired of war, or maybe they *too* were checking to make sure the ANZACs were still there

"What a bloody waste of good blokes! I mean, why would they work there, right in front of our eyes?" exclaimed Clancy.

"I don't know mate," replied Roo, "maybe a cuppa would help?"

"I doubt it, but get the billy fired up, it must be your turn anyway," joked Clancy.

On the 6th of October, Sniper's Ridge showcased a second demonstration where they utilised newly provided parachute rockets (flares). These flares produced a whooshing sound as they were propelled into the sky, illuminating Abdul's trenches all across the ANZAC line. With the area to their front lit up like day the soldiers poured rifle and machine gun fire at the enemy trenches, resulting in a significant exchange of gunfire.

Meanwhile, at Bolton's Ridge, the soldiers crouched down in their trenches as a couple of Turkish machine guns burrowed in to them. The sound of the guns, emanating from concealed positions on the right and left, was intense enough to unnerve anyone, with the rattling and cracking echoing through the air. The relentless shells, rifles and machine guns had the space along the top of their parapets almost whipped up to dust, causing the contents of the sandbags to spill out through bullet holes onto the soldiers who sought refuge at the bottom of the trenches. Some enemy soldiers even attempted a half hearted charge, but the 9th Battalion men simply mowed them down.

It was mid autumn at Gallipoli and the temperatures were definitely cooling, resulting in one good thing, less flies. But on the 8th of October fierce storms caused serious damage to the piers at ANZAC. This was the first warning of the coming winter.

The 16th of October brought demonstration number three. This time each man was ordered to fire one round only, which perplexed many of the ANZACs. There was also additional artillery fire, the bombardment courtesy of all the artillery on the peninsula, assisted by the warships, which came along for the purpose. For two hours the wildest furies of Hell were opened on the Turkish trenches, many Turks being blown out by bomb and shell. The air was alive with shrieking, whistling, groaning and the hissing of shells as they arrived like hail from the heavens, thick and fast. The soldiers were aghast as the mighty explosions tore the place to pieces; the hills almost appearing to be blown bodily into the air. The roaring of the guns and exploding shells was deafening, and seemed to the men who witnessed it, mightier than the loudest thunder.

But this time, despite this storm of artillery, there was only a limited response from the enemy.

The ANZACs waited in anticipation, bayonets fixed, but no one came.

Another significant event occurred on this day with General Hamilton being recalled to London, effectively ending his long and illustrious military career.

More storms followed throughout October and November and the temperatures dropped dramatically. The men were kept busy improving, and constructing, new shelters for the winter; but wood and metal were scarce. However, Percy and other 2nd Light Horsemen managed to procure iron and wood from the Engineers Dump at the Cove.

The endless daily digging, although tiring, kept the men warm, but sniping and shrapnel was as deadly as ever, with bivvies, the beach and even the hospital, becoming regular shelling recipients.

By the 25th of October the 9th Battalion had been in a war zone for six months, suffering one hundred and fifty one deaths, plus countless wounded, and on this date the battalion fielded just over a third of its full strength. In the last week of October they erected some dummy machine gun posts. Each was promptly destroyed by enemy artillery. Sapping and tunnelling continued and much sniping at the enemy was carried out.

Hill 60 represented the final significant assault by the Allied forces in the Gallipoli campaign. The lack of success in the August offensive heightened concerns about the campaign's future, especially considering the ongoing demands on the Western Front and at Salonika. The British authorities regarded the situation in Gallipoli as both embarrassing and inconsequential and, in response to Lieutenant General Hamilton's request for additional troops, earlier that month, the British government not only turned him down but also replaced him with Lieutenant General Sir Charles Monro.

To compound matters, the Central Powers' occupation of Serbia established a direct railway link between the Ottoman, Austro-Hungarian, and German empires. This enabled the Ottomans to receive substantial artillery support from Germany and Austria. Additionally, the Ottoman Fifth Army's numbers were growing, with a force of three hundred and fifteen thousand soldiers compared to the Mediterranean Expeditionary Force's one hundred and thirty four thousand. It didn't take long for Monro to recognize that the most prudent course of action would be to recommend an evacuation.

On the 3rd of November the 9th Battalion received orders in the afternoon to pack up and be ready to move off by 2000 hours. They were being relieved by the 1st Brigade and moved to a quieter spot; compared to what they would be leaving. As they got ready they were issued some rations, including cheese for the first time since they'd been at Gallipoli. The whole battalion, the men learnt, was to move off during the night and embark for Lemnos. Their rest period had finally come.

However, as with best plans made by mice and men, they did not depart that night, and just slept where they could. The next morning, the troops started cooking for themselves, as all the cooks' dixies were packed up for the move.

"That's a bugger," moaned Clancy, "I was hoping for some hot stew or something".

The battalion's departure ended up being delayed for days due to the wind getting up in the afternoon and raising sufficient sea to prevent anything getting in to the wharf. The rough seas continued for several days, and the wind was icy cold early in the evening.

The delay for the battalion meant that, on the 7th of November, they would be party to a historical event of the Dardanelles campaign.

Lieutenant Ponsonby and his platoon were enjoying some billy tea on the beach when a rowing boat arrived at the shoreline with a very important passenger on board. Very few had any previous knowledge of his visit, but the moment he stepped ashore the men tumbled to it, and a remarkable scene occurred.

Sporadic cheering and shouting was coming from near the pier, and attracted Clancy's attention.

"What's all that row?" he exclaimed, "is the King here or something?"

Ponsonby rose to his feet for a better look.

"My goodness," said Ponsonby, "it's better than that boys; it's Kitchener!"

How the knowledge could have spread so fast is unfathomable, but by the time Kitchener had reached the end of the pier men were tumbling like rabbits out of every dugout on the hillside, leaping over obstacles, and making straight for the beach. Aussie soldiers were not ones for showing excitement or cheering, but as Lord Kitchener, accompanied by Lieutenant General Birdwood and others, passed by the crowd along the beach, the men spontaneously called for cheers, and gave them again and again. It was truly a soldiers' welcome.

As Kitchener moved along the beach he stopped many times to speak to the men.

"The King has asked me to tell you how splendidly he thinks you have done," he said, "you have done excellently well; better even than I thought you would."

At first Clancy was in awe of the man, but these words really got his goat. He just could not help himself.

"What do you mean by that you bludger?" Clancy growled at the Field Marshall.

Lieutenant Ponsonby threw his left arm out in front of the sergeant major as if to hold him back.

"Clancy...no," he whispered.

But it was too late for that now. Kitchener stopped and turned to Clancy.

"What was that sergeant major?" he enquired.

"I want to know what *you* meant by saying that we've done better than you thought we would...er...sir," Clancy announced.

Kitchener was not flustered at all and pondered for a while.

"Yes, I suppose it was a little thoughtless of me, and I meant no offence," replied Kitchener, "really what I should have said is that I had my initial doubts about a brand new and untried army, but you have all done brilliantly".

"Well, why didn't you say that in the first place?" replied Clancy.

Kitchener smiled.

"What's your name sergeant major?" he asked.

"Clancy McBride. Pleased to meet you," Clancy responded, hand outstretched.

Kitchener took Clancy's hand and shook it firmly.

"I like a man not afraid to speak his mind. Too many yes men in my circles unfortunately," he said, looking his entourage up and down, "how long have you been at Gallipoli Mister McBride?"

"Me and my mates here landed on the first day. One of the first boats ashore, sir," replied Clancy, feeling very proud.

"Really? Walk with me sergeant major," said Kitchener.

Without a pause, Clancy by his side, his entourage, including Roo and Archie, in tow, Kitchener walked straight up the steepest road in the ANZAC area direct from the beach to the highest point. Striding forcefully up the steep and winding path, Kitchener was at the summit in around ten minutes. Each ANZAC knew that most who traverse this road arrive at the top breathless, the majority of whom certainly requiring a respite on the way; but Kitchener went straight up without a halt, and, arriving at the top, immediately spoke to the brigade commanders assembled there, without pausing for breath. Next he marched through the front firing trenches at Quinn's Post, Courtney's and the Nek, where the Light Horse had charged and died back in August. As he passed by, the troops could scarcely be restrained from cheering him, even though the Turks, in places, were within twenty yards. Birdwood and his staff experienced some moments of considerable anxiety as this tall figure, wearing a staff officer's cap, stalked down many awkward corners, where he was all too visible to the Turkish snipers, constantly stopping to speak to the men. The Aussie soldiers, fortunately, generally managed to keep their heads on these occasions.

Kitchener surveyed the entire ANZAC position from a good look out point, getting a quick grasp of the country.

"So, do *you* have any thoughts sergeant major?" asked Kitchener.

"Thoughts sir? About ANZAC?" Clancy replied.

"Yes. Has it been worth it? Should we stay? That sort of thing?" said Kitchener.

"Well sir for the army it has created in ours and the Kiwis then yes it has been worth it; perhaps not to the mates we've all lost, but," Clancy began, "if we had had twice the men and artillery from the start we would be in Constantinople by now. I mean, crikey, we reached those heights up there on the first day, but couldn't hold because we had no one to help us. I bet you didn't know that did you sir?"

Kitchener glanced towards his entourage.

"I most certainly did *not*," he replied.

"I think we've shot our bolt and it's time to go. We've done bloody well, fought off every Abdul attack, but if they get those big guns here we are done for. Besides if you send us boys to France the war will soon be won," said Clancy with a smile.

Kitchener chuckled and held out his hand to Clancy.

"Yes. Quite. Thank you for your invaluable insight Mister McBride...and good luck," said Kitchener.

"You're welcome mate...er...sir," replied Clancy as he braced up in acknowledgement of the Field Marshall.

Within two hours of his arrival, Kitchener was gone, having seen almost every important officer and taken a thorough look at the position.

Morale had certainly been boosted by his visit, but what would the outcome be?

Kitchener was a practical man and now that he had seen Gallipoli for himself he was finally convinced of the uselessness of holding on any longer. The whole peninsula *must* be evacuated.

Kitchener's decision would not be revealed for some time, but having been at Gallipoli without a break, the 9th Battalion was frothing at the mouth for a rest period at Lemnos. The next day, the advance party left for Lemnos and the rest of the battalion were relieved at 1000 hours by the 2nd Battalion, moving in to bivvies on the hillside west of Artillery Road.

"You know, I didn't think I'd get off here," said Archie.

"Soon be home eh?" Taff responded.

"Home? We're only going for a two week rest. Besides, the war aint over in France yet...how's yer French?" said Clancy.

"You mean after this we have to fight again?" said a confused Taff.

"Yes mate, you signed on for the duration," replied Clancy.

The 10th of November brought a period of rest too for one hundred and ninety five men of the 2nd Light Horse Regiment who departed for Mudros. But, despite the constant fighting since their arrival in May, Percy and his chums elected to remain as rear party, suspecting that something momentous was in the works. Those who remained were a handful of 2nd Light Horse soldiers, including signallers, plus Captain (former sergeant) Steele, the Adjutant, and also a squadron of attached 11th Light Horse.

After two weeks of waiting, at 1800 hours on the 16th of November orders were received "ready to move in fifteen minutes", and, at 1930 hours, the 9th Battalion marched out under cover of darkness, finally boarding small boats from number 8 Pier, which took them to the 'Abbassia'. It had been bitterly cold waiting to go on board, and then waiting on deck, and the men were stiff and numbed all over with the freezing temperatures, but they were happy to be leaving. To them it was the invasion in reverse, but not a shot fired.

At daylight on the 17th the battalion, aboard the 'Abbassia', entered Mudros Harbour after spending a very cold night without food, huddled together wherever they could find room. Upon completing six months of intense fighting, the men felt deserving of an extended period of respite; although uncertain about the duration of their holiday. Mudros Harbour was full of shipping, just as when they were there previously. The troops were quickly transferred to a ferry boat, and were taken ashore. Once on dry land they had to march several miles with all their kit on, but they were safe. The initial sensation was unimaginable as their weary legs struggled to carry them. Naturally, some expressed their discontent. On route they passed through a Greek village and numerous children of ten or twelve years of age came out to sell chocolates and oranges. The battalion was halted and fallen out to do their shopping, most of them not having had anything of that sort for six months.

Upon arrival at their camp, their spirits were lifted. The provision of splendid food, a stark contrast to the monotonous biscuits and salty tinned meat, elevated their hopes. Their breakfast comprised two eggs and bacon, while lunch consisted of fresh meat and vegetables, followed by tea, and in the evening they were even provided with a half bottle of stout...for medicinal purposes. With a month of such nourishment, they anticipated a recovery of their lost strength.

"Veges and beer?!" exclaimed Archie, "why couldn't we get this stuff on Gallipoli?"

"No idea mate, but they're probably just fattening us up so they can send us back," Clancy responded.

"Thanks for cheering us up mate," said Archie.

Within the camp, the Greek locals offered various goods for sale, including eggs, grapes, apples, tinned fish, candles, chocolates, and nuts, fulfilling their desires for delectable treats. The return to good food was truly delightful. The tranquility in the area made it difficult to fathom that the war raged only fifty six miles away. Their comrades' appearance being the only reminder of the hardships endured.

While some tents remained to be erected, the heavy rain had inundated the land, making the upcoming days rather unpleasant. At present there were eighteen men per tent, but, surprisingly, most of them were singing, exuding a sense of contentment. They intended to turn this trip into a genuine holiday, limiting themselves to necessary tasks and duties.

It was bitterly cold the first four days after arrival. A cold, snowy wind seemed to eat into you if you stood still. But the men were being well fed, the drill was easy, and being away from the dangers of the firing line was hard to realise. Cricket and football too were in full swing, with each unit having its own cricket and football team.

It was some days after the battalion arrived on the island before they could get accustomed to no firing going on, and for the men to realise that it was quite safe to walk about anywhere. In essence the break, away from Gallipoli, meant undisturbed sleep, amusement, bathing without the threat of Beachy Bill, plenty of food, and even a canteen. It was just like the school holidays.

It didn't go unnoticed that there were some fine ships in the harbour. What they were doing there no one knew, but what they *did* know was that every day after *their* arrival, troops were arriving from Gallipoli.

On the 26th of November orders were issued on Gallipoli for complete silence. There was to be no rifle or machine gun fire, and no bombs to be thrown. But, digging carried on, as did the continuous enemy shelling.

The silence was broken two days later when yet another demonstration was ordered along the whole line, again to remind the Turks that they were still there. Then, on the 28th, something new, and a bit of a novelty to most...snow.

The 2nd Light Horse awoke to find about three inches of snow on the ground. For several days prior the cold had been worse than anything any of the men had ever experienced. The snow started to fall at midnight and continued all through the next day. It fell pretty heavily and the men really enjoyed the sight. It was indeed pretty, but the novelty soon wore off. Snowstorms may be right enough viewed from the verandah of a nice cosy home with a nice cosy fire to sit beside, or nice warm bedclothes to get into, but having to stand about in the open trenches with no covering over you makes a different picture of it altogether. The men in the trenches had a very bad time in the slush and cold, with many having to be sent away with frozen feet. Percy had witnessed dozens of them going down to the hospital with their feet wrapped in pieces of blankets as their feet were too swollen to fit in to their boots. Food and water supplies were also greatly affected by the big freeze. The frozen water had ruptured the water tank pipes resulting in the troops being placed on quarter rations of water. The sea too was playing tricks making it too rough to land anything. The soldiers were without bread, and only once or twice got a bit of fresh meat. The unexpected cold snap had caught the high command by surprise and they weren't prepared for it.

Luckily for the Lighthorsemen they had their dugouts, which were as warm as toast, but when they were on duty outside it was a different story with the snow still falling lightly, and an icy wind blowing, cutting through overcoat, clothes, and body alike. The snow melted a little during the day, and what was left froze the following night. It was curious for the men trying to get water to make tea. It was frozen solid, and they had to belt the tin about, until the ice inside broke up a bit, then shake it out. Percy, Davo and Boggy, even ventured down to the beach to get a box of firewood, but there wasn't any to be had.

Just to add to the discomfort the Turks regularly shelled the trenches. During one event Percy heard a shrapnel shell burst away up in the air, and could hear the pellets coming, so ducked down under a bit of a bank. It was just as well he did, for a pellet just hit the top of his hat and fell about a foot away. Percy kept it in his pocket as a souvenir, where it was certainly more comfortable than inside his head.

December began with lovely mild weather, but when the rest of their regiment did not return as expected, the troopers could see that something was happening. At around the time of the first snow fall there was a cessation of hostilities on the allied side, and *all* of the fetching and carrying of provisions was done at night. With the lack of firing, the Turks became very cheeky, crawling right out of the trenches, only to be shot down. This went on for a few days, and then the Turks carried out a heavy bombardment of the trenches at Lone Pine, making a terrible mess of things. After this, things seemed to return to normal, but certain things, however, were taking place that showed some move was being contemplated.

On the 14th of December on Lemnos the 9th Battalion was feeling rested and fed, but still unsure of what lay ahead. Their thoughts were soon answered when Lieutenant Ponsonby asked for a small band of volunteers to return and assist in the evacuation of Gallipoli.

"So we're *really* leaving?" asked Roo.

"We are dear boy," he replied giving all present a glance, "but what is said here must not be repeated. There are spies on this island don't forget".

"Well, I'm in sir, and I'm sure these four strong blokes here are too," said Clancy looking over at Archie, Roo, Taff and Stowie.

"Too right we are," replied Stowie.

As they approached the shoreline of Gallipoli they could just make out the eerie silhouette of the Razor.

"I thought we'd come back," whispered Archie, as the small boat bobbed up and down, "but not like this".

"At least this time no one's shooting at us," said Clancy in a low voice.

As the hull of the boat scraped on to the sandy beach, there was total silence, yet the place was a hive of activity, pack animals being relieved of their burdens, stores being quietly loaded on to barges at the pier, rubbish being piled up ready to burn.

Forming up in their small squad, the boys were met by designated guides; others who had volunteered to remain behind.

"Archie! Roo! Fancy meeting you here?" exclaimed a quiet voice from the darkness, holding out a hand in greeting, "Clance, Stowie, Taff...good to see you".

"Percy! I didn't know you were still here," whispered Archie.

"Yeah, me, Davo and Boggy too," replied Percy, "we couldn't just sail away as if nothing had happened here".

"Yeah, same here," said Archie.

"Where's me old mate Chugger then? Too cold to leave his dugout?" enquired Clancy.

Percy and his two mates glanced at each other; the atmosphere turning solemn.

"He got knocked mate," replied Boggy, "back in August".

Clancy and the rest were stunned.

"He's not...you know?" asked Clancy.

"Dead?" replied Percy, "no, but he got hit pretty bad".

"He's probably sunning himself in hospital in Egypt, and making friends with the nurses too I'll bet," added Boggy.

All present smiled a relieved smile, but it was time to change the subject, for there was work to be done.

"So, what have you got for us...er..." said Clancy eying Percy's sleeves, "sergeant. Well done mate".

Percy noticed the crown on Clancy's sleeve.

"You too sir. Soon be an officer eh?" he whispered.

"No fear. Like I told Freddy, they'd have to take my brain out first eh?" replied Clancy.

"They'd have to undo your laces first though," said Roo, as Clancy gave him a quick slap across the back of the head.

There was much to do, even on their first night back at the Cove, and very soon the boys were trudging up to Destroyer Hill with bags of flour, lime and rolls of hessian.

Throughout the darkness, as they climbed up and down the steep pathways, which were illuminated by lonely camp fires, they noted many changes. The population had already decreased considerably and Mother Nature was at work re-clothing the brown earth, with many of the natural plants putting forth a few timid tender shoots. There was much litter lying about. At one corner a great heap of New Zealand weekly newspapers lay, unread. There were disordered heaps of the despised bully beef, each tin holed with a bayonet to let in the air and spoil the contents for the enemy. Discarded garments that had seen better days were also strewn about the trenches.

Some movement was permitted during the daytime so as to make things appear as normal as possible for the Turks. There too was the occasional respite when the men would sit drinking billy tea and warming themselves by the fire.

"How long have you known we were leaving Perce?" asked Clancy.

"About a month I reckon. There were rumours all over the place. Some said our numbers were being reduced due to winter feeding, and I even heard that Aussie soldiers would be replaced by troops from colder countries. But here we are," Percy explained.

"Well, we've done all we can here," said Archie.

"I'm sorry for the mates we'll be leaving behind," said Roo solemnly.

"Me too mate," added Stowie, "I just hope our poor pals who lie all around us sleep soundly, and don't hear us marching back to the beach as we go filing away from them forever".

"That's very profound mate," said Archie.

"It's how I feel," replied Stowie.

"Well cheer up me old mate because our sleeping pals will have the last laugh," said Percy, "here let me show you some of the gifts we have left them".

"Gifts?" exclaimed Clancy.

As Percy walked them through the maze of trenches he

pointed out the rare jokes which some of the troops had left behind for Abdul when he *did* come. There were tracks leading into a drop of fifty feet, certain death for anyone not familiar with the lay of the land. There were strings with bombs attached, and in the many dug outs were numerous little presents of watches, boots, hats, and so on, all with explosives enough attached to blow the surroundings to kingdom come.

"That'll give the bastards a nice surprise eh?" laughed Clancy.

"It *is* nearly Christmas after all," added Roo.

Davo checked his watch.

"Speaking of Christmas it's eleven o' clock and we're expecting something from Abdul soon, so get your heads down," said Davo.

The final few days may have been slow, but the Turks kept everyone on their toes with the usual daily few minutes of bombardments at 1100 hours and 1700 hours. This time some of the shells dropped short whilst others overshot the intended targets.

"They must have been at the boozer last night eh?" said Clancy.

Silent periods continued in order to mislead the enemy.

But the ANZACs were an inventive lot and spent their time creating ingenious devices which were then rigged to rifles and bombs to fire or lob at the enemy.

The boys were admiring one such device whilst setting it up.

"So what is this then mate?" asked Taff.

"It's a drip rifle, a bloke in the 7th Battalion, Lance Corporal Scurry, thought it up. Some blokes call it the pop off rifle too," replied Davo, "let's assemble it and I'll show you how it works".

"So fellas there are two ration tins, as you can see. We fill the top one with water, and attach the empty bottom one to the trigger with string or wire...see?" explained Davo, "then, just before we bugger off, or you want to set it, you poke a small hole in the top one, then water trickles in to the lower tin until it gets too heavy, falls over and, Bob's yer uncle, pulls the trigger".

The men were amazed, but Clancy, not really being technically minded was a bit confused.

"Look Davo, truthfully I didn't understand a word you said, but as long as it works then that is fine with me," explained Clancy.

"I'll tell you what let's get this one going so you can see it in action. Meanwhile we'll put a few more together and get the billy on," replied Davo.

"Won't the Turks think it strange that just a single shot is fired now and then?" enquired Roo.

"Don't worry mate we *are* allowed to take a few shots of our own as we wander round the line," replied Percy.

"What? Like this?" said Clancy as he suddenly cocked his rifle, stood on the fire step and emptied his magazine across no man's land.

As a Turkish machine gun spat rounds back in their direction Percy nodded and shook his head saying "yeah, something like that".

There was much mental strain and worry on those who remained too.

"What if the Turks attack?" asked Taff.

"Well there are twenty thousand of us and a couple of hundred thousand of them, so they'd better go get some more blokes!" laughed Boggy.

The uncertainty of what would or *could* happen played heavily on many of the men's minds and some enlisted the help of a gramophone, or even chocolates and sweets, to while away the time until they received the signal to move. A rear party Quick Reaction Force had also been formed in case the Turks realised what was occurring, and attacked. What with this and the goings on during the night, everything had been thought of and covered.

But the saddest thought of all for the men was that they were leaving over eleven thousand ANZAC graves in the keeping of the Turks.

Every day they were never absent from the cemeteries, men by themselves, or in twos and threes, erecting new crosses or tenderly tidying up the grave of a friend.

"Here he is," said Clancy as they searched for the grave of Private Devereux.

As they looked around they recognised the names of many whom they'd trained with, laughed and cried with. All gone before their time; never to see the shores of Australia again.

"Devereux? I don't think I met him. Was he a mate?" asked Percy.

"Yeah. He talked a load of shit though," replied Stowie.

"He did, didn't he?" laughed Clancy, "but he was killed by his own kindness in the end".

"Where are your mates buried Perce?" asked Taff.

"They're not mate," replied Percy, "they are lying where they fell in no man's land. It was too dangerous to get them…you know?"

"Yeah mate there's a few of those on the ridge," said Clancy, "I hope Abdul has the decency to bury them".

"Anyway, let's do what we can for these poor fellas eh?" said Percy.

The boys got to work with the tools that they had, carefully lettering in the half obliterated names of their comrades on rough wooden crosses, then gently raking the mounds and bordering them neatly with fuse caps from fallen shells.

The soldiers believed that the Turks would respect these graveyards and many had been writing letters to leave in their dugouts for "Abdul," telling him what a clean fighter they thought he had been, and wishing him farewell, asking them to look after their mates.

As they tidied the graves, they saw a Padre walking amongst the crosses sprinkling something over the soil. The man was Padre Walter Dexter, a veteran of the South African War, and military clergymen from Victoria.

"What are you doing Padre, if you don't mind me asking?" said Roo.

Walter smiled.

"I am doing God's work just like you men and ensuring that these dear souls always feel like they are at home," he replied.

"How are you doing that sir?" asked Archie.

"I have been scattering silver wattle seeds in the cemeteries and gullies," replied the Padre, "if *we* have to leave here, I intend that a bit of Australia shall be here".

"Good on yer Padre," said Clancy.

On the 18th of December the 2nd Light Horse was re-enforced by one, their Commanding Officer Lieutenant Colonel Glasgow, who had come to supervise the regimental evacuation. The colonel was impressed with the work that his men had done and was determined that the manner of their departure was a good one.

"We'll show them we can still march out spic and span," he said.

At midnight on the 18th, their last night, the 2nd Light Horse tore up blankets and put them on the ground, so that the enemy would not hear any unusual noise while they moved about in the trenches. Having prepared their weapons and booby traps they then slipped woollen socks over their boots, the object being to deaden the sound of their feet, then covered their fixed bayonets with hessian, in order to prevent them glittering in the bright moonlight. The route by which they were to go was very carefully marked out by means of lights, and in places where there was any possible chance of going astray, the ground had been strewn with flour and lime, so as to indicate the correct path; a kind of Hansel and Gretel trail. Each party was so well timed that just enough men to fill a barge arrived on the beach at one time.

As they passed the men of the 9th Battalion they shook hands warmly.

"See ya later boys, thanks for your help," said Archie.

"Don't be late for tea or mum will be spewing," joked Percy as he hugged his brother and cousin.

"First on, so we might as well be last off eh?" said Clancy, looking around at his mates.

The boys waved a silent farewell as the Lighthorsemen disappeared down the winding pathways to the beach.

Archie and the remaining troops were now the last hope.

With the rest of the covering party they manned the entire ANZAC front; one man to every eight yards. Gun devices fired every so often but, apart from that, the men kept quiet and still. Number 1 outpost was the last to be recalled. It was a bright moonlit night as the last men marched down to ANZAC Cove, making for an impressive sight, as parties came from all directions in silence, with padded feet to deaden any sound, all making for their appointed places like clockwork. To each man it concluded a real experience that money could not buy, with an enemy whom they admired for his fair and clean fighting. There was a myriad of emotions concerning the departure, with some simply accepting it as their lot for being a soldier. Others were visibly upset, but not sorry to be leaving, although when they filtered past the many cemeteries, many thought of the mates who would rest eternally on these shores.

"Bless you boys. Rest easy. Australia forever," whispered Clancy as he shed a tear for the fallen.

By the 17th of December, fifteen thousand troops had been taken off the peninsula. Twenty thousand remained, but were away by 0300 hours on the 20th of December 1915.

All abandoned stores on the beach had been soaked with petrol, ready for the defiant departing bonfires.

As Archie and the boys stood on the shore, ready to board one of the many lighters and trawlers, they looked around at the towering hills and mountains to their front.

"Got any good bye dances Roo?" asked Clancy with a smile.

"Not that I can think of mate, but I have got one of *these!*" he said as he calmly, but forcefully, threw a two fingered "salute" in to the air.

The soldiers laughed, each managing their own "salute" and a sigh of relief.

"Do you think it was worth it?" said Archie turning to his friends.

"This place *made* an army, as well as mates for life," said Clancy, "I just hope that what we are doing will save other blokes from having to do the same".

"Well it aint over yet boys," said Stowie as they climbed on to the boat.

As the last trawler pulled away from the Gallipoli shore, flames appeared all along the beach, the stores and explosives caught fire, and a mighty conflagration lit up the cliffs.

At 0400 hours on Monday the 20th December 1915 the evacuation was complete, and by some miracle there were no fatalities or people left behind, the only injuries sustained that night being a soldier who had his leg run over by a big gun and another who was shot in the chest. One man, a sentry from the 13th Battalion almost missed *his* moment. He had fallen asleep and ran to the beach just as the last boats were leaving.

As Archie gazed at the fires ablaze on the beach, casting light upon the familiar landmarks they had fiercely defended, a few miles away to the north, Samuel Ford found himself deep in thought while being rowed to safety in his small boat.

ANZAC and Suvla, once teeming with activity, now lay abandoned. On the night of the 8th of January 1916, the British forces departed from Helles, marking the end of the Gallipoli campaign.

Such was the remarkable evacuation of Gallipoli, an achievement that would forever be etched in memory; thousands of men, quietly withdrawn from right under the enemy's noses, and they, in absolute ignorance.

Some historians tell us that Gallipoli was a defeat, but it most certainly was not. The allies had won most of the battles and held their line for eight months. They were not defeated, but similarly there were no winners, each army simply being withdrawn to be utilised somewhere else at another time.

For the men of Queensland, the war was not over. The 9th Battalion would soon be bound for France to fight a new foe, the Imperial German Army, whilst the 2nd Light Horse Regiment was destined to continue the fight with the Ottoman Empire in the deserts and mountains of the Middle East.

The Taylor boys and their mates have yet to complete either journey, so, they will march again.

.

Tony Squire, originally from England, is now an Australian citizen and resides there with his wife Sheila. Following in his father's footsteps, he pursued a career as a professional soldier and dedicated a total of 21 years to his service. Throughout his life, he has held a deep passion for history, particularly military history, and from a young age, he aspired to craft a historical novel that would intertwine his characters with real life historical events. This dream has come to fruition multiple times through his books aimed at younger readers, featuring his beloved character Buckley the Yowie. However, in his latest endeavour, a novel intended for adult readers, Tony has embarked on his long awaited journey of chronicling the remarkable tales of the ANZACs during the tumultuous period of the Great War.

Milton Keynes UK
Ingram Content Group UK Ltd.
UKHW020629111223
434160UK00017B/1144

9 780645 450088